ISBN 978-1-8384254-0-1
This edition © PJ Shann 2021

The right of PJ Shann to be identified as the author of this work has been asserted by him in accordance with the Copyright, Designs and Patents Act 1988.

All rights reserved. No part of this publication may be reproduced, stored in or introduced into a retrieval system, or transmitted, in any form, or by any means (electronic, mechanical, photocopying, recording or otherwise) without the prior written permission of the publisher. Any person who does any unauthorised act in relation to this publication may be liable to criminal prosecution and civil claims for damages.

This is a work of fiction. Names, characters, places and incidents either are products of the author's imagination or are used fictitiously. Any resemblance to actual events or locales or persons, living or dead, is entirely coincidental.

Cover illustration by Jonathan Cusick
www.jonathancusick.com

THE QUEEN OF HEARTS

PJ SHANN

ONE

MY NAME IS Joel September, and until a few years ago I was a Detective Inspector in the Metropolitan Police Service. A pretty good one too, as it happens. I was strong, healthy and smart, I had a good clean reputation, an intelligent, attractive wife with her own blossoming career in the City, and I was generally considered by all — myself most definitely included — to be a shiny bright prospect for the future. I was 'one to watch'. I was what those people in the know might even have gone so far as to call a 'boy wonder', or a 'rising star'.

But as it turned out, I was sadly none of these things. I was only a nearly-man.

These days I'm a Hertfordshire-based taxi-driver, a single-father separated from the mother of my child, and on bad days I often walk with a bit of a limp, courtesy of the injury that allowed me to resign from the Met' without leaving too many red faces behind me. I no longer believe that I'm even *slightly* smart and my reputation (or so I'm frequently told) is that I'm about as reliable as a newsreader suffering from Tourette's Syndrome. The future, once so promising and assured, now seems endlessly uncertain. How are the mighty fallen.

Or as I believe it says in the Bible somewhere or other — bummer.

I didn't do anything wrong, I want to make that clear from the very start. I never once compromised myself, either professionally or personally. I didn't take backhanders from criminals or play hoopla with prostitutes. I didn't fabricate evidence or misplace it, either accidentally or deliberately. I never bodged an investigation through procedural ineptitude, or scarpered with the booty from a drugs raid.

In other words, I wasn't bent, or incompetent, or foolish.

In fact, my only real mistake seemed to be that I was possessed of a certain professional naiveté. Specifically, I was guilty of having a more black-and-white outlook on the enforcement of law than some of my more experienced colleagues. An "excess of zeal" I remember one particularly outspoken high-ranking critic calling it. And that, in a nutshell, is ultimately what led to my downfall — being caught red-handed in possession of an excess of zeal.

Or, as I preferred to think of it, doing my job just that little bit too well for comfort.

Anyway, to cut a long, depressing story mercifully short, I suspected a handful of undercover officers of taking their roles as villains a little too seriously, to the extent that they had become villains in their own right, and I tried to catch them at it. All well and good, you might say — after all, if I'd succeeded I would have been a hero. I'd have got a pay rise and a medal on my chest and my name in the papers.

But unfortunately, I *didn't* succeed. In fact, I failed miserably, and was badly injured in the process.

Afterwards, the very officer I suspected of being the ringleader of this corrupt organisation was not only cleared of all suspicion, he was actually *promoted*, which really rubbed salt into the wound. Meanwhile, I found myself immediately shunted sideways into a tedious, dead-end, desk-bound administrative post that was to the chance of career progression what the deadly flesh-eating disease *necrotising fasciitis* is to a full and active social life.

Even more salt for that wound of mine, which by that time was beginning to feel quite seriously over-seasoned.

Of course, the Powers That Be insisted that this shift in my duties was intended to be a concession to my diminished physical capability, although as far as I was concerned, all it really achieved was to hasten my exit from the Job. Stripped of the smoke and mirrors of the Human Resources jargon, I suspect that this was always its real purpose. It was the price of failure.

But as they used to say back in the day, that was then and this is now.

I've tried very hard indeed over the years since my resignation to put the past behind me, and mostly I believe I've been successful. It's true, I've never quite shaken off the habitual nosiness that appears to come part and parcel with being a cop, or the occasional God-like assumption of absolute moral authority that sometimes accompanies it. And while I'd be the first to admit that these tendencies have, from time to time, landed me in a certain amount of trouble, so far there hasn't been anything I couldn't handle.

So far...

But trouble, of course, comes in all colours, shapes and sizes, and as I was shortly to learn, from all different angles, too. Unfortunately, it seems that putting the past behind you doesn't always work out quite as well as it probably should.

In fact, sometimes, no matter how hard you've tried, the past simply *refuses* leave you alone.

I WAS ONLY working A half-day that Saturday, which meant that I would be home by two o'clock at the latest. It was a beautiful August day, one more in a long sequence of beautiful August days in what, to date, had been a textbook summer, the kind you fondly recalled from childhood and never expected to see again. The plan was to have a pleasant lunch with my in-laws, who minded my young daughter Victoria whenever I was working, and then she and I would have the rest of the afternoon and the evening to ourselves.

In theory, Victoria and I could do whatever we wanted with our quality free time together, which in practical terms meant that we'd be doing whatever Vic (a natural born autocrat) wanted to do. If I knew my daughter, this meant a trip to Stanborough Park to feed the ducks and geese, followed by a strenuous hour of horsey-horsey back at home in the living room — an activity otherwise known as the *Make-Daddy-Sweat-Like-A-Pig* game. This, no doubt, would be followed by a lengthy bubble bath and then Disney movies till bedtime.

It would be exhausting, of course, but then that's kids for you. They have the weird ability to make you feel both young and old at the same time, and along the way they also manage to knock seven shades of crapola out of you. By the time Vic was finally settled down for the night it would be just about all I could do to keep my eyes open long enough to turn out the lights. However, my daughter was virtually my sole reason for living these days, and I could deny her nothing. She was the apple of my eye, the owner of my soul, and the queen of my heart.

So, driving back home to Welwyn Garden City from Stevenage after dropping my last fare of the day, thinking about the small, precious pleasures to come, I was a happy man.

And why not?

The sun was shining brightly, my top-light and the meter were both turned off, and a refreshing, fragrant breeze was blowing in through my open window. The radio, tuned to an oldies station, seemed to be playing the entire soundtrack of my youth, each and every song like little memory capsules, relics from a time when music seemed to be an essential part of life itself rather than just the background static it had become over the years. Everything sounded so great, even the clunkers I'd hated the first time around.

All in all, it was just one of those fabulous afternoons when you feel as though you've been handed a get-out-of-jail-free card, and wherever you happen to be, or whatever you happen to be doing, you're just glad to be alive.

In retrospect, with thirty-six years of life-experience under my belt, I suppose I should have known that this good feeling wasn't going to last.

The QUEEN of HEARTS

∽

VIC AND I live in a little three-bedroom terrace house at the end of a cul-de-sac on a leafy estate a few miles from the city centre. It's a nice quiet place to live, as a rule, where nothing much ever seems to happen. But as soon as I stepped in the door, I knew that *something* had happened today, and that things were far from right.

At least Vic was in one piece, and that was something of a relief. Although she was now only a couple of months from her third birthday, the phrase 'the terrible twos' could have been coined precisely with my wildly precocious daughter in mind, and she was generally up to more mischief than her old man had ever dreamed of in his own salad days.

Currently, she was standing on a slew of old newspapers spread out over the kitchen floor, happily finger-painting at the easel her doting grandparents had recently bought for her. Usually a highly creative dresser, Vic at this moment in time was naked save for a pair of Day-of-the-Week knickers, which told me that today was *Wonderful Wednesday*, even though it was actually *Spectacular Saturday*.

Perhaps that's why they were inside out.

There wasn't much in terms of a recognisable composition on her current canvas, but Vic had done a really bang-up job of painting selected parts of her anatomy and the whole of her round face a deep cobalt blue. Her bright green eyes and perfect rows of sharp white milk teeth shone out at me like gemstones when she smiled.

The QUEEN of HEARTS

'Daddeee!'

She ran pell-mell into my arms, and when I lifted her up she stamped handprints on my cheeks like little blue starfish.

'Clown!' she said. 'Funnee!'

Yep, that's hilarious, I thought.

Over her tiny shoulder, I was looking at Henry and Maude Forrester, my estranged wife's parents, and wondering exactly what the trouble was. I couldn't smell lunch, and they were sitting at the kitchen table with long, stony faces. They looked like an advertisement for timeshare holiday villas on Easter Island.

'What's up?' I asked.

Vic, who was obviously in a very literal frame of mind today, immediately pointed at the ceiling. 'There!' she bellowed.

Henry and Maude glanced at each other, compressing their lips into angst-ridden frowns, and I groaned internally. Only one thing I was aware of (apart from the thorny subject of bogus asylum-seekers) made them share this grim expression, and that was their daughter, Lisa. My absentee wife. Vic's absentee mother. Everyone's nightmare.

'She's coming over this afternoon,' Henry told me in his dry, precise diction.

My heart sank. 'What for?'

Once again, Henry and Maude grimaced at each other. Whenever they did this they looked eerily alike, like ancient fraternal twins struggling to unclog a smelly blocked drain.

'She *says* she wants to see Victoria,' Maude replied in a voice laden with doom, as though she was expecting a call from the Grim Reaper, and quite naturally, wasn't all that enchanted with the idea.

I managed a shrug. 'Well, she's entitled, I suppose.'

'Mmmm,' they said together, harmonising their doubt.

Henry and Maude were still disgusted with their daughter's behaviour, and had sent her to Coventry on a long-term visa. I didn't kid myself that this was because Lisa had walked out on our six-year marriage, although I suppose it was that too, to a certain extent. Mostly it was because she appeared to have abandoned her infant child in favour of her high-flying career and a fast, flashy lifestyle.

It had been only a few weeks after Vic's second birthday when Lisa had made her hasty exit from the September household, leaving a brief and entirely unsatisfactory note of farewell stuck to the fridge door, and leaving me well and truly up a certain creek without a paddle. Thankfully, her parents had come down on my side of the marital rift and had given me about much help as I could possibly use ever since.

We were doing all right on our own now, Vic and me. Not *great*, but all right. And yet here I was, struggling to be fair to the woman who had walked out on us.

Talk about being a glutton for punishment.

'She is Vic's M-U-M, after all,' I said thoughtfully. 'Perhaps it's a good sign.'

'Good? Good in what way, precisely?' Henry asked sharply. Before his retirement a baker's dozen of years ago, he'd been a policeman himself, and sometimes he sounded like he missed the joys of the interrogation room.

'Well, I don't know,' I replied. 'Maybe she's finally getting herself sorted out. Maybe she's thinking about coming back, and wants to test the water first.'

Henry literally snorted in derision at this particular suggestion. 'You're an optimist, boy. I've always respected that quality in you. Unfortunately, when it comes to the subject of my daughter, you're also a blithering idiot.'

Thanks a bunch, Henry, I thought. Nice to know where I stand in the grand scheme of things. Hopeless optimist. Blithering idiot. That's me sorted out, then.

Maude was slightly more diplomatic.

'I know it's none of my business, Joel,' she said gently, 'but she's only visited once in nine months. If she genuinely missed either of you, I think you'd have known it by now.'

She was right, of course. There had been only the single visit, almost exactly one month to the day after Lisa had left. A duty call, pure and simple. It had been Christmas Eve and she had stayed all of twenty minutes. Maybe it had been as little as fifteen.

Maude shook her head and the startling green eyes her granddaughter had inherited from her darkened slightly. 'I don't pretend to know what this is all about, Joel, but I'm sure it can't be good. Maybe a child has become a desirable fashion accessory in the City, and Lisa's feeling left out?'

So there it was. Their greatest fear.

You see, even though I knew Henry and Maude were desperate for their skittish daughter to come back into the family fold, I also knew they were secretly afraid that if she ever *did* come back, the reconciliation wouldn't last very long. Mostly, they were terrified she'd eventually end up taking their granddaughter away from me and away from them, to an uncertain life of sloppy day-care centres and dodgy, unregistered child-minders with suspected Munchausen's.

This would be an action they would never be able to forgive.

As it happened, Henry and Maude's fears on this score were completely without foundation, but they didn't know it because neither Lisa nor I had ever told them the real truth about why she left. Lisa probably hadn't told them because she hadn't wanted to paint herself even darker in her parents' eyes than she already had. I suppose that I hadn't told them for much the same reason.

Let's call it an example of misguided loyalty, a known trait of hopeless optimists and blithering idiots worldwide.

The truth was that Lisa had turned out to have all the maternal instincts of a snake, and one of the less affectionate of the species, at that. Not only had she never loved her baby daughter, but I don't believe that she'd ever even *liked* her. As far as my wife was concerned, getting pregnant had been the second worst mistake of her entire life. There are no prizes available for guessing what the *first* had been… but yeah, that's the one.

So whatever Lisa meant to achieve by coming here today, I certainly didn't believe it was to get her hands on Vic. And by my reckoning a marital reconciliation would be a long-shot on a par with winning the jackpot on the European lottery. All of which begged the question, what was she *really* up to?

Henry and Maude abruptly stood up together as though joined at the hip, no longer just fraternal twins but conjoined too.

'We'll get out of your way now,' Maude said.

'There's no need for you to leave. I thought we were having lunch?'

'It doesn't matter. We should get back for Daisy, anyway.'

Daisy was the Forrester's old Golden Retriever, a real gutbucket of an animal who was also occasionally called Sausages, because freshly fried bangers were her favourite treat. I knew that if left alone for too long, Daisy was apt to eat the carpets. Also, the furniture and the doors.

They began to get into their matching lightweight summer jackets, fawn for Henry to match his socks, and powder blue for Maude to match her hair. I shifted Vic's bottom to the crook of my arm and opened the door for them.

Maude glanced up at the kitchen clock. 'She should be here in about an hour.'

'That girl has never been on time for anything or anyone in her whole life,' Henry said. 'She was two weeks late being born.'

'Eleven days,' Maude softly corrected.

Henry grumped, 'Be late for her own damn funeral, most likely.'

Maude gave me a final smile. 'If there's any trouble, call us immediately.'

Henry and Maude made their way to the door and gave Vic a series of affectionate goodbye kisses, miraculously avoiding getting themselves and their jackets smeared with paint. This was a clever trick I had yet to master, and the majority of the items in my limited wardrobe now looked like Jackson Pollock rejects.

Henry shook my hand, as always, with his trademark vice-like grip. Maude pecked at my cheek and squeezed my arm supportively. Once outside the door, she turned back.

'Don't forget to call,' she reminded me.

'You call *me*,' Henry snapped, 'I'll call my solicitors. We'll nip this nonsense in the bud.'

I spent the next quarter-of-an-hour or so cleaning both the paint-spattered kitchen and my paint-spattered daughter to the very best of my ability. I had just about finished getting the last of the paint out of Vic's fine blonde hair with a non-stick washing-up sponge when Albert the Cat bundled his way in through the flap in the kitchen door, obviously *en route* from some top-secret daytime lair to his favourite snoozing spot in the bottom of the airing cupboard.

Albert the Cat is only a couple of years older than Vic in human years, but on the feline scale of time he's something of a seasoned boulevardier — a veritable cat of the world — and he has been my close confidante on many a long and lonely night. In many ways it's an ideal relationship, in that I'm able to speak openly, and he listens without judgement. The best part of the arrangement is that Albert doesn't talk back. Or at least, he hasn't so far.

But right now all those chummy little tête-á-têtes we had shared may as well have never happened, and for a few moments Albert just stood glaring at me intently from beneath a furrowed brow, as though I were a baffling species of inedible mouse he'd never come across before.

Then he turned his cold green eyes accusingly on Vic.

I could see what was troubling him. Ordinarily, Albert is a tortoiseshell, but at this moment in time he was a tortoiseshell with a significant cobalt blue stripe all the way down his back and along his angrily twitching tail. The fur on his ears had been twisted up into stiff blue antennae, and he looked like a minor demon.

Vic had been in a generous mood, I guessed, and had chosen to share her paint with him.

'Hi, Albert,' I said. 'What's wrong, feeling blue?'

'Allie!' Vic, sitting on the draining board, all but screamed. She held out her chubby arms to the aggrieved cat and made a series of loud kissy-kissy noises with her mouth that sounded like someone trudging through ankle-deep mud in ill-fitting Wellington boots.

Albert winced under this sonic onslaught, his long whiskers twitching as he mouthed a series of silent feline obscenities. Then he swung about and stalked away to the corner of the kitchen where his food bowl lived. He hunkered down in front of his dried food with his back to us and started crunching.

Vic tugged at my sodden, rolled-up shirtsleeve until I looked at her. 'Allie loves me,' she said, nodding solemnly.

Behind me, I heard Albert theatrically choking on his kibble in response to my daughter's sadly misplaced sense of confidence.

'Of course, he does, darling,' I told her. 'In his own strange way...' I lifted her down from the draining board and gently set her on her feet. 'Just don't hold your breath waiting for a Christmas card, eh?'

The QUEEN of HEARTS

'DON'T HOLD YOUR breath' would have been pretty good advice for me too, as it turned out. Not with regard to cranky cats and Christmas cards, of course, but to estranged wives and promised visits.

If I had taken this simple phrase to heart maybe I wouldn't have bothered rushing around the rest of the house like a mad thing, tidying and straightening as I went. Maybe I wouldn't have bothered giving myself a swift wash-and-brush-up, just in case Lisa really had sorted herself out and was thinking about coming back to us. Maybe I wouldn't have wasted my time, or my physical and emotional energy.

Maybe.

But Henry was quite right about me, it seemed. I *am* a blithering idiot and a hopeless optimist, and I *did* hold my breath. And Lisa, true to form, let me down. She never showed. She never called to say she couldn't make it. She wouldn't answer her phone when I rang to ask why.

My only comfort as I carried Vic up to her cot later that night was that my daughter hadn't caught on to what was supposed to be happening, and so was spared the upset I was going through. Even so, before I went to bed myself, I left a couple of messages on Lisa's voicemail that would let her know, in no uncertain terms, exactly how I felt about this latest example of her chronic irresponsibility.

Hours later, just as I finally began to doze off, I found myself miraculously transported back to the sun-filled kitchen of that afternoon, just back from work, with starfish stamped on my cheeks and a half-naked, blue-faced child wriggling around in my arms. Maude had just told me that Lisa would be arriving in about an hour, and Henry had responded by saying that his daughter had never been on time for anything in her whole life.

'Be late for her own damn funeral,' he added ominously.

And his voice, now loudly echoing against the inside of my thick skull, seemed to follow me down into the darkness.

Two

IN SPITE OF this curious sense of unease (and the rather murky bad dream it developed into), it took a whole week for me to get really worried about Lisa's no-show. *Seriously* worried, that is. After all, even when things had been good between us, she had never been that great a communicator, and sometimes even the basic courtesy of a post-it note on the fridge door had seemed to be beyond her meagre capabilities.

To be honest, I didn't even remember that much of the dream, but the little I did recall wasn't at all pleasant, with something large, dark and thoroughly monstrous chasing Lisa through some kind of shadowy labyrinth. I didn't like it much. Lisa didn't seem to be enjoying it too much, either. Probably, I thought, her nose was put out of joint because *she* was used to being the only monster in my dreams.

The week passed me by in the usual sedate manner, which was basically an amiable blur with little in the way of surprises. I divided my time as well as I could between taxi-driving and child-rearing, ably assisted by my unpaid deputies, Henry and Maude. I made the usual round of supermarket runs, train-station pick-ups, and airport drop-offs at Luton, Stansted, and Heathrow. I took bubbly young people out to nightclubs in Hitchin, Stevenage, and St Albans, and brought dead-eyed drunks home from the same clubs several hours later, keeping out a vigilant eye for the potential pukers in the back seat.

On *Wonderful Wednesday* morning, a blue-rinsed, walking-frame-shuffling nonagenarian I drove to and from a chiropodist appointment kindly offered me the option of sex in lieu of payment (offer rejected). On *Fabulous Friday* afternoon, I transported a dour grey parrot with the demeanour of a caged serial-killer from the house of one embittered spouse to another, who then offered to pay me double the fare to take the bird back where it had come from (offer accepted).

Ah, love and marriage!

Driving back, I caught the parrot's eye in the rear-view mirror, and I could see that we were thinking much the same thing... which was a slightly disturbing discovery from my point of view.

But apart from these exciting highlights it was business as usual, and nothing else of any note whatsoever occurred. The world turned, and my world, my life, remained exactly the same.

Until the moment it changed, that is.

ON *SPLENDID SUNDAY* morning, I was jerked mercilessly awake by the sound of the telephone beside my bed shrieking into my ear, and for a few seconds, I thrashed about on the mattress like a mackerel on the deck of a trawler. By the time I was coordinated enough to bring the receiver to my ear, I'd managed to make out the glowing digits on the clock-radio, which told me that the time, unbelievably, was a few minutes before five.

Five o'clock in the bloody morning.

This was just my luck, all right, as it had been one of those rare nights when Vic slept right through and I had a chance to catch up on my much-needed beauty sleep. And then some inconsiderate bugger goes and calls me at dawn. *Pre*-dawn, in fact, robbing my *Sunday* of all its *Splendid* before it even began.

In the trees behind the house, whole colonies of birds still snuggled in their nests were looking askance at my bedroom window and wondering, 'Who's that noisy bastard?'

They weren't alone. So was I.

'Hello?' I growled into the mouthpiece. When there was no immediate reply, I said the same thing again, only louder, with just a touch more of the enraged timber wolf about it.

There was an even longer silence, which this time I did not break. It was not a complete silence, you see. It was the kind of silence where you know that someone is at the other end of the line, holding his breath, listening, waiting.

'Hello?' I asked in slightly tamer voice, less volume, less gargling menace.

There was another long silence, during which my sleep-addled brain finally, belatedly, began to work. It wasn't *his* breath, I realised. It was *her* breath.

'Lisa?' I whispered. 'Is that you?'

This time there was a faint rustling sound.

'Lisa, if it's you, don't worry about last week. It doesn't matter. Come today, if you can. Come whenever you like. Lisa? It's okay, we can talk about it. It isn't—'

The line was softly disconnected.

I immediately hit the call-back button, only to be informed by an automated message that my caller had withheld their number. I knew there was a way to do that, but I personally didn't know what it was. Probably, I thought, you needed a doctorate in advanced telephonic sciences to be able to do such a thing, which frankly was something I lacked.

I did know, however, that this withholding business frequently happened automatically when calls were made through a switchboard. A switchboard, for example, just like the one in operation at Lisa's place of employment.

Once again, I glanced at the time on the clock-radio, and then frowned doubtfully. I was all too aware that Lisa was heavily into her career, but would she be at work this early, and on a Sunday morning to boot? It seemed extremely unlikely.

But there was only one way to find out for sure.

I got out of bed, pulled on my dressing gown and made my way to the bathroom, quickly poking my head around Victoria's bedroom door along the way. Luckily, Vic was still fast asleep, a vast battalion of watchful soft toys standing guard over her as she lay snoring, with her chubby feet comfortably wedged up against the sidebars of the cot she had just about outgrown.

In the bathroom, I briefly studied my red-eyed, stubble-cheeked reflection in the mirror above the hand-basin, and rediscovered an old truth — I wasn't a morning person, and my face was not a morning face. After urinating for about a century or so, I quietly padded downstairs and sat on the sofa with my address book.

The QUEEN of HEARTS

First I dialled the number of Morgan-Matheson, the private bank Lisa worked for, but got only a recorded message asking me to call again during normal office hours, which was pretty much what I had expected. Next I tried her mobile number, which just redirected me to the voicemail service I had already used (and abused) quite extensively earlier in the week. Finally, I tried the number of the landline at her swanky rented flat in London, which was sending out an unobtainable signal.

I called the operator, who tested Lisa's line for me but could find nothing wrong with it. Maybe, he suggested, Lisa's phone had accidentally been left off the hook? I thanked him for this insight and then hung up.

Suddenly, all the worries that had been quietly growing inside me for the past seven days abruptly trebled. It was partly the bad dream, partly the early morning call and hang-up, and partly something else, a spookily tangible feeling of foreboding.

Something fishy was going on here. I knew it with a rock-solid certainty that I would never be able to explain or rationalise to any other person. You could call it ex-copper's intuition, I suppose. Or, if you were that sort of person, you could just get down off the fence and call it a premonition.

After all, as it says in the Bible — one nut's lower than the other for a *reason*.

The QUEEN of HEARTS

AT AROUND ELEVEN-thirty or so, Vic and I were scrubbed, polished, booted and suited, and already on our way to our luncheon appointment.

Three out of four Sundays each month, we spend the day with Henry and Maude at their cottage in Old Welwyn, which is about ten or so minutes' drive away from our house. But this Sunday, by a strange fluke of synchronicity, we just happened to be booked in at *my* parents' home in Maida Vale, west London, which was about twenty-odd miles away. And Maida Vale was only a small hop, skip and a jump across the Westway from Bayswater, where Lisa lived the highlife in luxurious, solitary splendour.

My idea was to leave Vic with her paternal grandparents while I popped off to see what — if anything — was happening with her mother. This hastily concocted but simple plan, however, depended entirely upon Vic's cooperation, which might have been a problem. She was absolutely fine with Henry and Maude now, but she'd had a lot less experience of my parents' company and had never been left alone with them before. There was a good chance that she might not take to the idea.

'Vic, how're you doing back there?' I asked her now.

I peered into the rear-view mirror briefly and saw her nodding as she happily flicked through the pages of an upside-down picture book. A second or two later, she began to run through her small repertoire of nursery rhymes at an eardrum-bursting volume.

Wing Awing Awoses.

She sounded like Elmer Fudd on helium.

A half-hour later, I double-parked outside my parents' house, a typical west London brick-built three-bedroom semi they had lived in since their marriage sometime back in the Stone Age.

My parents' names are Vincent and Rosalind September, and they have both long since retired from their careers in the lower echelons of the Civil Service. They're almost eighty-years-old now, which means that by the time they had me they were already in their mid-forties. Which also means that I was probably a mistake, and to be honest, there were times during my childhood when I felt like one. It wasn't that I was ever neglected or uncared for, I think it was just that my parents were too old for a first child, too busy with their shared careers and their shared interests and hobbies. Too wrapped up in their own intense, exclusive relationship.

In retrospect, my only surprise is that they didn't have me adopted at birth, or failing that, pack me off to some tenth-rate boarding school as soon as I was old enough. Instead they chose to keep me around, like a kind of pet gooseberry. I prefer to take this as a sign that in their own eccentric, unfathomable way, they sort of liked me.

I unhooked my seatbelt and turned around in my seat to face Vic, who was looking at me expectantly. She already seemed to know something was coming, she just didn't know what it was. I took a deep breath. I had a feeling that this was going to be tricky.

'Okay, little girl,' I said. 'Do you know where we are?'

'Vinny an' Rosie's.'

Henry and Maude were Granddad and Nana, but Vic called my parents by their Christian names, just as I always had. Nobody had taught her this, she'd just picked up on the distinction on her own.

'That's right, sweetheart, Vincent and Rosalind's. Now, I've got all your colouring books and pens in your backpack, and I've brought along a couple of DVDs as well.'

'Poo?'

'Yeah, Poo Bear, and The Little Mermaid.'

Vic clapped her hands enthusiastically for her current faves.

'Um, listen, Victoria. While we're visiting Vinny and Rosie, it looks like Daddy's going to have to pop out for a few minutes...'

I rushed on into her sudden, ominous silence.

'I won't be gone for long, I promise, but it's very important that I go for a little while. I will definitely be back in time for lunch, and I'll probably be back a long time *before* lunch, so there'll be no need to worry, will there?'

More deadly silence.

'So, what do you think, darling? Can you be a good girl for Daddy and stay with Vinny and Rosie for a little while?'

Today, Vic was wearing a pair of bottle-green cords, yellow SpongeBob socks with a pair of red jellies, a pink t-shirt with the legend 'Pop Goddess' sequinned in gold across her narrow chest, and a lime-coloured felt beret snugged down tight on her peanut head. Also, a set of Power Ranger water-wings. She stared at me for a long, long moment with huge green eyes that seemed to look inside me like an x-ray.

Then she sighed heavily, like the out-of-patience and much-put-upon child-minder she sometimes pretended to be to her dolls and action-figures.

'OK,' she said.

The QUEEN of HEARTS

I WON'T BOTHER pretending that I've never seen the place Lisa now calls home. In fact, I freely confess that I have. I was absolutely broken-hearted when she first left me, and I must have spent more than a few miserable, lonely hours sitting in my car outside her building, just hoping for a glimpse of the woman I thought I still loved.

Actually, to be totally truthful, it was a *lot* of hours. (Or, to be totally, *totally* truthful, I guess I'm lucky I wasn't arrested for stalking.)

But back then, of course, I was being driven solely by my screwed-up emotions, and my usually analytical mind didn't get much of a look-in. The only valid observation I can recall making at the time was that although Lisa's flight seemed to have come out of the blue, in reality she had to have been planning it for quite a while. Long enough to get herself comfortably set up, anyway.

The 'instant' apartment's existence had been too good to be true. The 'instant' apartment's existence had spoken to me of long-term betrayal, not short-term expediency. But seeing the place again now, studying it from my idling car, I discovered that it was saying something else entirely: now it was saying — actually, it was virtually screaming — *money*.

Lisa's home was on the sixth floor of a smart, modern eight-storey apartment building just off the Bayswater Road, only a street or so from the place where Bayswater became Notting Hill. It was set back from a busy main road by generously proportioned and immaculately landscaped grounds. It had CCTV security, an underground car park for residents, and the ground floor was taken up by various communal facilities, including a gym, a sauna, and a small swimming pool, that wouldn't have been out of place in a luxury hotel.

I couldn't know for certain, having never been up there in person, but I guessed that the view from her sixth-floor balcony would be exceptional, with Regent's Park to the left, Hyde Park to the right, and central London itself, bisected by the gleaming Thames, straight ahead. She'd be able to see it all — the Shard dominating the horizon south of the river, and the Palace of Westminster, Big Ben, and the Abbey crowded together to the north. Somewhere behind them, the dome of St. Paul's would be floating in mid-air over the City, like an ascending balloon.

It was one hell of an address, and — without the slightest shadow of a doubt — it would have one hell of a price tag. Never mind the monthly rent, which was probably four or five times the cost of the mortgage on the house in Welwyn Garden City, even the annual service charge that maintained all those top-of-the-line facilities must have run into the thousands.

And as well paid as Lisa undoubtedly was, what with all her bonuses and commissions and dividends, I couldn't imagine how she managed to make both ends meet.

I mean, it wasn't as if she had ever learned to skimp in other areas of her life. Lisa still liked expensive clothes and expensive cars. She liked eating out and socialising in all the fashionable places. She demanded an absolute bare minimum of two luxury holidays each year, and generally required as much comfort as she could lay her manicured little hands on.

From time to time over the months since she walked out on us, it has crossed my mind to ask her exactly how much it costs to maintain this kind of high-flying lifestyle... but then I've taken a very deep breath and reminded myself that it isn't really my business anymore.

But if Lisa *isn't* my business anymore, I suddenly thought, what am I doing here now? Which was a pretty good question. All I needed now was an equally good answer and my work here would be done.

I took a last look at the front of the apartment block, and at Lisa's windows in particular. I revved the engine a few more times, more aggressively than was strictly necessary, and then followed the driveway around to the back of the building. I parked in one of the dozen-or-so above-ground bays that had been specially designated for the use of visitors, tradesmen, and snooping ex-husbands.

Back at the front entrance, I was confronted by a neat panel of steel buttons, one for each of the thirty-two apartment. Hoping for the best, I pressed as many buttons as I could reach all at the same time — just about every one, except Lisa's. Seconds later, a confusion of voices started to ask questions from the intercom's speaker, which quickly went into overload and began to howl with feedback. As I had hoped, someone up there lost patience and simply buzzed the door open, and *voila!* — I was in.

The imposing lobby was all Italian marble and smoked-glass and brushed-steel accents, and immense pot plants so succulent that the addition of a vinaigrette would have made them edible. The wall to the left was taken up with banks of inset mailboxes that exactly matched the buttons on the panel outside. The opposing wall featured a large sliding glass door that opened with a key-card and through which I could see a part of the building's communal gym.

Inside the gym, a lone woman wearing black Lycra and white iPod headphones ran endless laps on a treadmill. She raised the hand not clutching a bottle of mineral water and gave me a friendly little wave. I waved back and moved toward the two elevators in the wall facing the entrance, one of which opened immediately the second I pressed the call button.

The six-floor ride was smooth, swift, and completely silent, the Rolls Royce of elevator travel. The corridor outside was a rectangular marble tunnel running the entire length of the building. Natural light entered through large windows and was amplified by equally large wall mirrors. The hard edges were softened by planters set under the windows, and by more lush pot plants breaking up the walls between the four widely-spaced apartment doors.

I went to Lisa's door and rang her bell. I heard it ring inside the apartment, a tasteful double chime that managed to sound traditional even in this aggressively modern setting, but it was not answered. I rang the bell once more and then began to knock. I was still knocking and ringing almost five minutes later, long after a more sensible person would have stopped.

But sensible people don't go snooping around their estranged wife's home just because they get a funny feeling, do they? Sensible people don't stare at the front of buildings for long minutes on end, wondering why their estranged wife's curtains are the only ones still closed at this advanced time of the day. Sensible people don't rev their car engines repeatedly until they see those closed curtains give a tell-tale twitch.

No, only blithering idiots like me.

I was beginning to get a really bad feeling in the pit of my stomach, which was either nervous tension or a late reaction to last night's home-cooked nightmare. (My own take on risotto, which Vic claimed tasted the way my socks smelled at the end of the day.) Then something happened. I didn't hear anything or see anything, but somehow I sensed change. I felt the presence of another body at the other side of the door. I felt myself being *observed*.

I looked at the cyclopean eye of the door-viewer and smiled, trying to project a supreme sense of confidence through the tiny aperture.

'Come on,' I said to Lisa. 'I know you're in there, I saw you at the window earlier, peeking through the curtains to see who was making all the noise with their car. Open up and we can talk. That's all I want, to talk to you face to face. I'm not leaving until I do.'

Once again, I sensed movement behind the door. I continued to smile pleasantly, hoping that would work. If it didn't, I'd try something else. One way or another, I was determined I would get that door open.

Suddenly, the lock snapped and the door clicked open. A thick security chain stopped the door opening any wider than four inches, but that was quite wide enough for me to see the face peering out and up at me from the dark cavern of the apartment.

The pallid face was simultaneously puffy with tiredness and drawn with worry, the whites of the eyes suffused with tiny broken veins — and it was a face I had never seen before in my life.

The smile dropped from my lips. The expression that replaced it must have been rather forbidding, because the man in Lisa's apartment tried to slam the door shut again. Luckily, I caught it just before the lock engaged, and found to my surprise that I was able to hold it open against the other man's weight and strength using just one hand.

I used the other hand to direct a finger at the narrow space directly between his shadowed eyes, which were now rapidly filling up with panic.

'Who the hell,' I asked, 'are you?'

Three

THE MAN DIDN'T bother to answer, just continued his feeble attempts to slam the door in my face, but it was a contest he could never hope to win. I'd be the first to admit that my body wasn't anywhere near as toned as it was back in my heyday, but at least I still had some muscle to my name. My opponent, on the other hand, was about a foot shorter than I was, with a physique something along the lines of a stick insect — and a fairly malnourished specimen, at that.

I guess it might have made for an amusing moment in a knockabout comedy film, the little guy struggling heroically, every muscle strained, while the bigger guy yawns with boredom. But this wasn't a film, and I could see nothing funny in the other man's careworn expression. In my estimation, something had recently put the fear of God into him, and I wasn't convinced that my admittedly less-than-subtle brand of cold calling was entirely responsible.

In any case, I quickly dropped my accusing hand, hoping to calm him down.

'Hey, I'm sorry,' I said. 'I didn't mean to alarm you, it's just that you surprised me when you opened the door. I was expecting someone else, and I overreacted. I apologise, okay? Sir?'

That 'sir', that short grace note of respect, got to him more than the gentle apology had. I saw a little of the panic and tension leave him, and he reluctantly gave me some eye-contact.

'Sir,' I repeated, giving his ego another little stroke, 'I wonder if you could help me. I'm looking for Lisa.'

'Lisa?' He still looked wary, but at least he had stopped trying to close the door on me.

'Yes, Lisa September. It's possible you may know her as Lisa Forrester?' When he didn't respond to Lisa's maiden name, I bluntly added, 'This is her flat you're in right now.'

'I know it is. Of *course*, I know.' He quickly tugged the rumpled jacket of his grey pin-striped suit back into some kind of shape, ran a still-shaking hand through his disarranged crop of prematurely salt-and-pepper hair, and then, with all the dignity he could muster, drew himself up to his full, diminutive height. 'I'm Andrew Lipton,' he said — he *announced*, in fact, as though his was a name I should have been familiar with, which I was not.

I looked back at him, eyebrows raised in expectation.

Then he said, 'I'm Lisa's boyfriend.'

Boyfriend?

The word was like a slap in the face with a wet fish. Like being sandbagged, cold-cocked, ambushed. Like standing on the teeth of a rake and having the handle swing up to bonk you sharply on the forehead, making you see a spinning constellation of stars. All of the above, but worse. Infinitely worse.

Jesus, I thought, I should have been ready for this.

I mean, I'd already assumed that there must have been other men in Lisa's life since she left me, of course I had. But knowing it on an intellectual level isn't like finding out for sure. It isn't like being face to face with the cuckolding arsehole himself.

'You're her boyfriend, eh?' I asked, and when Lipton nodded, I said, 'Good for you — I'm her husband.'

I was hoping for a big reaction to this revelation, but Lipton merely nodded wearily again.

'I know who you are,' he said quietly. 'I'm afraid Lisa's not here at the moment.'

'Where is she?'

'I don't know.'

'When did she leave?'

'I don't know.'

'When will she be back?'

'I don't know that, either.'

'You don't know much, do you?' I asked.

'That's the story of my life,' he replied, with a small, almost bitter smile.

Nine times out of ten, I would have left it at that. I would have politely walked away, and maybe asked him to pass on a message the next time he saw Lisa — if it didn't put him to too much trouble, that is. But this was the tenth time, and my ex-copper's intuition was still sounding the alarm bells.

I found Lipton's manner strange, but strange in a way I had seen often enough in the past to recognise it for what it was. This man was not telling me the truth, the whole truth, and nothing but the truth. Maybe he wasn't telling outright porkies, no, but he was definitely skimping on the *actualité*.

'What are you hiding?' I asked him abruptly, and I knew from the sudden widening of his tired eyes that I was correct.

'Hiding? I don't know what—'

'Open this door, right now,' I said, leaning toward him menacingly. 'Open it, or I'll open it for you.'

He stared into my eyes for a few moments, prominent Adam's apple bobbing away on his scrawny, ill-shaven throat as he nervously swallowed. Then his eyes dropped and he began to unlatch the door.

I allowed myself a brief smile of satisfaction. My old knee injury meant that all my door-kicking-in days were long, long behind me, but Andrew Lipton wasn't to know that. Years in the Met' had helped me perfect this kind of empty threat (empty threats being pretty much all we had left in our arsenal) and it was nice to see that I hadn't lost the touch.

'Let it be noted,' he said querulously as he opened the door, 'that I'm doing this under protest.'

'Okie dokie,' I replied, and stepped past him into the gloomy hallway.

I WAITED WHILE he carefully locked up again and then followed his slight figure along the dim hallway and into the main body of the open-plan apartment, which was almost pitch black. The heavy, double-lined curtains blocked out just about every bit of daylight, except for the small chink where he had sneaked a peek earlier in response to my engine-revving activities. A wafer-thin band of white light sliced the large area in two like a laser beam, with me on one side and Lipton on the other.

The air in the apartment was stale, as though it had been unoccupied for a while. It also had a faint but thoroughly unpleasant underscent, and I have to say that I strongly suspected Mr. Lipton of farting just before coming to answer the door.

I opened my mouth to speak, but then just froze.

All the while my eyes had been slowly adjusting to the apartment's ambient darkness, and suddenly I was able to see why Lipton hadn't wanted me to come in. The whole apartment had been comprehensively wrecked.

Drawers had been yanked out of cabinets and their contents explosively scattered. Furniture had been overturned and broken into pieces, and upholstery had been viciously slashed open. The screen of an enormous wall-mounted TV had been hammered to bits, the guts had been ripped out of books, pictures had been torn from the walls and their frames smashed to kindling.

'What the hell…?'

I went to the window and snatched open the curtains. In full daylight the damage seemed even worse. It looked as though a hurricane had blown through the apartment, a hurricane with an evil personality.

I looked at Lipton. 'Did you do this?'

'Of course not,' he said, with such a complete lack of conviction that I instantly believed him.

'Then who did?'

'The police say that it was a burglary that went wrong.'

He glanced away from the wreckage as he spoke, looking out through the floor-to-ceiling windows at the spectacular view the curtains had hidden.

'In an upmarket address like this,' he went on, 'the burglars must have been expecting to find a lot of valuables like cash and jewellery. When they didn't, they smashed the place up out of spite. The police say it's a local gang who are trying to finance their drug addictions. Apparently there's been a spate of similar break-ins in the area.'

'Was Lisa here when it happened?' I asked. 'Was she…?'

'No, thankfully she was away. On business.'

'And now?'

Lipton shook his head and let loose with a heavy sigh. 'I already told you, I don't know where she is right now. All of this…' He waved his arms around generally. 'It upset her so much, she said she needed to take a short holiday to get over the shock. She wouldn't tell me where she was going.'

'Funny she didn't want her boyfriend tagging along for emotional support,' I said.

Lipton twitched a little. 'Well, I promised her I'd stay here and get things cleaned up. Put everything back in order, for when she comes home. That's why I came this morning, to make a start.' He turned back to me. 'Why are *you* here?'

'She was supposed to come see me and our daughter last weekend, but she never made it, and I haven't been able to contact her since. I was worried.'

At this, Lipton's face seemed to go a shade paler, and the purple shadows beneath his eyes to darken. It might have been my imagination, but I didn't think so.

'There's no need to worry,' he said, although it sounded like he was talking to himself, not me.

I began to walk around the apartment, slowly taking in the true scale and scope of the vandalism.

Looked at closely, it was truly awesome. Everything that *could* be smashed *had* been smashed. In the kitchen, all the cupboards and drawers had been emptied, their contents tossed, shards and fragments of plates and glasses everywhere over the floor like frozen confetti. Knives had been used to score the plasterboard walls and then been hammered through the cabinet doors. Packets of cereal and jars of sauces had been broken open on the tile floor and then walked through on to the light-cream carpets. Someone had used a screwdriver to etch the word BITCH half-a-centimetre deep into the polished surface of a mahogany dining table.

As I made my way back into the living room area, I realised that Lipton had been following me about the apartment like a dog at heel, and I imagined that he'd follow Lisa around in just the same way. Knowing Lisa, she probably liked it. There had always been something of the *femme fatale* about Lisa, a sort of *film noir* quality that attracted a certain kind of man, the worshipful, lap-doggish types. There had been a couple of them sniffing around when I first met her, and Lipton reminded me of them a great deal.

'How did you two hook up?' I asked him.

'We used to work together at the bank. Morgan-Matheson?'

I nodded. It made sense. I could imagine Lisa using Lipton's attraction to her to shin a little farther up the greasy pole. I could imagine it all too easily. '*Used* to, you say?' I asked. 'You've moved on, then?'

A pause. 'Er, yes, that's right. Pastures new and all that sort of thing.'

'Been seeing each other for long?'

'No. No, not long at all...'

I smiled to myself — as if he'd tell me otherwise.

I made my way across the badly soiled carpet towards the door that led to the master bedroom — one of the very few doors in the open-plan apartment, and the only one that was actually closed — and noticed that for the first time since I'd entered the flat, Lipton was hanging back. The unpleasant smell like bad drains that faintly perfumed the rest of the apartment seemed much stronger here.

I looked back at Lipton questioningly.

'You'll see,' he said with a small shrug.

I opened the door and instantly grimaced. Lisa's bedroom was clearly the epicentre of the carnage. It was exactly the same pattern of destruction as in the rest of the apartment, but on a far greater scale.

Once again the BITCH motif was apparent, this time scrawled in blood-red spray paint across one of the walls. The same paint had been used to write the c-word on the wall above the bed — along with a crude supporting graphic, just in case the meaning wasn't already clear enough. All Lisa's clothes had been pulled from the wardrobe and drawers and then slashed to pieces, her underwear first ripped up and then kicked into ragged mounds that lay in the room's corners like dead birds.

And in the exact dead centre of the sliced-open mattress, which had been left twisted askew on the base of the kingsize bed, someone — a someone who obviously believed in getting their daily roughage, and plenty of it — had taken a very, very large shit.

Nestled cosily beside a fluffy cloud of mattress stuffing, this enormous, prize-winning turd was fully curled around itself like a juicy Cumberland sausage. Lodged into its exact centre was a knobbly fluorescent pink vibrator, which had presumably been taken from the wreckage of the bedside cabinet at my feet.

I gaped. I couldn't help it, like staring at the aftermath of an RTA as you drove past. I couldn't *not* look.

'Rather disgusting, isn't it?'

I started a little. I had been so transfixed by this perverse tableau that I hadn't heard Lipton come up behind me.

I turned and saw him standing in the doorway, staring at the bed with a kind of fascinated horror, an expression which I'm sure exactly mirrored my own. I didn't know whether to pull on a pair of Marigolds and clean the appalling mess up, or try to sell it as an art installation to the Tate Modern.

I nodded in silent agreement. Yes, *The Behemoth Bowel-Movement of Bayswater* was certainly a disgusting sight. It wasn't the *worst* thing I'd ever seen, but it was definitely up there in the top ten.

Then, just as I was about to leave the bedroom, something I recognised caught my eye. I bent down and scooped up a book with a pink sequinned cover out of the flotsam and jetsam littering the floor.

The book was actually a small photo-album, and I recognised it because I had made it up myself especially for Lisa, about a month or so after she'd walked out on us. It was filled with a collection of photographs of our small family from the first two years of Vic's life, which I had carefully compiled to show Lisa what she was missing.

In my mind's eye, I suppose I'd imagined her brooding over these cunningly selected images during the long, lonely nights up here in her smart London eyrie. Brooding as she sat in high-powered meetings in the City, hardly able to keep her mind on the day's agenda for thoughts of the family she had left far behind.

I had imagined her going to her cold, lonely bed every night just a little bit sadder than she had the night before, and then further imagined that all those sad and lonely nights would slowly add up, and that it wouldn't be long before their combined emptiness would prove overwhelming. And then Lisa would finally understand, once and for all, that her place was back at home with us, with her husband and daughter, who loved her so very much.

But *nah!* Not *my* Lisa. *My* Lisa had just stuffed the photo album away at the back of the wardrobe, and if not for the intervention of a burglar it would never have seen the light of day ever again.

I flicked through the album briefly. The cover was scuffed and one of the last photographs had been torn out, but apart from that there was no damage. I put it away in my pocket, unwilling to leave images of my daughter in these dismal surroundings. Lipton saw me take it, but very wisely made no comment.

For the next few moments I kicked around looking for the missing photograph, unfortunately without success, until the stale smell from the bed finally drove me out. Lipton obediently trailed me to the front door, unlocked it, and then held it open for me like a doorman.

'Would you like me to pass on a message, if Lisa should call?' he asked as I passed him.

I paused in the corridor for a long moment, thinking, looking back into the ruined apartment.

'Actually,' I told him, 'I believe everything's already been said. I just didn't know it until today.'

As I drove back to Maida Vale, I very carefully thought my way through everything I had seen at Lisa's apartment and everything Andrew Lipton had told me while I was there. All in all, I didn't believe that I'd been lied to so often or so badly in such a short space of time. It must have been some kind of record.

To begin with, if Lipton was Lisa's boyfriend in the romantic sense of the word, as he clearly wished me to believe, then something fundamental had changed in the very fabric of the universe. I was well aware of the kind of male characteristics Lisa found sexually attractive, but as far as I could see, Lipton hadn't been blessed by any one of them. The only quality that might have made him desirable in her eyes was extreme wealth, and somehow he just didn't give off those kind of vibes.

Secondly, his story of the botched burglary, complete with drug-crazed gang members and its subsequent slipshod investigation by the police, simply didn't add up.

For starters, the forensic examination of a crime scene leaves its own tell-tale marks, and I had seen not a single one of them in Lisa's apartment, which suggested that the police had never been summoned in the first place. (If nothing else, *The Monster Turd of Olde London Towne* would most certainly have been taken into custody.) Also, while gangs of the kind Lipton had described certainly *did* exist, on the whole they tended to stick to their own turf — usually one of the sink-estates where their type of urban camouflage is more effective. In my opinion, they would have stood out on that swish apartment building's CCTV system like the proverbial hard-on in a convent.

But just for the sake of argument, even if a gang like that *had* gone walkabout and somehow managed to get into Lisa's ultra-posh building without alerting the security system, they certainly wouldn't have smashed the place up because of the absence of valuables like "cash and jewellery", as Lipton had put it. Domestic appliances like TVs and Blu-ray players and lots of other basic household goods are very easily converted into ready cash, and the gang would have been more than happy to take them. No way would they have trashed them in a fit of pique.

So, no official police investigation, no drug-crazed gang of burglars, and — as far as I could see — no actual break-in, either. Because barring a human-fly type of approach from the roof, Lisa's apartment was only accessible through its front entrance, and neither the heavy door nor the high-spec' lock appeared to have been forced or recently replaced. Therefore, the lock had either been expertly picked (a skill unknown to eight-out-of-ten drug-crazed gang members) or, as *I* now firmly believed, simply unlocked by someone who had their own key.

In fact, there was only one irrefutable fact in the whole fairy story, and that was the reality of the sickening vandalism. In my view, this was probably the work of an individual, definitely a man, and it was deeply, *deeply* personal. It was a message. The repetition of the word BITCH was significant, as was the defiled bedroom, and the undercurrent of sexual rage that ran through it all.

I could pretty much guess the real story.

Lisa had got herself mixed up in a relationship with the wrong sort of man, probably the sort of man who was both willing and able to subsidise her extravagant lifestyle with his dodgy, unexplained income. But at some point Lisa had forgotten — or perhaps she had never truly realised — exactly what sort of man he was, and had begun to treat him the way she was wont to treat her men.

Maybe she'd unkindly dumped him, or blatantly cheated on him, or spent too much of his money on the wrong kind of thing. Or (as is more likely, bearing in mind this is Lisa we're talking about) all of the above. She'd done something, anyway, to piss him off bigtime, and it had been enough to spark the apartment-trashing response.

Lisa would not have called the police under these circumstances, all her instincts of self-preservation would have urged her not to. But she obviously wasn't above calling up her little puppy dog, her biggest fan, Mr. Andrew Lipton, to clean up the mess for her while she sunned her shapely, pampered derrière on some foreign beach — recovering from the shock, darling. When she came back, she'd give him a pat on the head and tickle his belly, and the poor chump would think he was in heaven.

By the time I found a parking space a couple of hundred yards from my parents' house and turned off the engine, I realised that I had been gone the best part of two hours. I really should have gone straight in, because it was a certainty that either my daughter or my parents, or both, weren't coping with the unusual situation I had placed them in. But for a while, I simply stayed where I was.

Mostly I guess I was trying to come to terms with the way I was feeling — the growing realisation that the last thing I had said to Lipton as I left Lisa's flat was more truthful than I had known at the time. The last word on our marriage *had* been spoken a long time ago. It *was* over. It had finally got through to me, as though a switch had been thrown.

I wasn't exactly sure which particular detail had finally tipped me over the edge. Maybe Lipton's assertion, ridiculous though it seemed, that he and Lisa were lovers had something to do with it. Maybe it was the nauseating destruction Lisa had brought upon herself, clear evidence of the circles she now moved in and the company she kept. Or maybe it was the sad little photo album, filled with pictures of our innocent daughter, abandoned in the midst of it all. Maybe that was the final straw.

Or maybe it was just this: I had looked at Andrew Lipton and suddenly seen myself.

I mean, our physiques aside, what was the real difference? Both of us came running at Lisa's merest whisper. Both us were ready to do absolutely anything for her, and to forgive her absolutely anything. She knew that she could walk all over us, so that's what she did. In reality, I was no different to Andrew Lipton, or to any of the other little lapdogs and puppy dogs who I had sneered at for allowing themselves to get sucked into Lisa's dark gravity.

In fact, I was worse, because I knew better.

Well, not any more, I decided. I was done. I no longer cared where Lisa was, what she was doing, or who she was doing it with. I didn't care if she was happy or sad, safe or afraid, dead or alive. This was astonishing to me — I simply didn't *care* anymore. I felt amazingly light and pleasantly numb, the way I imagined a man who has been falsely imprisoned for years must feel as he steps out of the prison gates, having finally been vindicated and pardoned.

I felt *free*.

But little did I know, I was only on parole.

Four

My parents are very old and their house is very dusty, and — to tell you the absolute truth — *vice versa.*

The house is absolutely crammed from basement to attic with ancient 16mm and Super 8mm film reels and associated projection systems and accessories, extinct-format videotapes and slides, thousands and thousands of obscure books, newspapers and periodicals from around the world, and actual filing cabinets full of correspondence from their many friends and former colleagues in the Civil Service.

My parents' minds are likewise crammed with two long lifetimes of facts and figures and arcane strategies. They have always loved games, quizzes, and puzzles of all descriptions, and have for many years contributed crosswords to newspapers as lofty as The *International Herald Tribune,* and as humble as the local free papers. They never seemed to differentiate.

One of the most abiding memories of my youth is watching them indulge their hobbies, which they seemed to take just as seriously as their work for the Civil Service, and which were hardly ever (for which read *never)* deemed suitable for my involvement. I have a number of memories (vague, and no doubt slightly false memories) of doors being closed on me, and books being snapped shut if I tried to read over their shoulders.

Like I said, my parents weren't what you might call kid-friendly.

So imagine my surprise when I walked into the living room and saw that Rosalind and Vincent appeared to be trying to teach Vic the rudiments of chess. It seemed so out of character that my surprise was almost shock. Where was all this patience and tolerance when I was small, where was this sense of inclusion?

Any measure of resentment I might have felt, however, was immediately blown away by the happiness I saw on Vic's face when she looked at me, the excited light in her green eyes. Improbable though it seemed, she had really enjoyed my parents' company, and they had clearly enjoyed hers.

It came to me then that it really was possible for people to learn from their mistakes. Seeing them interact with their granddaughter this way, it looked as if my parents might have learned something over the years.

And I realised that if *they* could, so could I.

'Everything okay?' I asked them.

'She's very bright, Joel,' Rosalind said immediately.

'Remarkable,' Vincent agreed.

I nodded. Maude was always telling me my daughter was a bit of a prodigy, and was destined to be a genius.

'Look, Daddee,' Vic said, snatching up a double handful of chessmen from the board, totally destroying the game. 'I got *prawns!*'

WE GOT HOME at around five-thirty and I put Vic straight in the bath. While she was still making bubble beards and telling me how funny and smelly my parents were, the phone rang. It was Maude, who was checking up on the arrangements for the following day, when Vic was due to begin her twice-weekly attendance at a local playgroup.

I sat on the toilet seat to keep an eye on Vic while she bathed, and told Maude about my visit to Lisa's apartment, all the while carefully moderating my language because of Vic. Not that what I told Maude was the full, unexpurgated version of the visit, anyway. Not by any means. It was more like the PG version of an 18 Certificate visit — heavily censored for sex and violence. And poo.

Nevertheless, even with this swathe of editorial cuts it might still have made for an exquisitely awkward conversation, confessing to my mother-in-law that I had finally fallen out of love with her daughter. But I had learned over the years that beneath the stereotypical mother-in-law persona she sometimes adopted, Maude was actually a very compassionate and understanding woman. She was wise, warm-hearted and incredibly fair-minded. In short, she was everything her daughter was not.

It was my fervent hope that all these marvellous attributes, which had obviously skipped a generation with Lisa, would be passed on to Vic along with her green eyes.

'Well, it's none of my business, of course, but I'd say it's about time,' was Maude's first reaction after I had finished speaking.

Despite my belief that she would understand, her words still filled me with relief.

'You know, we used to worry about Lisa so much, Henry and I,' she went on. 'She was such a beautiful child, just an angel from day one. But from puberty onward everything seemed to go wrong. Almost overnight she turned surly, deceitful, rude, incommunicative — and dishonest, too. She didn't only lie, she *stole*. From us, and from our friends and relatives, and as a policeman, you can imagine how Henry felt about that!'

I could.

'I can't remember how many boyfriends she had at that time, I don't think I *want* to know, and the ones I met were all highly unsuitable. Goodness knows what the others were like — a bunch of criminals, probably, Henry always said. We thought it was just the usual teenage rebellion at first, the same sort of behaviour we'd seen before in the children of our friends. So we battened down the hatches and waited for it to fizzle out on its own...'

She paused, and I heard a regretful sigh.

'...but unfortunately, it never did, not even when she ceased to be a teenager. In fact, as she moved into her twenties, she seemed to get even worse. She became a person I wasn't sure I wanted to know anymore. Then she met *you*, Joel...'

'And it all went downhill from there,' I joked weakly.

'Exactly the opposite. Everything got so much better almost instantly. It was as though our daughter had been returned to us. Our *real* daughter, that is, the one we'd raised — not that awful changeling. She loved you so much, Joel, she really did, and it brought all her better, finer qualities flooding back. Henry and I were so happy. I thought it was very telling that you were a crucial few years older than her, and that you were a policeman just as her father had been, as if it had a stabilising effect on her.'

'So you think that my leaving the force the way I did *destabilised* her?'

'Not on its own, no. But if I'm honest, I do think it contributed a little. Then Victoria came along, quickly followed by the move out to Hertfordshire. With the benefit of hindsight, it was a little like a line of dominoes tumbling. I think she tried to fight it as long as she could. But for the last few months before she left, I swear I could see her reverting. I just hoped that I was wrong…'

This made me feel guilty all over again, because the dominoes Maude had mentioned were all mine, every single one of them. I had set them up and I had knocked them down.

I hadn't needed to leave the police when I did. I could easily have gone on with the piss-poor desk jobs they were offering. But pride and resentment were eating away at my ego every day, and when I was given the option of a golden handshake on medical grounds, I grabbed it. In much the same way, I hadn't needed to rush into getting my suburban licence to become a taxi-driver. But I'd wanted to do something quickly, before I began to stagnate, and it was the first thing to appeal to me — partly because I already knew London like the back of my hand, but mostly because it was a way to be my own boss, a one-man-band, a private operator. A rock. An island.

My reasoning was that if there was no one to trust, there was no one to betray me.

Furthermore, later on I was the one who really wanted a child, and now that I look back on it, maybe I'd unconsciously coerced Lisa into conceiving, in just the same way as I very consciously coerced her to give up smoking, for the sake of the maybe-baby. And I was the one who had decided, and implacably insisted, on the move out of London against all Lisa's objections. I had my reasons for the move, of course, all of them good.

The main reason was that over the previous year or so, I had come to learn that taxi-drivers get to see a lot of the same things that coppers do. This means that we see human nature in the raw. Human nature down and dirty. And let me tell you, a lot of the time it really stinks. The difference is that when you're a copper, at least you feel you have *some* small measure of control over the ugliness.

But as a taxi-driver, you have *nothing*. No power, no authority, only the crushing awareness that you're an unarmed civilian in an unacknowledged civil war. I had begun to look at London in a totally different way, and I realised that I didn't want my child growing up in that kind of environment.

As luck would have it, Lisa's parents already lived in leafy Hertfordshire, so I had moved us out to be close to them. I sold the black cab, bought the Scenic, got my hackney carriage licence from the Welwyn-Hatfield Borough Council, and went back to work. It had seemed to me like the best solution for us all.

Ah well — as it says in the Bible, the road to hell is paved with good intentions. What it *doesn't* say, of course, is that it's possible to drive down the bastard with the meter running.

All the time I'd been brooding, Maude may as well have been reading my mind.

'Joel, *none* of this is your fault,' she said firmly. 'Don't think for one moment that I blame you for what happened. As far as I'm concerned, you left the Job with your integrity intact. Henry thinks so too. You did the *right* thing. You always have. We're proud of you and your achievements. First you found an alternative way to make a decent living, and then you wanted a family, and you wanted a safe place to raise that family, and you made it all happen. It wasn't your fault our daughter was cracked. You were a good husband then, and you're a good father now.'

I got this curious little tickle in my throat just about then, and Vic peered at me from a mane of bubbles and asked me what was wrong with my eyes, had I got soap in them?

Yeah, that's right, Vic, I got soap in my eyes.

'What I'm saying, Joel,' Maude said, 'is that I'm *glad* the scales have finally fallen from your eyes. The years that you and Lisa were together were the best of her life, I'm sure, and I bless you for them even if she doesn't. But now you can move on. It's time. You've done your duty.'

AN HOUR OR so later, while Vic and I were snuggled up on the sofa in our jimjams watching *Mary Poppins* for about the eight-thousandth time, the doorbell rang. I left Vic trying to copy Dick Van Dyke's attempt at a Cockney accent, and exited the living room pulling on my dressing gown.

I opened the front door on to my poorly maintained garden and was momentarily struck dumb. Standing on my doorstep, literally dwarfed by the line of overgrown miniature conifers that ran alongside the garden path, was just about the shortest, ugliest man I had ever seen in my entire life.

Dressed in a sharp grey suit in a style that was much too young for him, he was about four-eight or four-nine, with greying mousey hair that had been shaven almost to the bone of his wide, flattish skull. He had so much scar tissue on his face that he looked, at first glance, like a burns victim. But then I saw the squashed tomato nose and the cauliflower ears, and recognised the more obvious signs of a boxing history — one where he had clearly developed an intimate, long-term relationship with the canvas.

Being so short, he looked somewhat like a child wearing a rubber mask, and when I finally managed to mutter a greeting, I half expected his response to be, 'Trick or treat?'

Instead he grunted, 'You September?'

I nodded.

Then he said, 'I'm looking for Lisa.'

I frowned. 'Lisa?'

'Yes. Lisa Forrester-September. This is her house, isn't it?'

I felt strangely off-balance. Apart from a few minor dialogue changes, this was exactly the same uncomfortable conversation I'd had with Andrew Lipton this morning, only now I was on the other side of it.

'It *was* her house,' I told him, 'but she doesn't live here anymore.'

'Where is she now? I need to speak to her.'

I shook my head, more to clear it than in reply. I wasn't enjoying this version of the conversation any more than I had the first.

'Who are you?' I asked him.

'I'm her boyfriend.'

Boyfriend? Déjà vu, I thought.

I'm afraid I began to laugh.

All right, I know it was cruel and unfair and bang out of order, but come on! If the union of Luscious Lisa and Andrew Lipton was too ridiculous for words, what on earth was this?

I was familiar with the story of *Beauty and the Beast*, of course... but *Beauty and the Mangled Pixie*? Really?

I'm fully aware that women sometimes choose the most unlikely of men as partners, perhaps out of the belief that they can change and improve them. But Lisa certainly wasn't that kind of women. In fact, the only kind of woman I could imagine being up for *this* job would have to be a top plastic surgeon — perhaps one who specialised in miniatures.

'What's so funny, fella?' he spat when I couldn't seem to stop chuckling. 'What's so fuckin' funny?'

By now he was really angry with me — actually he was more than just angry, he was completely *enraged*, doing his absolute nut. Perhaps justifiably. I had to bite the inside of my cheek hard enough to draw blood.

'I'm very sorry, I shouldn't have laughed,' I apologised, 'but I just don't see you as Lisa's type.'

He glowered up at me from beneath a Neanderthal-heavy brow broken by old scars. 'Yeah? Well, little Lisa's standards might have dropped recently.'

The QUEEN of HEARTS

Now this was well below the belt, and all my good intentions instantly flew away like little birds. Flap, flap, flap.

'I can't imagine they'd drop low enough to include you,' I replied coldly.

'You'd be surprised.'

'Mate,' I said, 'I'd be absolutely bloody *astounded*.'

Then it suddenly occurred to me that this thug, this squat little troll of a man, seemed like exactly the kind of person who would be capable of violently trashing an apartment, spraying vile sexual graffiti on the walls, and then squeezing out a large-economy pony-and-trap on someone else's bed.

'She really likes it, your wife, doesn't she?' he sniggered. 'She likes it rough and ready?'

Goaded despite myself, I stepped out through the doorway to confront him. It was his turn to laugh now, his wide grin showing me a sprinkling of gold crowns where his real teeth used to be. But at the same time he backed up a couple of steps to maintain the distance between us. His fists came up in a mocking defensive guard position. He tapped his knuckles together as though he had the gloves on and then thumbed his nose at me like Bruce Lee.

'Want to try your luck, Sonny Jim?'

'No, thanks,' I said. 'I've never hit a midget before, and I'm not about to start now.'

His grin evaporated fast.

'Who are you?' I demanded. 'What do you want with Lisa?'

'You can consider yourself a lucky man, September,' he growled, rolling his shoulders to relieve the uncomfortable tension of holding his aggression in check. 'Nobody talks to me like that. If I didn't have my orders, I'd—'

'Yeah, you'd bite my ankles off.'

For a second his piggy little eyes looked ready to shoot laser beams. 'No,' he said. 'What I'd do is, I'd introduce you to the Lightning Bolt.'

'The *what?*'

He clenched his right hand into a tight fist and held it up like a golden trophy for my inspection. 'Once you ride the Lightning, baby, you go down and you *stay* down.'

'Stop it,' I yawned, 'you're scaring me.'

'You'd be scared, all right, if I didn't have—'

'Your orders, right. So let's talk about who's *giving* the orders, shall we?'

He immediately dropped his fists and began to back off. 'Tell Lisa the Big Man wants to talk,' he said.

'The *Big Man?* Who's that? Not *you*, surely?'

'Just do it,' he scowled.

I watched him retreat backwards all the way to the gate, swiping at the conifers as he passed with little feints and jabs, and then scuttle out into the street like a garden gnome on the lam.

'Tell Lisa to get in touch,' he called out. 'Tell her to do it before someone she cares about gets hurt.'

'Are you threatening me?'

He laughed nastily. 'Not you, September — I said someone she *cares* about...'

His eyes momentarily dropped from my face to a point both below and behind me, and he waggled his ruined eyebrows at whatever he saw there. When I looked down, I saw that Vic had joined us, and was now standing in the doorway watching the proceedings with considerable interest.

'Cor, guvnor,' she said, still in character from the movie, 'you're a toff, an' no mistake!' And then, pointing at our unwelcome visitor, added, 'Look, Daddee — a goblin!'

'Get it *now*, September?'

I thought of the photograph of Vic missing from the album I'd found at Lisa's apartment, and suddenly I *did* understand.

'Hey!' I yelled. 'Come back here! Come back right now!'

He began to jog away down the street, bearing his gold teeth at me again in a vicious grin, and I ran after him as well as my knee would allow, which wasn't all that well.

'Hey, you! Stop there!'

By the time I had reached the gate, he was halfway down the street, and as I watched he jumped into the passenger seat of a black Rover that was parked facing away from the house. The engine immediately roared to life and the car lurched away from the kerb. Seconds later it had turned the corner and had left the cul-de-sac.

I stood at the gate, breathing hard and shaking with pure anger. Vic, seeing that the show was over for now, toddled back inside to catch up with *Mary*, and I was alone. Or at least, I thought I was.

'What was all that about?'

I turned and saw that old Mrs. Webber from two doors down had ventured out on to her own doorstep, and now stood looking at me with the gravity of a judge in a murder trial. We weren't the closest of neighbours, truth be told, having had a few run ins over the years, most of them regarding Albert the Cat's interest in Mrs. W's pretty little tabby, Alice — said interest being extremely carnal. Mrs. Webber didn't like it. But my argument had always been that Alice seemed to like it just fine.

'I don't know,' I replied, 'I'm not sure.'

'I *wondered* who that car belonged to,' she said. 'It's been hanging around for nearly a week now, off and on.'

I looked at her more closely. 'Are you sure?'

Silly question. Mrs. Webber was a notorious neighbourhood snoop and gossip, and virtually nothing happened in the cul-de-sac without her knowing about it. She could probably tell me which pair of socks I'd worn today, and if they had any holes in them — and, if pressed, how long the holes had been there. It was tempting to believe that Mrs. W had been a resident here in the cul-de-sac since the dawn of time, but actually we were here first, moving in a few months before she did. Yet somehow she always managed to make me feel like the newcomer.

'Of course I'm sure,' she replied indignantly. 'Oh, they parked in different places each time,' she added with a small moue of disdain, as if anyone imagined she could be fooled so easily. 'In the cul-de-sac one day, just outside it the next. One side of the street one day, the other side the next. But it was the same car, all right.'

'You say *they* parked? How many men were there?'

'Two, but I never saw the driver because of the tinted windows, just the little one when he got out.' She paused for a moment, frowning. 'What happened to his *face*, do you think? Was it an accident?'

'I should think it was probably done on purpose,' I replied. And might be again, I thought, if he ever had the nerve to come back.

I began to make my way back up the garden path, feeling the old lady's eyes on me all the way. I don't think she was terribly impressed by my tatty dressing gown.

Thinking hard, I paused on the threshold.

'Mrs. Webber, this might sound like an odd question, but I don't suppose you made a note of the car's licence plate number, did you?'

'Of course not. Why would I do something so strange?'

'No reason,' I said, trying not to sound deflated. 'No reason at all.'

No reason except that license plates could be traced to their owners, and I would have dearly liked to know the name of the ugly little bastard who had just threatened me and my daughter.

AFTER VIC WAS asleep, I snuck up into the loft and retrieved from the dust and the cobwebs a large cardboard box that had once contained our microwave oven. Now it contained everything that was left in the house of my wife's possessions.

I carried it down into the kitchen and used a paring knife to slit the wide packing tape that held the box together. When I'd originally sealed it up, it had felt like I was throwing the last clod of earth on the grave of our marriage. What I was doing now felt like raising an evil spirit.

The top of the box was padded out with clothes, including a couple of sweaters that had been worn but never washed. As a result, the smell of Lisa's favourite perfume rose out of them as if she were here herself, and I could feel my heart walloping away in my chest. I pulled out all the clothes and put them to one side, then picked through the rest of the stuff, knick-knacks and other odds and ends mostly, until I found what I wanted.

It was something I had found a few months after Lisa had left, when I was moving furniture to repaint a wall. She hadn't left it behind deliberately, it had fallen down the back of a chest of drawers and been lost. It was an old address book that spanned a time from long before we met to shortly after we married.

I began to flick through the book, just as I had when I had first found it, but this time there was a major difference. Then it had been idle curiosity, and soul-searching, and a weird kind of self-punishment. Now it was an investigation.

This was *Operation Find Lisa*.

It wasn't that I was worried about *her* anymore, I told myself (although of course I was), but I *was* worried about our daughter. And I was worried about the man she'd called a goblin. I didn't want him coming around here anymore, making his threats. I wasn't going to let that happen, and if I had to find Lisa and get her to call this so-called Big Man to put a stop to it, then that was exactly what I was going to do.

So... It turned out that a lot of the names in the book were mutual friends of ours, most of which I realised I hadn't spoken to in a very long time. In fact, to be honest, I'd lost touch with them all. Whenever I read a newspaper report about another old person being found in their home, having died and laid there for

The QUEEN of HEARTS

weeks afterward, undiscovered, I always think, how did that happen? How could someone be so alone?

But I think that *this* is how it begins, with simple laziness. If you don't make the effort to maintain them, all your friendships soon begin to crumble, and then your world diminishes, gets smaller and narrower, until there's only you. And probably a cat, who will most likely begin to eat you only minutes after you've expired in your armchair, the ultimate TV dinner.

You know, it's cheery thoughts precisely like this that make me as popular as I am.

I started calling the numbers, not knowing what to expect.

For the most part those mutual friends seemed happy to hear from me, and sounded just as guilty about having lost contact as I was, which was sort of a comfort. Everyone was friendly and eager to know how Vic and I were getting along now. But it was noticeable that very few of them asked about Lisa. Even those people who had been her friends more than mine. In fact, a couple of them reluctantly broached a sensitive subject.

It appeared that Lisa had borrowed money from them over the last six or so months, and had yet to pay it back. In most cases the sum was a few hundred pounds. In a couple of cases it was a few *thousand* pounds. I promised to do what I could about getting her to pay it back, but I'm sure they could hear the doubt in my voice. When was the last time, I could almost hear these people thinking, you were able to make Lisa do anything?

All of these calls were very interesting, but they brought me no closer to Lisa, so I moved on to the names of people I *didn't* know.

The QUEEN of HEARTS

In many cases (an alarming number of cases, in fact) these were simply men's forenames and their phone numbers, and I remembered Maude saying that she didn't like to think how many boyfriends Lisa had enjoyed in the years before I came along. Neither did I, but now I had to. Some of the names in the book were underlined or circled, and some of them were highlighted with suggestive little stars.

I found my own entry, which said, Joel (Cop). September (?). I got five stars, but the high rating gave me no pleasure whatsoever.

I soon discovered that lot of these second-string numbers no longer existed. Or if they did still exist, Dave or Stevie or Michael no longer lived there. Or Derek or Marlon or T.J. heard me say Lisa's name and just hung up — or laughed, or swore, and *then* hung up. Finally, I was left with only one more number, a landline with an area code that rang a bell somewhere at the back of my mind.

It belonged to a man called David. He had two stars, one either side of his name.

I dialled the number. Somewhere a phone rang five times before being answered by what sounded like a very well-bred pre-teens girl. I told her I was looking for David and the phone immediately clattered on to a table, making me wince. I heard her shouting, 'Daddy, someone on the phone for you!'

A moment later, a very deep, measured voice said, 'Hello?'

'Hi,' I said, 'is that David?'

'It is.'

'Hello, David, I'm wondering if you might be able to help me.'

The QUEEN of HEARTS

By now, after all the calls I had already made, I felt as though I were reading from an over-familiar script, and was speculating on ditching taxi-driving and taking up telesales as a career.

'I'm trying to locate a woman called Lisa September, and your name came up. When you knew her, she may have been going under her maiden name of Forrester?'

After a long silence, he quietly asked, 'Who is this?'

'I'm sorry, my name is Joel September. I'm—'

I was about to explain my relationship to Lisa and how I came by his name and number, but he suddenly broke in.

'Joel? Did you say Joel September?'

'Yes.'

'Well, for Heaven's sake! Joel, this is *David* — David Handley!'

Click, click, click, it fell into place.

Handley was the chairman of the board at Morgan-Matheson, Lisa's boss at the bank. No wonder the area code seemed familiar. In addition to meeting Handley at various company functions over the years, Lisa and I had also been along to a couple of New Year's Eve parties at his home in the country, a large, expensively renovated barn on the outskirts of a small, exclusive Hampshire village.

His daughter was a chunky, horse-faced thing, I seemed to remember now, a scale-model version of her mother. Handley himself was exactly the tanned, distinguished-grey executive he sounded like. At home in the Nineteenth Hole, on the decks of yachts, and at luncheon in The Ivy.

I quickly explained how I had found his number, and told him that I needed to contact Lisa urgently and by now was clutching at straws.

'I don't suppose she happened to mention to you where she was planning to go?' I asked.

'Go?'

'For her vacation. You know, to get over the shock of the break-in.'

In the background, I heard the horsy daughter canter by, bugling voice at full volume. 'Hang on a moment, will you, Joel,' Handley said.

I heard him get up from his seat, and a woman's Home Counties voice asking who he was speaking to at this time of night. Handley, the receiver pressed against his chest, rumbled that it was just business. I heard a door close and then Handley came back on the line, speaking into the silence of a bank vault.

'Sorry about that, couldn't hear myself think there for a moment.'

'That's okay.'

I waited for Handley to speak, but I had to wait for an uncomfortably long time. Eventually, he said, 'Joel, I think we need to have a conversation, but I am not prepared to do it now, not over the phone. I think this is something that needs to be said face to face, privately. Is there any chance that you could come down to the bank, say tomorrow morning?'

I had to drop Vic at her first playgroup at nine o'clock, and Maude would pick her up for me just after eleven. Not too much of a problem. This kind of flexibility was what made my life viable.

I told Handley I could be with him by about ten o'clock.

'That'll be fine. I'll leave word at reception for you to be brought straight up to me. I'll see you then, Joel. Goodnight.'

'Goodnight.'

I put the phone down. Handley had sounded his usual confident self, but I was convinced that most of it, maybe *all* of it after that initial, inquiring 'Hello', was pure bluff. There was a lot of stuff going on under the surface. I was convinced that some of it was embarrassment. The rest of it was something else, something I was going to have to wait to find out, and it was pointless to speculate.

But all the same, I was betting it had something to do with his home telephone number being in Lisa's private address book. That and the two stars which bracketed his name.

I went to bed, but I didn't sleep for a long, long time. When I did, I dreamed of Lisa lost in the maze again, desperately twisting this way and that, terrified eyes wide in the darkness as the circling beast drew ever closer.

I wasn't altogether surprised to note that my suspicious mind was beginning to root for the beast.

FIVE

'SO, HOW WAS it?' Maude asked when I phoned her from the car the next morning on the hands-free. 'How did it go?'

In the run up to Vic attending her first solo playgroup session, I had admitted to Maude that I found the prospect of actually leaving her in the care of more or less complete strangers a very frightening prospect. I was convinced that at least one of us was going to burst into tears, and that it might well be me blubbing away like a fool.

Fortunately, the reality had been easier to bear.

'It wasn't too bad,' I said, weaving through the city-wide *Magnificent Monday* morning congestion. 'You remember I went in with Vic last week to get her used to the place, and she really took a shine to the playgroup leader, Elaine? Well, the very second that Vic saw Elaine's face this morning, she ran in at top speed and never once looked back.'

'How did that make you feel?'

'Proud,' I said. 'Proud... and slightly redundant.'

'Oh, you're far from redundant, don't worry about that,' Maude assured me. 'Were you the only man there again?'

'Yeah, and all the mums still look at me like I'm some kind of monster.'

'They'll get used to you soon enough.'

'I suppose so.'

Privately, I doubted this. Most of the women I had seen there obviously regarded me with extreme suspicion, as though at any moment I might rip off my Charming Single Daddy disguise to reveal the slavering child-molester beneath, and then carry off their snot-nosed rugrats to my wicked lair for a spot of cannibalistic perversity.

'You never know how things are going to work out, Joel,' Maude continued. 'This isn't just the beginning of Victoria's introduction to education, it's also the start of her social life. She's going to make friends, and be invited to parties and to other girl's houses for teas and sleepovers. Maybe you'll get invited places, too.'

'I don't think so,' I laughed, recalling the horror with which the mums had viewed a man in their midst. I didn't rate my chances of being invited to many sleepovers, anyway.

'Well, of course it's none of my business, but you've got to keep an open mind. You're still a young man, a devoted single-father who, in my humble opinion, could use a little TLC — or, if nothing else, some intensive sexual healing. Mark my words, Joel, somewhere out there is a single-mother with the same needs.'

'Maude, please, you're embarrassing me!'

I was kidding around a bit, trying to sound amused, but the truth is that I really was embarrassed. That none-of-my-business act of Maude's was almost her trademark, and I could hardly recall a single conversation where she hadn't used it at least once. But the thing was that despite all her denials, she sincerely believed that my business, no matter how sensitive and personal, *was* her business.

I heard her take another deep breath, and God alone knew what she would come out with next. All I knew was that I didn't want to hear it. There's only so much a man can take.

'Listen, Maude,' I said quickly, 'I've got to go.'

'You should listen to me, Joel. It may be none of my business, but I *am* a woman, and I know what I'm talking about.'

'I'm sure you do, but I've just found a parking meter in central London, and the bloody thing makes more an hour than I do. I'll see you this afternoon.'

I terminated the connection quickly.

As kind as Maude was, and as much as I liked her, I had to be careful not to listen to her too much. Give her enough time and she could talk a ravening werewolf into being a nut cutlet-scoffing veggie, and the other way around, too, if she was so inclined.

I've often thought that the United Nations should send her to the Middle East. She might not be able to bring peace to the region, but she might at least manage to unify them against a common enemy — the Women's Institute.

TWENTY MINUTES LATER a clerical minion with a bad case of designer dandruff, who'd been impatiently waiting for me in the bank's lobby area, was leading me to David Handley's private office. He'd ascertained my identity by asking my name but never got around to offering his own, and as he rushed down the long, plushly carpeted corridors ahead of me, I had to stay clear of his slipstream to avoid inhaling fragments of his disintegrating scalp.

Two minutes after that I had been deposited in Handley's office, and Handley himself came in a further minute or two later, spouting effusive apologies for his tardiness, which I politely brushed off.

Handley was a little heavier than I remembered, and his tan was a little heavier, too, but his once grey hair had gone beautifully, photogenically silver. He looked like one of the mature male-models from those old mail-order catalogues, the guys who used to stand around in smiling groups of twos and threes, showing off the piping on their matching pants-and-vest combinations while pointing into the distance and checking the time on their wristwatches. He smiled and shook my hand warmly and offered refreshment, and he was charming and amusing and twinkling — and under it all, he was nervous as hell. I could smell it, like an underscent to his expensive aftershave lotion.

We chatted meaninglessly for a while, and finally, after his secretary had brought in a tray of coffee and we had poured and spooned and stirred, he sat down behind his impressively wide desk and nervously cleared his throat.

'How long did your affair with Lisa last?' I asked before he could speak, and the wattage of his bright smile succumbed to a sudden and drastic power shortage.

'Ah,' he said. 'So you've guessed.'

'It wasn't too difficult a deduction. When did it begin?'

'Over a year-and-a-half ago now. It only lasted for a few months, thank heavens.'

Handley was studying the ceiling, the wall, his coffee cup, his buffed fingernails, anything to avoid looking me in the eye. He was talking about a time period when, to all intents and purposes, Lisa and I had still been happily married (or so I had believed) and trying to get the hang of being parents, and he knew it.

'Was it serious?' I asked. 'Was it a relationship, or was it...?'

He paused before replying, and then said, 'I won't lie to you, Joel, it was just sex to begin with.'

I somehow resisted the urge to jump across the desk behind which he had hidden and thump him one. My calm reaction seemed to embolden him further, and he went on more confidently.

'It was the old story, of course, two highly-ambitious, highly-driven professionals working closely together for extended periods of time, often long into the night. It was the moments of eye-contact that became longer and longer, the relationship becoming increasingly familiar and tactile as we bonded. And then slowly, almost unconsciously, we began to... well, *seduce* each other. In the end, I don't believe that either of us was truly to blame. It was pure chemistry, it was human nature, it was circumstance, it was a heady, irresistible combination of them all...'

Before this meeting, while dwelling upon my dark suspicions, I'd imagined that this kind of self-serving, self-justifying speech would have incensed me, pushing me over the edge — but now, perversely, it just made me want to laugh out loud.

I imagined Handley lying awake in his bed last night, his pony-club matron of a wife snoring away beside him as he practised these lines of dialogue under his breath, sharpening his delivery, and wondering how the piece would play to a hostile audience of one.

I was about to respond, but Handley hadn't quite finished.

'But then I got it into my head that it was something more than just a bit of fun,' he continued, and somehow he sounded hurt, and therefore slightly more sincere. 'I did some silly things, I admit. I started to make a dreadful fool of myself, before realising what a terrible risk I was taking, with my career, with my family. It was my mid-life crisis, I suppose. Needless to say, I now bitterly regret my inappropriate behaviour and any pain I may have caused to others.'

Yeah, yeah, yeah, I thought, sincerity bit over and done with. Now Handley sounded like the counsel for the defence doing the pious bit in their summing up, which I'd seen so often in the courts. As if saying sorry made it all better, no harm done. Admission as absolution.

'And this is why you wanted to speak to me here, rather than at home?' I asked.

'Yes, for the most part. It would not have been a good idea for my wife to hear me discussing anything concerning Lisa, even now. I don't think she knew about the affair, not for sure, but she probably suspected. My wife has a very good friend in our overseas bureau and gets frequent updates on company gossip.'

He smiled to himself.

'And, of course, Lisa had…'

He abruptly stopped himself going any further with this line of thought. The smile vanished back into his box of tricks. I think that just for a moment, he'd forgotten exactly who he was speaking to.

'And Lisa had what?' I prompted.

'Lisa had developed a reputation as...' He was colouring up nicely now beneath his tan. 'Well, as something of a... a flirt.'

'A *flirt?*'

He shrugged uncomfortably, and we both knew he was talking about more than simple flirting. Did I want to know who else in the bank Lisa had screwed to further her precious career? Did I want a damn *list?* No, I did not. What I really wanted to do was get out of this office and puke into a bucket until my socks came out of my mouth.

I was about to rise from my seat when something small and indistinct that had snagged on my subconscious earlier finally came clear.

'*Had,*' I said.

'I beg your pardon?' Handley replied.

'You keep saying *had*. You keep referring to Lisa in the past tense. Why is that?'

'That's the other reason I wanted you to come here today, Joel. You asked me last night if I knew where Lisa had gone on holiday.'

I sat up a little straighter. 'Yes?'

'I thought you should know that she *isn't* on holiday. Or not from Morgan-Matheson, at any rate. The truth is that Lisa doesn't work here anymore. Lisa hasn't worked here for approximately five months.'

I absorbed this surprising news for a few seconds, and then asked, 'Did she move to another bank? Was she headhunted? I know she was always talking about receiving job offers from all kinds of companies based in the—'

The QUEEN of HEARTS

'No, she didn't move to another bank, Joel. Quite the opposite. I'm afraid she was dismissed.'

'You sacked her? Why?' One reason immediately presented itself. 'Oh, I get it, you got rid of her because you couldn't face seeing her every day after your affair ended, and you didn't want your wife to find out about—'

'No, no, it wasn't that at all.' Handley's weary manner quickly diffused my rising anger. 'What happened between Lisa and I was personal, and it was in the past for both of us. It didn't affect our business relationship.'

'So what happened?'

Handley sighed. 'Lisa brought a lot of new business to Morgan-Matheson, introduced us to many wealthy new clients, and as a result she was a highly-valued member of our team. She was in line for another promotion, another substantial pay-rise, and another bonus — all fully justified in light of her achievements.'

'But then?'

'But then, quite by accident, a few irregularities were discovered in one of the accounts she managed. These irregularities were serious enough to prompt a full-scale internal inquiry. And, as a result of that inquiry, the board reluctantly decided that Lisa's position at the bank was untenable.'

I stared at him. 'Are you saying that she stole the bank's money? She embezzled from you, or from your clients?'

'No, not exactly. But it seemed that a number of the new clients she brought to the bank were of... well, shall we say, dubious character? I'm thinking of one client in particular. We could prove nothing in the end, but we strongly suspected that this individual may have been using Morgan-Matheson to launder money from illegal activities, and also that Lisa was running the operation for him.'

I closed my eyes briefly, suppressing a groan. This was worse than I had expected. I had been ready for the infidelity. This was something else entirely.

'Something's telling me that you didn't report this to the police,' I said.

Handley shook his head. 'The board thought long and hard about that option, but eventually decided that a public scandal was not in the best interest of either the bank or its clients.'

'I see.'

The board had decided. Which meant that Handley, as its chairman, had decided. Which meant that Lisa had probably blackmailed him over their affair. There was no doubt about it, I thought, my wife was a real charmer.

'So Lisa walked away scot free,' I said.

'I wouldn't say that, exactly. There were consequences. Very grave consequences, in fact. She lost her livelihood, for one thing. Banks are like elephants, Joel, they have very long memories. Lisa will never work in a legitimate financial institution ever again. We thought that was probably punishment enough, for someone...'

'For someone like Lisa?' I said, finishing his sentence for him.

'Yes.'

'What about the dodgy client? Who was he?'

'I'm afraid I am unable to divulge that information at this time.'

Handley saw my irritation and softened his stance a little.

'As far as our inquiry was able to ascertain, 'he' was in fact a number of false identities, shell companies, and dummy corporations, none of which we were able trace to their true source. If there ever were any files in existence that might have pointed to a real identity, we believe that Lisa must have destroyed them.'

Or *hidden* them, I thought. Somewhere in her swish apartment, for instance.

I saw again in my mind's eye all those emptied drawers and cupboards, the scattered papers, and the ripped upholstery. It hadn't been a case of simple vandalism bought in by a vicious sugar-daddy, after all. It had been a search party ordered by a desperate criminal.

I stood up. Handley also rose and began to show me to the door, but hung back a little, not daring to offer his hand, just in case I was feeling vengeful. I had just reached for the door handle when something else occurred to me.

I remembered asking Andrew Lipton how he and Lisa had met. He had told me they'd worked together at the bank, but then he'd left for "pastures new", I believe it was. But the reality was that *Lisa* was the one who had left. Did this mean that Lipton was still working here? If so, I wanted another word with him, and I wanted him to tell me the truth this time.

I turned back to Handley. 'Andrew Lipton? Where might I find—'

Handley's face immediately creased with concern. 'I know, isn't it terrible? I was so shocked when I heard. It just shows you — it doesn't matter who you are or what you're worth, no one is safe in this city anymore. Thank goodness I live in the country.'

'What are you talking about?' I asked, frowning. 'Isn't *what* terrible?'

Handley blinked. 'Didn't you hear? Poor Andrew was mugged yesterday evening. Beaten up in his own home by a gang of burglars, a completely unprovoked, vicious attack...'

LIPTON WAS IN a private room at the Royal Free Hospital. The care was top of the line, but the security was surprisingly lax. With a little guile anybody could just walk in and make themselves at home, and so that's what I did.

I found Lipton fast asleep, quite probably medicated, with an IV line plugged into one of his arms feeding him fluids. I ate some of his grapes and drank half a jug of his orange squash while I waited for him to wake up, and I thought about how I had managed to get him so wrong.

Before leaving Morgan-Matheson, I'd had David Handley explain that crack of his about it not mattering who someone was or what they were worth, and what do you know — it turned out that Lipton *was* rich, after all. Or at least his parents were. They were super-rich. That's mostly what he was doing at the bank, learning how to look after the family fortune. It wasn't a real job, because he didn't *need* a real job.

That's what I'd got wrong. Through Lisa, I was used to meeting bankers, brokers and share-dealers, many of whom, in my experience, were little more than yobs with cash on the hip. But Lipton was born rich, had never known anything but rich, and he probably never gave money a second thought, except to speculate on how he could use the moolah he already had to make even more.

Lucky for some, eh?

Not that this helped him much now, even with a private room and private care. Poor-little-rich-boy, all alone in the big bad world.

Lipton, it had to be said, was a mess. A swathe of bandages had been wound over and around his head like a white turban, and below this starkness were two well-blackened eyes, a broken nose, and shredded, swollen lips. The rest of his face was covered with lots of small dark bruises, as though someone had repeatedly jabbed him with an umbrella, or as if he were mutating, rather painfully, into a Dalmatian dog.

He was still unshaven and there was grey in his stubble that I would have sworn wasn't there the day before. The arm not hooked up to the IV line lay across his thin chest in a sling. One of his legs was in plaster and elevated. Every time he breathed, he winced in pain, even in his sleep. Broken ribs, I thought. This man hadn't been mugged, he'd been worked over by someone who really enjoyed the work.

I could guess who that had been.

At that moment, Lipton's eyes fluttered open, showed instant, instinctive fear, and darted about the hospital room like a pair of trapped birds. Then he remembered where he was and began to calm down. When he finally noticed me sitting beside him, he didn't cry out in alarm, as I had expected, but simply closed his eyes again, as if that would make me disappear.

'How are you feeling?' I asked, and watched him shudder. 'Okay, so *that* was a fairly stupid question,' I admitted. 'Sorry.'

He opened his eyes. 'Please, go away.'

'What happened?'

'I'm not going to speak to you. You may as well leave.'

'But you *are* speaking to me,' I smiled. 'Don't stop now, I'm just beginning to enjoy myself.'

He glanced around for the call button so that he could summon a nurse to chase me away. Then he saw the handset on the chair beside me, well out of his reach, and seemed to slump in resignation. As best he could the way he was strapped up, he angled his body away from me, facing the opposite wall.

'Why won't you talk to me, Andrew? Do you think I had anything to do with you being attacked?'

I saw his head waggle fractionally. No.

'So what's the problem?' I thought for a moment. 'Did someone *tell* you not to speak to me?'

Another minute head movement. This one looked like a nod.

'Okay,' I said, understanding. 'All right, then I'll do the talking. All you have to do is listen. How's that?'

He nodded.

'I'm guessing you told the police that you didn't see the face of the person who mugged you, and you wouldn't be able to identify him.'

Nod.

'But you *did* see him, didn't you?'

A hesitation, then another reluctant nod.

'Okay, let me describe him for you. This guy's very short and he's very mean and he's very ugly. He was waiting for you in your flat when you got home. He'd picked the lock to get in and really ripped the place to pieces. He had lots of questions to ask you, mostly concerning the whereabouts of Lisa and some files she was supposed to have hidden.'

Lipton was now looking at me in amazement, as though I were a fortune-teller and I had the whole of his future on view in my crystal ball. Now, if I could only give him the name of his favourite colour...

'When I saw you at Lisa's,' I continued, 'you hadn't just gone around that morning to clean up, had you? No one cleans an apartment wearing a pinstriped suit, even if they had slept in it the night before, like you had. You were hiding out there, weren't you?'

Another small nod.

'What was the theory, you thought he wouldn't come back to Lisa's place again, because he'd already searched it?'

'Yes,' he whispered.

'Not bad thinking,' I acknowledged. 'But then you went back to your own flat because you thought the coast was clear. Unfortunately, it wasn't. He was there waiting for you. Who is he, Andrew? What's the name of the man who did this to you?'

'I think I heard her say his name was Greg,' he mumbled.

'Greg? Greg *who?*'

He shrugged carefully, mindful of his arm resting in in the sling, and then he quietly mumbled something else — something that was hard to believe, and even harder to stomach.

'He's *what?*' I said, aghast.

'He was Lisa's boyfriend,' Lipton confirmed, sounding almost as nonplussed as I felt myself.

So the Goblin had been telling the truth about that?

'Not for long, I don't think, just a couple of weeks or so,' Lipton added. 'This was on the rebound, after that other guy dumped her.'

'*What* other guy?'

'His boss, the Big Man.'

'Lisa slept with him, too?'

He nodded sadly.

'Jesus Christ!' I couldn't help myself exclaiming. 'Is there anybody in this whole mess my wife *hasn't* shagged?'

'Yes,' Lipton answered miserably. 'Me.'

He wasn't a great deal of help after that. He claimed not to know any of the names involved in the money-laundering scheme, and also that he'd known nothing of Lisa's illegal activities at the bank until the results of the inquiry were revealed. He knew Lisa had files of some kind hidden away — or at least, she had hinted to him she had — but not where they were, or what kind of damning evidence they contained.

He also repeated his claim that he didn't know where my estranged wife had gone to ground. I still wasn't sure that I believed him on that one.

'If I'd known where she was,' Lipton said, 'don't you think I'd have told that gorilla while he was busy breaking my leg? And if I knew, and still didn't tell him when he was breaking my leg, why would I tell you now?'

'What about,' I suggested after a moment's thought, studying his injured limbs, 'if I were to try a little bit of amputation? After all, we are in a hospital, and all the tools are close to hand…'

It took him a while to realise that I was joking, and then he turned his head away from me again, this time to hide a small, shy smile.

'Incidentally, Andrew, why *didn't* you tell them? Why are you so loyal to her? She isn't your girlfriend, she hasn't even slept with—'

'Because I love her,' Lipton said simply. 'And because I owe her.'

'Owe her what?'

'I was the one who discovered the irregularities in her accounts at the bank. She was out for the week, I didn't know what I was looking at, so I took it to Mr. Handley. I got her into trouble.'

'No,' I told him. 'She did that all on her own.'

I said goodbye not too long after this. In the first place Lipton was still pretty weak from the pasting he'd taken and was quickly tiring again. And in the second place, I was beginning to like him a bit too much.

Not only was he one of the few men on the face of the planet who apparently hadn't exchanged bodily fluids with my wife, but he also managed to make me look good. Lisa's father, Henry, thought that *I* was a hopeless optimist (and he's right, I am), but in comparison, Lipton was just a doormat with a birth certificate.

I DROVE BACK home to Welwyn Garden City in a pretty strange mood.

It was something like that feeling you get when a combination of mental and physical exhaustion has forced you into an almost hysterical state, and as I'm sure you know, this is a bad place to be. You cry when somebody does something nice for you. Things that shouldn't be funny suddenly are, and you laugh when you really want to cry. You suddenly notice there are signs, omens, and portents everywhere; hidden in the lyrics of songs on the radio, in the shapes of clouds in the sky, and on advertisements pasted to the back of buses.

The songs on my oldies station were all about people who had fallen in love with the wrong person, and the clouds I could see building on the horizon were huge, swollen and black, and looked as though they contained a sizable summer storm. On the back of the bus I followed out of the City and into the West End was a poster advertising a National Theatre revival of an old musical called *The Boyfriend*.

See what I mean?

I spent the rest of the day working as normal, but for the life of me, I wouldn't be able to tell you where I drove or who my passengers were. For all I knew, I could have been taking the ghost of Elvis Presley on a tour of the Welwyn/Hatfield burger restaurants, or transporting a group of extra-terrestrial commuters from their crop-circle landing site to their place of employment behind the cosmetics counters at John Lewis.

The point I'm trying to make here is that I was preoccupied. I was extremely preoccupied.

When I got home both Maude and Henry were there. Vic was on me almost before I was even in the door, and she was still absolutely full of her morning at the playgroup. She was babbling about playing with water, playing with sand, playing with blocks, playing with Elaine, and all the other boys and girls she'd met, and she showed me the painting she'd made that morning, which I think was supposed to be a horse in a field, but looked to my untrained eye more like a squid driving a mustard-yellow 1978 Ford Capri over a cliff.

My in-laws were also speaking to me, but I didn't catch too many of their words. Mostly I saw their mouths opening and closing silently, like those of goldfish in a bowl. Probably they were expecting me to tell them about my day, which was something I usually did, but obviously I couldn't do that today. I knew what they *said* they thought of their daughter, but I also knew that deep down, they still loved her far too much to want their worst expectations not only confirmed but totally surpassed.

So I did my best, and kept schtum.

Shortly before they left, Maude told me what a nice surprise she'd had when she picked Vic up from *Tiny Minds* — *Tiny Minds* being the name of the playgroup Vic had just begun attending. Its full name (rather better-sounding than its abbreviated form) was *Tiny Minds, Big Ideas*. It turned out that Elaine Leigh, the woman who ran the place, was the daughter of a dear old friend of Maude's who'd moved away from the area years ago due to a job relocation. In fact, it seemed that Elaine and Lisa had actually been in the same form at school for a number of years, and at one time had been fairly close friends.

Well, nobody's perfect, I thought.

As we waited for Henry to put his coat and shoes on, she took me aside to ask me if I thought that Elaine was an attractive woman. When I mumbled something non-committal about her seeming 'nice', Maude seemed overly, if not disturbingly, pleased. She had somehow found out that Elaine was presently unattached, and might be open to offers from a similarly attractive and practically unattached young man (Maude's fulsome description of me) who might be interested in taking her out on a date.

What did I think?

It was a typical Maude-ish performance, half-joking and half-serious, but she seemed to sense that I wasn't in the mood for the act today. She must also have sensed that I didn't want to talk about *why* I wasn't in the mood for it, and soon gave up.

'Sorry, I know it's none of my business, but I don't mean any harm,' she said, squeezing my arm. 'It was just a thought.'

'It's possible to have too many thoughts,' Henry said, finally shrugging into his jacket.

Maude smiled sweetly. 'Not for you, my darling, not for you.'

As Vic and I were waving them to their car, I suddenly had an idea and called Henry back. I knew from past experience, and from Maude's occasionally exasperated conversation, that whenever he wasn't helping to look after my daughter or tending to whatever gardening project was currently spinning his wheels, Henry spent a great deal of his time glued to the TV sports channels. It was quite possible that he had the kind of specialised knowledge I lacked.

While Maude busied herself starting the car, I asked him if he knew a boxer fitting the description of my thuggish caller of the night before. First name possibly Greg. Short, face like a smashed vegetable basket…

'Could be any one of a hundred journeymen fighters from the past twenty years,' Henry shrugged, pushing back a stray conifer branch that had tickled his ear. 'The truth is that boxing's not really my sport, and never has been. Football, rugby, golf — even the gee-gees, at a push — those have always been my areas of interest.

The QUEEN of HEARTS

Never could get myself too excited about a couple of young men knocking lumps out of each other. Of course,' he added, 'it might have been the criminal element that put me off, too — there always seemed to be a lot of crooks around boxing. Why'd you ask, anyway?'

'Oh, it was just someone I passed in the street today,' I answered vaguely, disappointed with his response. 'He looked like a boxer, seemed a bit familiar, and I wondered if I'd ever seen him fight for a title.'

'Mmm,' Henry said. 'You know, if *I* see someone on the street and their face is familiar, I tend to assume that the place I've seen them before was in a mug-shot.'

In the car, Maude pipped the horn. 'Today, if you can manage it, Henry!'

'I tell you what I'll do,' he said suddenly. 'I'll ask one of The Boys for you.'

Silently, I groaned. The Boys were Henry's golf cronies, most of whom, like Henry, had once upon a time been members of the Hertfordshire constabulary. Their average age, I guessed, was somewhere around a thousand-years-old. Henry was the youngest and the liveliest by far. The others, as far as I had seen, were just ancient blocks of wood with only an accidental similarity to men.

Henry snapped his fingers. 'Charlie will know. You know, old Charlie Noble? I think you must have met him at least once.'

Probably not, I thought. But even if I had, it was doubtful I'd remember. After all, one thousand-year-old tree stump looks pretty much like another.

'Yes, Charlie's the man for you,' Henry enthused. 'Used to box for the police force himself, back in the day. Knew everything about everybody in the game.

Might take him a while to get back to you, though. Bloody fool got married again recently. Fourth time around and he's already—'

'Henry?' Maude was revving the engine loudly, reminding me of myself outside Lisa's apartment building. 'Daisy will have eaten the television set by now.'

Henry rolled his eyes at me. 'I'll call Charlie soon as I get home. He'll sort you out.'

I was sure he would. With my sort of luck good old Charlie Noble probably remembered every single boxing contest on the planet since the dawn of time, all the way from the David and Goliath showdown right up to the latest Las Vegas World Title extravaganza, blow for blow, and would want to tell me about every one of them in detail, in chronological order.

I couldn't wait.

Six

Both Vic and I were pretty tired after our respective days. We ate dinner (fish-fingers and waffles with marmalade) and bathed far earlier than usual, and it wasn't long before we were settled down on the sofa for our nightly Disney binge. My daughter's choice for the evening's feature presentation was *Snow White*. When the phone rang mid-movie, I went to answer it with a marked lack of enthusiasm. I just knew it was going to be Henry's pal with seventy-odd-years' worth of bottled-up boxing reminiscences and all the time in the world to share them with me.

It was at times like this that I wished I still smoked cigarettes — I could have used the filters for earplugs.

When I said a guarded hello into the phone and received only silence in reply, I sighed heavily. Already been there, I thought. Been there, done that, bought the t-shirt, worn it, washed it, shrunk it, and donated it to Oxfam.

'You may as well speak,' I said irritably, 'you're paying for the call anyway.'

'I'm sorry?'

It was a woman's voice, a little faint, a little restrained in the face of my belligerence. It could have been my wife's voice, it was the right age, but it wasn't her. Lisa had never apologised for anything in her life, and she knew me far too well to ever be afraid of me.

'Hello, Mr. September? I'm sorry for disturbing you at this hour, but I felt I should call because I wanted to—'

'Who *is* this?' I barked.

'Oh!' my caller said, sounding more uncertain and flustered than ever. 'Sorry! Mr. September, this is Elaine Leigh. From *Tiny Minds*?'

Now it was my turn to say, 'Oh!' as I played for time. Although in my case it was 'Oh! as in 'Oh shit!', as I wondered what on earth old Mischievous Matchmaker Maude had been suggesting to this woman on my behalf.

'Hi, what can I do for you?' I asked cautiously, and if the answer I received was anything at all like, 'Give me an orgasm,' Maude and I were definitely going to have words.

'I just felt that I needed to tell you something.'

'Like what?' I was listening hard, but she certainly didn't sound like she was flirting. If anything, she sounded quite serious. 'Is this about Vic?' I asked.

'Well, yes it is. You see, I meant to speak to Mrs. Forrester when she arrived to pick Victoria up today. But once she recognised me, we were so busy catching up that the time just flew away…'

I bet it did. Once my mother-in-law got a choke-hold on a conversation, escaping from it took more than a simple tap-out.

'And after we'd caught up …well… let's just say that Mrs. Forrester seemed to have developed her own agenda, and wasn't in the mood to be distracted from it. She seemed *very* interested in my status as a single woman.'

'Ms. Leigh, please don't take it personally,' I told her. 'Mrs. Forrester's my mother-in-law. I'm currently separated from her daughter, and—'

'Oh, I know *that*,' she said dryly. 'Maude told me *all* about it.'

Maude. Right.

'I'm so sorry that you and Lisa couldn't make it work. I remember her from when we were just little girls with pigtails and scabs on our knees. But you know what they say — onwards and upwards, tomorrow is another day, whatever doesn't kill you, and all that stuff.'

'Yes, thanks. But the thing is, Maude has set herself up as my social secretary. She seems determined to get me hooked up with someone as soon as possible. I'm sorry if she was pushy with you.'

'Oh, Maude's too nice to be really pushy,' she said with a little laugh. 'But she's sneaky as hell, isn't she?'

'Yes, she is.'

'She stares at you with those big green eyes, just like butter wouldn't melt, and she does that old I-know-it's-none-of-my-business line. Then, before you know what's what, she's twisting one of your arms up between your shoulder blades, and you find yourself agreeing to everything she says.'

I could hear the smile in her voice. I was smiling and nodding. I liked her, and the picture she had just painted of Maude was both accurate and amusing. It was all the more unfortunate, then, that I was about to dash her good mood to smithereens.

Quickly, before she could get any chattier, I began to explain myself.

I told her that despite what Maude believed, I was in no way ready for another relationship, no matter how casual it might be or how few strings might be attached.

I thanked her for her interest (very much appreciated, of course), but added that at this moment in time it was my daughter, not myself, who had to be my number one priority.

I only stopped speaking when I realised she was making an odd sound down the line.

'Ms. Leigh, are you alright?'

It sounded like she was choking on something unfeasible large, like an entire side of beef, or perhaps trying to restrain a persistent hacking cough. After another few seconds, however, I eventually recognised the noise. It was muffled laughter.

'You know,' she said when she'd recovered, 'when Maude was busy listing all your many wonderful qualities for me, she never once mentioned that you have an ego the size of the Titanic.'

'What?'

'Did you honestly believe that I called to ask you for a date because your mother-in-law *said* I should?'

'Err... well...' Yes, I obviously had, and at this stage it was pointless to deny it.

She had another giggling fit, this time completely unmuffled, and I could feel my whole face burning with embarrassment.

'I'm so sorry,' she said, suddenly calming herself very deliberately. 'But if you knew me better, you'd realise I'm not the sort of person who'd do something like that.'

'Ms. Leigh, if I've—'

'Please, call me Elaine.'

'Elaine, I didn't mean to—'

'I mean, quite apart from anything else, you're the parent of one of our children, so nothing could ever happen between us, it just wouldn't be professional.

The QUEEN of HEARTS

Not even though you have, and I quote, "lovely eyes and a cute little bum".'

This was the moment when my jaw hit the floor with a clang. I was surprised Elaine didn't hear it.

'My God, did Maude really say that?'

'That and more — it was the real hard sell.'

'My *God,*' I repeated, thoroughly mortified.

Then, in the background on Elaine's end of the line, I heard a doorbell ring. 'Sounds like you have company arriving,' I said.

'Yes, it's this guy I know, been seeing him for about a year now. He comes around once or twice a week. Pops in, pops out, leaves me satisfied. My idea of a perfect man.'

So Maude had been wrong about her being available in any case, I thought, and then wondered why I was feeling a slight pang of disappointment.

'I better let you get off, then,' I said.

'Okay, well, it was nice talking to…' I heard another noise over the line, one that sounded like a hand slapping against a forehead — which turned out to be just what it was. I heard her whisper the word *dumbbell* under her breath, and then she said, 'I completely forgot to tell you why I called in the first place, didn't I?'

I'd forgotten that she'd forgotten.

'I wanted to apologise,' she said.

'For what?'

'For having to turn your brother away when he came to pick Victoria up this morning. I know he was angry, but rules are rules, and I'm afraid he didn't know the password.'

For obvious reasons, children were only allowed to be collected from the playgroup by anyone other than their parents upon the presentation of an agreed password. The password changed from week to week for added security. Vic's password this first week was *Broomsticks*, as in *Bedknobs and*, and only four people in the whole wide world knew it, and that would be Elaine, Henry, Maude, and myself.

My brother *didn't* know it. Which was unsurprising really, as I don't *have* a brother.

'Mr. September?' Elaine said into my continuing silence.

'Joel,' I said absently. 'Call me Joel.'

'Joel, are you all right?'

'I'm fine,' I said, even though my brain felt as though it was frozen solid.

'I must say,' Elaine said hesitantly, 'I couldn't see *much* of a family resemblance.'

'Well, I suppose he's more of a step-brother, actually,' I replied. 'We were never really close. We had different fathers…'

Different mothers, too, I thought.

'He used to be a boxer.'

'Oh, that would explain—'

'The face, yes, I know.'

I heard her doorbell ring again.

'Elaine, will you do me a favour?' I asked. 'My brother isn't exactly the most responsible person in the world, so if he, or any other member of my family apart from Maude or Henry, should ever turn up to collect my daughter — even if they *do* have the correct password — would you please give me a call before letting them take her?'

'Of course, if that's what you want.'

Elaine's doorbell was ringing ten to the dozen now, but she didn't seem in a hurry to answer it.

'Joel, is something wrong?' she asked.

'No, everything's fine. You'd better go. Don't want to keep your perfect man waiting.'

'Perfect man?' she asked, sounding confused for a moment. Then, 'Oh, right, my perfect man. You want to know the truth? It's the delivery guy from the Pizza Palace. I open the door, he gives me a satisfying pizza, and then he leaves — that's why he's perfect.'

I smiled, said goodbye, and hung up.

The smile didn't hang around for long, obviously. A millisecond at most. A few minutes later I returned to the sofa on rubbery legs that could hardly support my weight.

On the TV, the evil queen disguised as an old crone was offering a poisoned apple to Snow White, and my daughter was shaking her head as if to say, 'Don't do it, Snow, don't take it!' I put my arm around her and she slumped against me, her eyes already glassy. She popped her thumb into her mouth.

I stared at the TV without seeing it. I was numb, completely and utterly numb. It was almost beyond belief. Greg the Goblin had actually tried to *kidnap* my daughter from her playgroup. And if *Tiny Mind*s' security protocols hadn't been as tight as they were, or if Elaine had been lax at enforcing them, he might well have succeeded.

Abruptly, I amazed myself by yawning, a great jaw-cracking yawn that seemed to drain all my remaining strength.

'Daddee go sweep now,' Vic sing-songed around her thumb.

'Okay,' I said. 'Let's both go sweep.'

But the truth was that after Elaine's phone call, I doubted that I'd ever be able to sweep again.

S o... I woke up many hours later, still sprawled out on the three-seater sofa. I was propped up against a cushion with my head wedged at an unnatural angle to my body, like a corpse in a crime novel, and I had a crick in my neck of the approximate severity of the San Andreas Fault.

It was about one in the morning, and as I slowly came around, I glanced at the TV in time to see a curvaceous blonde wearing a scarlet basque and black fishnet stockings assisting a well-muscled gentleman, who was already stripped to the waist, to unbuckle his trouser belt.

Mmm, I thought. *Snow White* certainly has changed since the last time I saw it...

But no — reason swiftly reasserted itself, and I saw that what I was watching was really a late-night film on one of the lower-ranking digital channels, the sort of entertainment they billed in the TV guides as an *erotic drama*. The Disney DVD must have finished hours ago and the TV automatically switched inputs.

On the screen, I saw that the helpful young lady was now lowering the man's zipper in steady, deliberate increments, and licking her lips a great deal. I suppose it says a lot about the current state of my libido that the first thought to enter my mind was that if the blonde carried on like this, she was soon going to be in the market for a good chap-stick.

Thankfully, my second thought was a good deal less innocent, and for a few moments I weakly allowed myself to be drawn in by the thematic complexity of the film's underlying structure, the superb lighting, the bravura camerawork and incisive editing, the understated irony and emotional pathos of the script, and the subtle nuances of the actors' layered, multi-faceted performances.

Then it belatedly occurred to me that *Purple Passion Part 5, or Alison's Amorous Adventures* probably wasn't the best thing for my two-and-a-bit-year-old daughter to be watching — particularly at this moment, when the eponymous Alison had dispensed with her basque altogether and seemed to be urging her co-star to confirm, at close quarters, that she was not a natural blonde.

I retrieved the remote control from the coffee table and snapped the TV off, yawning to Vic that it was time for bed. Then I glanced at the sofa to my left where Vic had snuggled down, dribbling on the upholstery, all glassy-eyed and adorable.

But Vic wasn't there now.

I glanced at the sofa to my right — again, no Vic.

I leant over to peer beneath the coffee table, where she was occasionally to be found asleep curled up with her comfort blanket, but all there was under there right now was an old dummy wearing a beard of carpet fluff.

That's when I began to panic.

This is something no one ever tells you about when you're going to have a child. It's like information covered by the Official Secrets Act. People tell you about the nice things, sure — the smiles, the cuddles, and the cute things kids say. *Ahh!* They tell you about the terrible things, too — the disturbed sleep patterns, the incessant noise, and the full-stop sex life. *Boo!*

But they never once tell you about the *fear*, and they really should, because as far as I can see a parent's life is all about fear.

Every second of every minute of every day you're aware of the vulnerability of the tiny person you've assumed responsibility for. You're aware of every possible danger with which the world, and even your own home, seems suddenly filled. Unshielded power points, staircases, open windows, a gas ring left alight on the cooker, a bathtub left undrained... the list never ended. Above all, you're constantly aware that a moment's inattention could be fatal, and every news report about stupid or careless parents you ever shook your head over in the past comes back to haunt you like a vengeful wraith.

Even worse, you begin to have some understanding of your own parents' previously incomprehensible behaviour, which can be a really spooky feeling.

'Vic?' I stood up. 'Vic?'

I didn't wait for a reply.

I rapidly checked out the whole of the ground floor, snapping on lights as I went. I lingered longest in the kitchen, making sure that Vic hadn't climbed into the washing machine, or the oven, or even the microwave (those urban legends die hard, don't they?). The back door was firmly locked and bolted, but God help me, I actually went down on my knees to look out through the cat-flap.

'Vic? Victoria?'

Suddenly, a horrible fantasy — a literal Grimm's fairy tale — sprang full-blown into my mind: while I had been asleep, Greg the Goblin had broken into my house and stolen my daughter. I experienced a wave of anger more powerful than anything I'd had for a long while, not since my days on the Force.

I stomped out of the kitchen in a rage, heading for the phone. I'd call my in-laws first. As an ex-Hertfordshire police officer — Brass, no less — Henry would be able to tell me who to speak to at the local cop-shop, and dropping his name would mean that my report got priority attention. Or so I hoped.

But on my way back to the living room, I halted by the front door.

After the shock Elaine Leigh's phone call had given me earlier, I had made sure to lock the house up tighter than usual. Every window lock in the house was engaged, and I could see that the front door, just like the back, was not only locked, it was actually bolted. For good measure, it had the safety chain on, too.

Therefore, I reasoned, even if Greg the Goblin was a lock-picking genius of a sub-human, he *still* wouldn't have been able to get in. Therefore, I further reasoned, Vic was still in the house.

And then I noticed the stair-gates.

The stair-gates, both top and bottom, were equipped with childproof locking systems, and for obvious reasons (no one wants to see their infant child cart-wheeling down the stairs) I always kept them locked tight, checking them religiously whenever I passed through. Now, however, they were wide open.

Shit! I thought. *Shit!*

I ran up the stairs like a loon, limbs flying everywhere. But as soon as I reached Vic's bedroom door, I paused, and it wasn't just because my bad knee was threatening to lock up on me. It was my old friend, fear.

Hello again, fear whispered..

The QUEEN of HEARTS

Simple common sense told me that no one could have got into the house without walking through the walls like a ghost. But at the same time, simple common sense was also busy telling me that Vic just wasn't capable of unlocking the stair-gates — they were childproof and she was a child.

The result of all this SCS was total confusion, and a rapid escalation of my Grimm's fairy tale into outright horror.

The door was already open about an inch-and-a-half, and as I pushed it open wider, I half expected to see a dark figure hunched menacingly over Vic's cot, its long claws reaching down towards her throat, the amber glow of the nightlight making its bulbous eyes glow insanely. Some gruesome beast of the netherworld, some evil fiend of the night... or perhaps just some fugly goblin of an ex-boxer.

I cautiously stepped into the room, which at first glance appeared to be completely fiendless.

To my amazement, Vic was fast asleep in her cot. As usual her feet were comfortably propped up against the vertical sidebars to accommodate the profusion of soft toys piled at the foot of the mattress. One arm was wrapped around her bunny blanket. Her narrow chest rose and fell in peaceful respiration. Her tiny rosebud lips fluttered sweetly on every gentle exhalation.

I let out a shaky stream of air in a sigh of relief, and I wondered how long I'd been holding my own breath.

I didn't know which explanation was scarier, that I might have put my child to bed while in the grip of some kind of trance and then forgotten I'd done it, or that Vic was living up to her genius-in-waiting reputation by mastering the childproof locks on the stair-gates and putting herself to bed after I'd fallen asleep on the sofa. Didn't know and didn't care. Right now, all that mattered to me was that she was safe and sound.

I stood above the cot and stared down at my beautiful girl.

'If anything ever happened to you,' I whispered to her, 'I don't know what I'd do.'

I bent forward and placed a gentle kiss in the centre of her smooth forehead, the whole essence of my enormous love for her distilled into one simple, heartfelt gesture. In her sleep, Vic turned her head away from my lips and loudly farted.

'Yeah,' I said. 'I love you, too.'

As I began to turn away, a small, unexpected movement among the soft toys sent my heart slamming against my ribs again. I was startled, only a single fraction of a second away from making a shamefully unmanly sound of alarm (like a high-pitched squeal) before I realised what it was. It seemed that I had been mistaken — the room wasn't entirely fiendless, after all.

From amidst the shadowy pile of bears and pandas and dolls at the foot of Vic's cot, a pair of luminous green eyes had opened and were now studying me dispassionately.

'Jesus!' I whispered. 'Albert, is that you?'

The cat's eyes remained fixed and unwavering, as if to say, 'Yeah, you got a problem with that?'

'What are you doing in here?'

The eyes abruptly closed, dismissing me. My question was an affront to Albert's dignity and he was above answering it. Who on earth did I think I was?

That was it for me. I'd had more than enough for one day. I lifted Albert out of the cot and chucked him out of Vic's bedroom. I tried to shoo him downstairs and outside, but he dashed away and took sanctuary in the airing cupboard, and nothing could induce him to come back out again, not even half-a-can of leftover tuna fish.

I took a quick shower and went to bed, falling asleep almost instantly. Shortly after two o'clock in the morning, Albert's instincts were again proved correct, as the heavy rain the storm clouds had earlier promised finally arrived, lashing the windows, swamping the guttering, and seething into my ragged, overgrown lawn. Lightning flashed and thunder boomed.

The storm lasted half the night, apparently, but I managed to sleep through it all. There were no dreams, or if there were, I didn't remember them in the morning.

Seven

THE FOLLOWING MORNING, I tried to get the straight story on *The Great Stair-Gate Mystery of Welwyn Garden City* from my daughter, but Vic was in an incommunicative mood, having already emotionally committed herself to an especially thrilling episode of *Scooby Doo*, which she was watching with a frightening intensity.

Still, I gave it a go.

Did she put herself to bed last night? *Yep.* Did she open the stair-gates? *Yep.* How did she open the locks? *Yep.* How long had she been able to do that? *Yep.* Am I wasting my time here trying to get sense out of you, am I just talking to hear the sound of my own voice, should I simply accept the self-evident truth of the situation and try to live with it? *Yep* and *yep* and *yep.*

Not that it mattered, really. I knew she'd done it, and I knew how, too. The same way she'd figured out how to use pretty much all the functions on all the remote controls in the house better than I ever would. She was bright, that's all, and she'd figured it out. Maybe she'd inherited some of my parents' love of puzzles the same way she'd inherited Maude's vivid green eyes.

Shortly after breakfast (my own special recipe porridge, which Vic calls 'the white mud'), I was more than a little surprised to receive a phone call from

Andrew Lipton, banker, punch-bag, poor-little-rich-boy, and lapdog extraordinaire. I recognised his voice instantly and my spirits began to lift. It was my hope that he was calling with information regarding Lisa's current whereabouts — or maybe he even had a message from the woman herself — but sadly that proved not to be the case.

Mr Lipton had something else on his mind, it seemed. He wanted a favour.

Despite having only been admitted the night before last, it turned out that he was due to be discharged from hospital around lunchtime today, and he wished to engage my professional services in order to convey him (him and his various plaster-encased and bandaged limbs, that is) from the Royal Free Hospital to his basement flat in faraway Crouch End.

In other words, he needed a taxi to get him home and he wanted the comfort of a friendly face to go with it. The fact that he would choose *my* face, over all others, for this purpose only served to illustrate just how empty and pathetic his life had become.

But who was I to judge how empty and pathetic people's lives were? I had my empty and pathetic side too, like anyone else, didn't I? So naturally I agreed to help him.

To the honorary titles Hopeless Optimist and Blithering Idiot we can now confidently add a distinguished third — Soft Touch. At last, a hero you can believe in.

I delivered Vic to Henry and Maude's, worked for a few hours in Welwyn, and then made my way, once again, into London. I picked Lipton up at the hospital a few minutes after one o'clock. As soon as I saw him, I was immediately convinced that some kind of serious administrative mistake had been made deep in the bowels of the hospital's workings. Lipton didn't look a whole better than he had the last time I'd seen him, laying helpless in his hospital bed. To be honest, he probably looked worse.

True, the bandages that had been wound around his head yesterday had been removed and replaced with a slightly smaller dressing that made him look like he was wearing a small white bonnet (not a good look, incidentally, for anyone not playing a chambermaid in a period drama), and his arm was no longer wrapped up and strapped to his body like an Egyptian mummy's. That was on the plus side.

But on the minus side, the umbrella-point bruises on his face were coming out now in a hectic pattern of poisonous blues and purples, not to mention bilious greens and rancid yellows, that made his haggard fizzog look like an alien sunset. Furthermore, he could only move by lurching along on a pair of crutches, his plastered leg alternately dragging and swinging, like something out of a third-rate zombie film.

When there's no more room in hell, I thought, the chinless wonders shall walk the earth.

'Andrew,' I said doubtfully, 'this can't be right, mate. They can't send you home in this condition. You need a second opinion. Which idiot was it decided you were fit to be discharged?'

'I did,' he replied.

'You discharged yourself? Why?'

'I can't stay here anymore. I don't feel comfortable, I don't feel safe. Nothing feels right. I can't eat. I can't sleep.'

He gave me the puppy-dog eyes, which was a bit weird — I've never seen a puppy-dog with black eyes before. But I knew exactly what he meant about hospitals. They weren't my favourite places either. I'd spent too long in them.

'Okay,' I said, 'I'll take you.'

Lipton maintained a complete silence during the journey from A to B, despite my attempts to get him talking, and it suddenly struck me that he was incredibly nervous. And then I thought, well of course he is, you fool. I didn't doubt that he hated being in hospital, but the real reason he had asked me to take him home rather than a complete stranger was because he was afraid to go in there alone.

His home, his place of safety, had been violated. He had been *attacked* there.

This theory was fully borne out as I unlocked his front door for him and swung it open. Lipton, shakily supporting himself on his crutches down the last few steps to his basement flat, gasped at the mess still evident in the short hallway.

On the doormat, his personal mail had been torn open and the sifted contents scattered. Further along the hallway, I saw that a selection of the framed pictures his walls were literally covered with had been knocked down and smashed on the carpet runner, and broken glass had been ground into the weave. There were dusky spots of old dried blood here and there, both on the carpet and on the floorboards to either side, the blood obviously his.

I sensed Lipton's reluctance to enter, but I took his arm anyway and all but hauled him over the threshold. 'Come on, Andrew,' I said. 'It's like getting into a freezing cold swimming pool — easier if you just dive in.'

The QUEEN of HEARTS

I gently led him through a scene of chaos, which, although highly reminiscent of Lisa's flat, wasn't nearly half as bad. The place had been similarly ransacked, I could see that, but apart from all the broken photograph frames there appeared to have been little or no real vandalism.

Nobody had done a colossal poop on his bed, that was for sure. And nobody armed with a can of red spray-paint thought he was a bitch.

I lowered Lipton into the armchair of the large three-piece leather suite that dominated his tiny, dark living room. Many more framed pictures glittered on the walls, most of them smashed, and a layer of powdery broken glass lay like a fine coating of castor sugar over the backrests and arms of the dark furniture.

'Couldn't someone have come around and tidied up before you came home?' I asked.

He shook his head tiredly.

'Friends, relatives…the trusty old family retainer?'

Again, he shook his head.

'Christ.'

I went through into a narrow galley-style kitchen and put the kettle on, thinking that the least I could do before leaving to go back to work was to make him a hot drink and a sandwich. It seemed that no one else was going to.

'Are you hungry?' I called through.

'Not yet,' he called back.

'What about for later?'

'I don't know, I hadn't thought about it. I suppose I'll order a takeaway.'

I examined the contents of the cupboards and drawers, which didn't take long. There were a few pieces of crockery and some basic utensils, but not much more. If Lipton ever had more than one guest, or wanted to eat anything more complicated than a fried egg on toast, he was going to struggle. I found a couple of saucepans under the sink, but not a scrap of food anywhere, not even a can of baked beans. The small, under-the-counter fridge, although turned on, looked as though it had never been used to store anything except milk. This seemed like a very strange home for someone with Lipton's financial resources.

'Yeah,' I said. 'A takeaway sounds like it might be a good idea... This is all a bit basic, isn't it?'

'Well, I don't live here full time. Mostly I live in the country with... with my parents...'

I realised he had been about to say that he lived with his Mummy and Daddy, and had then thought better of it.

'Really,' he insisted, 'I only stay here when I'm working at the bank.'

No need to wonder why he wasn't going to ask for his parents' help now. He'd be too ashamed.

As the kettle began to roar, I stepped back out into the narrow hallway and stooped to pick up a few of the smashed picture frames from the floor, careful not to slice my fingers on the broken glass. The pictures inside the frames — surprise, surprise — turned out to be photographs of Lisa. Two of them were fairly recent shots I had never seen before, and the third was one that I had seen many times.

This last was a picture of Lisa wearing a dark red ball gown she had bought for the Morgan-Matheson Christmas party one year, a dramatic, plunging low-cut number which showed off her already highly impressive cleavage to maximum eye-popping, groin-jolting effect. Before being framed, this picture had first been enlarged slightly and then carefully cut down to exclude the man whose arm Lisa had been clinging to at the time — which had been me.

Thanks, Andrew.

Then I looked at the other framed pictures in the hallway, and realised with a small shock that they were *all* photographs of my wife, everything from informal snaps to studio portraits, all of them cut down to fit clip-frames and simply attached to the walls with sticky pads. Andrew Lipton appeared in a lot of the photographs too, leaning intrusively close to Lisa, like a tourist who unexpectedly finds themselves in a photobombing opportunity with a celebrity and intends to make the most of it.

Hey, Mum! Dad! Everyone! Look who I'm with!!!

Here they were as part of a larger group sitting around a nightclub table; here they were in an office decorated with a few scraps of tinsel and a cluster of balloons; here they were clinking champagne flutes while standing on the deck of a small yacht, the masts and pennants of even larger vessels visible in the background; here at a West End movie premiere; there dressed to the nines at Royal Ascot, Lipton looking like he'd just stepped down from the top of a wedding cake, and Lisa looking like she'd just jumped out of a cake at a stag party to a chorus of ribald wolf-whistles.

There were a lot of others that I just couldn't make out. Whoever had broken in that day had spent a lot of time simply whacking the frames one by one, perhaps with the same umbrella-point with which they later bruised Lipton's face, so that the glass was shattered in little milky starbursts, obscuring fine details. It seemed to me that more often than not, the epicentre of these starbursts lay directly over images of Lisa's face.

I saw just one more photograph that had survived unscathed, this one aboard the yacht again, and at the edge of the photograph, almost but not quite cut off, was David Handley. His head was turned as if to watch Lisa smiling for the camera, but his eyes (and clearly his thoughts) were elsewhere on her anatomy, and he had an expression on his face that he would never, ever, want his wife to see.

'This's Handley's boat you were visiting?'

'What? Oh, the pictures. Yes, I think so,' Lipton replied after a long moment's pause. He sounded very, very tired, and I wondered if I'd woken him from a cat nap.

I looked down at the loose photographs in my hands and I realised something else. To confirm it, I went back through into the small living room and looked around in amazement.

All the framed pictures in here were *also* photographs of my wife. Every single one. There must have been hundreds of them, at least. Maybe even a thousand. The whole flat was a shrine to all things Lisa. I couldn't begin to imagine what the bedroom was like… and I wasn't sure I wanted to find out. This flat wasn't a place where Andrew came to crash during the working week. This was his church, the place where he came to worship.

I looked at Lipton, *The Grand High Priest of the Besotted Cult of Lisa*, and shook my head. I felt bad for him.

'Andrew,' I said. 'Mate… this is a sickness.'

'I know,' he replied, and then burst into tears.

I have such a way with words.

The QUEEN of HEARTS

NOTHING AT ALL happened for the next two days. Then, on the third day, and despite it being *Fabulous Friday*, nothing happened all over again. But the following day something truly incredible happened, something so thoroughly unexpected, so absolutely extraordinary, that I could scarcely believe it myself — I somehow managed to wangle myself a date with a gorgeous woman.

It really was a *Spectacular Saturday*.

It was about nine-thirty in the morning and I was parked in the taxi-rank in front of the Howard Centre, a two-tiered shopping mall that incorporates the entrance to the Welwyn Garden City train station. A lot of the other drivers were out of their cabs, chatting together while drinking takeout coffee, and enjoying the fresher breeze the recent rains had brought with them.

The big topic of conversation this morning seemed to be the sentencing of yet another politician to jail-time after being found guilty of financial and moral corruption, but having moved up to first in the rank, I stayed in the Scenic and kept out of it. I have a weak stomach, so politics don't interest me.

In any case, I was deeply immersed in my own thoughts, the waters of which remained decidedly murky. The fact that everything seemed to have gone quiet over the last few days hadn't reassured me very much, and I was in a state of subdued dread. Never mind the weather forecast, this felt like the lull before the storm.

I was still undecided what (if anything) I could do about Greg the Goblin and the threats he had made against me and mine. I couldn't see myself going to the police just yet, as I didn't even know his full name. Nor was I in a position to prove that he had threatened us, and Elaine Leigh's testimony that he had tried to take Vic from the playgroup was easily refutable.

There were no other witnesses in either case. And even if he could be identified and located (from a physical description that read like the Frankenstein monster's shorter, uglier brother), all he'd have to say was that we had misinterpreted his words and his intentions.

I was just wondering, for the hundredth time that day, what else I could do to find Lisa, when one of the Scenic's rear doors opened and someone climbed into the back seat. The door closed and I, in Pavlovian reflex, started the engine. I caught a glimpse of long blonde hair swaying in the rear-view mirror. I caught a trace of musky, expensive perfume.

'Where can I take you?' I asked.

The answer was an address just outside the village of Datchworth, a journey of about fifteen or twenty minutes at most. I turned on the meter and pulled out into traffic. I'd been driving for less than a minute when I heard the first sob. I did my best to ignore it — I had a few troubles of my own, and then some — but I couldn't ignore the second.

'You okay back there?' I asked.

My passenger cleared her throat and mumbled something about being fine, but then spoiled it by sobbing again. I pulled over to the side of the road, engaged the handbrake, and turned around in my seat.

I told you I was nosy, didn't I?

I estimated that the woman in the back seat was probably around about my own age, but she didn't look it. Certainly, her journey through life seemed to have taken a much nicer route than mine. She was dressed in a simple but stunningly cut black business skirt suit, and wore heels so high they would have given a base-jumper an attack of vertigo. A couple of inches below the hem of the pencil skirt, her stockings were ripped over both knees, and tiny beads of blood were welling up out of matching grazes.

She was dabbing at the wounds with a pad of tissues she'd removed from a serious-looking black leather briefcase on the seat beside her. Her blonde hair partially hung over her face, but I could still hear her hiss of pain as she touched the tissue to her knee again.

'What happened to you?' I asked, but I thought those heels of hers told a lot of the story.

She raised her head and looked at me, offering the distant cousin of a wry smile, and it was like the sun coming out from behind clouds. Despite the tear streaks down her face and the pain evident in her blue eyes, it was obvious that she was a very beautiful woman. Ordinarily, I'm sure, she would have noticed me noticing her — not least because when those stunning blue eyes first hit me, I almost swallowed my tongue. But at that moment, she was understandably preoccupied.

'I think I was mugged,' she said.

'You were *what?* Where? Here in town?'

'In that shopping centre, where the train station is.'

'The Howard Centre.'

'Yes, coming down the escalator. Two teenage girls came past me, moving quickly, and they knocked me to the side. One of them tried to grab my case.'

'You should report this. Do you want me to take you to the police station?'

She looked at me for a long moment, and I felt the amazing depth of those blue eyes again. It's been my experience that blue eyes can often look empty, shallow as a puddle, but this pair certainly weren't. There were all kinds of interesting things floating around in them.

In response to my question, she eventually sighed and shook her head. No.

'Why not?'

'Well, maybe I was wrong about being mugged. Maybe I overreacted a little. Or a lot. Maybe I'm still overreacting now.' She gave me a tiny, shamefaced smile through the tears. 'To be honest I was a million miles away coming down that escalator, and I jumped another mile when those girls came rushing past me. I thought they... well, you know very well what I thought.'

She reached down into the footwall behind my seat and came back up holding her right shoe, from which I could now see the four-inch heel was hanging by a single thread of stitching.

'I came down on my ankle, which twisted when this happened, and I started to fall. One of the girls tried to snatch my case, or seemed to... but now that I think of it again, it's possible she was actually trying to *catch* me.' She tried to smile again. 'But they disappeared pretty quickly after that, so I really don't know for sure. Someone else helped me up, an old couple, I think. They were very kind.'

'Are you missing anything?'

She thought about it for a second or two, taking stock of herself, and then sighed again and said, 'Only my dignity — which, based on how I'm behaving right now, may only have been an imaginary quality anyway. Would you take me home, please?'

'Are you sure you don't need to go to an A&E? Or to see your GP?'

'No,' she said, firmly shaking her head. 'All this girl needs are a hot bath and a stiff drink, in that order. Home, please.'

As I said, it wasn't a long drive from the town centre to our destination, but I was still able to gather a surprising amount of information during the journey.

My passenger's name was Barbara Rawlings. She lived in London (by the river) and worked for a communications group (which, she said, quite often meant the exact opposite), and had been chosen to come out to Hertfordshire to scout locations for new premises because she had links with the area. It turned out she was a local, of sorts. She had been partially raised in the house we were heading for, and had inherited it after her parents had passed away. She had one brother, Roger, who had emigrated to Australia about a dozen years ago, and whom she still described as "the walking, talking migraine". She had been married once, and quickly divorced. She was single now.

'No,' she replied when I asked if she had kids. 'Although, I do want my own children eventually — I just adore them. I suppose time isn't really on my side anymore, but it'll have to be the right man next time. My mother always used to say any man can father a child, but it takes a special man to be a good father. I guess I still believe that, and I'm prepared to wait. In the meantime, I have my friends' children to have fun with.'

'With the added bonus that you can hand them back at the end of the day,' I said.

'That's right,' she agreed, laughing. 'What about you? Wife? Kids?'

I told her about Vic, and that I was separated from her mother.

'Separated as in taking a break, or separated as in…?'

'As in the marriage is dead as a doornail.'

'Ah!'

I wasn't precisely sure what 'Ah!' meant in this instance, but she didn't seem to say it with any great sadness.

The house was a bit of a surprise when we got there. I had already assumed from its location that it would be a large house set in even larger gardens, as a lot of the properties in this specific area were, and that proved to be the case. Built over three floors, it was set well back in its own large walled plot at the end of a long, tree-lined lane, but it was a far newer building than I had anticipated. Probably less than ten years old, judging from the design and materials.

Thoughtlessly I shared this stunning observation with Barbara as I turned the car around on the gravel forecourt.

'Well, a lot of it had to be rebuilt, after the fire,' she said in a quiet little voice before falling completely silent.

I quickly connected the dots and filled in the gaps for myself, cursing myself freely (but silently) as I did so. Youngish woman, major house fire, both parents dead. I could all but hear the pop as I pulled my big foot out of my fat mouth.

I turned off my meter as Barbara began to get out of the back seat. There was no way I was going to charge her for this journey. It would be my silent apology for my tactlessness. She hobbled around the car to my window, clutching her briefcase, going up on her single heel, coming down on her bare foot, like she was a drunk walking along a kerb.

'Are you sure you're okay?' I asked. 'Can I help you inside?'

'No, I'm perfectly fine, thank you,' she said, and then immediately fell down as her ankle gave way again.

I was out of the car in an instant, helping her to her feet. She was crying again, but at the same time she was laughing.

'You know, I don't think I'm quite as tough as I used to be,' she said with another of those charmingly wry smiles.

'Don't worry,' I told her. 'Nobody is.'

She looped her arm around my shoulders and I helped her over to the front door, holding her heavy briefcase while she unlocked. I didn't quite carry her over the threshold, but it was pretty close, a humorous moment that wasn't lost on either of us. We'd both been there before, obviously. We shared a small smile over it.

I helped her up a wide staircase to the first-floor bathroom and then went back down to locate the kitchen. I mixed the scotch and soda she had requested and then made a cup of instant coffee for myself, listening to water running and gushing through the pipes.

I kept thinking that I should make my excuses and leave, and I kept on not doing it.

About a quarter-of-an-hour later, in a much-improved physical condition, Barbara came back downstairs dressed in a thick white towelling robe.

Beneath the hem, her injured knees had been patched with large sticking plasters that looked comically symmetrical.

She found her drink on the counter where I'd left it, and raised the glass to toast me. 'Well, here's to a very unusual taxi-driver,' she said. 'To... what's your name again?'

I told her and she smiled.

'To Joel September, my knight in shining armour.' She drained half the glass at a single pull, and then sighed ecstatically, her eyes tightly closed, and for a moment I was able to study her at my leisure.

Her dip in the bath had done more than ease the pain in her knees and drain some of the tension from her muscles. It had washed away every trace of the carefully applied make-up she had worn, and her once skilfully-teased coiffure was now a maze of glistening rat tails that clung unflatteringly to her neck and coiled over her shoulders. Every curve of her body was hidden in the thick shapelessness of her robe. I was seeing her now with all the artifice gone and the sheer intimidation of her beauty faded.

And typically, it was at this moment that I began to find her really attractive.

FOR THE REST of the morning, and a fairly sizable portion of the afternoon, I have to admit that I was sort of out of it — on Cloud Nine, so to speak.

I had almost forgotten what it was like to be attracted to a strange woman. Strange as in unfamiliar, I mean, not peculiar. And I had definitely forgotten what it felt like to be fancied back in return, because (except in rom-com movies) men within hailing distance of their fortieth year with an ankle-biter in tow aren't really what you could call babe magnets.

But over the hour I had spent in Barbara Rawlings' company, it had quickly become very obvious to me that attraction was occurring, and that it was entirely mutual.

Nevertheless, it was Barbara who'd had to take the first step in the dating game, because my nerves were shot. I was well out of practise. In all probability, the only person *more* out of practise had been introduced to the general public by a plume of white smoke from the Vatican chimney. The last woman I'd actually asked out on a date was Lisa, more than seven years ago, when both the world and my few meagre chat-up lines were young.

In those days, dinosaurs still walked the earth, and I'd probably been out with most of them.

I'd finished my second cup of coffee, said my goodbyes, and was almost out the door when Barbara asked if she could buy me dinner to thank me for my kindness. And, being a generally magnanimous sort of guy, I said that she could (although I had no intention of really letting her pay for anything). We fixed a time for me to pick her up, and that was that, all done and dusted.

It was so simple. It felt so natural. It felt so good.

I drove off with a slight sheen of perspiration on my forehead, the pleasurable tickle of butterflies in my stomach... and guilt like a corkscrew already beginning to twist into my heart.

The QUEEN of HEARTS

Lisa might be able to bonk the entire male population of the free world in a carefree, guiltless oblivion, but it seemed that one single dinner date lay on my conscience like a slab of stone.

EIGHT

IT WAS PROBABLY because my mind was so taken up by arguing with itself, over whether I should have accepted Barbara's invitation or not, that it took so long for another observation to penetrate the veil of my guilty thoughts. This observation was that as I drove hither and thither along my merry way, taking my fares from wherever they were to wherever they wanted to be, I was being watched.

I was being *followed*.

Try as I might, I couldn't actually spot my shadow or shadows, but that hardly mattered, because I *knew* they were there. It was that old ex-copper's intuition again, you see. Occasionally, it's like being able to see in the dark.

This was a wake-up call, in case I needed one. A sharp reminder that I couldn't let a little bit of good fortune like a date with a beautiful woman make me forget my immediate responsibilities. This thing with Lisa wasn't over, and it wouldn't be over until I made it over. I had to find Lisa, and I had to make her put right whatever had to be put right to ensure our daughter's safety.

The only trouble was that *Operation Find Lisa* had ground to a halt. I had run out of ideas. All save one, and I was reluctant to explore this one remaining avenue.

Why? That's an easy one.

It was Pride, of course. Pride, one of the seven deadly sins, which (as I'm fairly sure it says somewhere or other in the Bible) is one of the biggies, right up there with Envy, Sloth, and Doner Kebabs with extra chilli sauce.

When I left the Job under such a dark cloud, I was a bitter man. I deplored the justice system and the Police Service, and all their inadequacies. I despised my superiors and their shortcomings, and I distrusted my colleagues' honesty — not to mention their morals, dress sense, and standards of personal hygiene. To be honest, I wasn't in the mood to cut anyone slack on anything. I just walked (well, limped) away and cut off all communication with everyone I had known in the Service.

Nevertheless, there were a few men I had worked with over the years, people I had once looked upon as friends as well as colleagues, who had all taken great pains to keep in touch with me after my disgrace and resignation. The man who kept calling for the longest time, the one who even now still sent me a Christmas and birthday card each year, was a guy called Scott Vaughan. Scott was the only member of my circle who had known me well enough to have recognised my secret weakness — that weakness was *anger*, also known in some elevated circles as "an excess of zeal".

I've heard other people refer to their anger as a rising red mist, but mine was more than just mist, mine was like an entire atmosphere — the atmosphere of the Red Planet — and Scott had coined his own nickname for me at those times when I well and truly lost it. He used to call me the Man from Mars.

Scott and I had come through training at Hendon at the same time, and then up through the ranks together until postings had separated us. He had been my closest friend on the force, perhaps my closest friend ever, and yet for years I had treated him like the enemy.

But now I was going to ask him for a favour.

I took a break around two in the afternoon, and headed for the Howard Centre. I went to a coffee shop on the first floor, bought myself a coffee and a BLT sandwich, and took them out on to the open-air terrace. I chose a small circular table a little aside from the other customers and took out my mobile phone and my wallet.

My wallet is a great bulging satchel of a thing, and isn't so much for carrying money (what money, ha-ha?) as storing information — information like phone numbers and addresses, usually scribbled on sections of torn beer-mats, the backs of supermarket receipts, dog-eared post-it notes, and other assorted pieces of flotsam and jetsam. If examined carefully, its contents would reveal the layered history of Joel September, all of it, both BL (Before Lisa) and AL.

I opened it up now and let my fingers have their way, flicking through the strata of my life until they found what they were searching for. It was a matchbook cover from some long-forgotten nightclub, on the back of which was written the last office number I had for Scott Vaughan.

I took a deep breath and began to dial.

At the other end of the line, the phone rang four times and was then answered by a man who sounded like he was in the process of eating his own sandwich and didn't care who knew it. I don't know what the filling was, but it sounded extremely *moist*. For the record, my money was on tuna mayonnaise.

I asked if I could speak to Scott.

'Vaughan?' he said, lips smacking noisily. 'Not here no more, mate, not for mumfs. Hang on, I got a number somewhere…'

The number he gave me led only to another office Scott had passed through, and the same thing happened another five times as I was redirected through a string of CID suites and incident rooms dotted around the capital. When a police officer is shunted about this much it can only mean one of two things. He's either in favour or out of favour. That is, either going up in a hurry or down in a hurry. Not one of the people I spoke to dropped the slightest clue as to which it was.

The final number I was given rang ten or twelve times, and I was just about to hang up and finish eating my lunch when it was finally answered.

'Yeah?'

Despite asking a question, the cold, male voice sounded about as incurious as anyone could sound without actually being dead.

I asked to speak to Scott Vaughan.

'Who is this?' the voice asked after a lengthy silence. The voice was still frosty, but now it was *intensely* curious. 'How did you get this number?'

I debated for a few seconds about giving my name, but then gave in. I needed help and Scott was probably the only person in a position to help me now, as well as being the only person who might be *prepared* to help me.

'My name's Joel September,' I said, and began to explain how I'd got this far down the line. 'I'm ex-Job.

Scott and I are old friends, we came through training together, and I—'

'Did I ask for your fucking life story? Shut up a minute. Wait.'

There was a long silence, then the voice came back on and grudgingly asked for my number. I reeled off the number of my mobile and he immediately hung up on me.

I stared at the dead phone in my hand, wondering what the hell was going on. I'd heard that in my absence the Service was supposed to have gone all touchy-feely (there were no more villains or victims, now they were all 'customers' of varying degrees of importance). But if that was the case, I'd noticed no trace of it in the conversation I'd just had.

Once again, I got that feeling — the feeling that I was being watched — but a quick glance around the other tables on the terrace revealed no suspicious characters. Looking back through the glass doors into the interior of the coffee shop, I saw no one lurking in corners or behind pillars. I drank my coffee and ate my BLT.

Then my phone rang. 'Hello?'

'Joel?'

'Scott?'

'Yeah, what's going on, pal?'

Pal? I thought.

Scott had never called me *Pal* before in our entire acquaintanceship. He'd called me a lot of things over the years, most of them unrepeatable in polite society, but never, ever, *Pal*. *Pal* was what you called a snitch to keep him sweet, and because you couldn't be bothered to remember his name. Is that how Scott thought of me now?

But then I imagined him sitting in the middle of an office full of curious, big-lugged coppers, trying not to sound off-balance as they eavesdropped on his conversation with a disgraced former officer.

'Sorry for calling you out of the blue like this, Scott. I don't mean to cause you any trouble.'

'No trouble at all,' he said. 'It's good to hear from you — been a long time since we talked.'

I remembered all the times I'd never returned his catch-up calls, all those ignored let's-get-together-for-a-drink-soon messages, all those unanswered Christmas and birthday cards, and felt like a prize shit.

'Scott, I think I probably owe you an apology,' I said. 'A *lot* of apologies. I suppose you have to do that sort of thing when you've been as big an arsehole as I have.'

Scott laughed shortly, and then his voice hardened. 'I like a man who knows how to grovel. What is it you're after, Joel?'

Scott had always been sharp, and he still was. I decided he was on the way up, not on the way down.

'I need some help finding my wife.' It was blunt, but sometimes blunt is best.

'Oh? So Lisa's run off, has she?' Scott asked, not sounding terribly surprised.

'She ran off a long time ago, but she wasn't missing until recently.'

'Mmmm...' I could almost hear him decoding this sentence, weighing up the information it imparted. 'What are you thinking, Joel, that she's in trouble, in some kind of danger?'

'God, no, nothing like that,' I lied. 'But it's one of those things, isn't it? I'm worried and I'm not worried. You know what I mean? Plus, there's Vic — our daughter, Victoria — to think about. I *am* worried about her learning that her Mum's disappeared.'

I felt terrible using Vic as a bargaining chip, but I really had my eyes on the prize now. The end justifies the means, or something like that. Scott had access to the police computers, which, loosely speaking, meant that he had access to just about every database in the country. Or could have it, if he really wanted to.

I knew that it was a fairly simple procedure to track someone around the country, even around the world, purely by their credit transactions. And as Lisa tended to use credit cards the way other people breathed, I thought Scott would be able to nail down her general location for me in a matter of hours. If he agreed, that was.

But the way it was sounding now, that was a *big* if.

'I'm not so sure that I can help you, Joel,' Scott said, speaking so carefully that I was now absolutely positive someone was listening closely to his end of the conversation.

'Why's that?'

'Things have changed a lot since your time. It's not the Wild West anymore. We can't go charging in and chasing someone through cyberspace just because we feel like it, without any evidence, or some kind of probable cause. The law is the law, and unsanctioned favours are severely frowned upon. There are all kinds of rules and regulations now, and the penalties for breaking them can be harsh.'

'So you're not going to help me?'

'I didn't say that,' Scott answered after a pause. His voice had dropped almost to a whisper. 'Look, I can't promise anything, Joel, but I'll do what I can, when I can. I'll call you if I find anything. If you don't hear from me, don't call back. Wait for me to contact you. Understand?'

'Scott,' I said, 'thank you so much,' but he had already gone.

'A DATE? THAT'S wonderful, just what you need!' Maude was smiling warmly, and if she thought it was fast work on my part, then she didn't let on. We were in the kitchen, where she was heating water in a pan for pasta. Vic was sitting on the floor beside Albert as he gobbled down a blob of leftover salmon, and she was regaling him with the highlights of the old *Barney* DVD Nana had found for her that morning in the supermarket's bargain bin.

Albert, it has to be said, didn't seem overly interested in Vic's conversation, cats being more or less impervious to the charms of large purple dinosaurs with the voices of adenoidal eunuchs.

'You don't mind?' I asked.

'Babysitting my own granddaughter? Not in a million years.'

'I meant do you mind me *dating?*'

'Why in heaven's name would I mind,' she said, pouring a little oil into the pan of simmering water, then adding a pinch of salt. 'After all, you're only doing what I said you should, and there's nothing in the world that makes an old woman happier. I'll call Henry and tell him I'll be staying over. He won't mind — not that he has much of a choice. Now, where were you planning to take Elaine for dinner? Because there's a lovely new restaurant in Knebworth I've just been reading about…'

Ah, I thought. Time to break the bad news.

'Well, actually, my date isn't with Elaine Leigh.'

For the first time, Maude's smile faltered slightly. I quickly explained what had happened, my meeting with Barbara and all, and the smile came back most of the way.

'Well, that's nice. Pity about you and Elaine, though,' she added with a small sigh. 'Not that it's any of my business, but I thought you'd have made a lovely couple. Very easy on the eye.'

She seemed to shrug off her disappointment easily, and then left me in charge of Vic's dinner while she took the girl herself upstairs for a quick dip in the bath, because she was absolutely filthy. When I'd pulled up outside the house, Vic had been standing in the bay window waving to me, making melted-face shapes against the panes of glass. I'd seen at once that she and Maude had been playing at dressing up, but had less luck identifying exactly what Vic thought she was.

Today my daughter was wearing about five different layers of grimy clothes, and two different kinds of footwear — one of them flippers. My best guess was that she was supposed to be a crime-fighting, fashion-modelling, duck/frog hybrid ninja type of thing. With a monstrous craving for tomato soup lunches, because most of her chest appeared to be spattered with dried quantities of it.

When I asked Vic what she was meant to be, she'd screamed, 'I'm a Queen!'

Which sounded about right.

I waited until Vic was in the bath and I knew that Maude wouldn't leave her, then headed for the phone and called old Mrs. Webber, super-snooper *par excellence*, to get her daily report.

'No,' she said, 'I've seen neither hide nor hair of it today. That makes four days in a row.'

At my request, Mrs. W had been keeping a watch out for the black Rover in which Greg the Goblin had fled earlier in the week. I wanted to know if he was checking out the house when I wasn't here.

'There was *another* car hanging around earlier, though,' she added. 'A metallic-blue Saab.' She was obviously reading from notes she had jotted down at the time, reminding me of a copper reading from his notebook in court. 'The registration number was—'

'Was it the same man?'

'No, it was two different men. *Normal* men. The windows weren't tinted this time, and I could see them both very clearly. One was very fat and had scruffy grey hair that badly needed cutting, and the other one was much younger and much thinner, with short brown hair and a face like a smacked arse — nasty piece of work, he looked. They were wearing shirts and ties, and it looked like they were studying a map, like they were lost.'

'What did they do then?'

'After a few minutes of dithering, they turned the car around and drove away.'

'Did they come back?'

'No.'

I sighed. 'Didn't it occur to you that they were probably just a couple of lost salesmen?'

'Yes, of course it did. But I thought you said we couldn't be too careful, not if…'

She tactfully left the rest unsaid, but she was right. You couldn't be too careful when your child had been threatened.

All the same, there had been no actual sightings of Greg the Goblin for the best part of a week now, which, as far as I was concerned, was all to the good. If you looked at it a certain way, his vicious parting words to me could have been nothing more than an empty threat — payback, perhaps, for the way I'd taunted him about his height, his looks, and his pulling power in general.

And that feeling of being followed I'd been getting?

Well, it was entirely possible that I'd been mistaken, and what I had taken for ex-copper's intuition was really its idiot half-brother, otherwise known as baseless paranoia. Also known as the heebie-jeebies. I'd certainly been known to suffer from that curious ailment from time to time.

'Do you still want me to keep an eye out?' Mrs. Webber asked, breaking into my thoughts.

'Yes, if you don't mind. I think the trouble's passed, if there ever *was* any trouble. But if you're sure...'

'Makes no difference to me,' she said, which made its way through my translation filter as, 'spying on the street is pretty much what I'd be doing anyway, so why not?'

LATER, AFTER MAUDE and Vic had eaten dinner and I had been through a personal and intimate refurbishment process, I spent a long time in my bedroom wrapped in a towel while I tried to find something appropriate to wear.

This was a much more difficult task than it sounds, I assure you.

It wasn't so much that I was overly anxious to impress my date, it was more that I simply had no decent clothes from which to choose. Those few items which were neither scarred by child-rearing, nor faded by countless runs through the washing machine, were either so out of fashion that to wear them in public would be to become a universal laughing stock, or so hideous they had scarcely been worn after the rash initial purchase.

In fact, the single smartest set of clothes I now owned — by a country mile — was my wedding suit, and although it still fit me almost perfectly, there was no way I was going out on a date wearing that cursed thing. It'd be like wearing a monkey's paw as a tie pin.

All the while, Vic lay on her belly on my bed watching me dither, her green eyes wide and both tiny hands cupped like a respirator over her nose and mouth, in silent condemnation of the amount of uncoordinated smellies I'd used so indiscriminately.

Cherry Blossom kids' shampoo. Coal tar soap. My menthol shaving cream. Her bubblegum-flavoured toothpaste. The skin of my face was tight and stinging with decade-old aftershave, and my eyes were still watering from its unaccustomed vapour. Clouds of a cheap sports deodorant that smelled insect-lethal were still actually visible, billowing under the overheard light like a thin drizzle.

Albert was there too, keeping a curious eye on the proceedings while perched on the chest of drawers. 'What a lot of fuss you're making,' he seemed to be saying, one rear leg suspended over his head as he licked his nether regions.

If I could do that, I thought in his direction, I wouldn't *need* a date.

I realised that my daughter had never seen me like this before. Nervous. Self-conscious. Apprehensive. Even a little afraid. I wondered what she thought of it all. I wondered if she felt that in some way I was cheating on her mum, but I didn't dare ask.

Finally, I narrowed my choices down to two possible outfits, both of which had their downsides. First, I had a clean-ish pair of blue jeans and a kind of Bermuda shirt with an abstract pattern of yellows, reds and oranges — which was sort of okay, but if I happened to wander under a bright light, it was going to look like my torso was on fire. Or I had a pair of black double-pleated trousers that were slightly too tight around the waist and a plain blue linen collarless shirt that would work fine — just so long as I rolled the sleeves up so the iron burn on the right cuff would be invisible.

Unable to decide between these riches for myself, I held both outfits up for Vic's inspection.

'Which one?'

She pointed at the blue jeans and the red and orange shirt immediately.

'Daddee wear the clown suit!' she said.

So, the blue shirt and black trousers it was.

NINE

IN PREPARATION FOR my date, I'd made sure that I called at the ATM to get some cash while I was in town. You couldn't go far wrong with cash, which was something I had learned the hard way. I used to be a naturally lucky person, but now the only luck I seemed to have was bad luck, as though Lisa was a black cat that had crossed my path and jinxed my whole life.

Now I'm one of those people whose credit cards never work just when they need them most. I'm the guy whose pen runs dry when he gets his one chance to sign on the dotted line, whose watch stops ticking the very second the guarantee expires, and whose shiny new shoes automatically become dogshit magnets the first time they're worn outside the house.

But now I had a feeling — just a *little* feeling, mind you — that my luck was finally changing.

It turned out to be one of those rare evenings that don't happen very often during the course of a man's life. Well, they hadn't happened very often in mine, anyway. It was an evening where everything went absolutely right. Wonderfully, perfectly, *astoundingly* right. All the way.

All the way, that is, up till the moment it went so dreadfully wrong.

The QUEEN of HEARTS

∽

AT THE BEGINNING, I was worried that everything that was happening at home would conspire to drain some, if not all, of the pleasure out of my date. Before I even thought of leaving the house, I had debated with myself long and hard about whether to warn Maude about Greg the Goblin. In the end, I decided not to.

In the first place, I didn't want to worry Maude unnecessarily. After all, I had seen neither 'hide nor hair' (as Mrs. Webber would have said) of the sawn-off pug-ugly since he'd made his threat. Secondly, if I did tell Maude, she would immediately turn around and tell Henry, and Henry would immediately turn around and involve the police.

Needless to say, that involvement would be on a whole other level than I had risked by trying to get Scott Vaughan to do me a favour. But Maude and Henry didn't know what I knew, which was that involving the police in our business on an official basis would probably lead to the exposure of Lisa's illegal (but so far unreported) activities at Morgan-Matheson, which would inevitably land their daughter in more hot water than she already was. Misery pretty much all around, in short.

Leaving the house was easier once I'd made this decision, and things only got better from there.

Barbara was ready and waiting for me when I pulled up outside her house, and I immediately began to drool. Despite her accident earlier, she was wearing a pair of strappy shoes with stiletto heels that made her smooth, shapely legs look about six feet long. In addition, she wore a long black belted silk dress that clung to her lithe body like perspiration, and had a kind of shawl made of the same material decorously draped over her creamy shoulders. Her hair was immaculate once again, long, flowing and golden.

I held the car door open for her, and she gave me a peck on the cheek as she climbed into her seat. I drove away feeling like a prince — or, let's say, like a frog that's just been mistaken for a prince, and isn't in a hurry to have the mistake rectified.

I had managed to book a table at the new restaurant Maude had suggested in the nearby village of Knebworth, an arrangement only made possible because there had been a last-minute cancellation just before I called — another example of that change of luck, perhaps? When we walked in and sat down together, I swear that every single (and not so single) man in the place had their eyes on Barbara. Most of the women seemed to be staring too, only theirs was a slightly different kind of stare. Put it this way, if looks could kill, I would have ended up eating dinner opposite a corpse.

I caught Barbara smirking at me after I'd ordered a bottle of wine, and I asked what was funny.

'It's your accent,' she explained. 'Sometimes it makes you sound like a character from one of those Cockney gangster films.'

I was slightly surprised to hear that I had any accent at all, but the observation made me listen all the more carefully to her voice, which was classless but totally classy. She sounded how she looked, and she looked like the women you see in magazines (no, not *those* kind of magazines), the posh, glossy ones, all fashion, lifestyles, and aspirations. Beautiful people whose lives, bodies, and faces, their very *existences*, seemed custom-tailored, elegant, and almost regal. Powerful women with jobs — careers — that let them earn umpteen thousands without ever breaking either a sweat or a nail. I really wished that I was that smart myself. I'm not a naturally sweaty person, but I *do* hate to break a nail.

I don't really know how to describe what happened next, but I'll try because it seems important.

After the small talk had dwindled out, Barbara began to ask me questions about myself, and for the first time in literally years, I found myself opening up about my life and my feelings to another person. (A *real* person, that is — one who didn't have a long, twitching tail and a bad case of fish-breath.) The courses came and went and I was hardly aware of them, although the food was as good as Maude had promised.

I spoke of my career in law enforcement and my regret over its unsavoury end. I spoke of the thought-processes that had led me to uproot my small family from the capital. I spoke of my failed marriage to Lisa, my relationship with her parents, my relationship with *my* parents, and, of course I spoke about Vic. I spoke about everything. The dam had well and truly broken.

And if it sounds like Barbara got the worst of the deal, going out on a date only to end up being on the wrong end of an overdue therapy session, then I'm not describing it right. It wasn't like that at all. We made a real *connection*.

Barbara also spoke at length to answer my questions, although she seemed shy of going into too much detail about her deceased parents, and of course I didn't press her on that. She told me a little about the men in her life, a little about the places she had been and the things she had done, and literally next to nothing about her work — 'Work, phew, the least said about *that* the better!'

And we laughed. Oh my God, we laughed such a lot.

Then, when the last course had been consumed, the plates cleared away and the coffees almost drained, Barbara had taken my hand over the table and invited me back to her house for a nightcap. I saw the promise in her candlelit eyes, and I accepted.

And that was when the evening began to go wrong.

I HAD EXCUSED myself to visit the men's room. I had been gone for slightly longer than might have been expected, but then I imagine that most men find it difficult to urinate efficiently with a raging hard-on. It had been a long time coming, and now that it was here, it seemed reluctant to leave.

I had to wait quite a while for my excitement to ebb a little, my forehead pressed against the cubicles' cool white tiles as I desperately tried to think of passion-free subjects. Helping Henry spread his garden with manure, the future of the country in a post-Brexit world, old Mrs. Webber's underwear flapping around on the washing line...

On the way back, I noticed that the short corridor outside the toilet ended at a door which opened on to the car park at the rear. Someone had wedged this door open earlier to allow a breeze to flow through the over-warm restaurant, and suddenly a cool refreshing breeze was what I wanted most. On a whim, I stepped outside into the night.

The small car park was hemmed in on three sides by trees, some of them in blossom, lending to the night their own subtle fragrances, which mixed and merged with the good food smells coming from the restaurant, and with Barbara's perfume, which I could smell now on my hands and clothes, bringing us ever closer.

The only thing spoiling this olfactory pleasure was the intrusive presence of the large green dumpster parked a few feet away to my right, from which I caught an unwelcome waft of rotting vegetation. As I turned to go back into the restaurant, I saw a flicker of movement behind it.

I froze.

There was a brief moment when I tried to convince myself that I simply couldn't have seen what I thought I'd seen — no, it was just a shadow thrown by a tree moving in the breeze, just a cat mooching for scraps of food in the garbage, or maybe a waiter having a crafty fag between orders. But in the end, I had to admit that it was none of those things. It was what it was.

It was the man who had been shadowing me.

I quietly stepped around the corner of the dumpster, and there he was, looking back at me like a schoolboy caught with his hand in the cookie jar. He was about the same size as a schoolboy, too.

'What do you think you're doing?' I asked Greg the Goblin.

There was a strange duality to my voice, I noticed. My *mind* believed that I was speaking quite calmly and reasonably, but to my *ears* that voice sounded suspiciously like it was shouting its bloody head off.

Greg the Goblin opened his mouth to respond, but anger, the Red Planet's crushing gravity, now had me firmly in its grasp. It had finally happened. I'd returned to Mars.

I thought of the war-zone he'd turned Lisa's flat into, and the fragrant little gift he'd laid on her bed. I thought of his theft of Vic's photograph from Lisa's album, and his ugly threat on my own doorstep. I thought of him following me here tonight, spying on Barbara and I as we got to know one another.

To my surprise, an arm suddenly came into view, and the fist at the end of it struck the Goblin smartly in the centre of his chest, driving him back a step or two. To my greater surprise, I recognised that the arm was mine.

Greg stepped forward again, rubbing his chest. 'Now you've asked for it!'

He quickly dropped into a squat fighting stance, reducing his height still further, and then started doing that aggressive exhalation thing through his nostrils that boxers do, which always sounds like someone with a persistent cold attempting to clear their noses. He tried a bit of an Ali-shuffle next, his little legs riverdancing their way through the garbage spilling from the dumpster. His fists were up, circling defensively, and occasionally shooting out in jabs and abbreviated uppercuts.

'I'm gonna introduce you to the Lightning Bolt now, smart-arse,' he said. 'Prepare yourself for shock and awe, September — there's a storm coming your way!'

My fist shot out, once again entirely of its own accord, and went through his defences as though they weren't there. My knuckles caught him on the point of the chin, and Greg the Goblin instantly went down like a sack of coals.

I took a swan dive into the rolling red surf and followed him down.

It could only have been a matter of seconds before a couple of waiters waded in and dragged me off him, but in that time I'd managed to do quite a bit of damage. He was bleeding from both his nose and mouth, and I'd reopened an old cut above his right eye. It was a very satisfying sight to anyone of the Martian persuasion — one that could only be improved, in my estimation, by the absence of a number of those gold-capped teeth. As the Goblin tottered to his feet, swaying, I made another attempt to get at him, but the waiters held on tight.

'What on earth is going on here? Do I have to call the police?'

At the mention of the word *police,* the Goblin emitted a small yip of alarm, like a Yorkshire terrier scenting an invading postman, and he immediately scuttled away behind the dumpster and legged it.

I glanced at the man who had spoken. It was the restaurant's manager, who had so charmingly seated us an hour-and-a-half earlier. Now his face was like a slab of concrete, and he didn't look so charming anymore. With him were a fair number of the restaurant's other patrons, and, hovering at the back, Barbara, who looked utterly shocked at the turn of events.

I shook the waiters' hands off my arms, tucked my shirt back into my trousers, and asked for the bill.

The QUEEN of HEARTS

I DROVE BARBARA home immediately, but I honestly don't recall one second of that journey.

It had been years since I'd been involved in any real violence, and I was completely unprepared for the deluge of adrenaline that flash-flooded my system in response. The next thing I knew, I was standing in the centre of Barbara's living room, my knuckles still clenched, and the muscles in my arms and legs quivering with tension. Barbara had poured me a snifter of brandy and was trying to get me to take it.

Finally, she was able to get me sat down on the settee beside her, and slowly — very slowly — I began to come back down to earth.

She didn't ask me anything about Greg the Goblin, or about what had caused me to slip into such a rage. She spoke in a calm, even voice, telling me to relax, telling me that everything was fine, that everything was safe now, as though she were talking to someone in shock — which to some degree, I suppose she was. After a while, every muscle in my body seemed to relax at the same time, like an elastic band had snapped, and if I hadn't been sitting down already, I would have fallen down.

The first time her lips touched my face was on the cheek, the sort of kiss you'd give to calm or reassure someone. The second time, her soft lips touched the corner of my mouth, and lingered. The third time, our mouths met and locked.

It was extraordinary. It was like the first inhalation on a cigarette after a year-long abstinence, a giddy, dizzying experience.

Then Barbara opened her mouth to me. Her tongue found mine and performed a sort of undulating shimmy that made my toes curl. I felt her hand settle at the back of my neck, and then she reclined on the settee, pulling me down on top of her. I ran my hand up the front of her silk dress and realised that my eyes had not deceived me earlier; beneath the sheer material she was entirely naked, not so much as a scrap of underwear on her, not a single stitch. Her whole body felt hot, feverish, as though there were a furnace burning away deep inside her. I had forgotten that this was the way women felt in moments of passion.

In another way, I had forgotten nothing.

The belt that held the dress together was suddenly in my hand. I pulled at it and the dress unravelled, gaped wide, melted away. The most substantial parts of Barbara's clothing now seemed to be the straps on her shoes. Her free hand was wrenching at my belt buckle, and in a few short movements we were both of us half-naked, pressed together, just one more movement, just one slick and easy movement, from complete union.

And I stopped.

I pushed myself up above her, both of us breathing hard. I was trembling, my arms shaking as they supported my weight. My hair fell over my brow in a sweaty lop. She stared up at me, the pupils huge in her blue eyes.

'What is it?' she asked breathlessly. 'What's wrong?'

'I'm married,' I said. I sounded strangely surprised, as if this was something I hadn't realised until just this moment.

She frowned. 'I know, but you told me you'd separated?' She reached down between our bodies and found me. 'And anyway, I don't mind.'

'I know you know. And...'

I pulled away from her and collapsed back, putting my head in my hands.

'…and I think I *do* mind.'

Of course, it was the conversation we'd had in the restaurant which was mostly responsible for this sudden attack of the guilts. Talking about how it had gone so wrong with Lisa had inevitably involved describing how it had been between us *before* it all went wrong — and then I'd been forced to remember all the good things about her, which were identical to all the wonderful qualities that I saw in her mother now and hoped to see in our daughter in the future. Those things and more besides. I remembered all the things that had made me fall in love with Lisa from the beginning, and discovered that there was a big part of me that *still* loved her, no matter what she'd done or how angry with her I was.

I felt Barbara shift on the seat beside me, felt her snuggle up to me again, her arms slipping around me, her small soft hands, her long slim fingers, insinuating themselves in bad places, places where I felt they shouldn't go. Places where I *wanted* them to go.

'I thought I was ready,' I said, 'but I'm not. I'm sorry, Barbara. It just feels completely wrong.'

Her lips moved against my ear. 'You feel ready to me,' she said, softly squeezing.

I took her hand away from me, brought it to my lips and kissed it.

'That isn't where the problem is,' I told her sadly. 'I tapped a finger to my temple. '*This* is.'

It took a while for it to sink in that I really meant what I'd said. Then there was a good deal of mutual embarrassment as we began to pull our clothes back into place and tuck our bits and pieces away as best we could. This was particularly embarrassing for me, as it was obvious that a certain part of my anatomy did not agree with the decision I had made on its behalf. My penis and I were not seeing eye-to-eye (so to speak), and this time it steadfastly refused to return to a state of hibernation, no matter how many passion-killing thoughts I ran past it.

Barbara sat back on the settee and sipped the remainder of the brandy in the glass she'd poured for me, and seemed somewhat stunned by the turn of events. Her eyes had taken on the same sort of glazed faraway look as Greg the Goblin's when my knuckles had connected with his chin.

I didn't blame her. She had been hit for six. I didn't imagine that anything like this had ever happened to her before, unless she made a habit out of dating crazy men.

'I'm sorry,' I said. 'I'm really, really sorry.'

Barbara looked at me. Then she looked down at the front of my trousers, which still looked like a freshly erected wigwam. Then she started to laugh.

Half-an-hour later, I was home again, and I was quietly (and, yes, hopelessly) optimistic about how the evening had ended. Okay, it had been a disaster, but it wasn't all bad. I'd had a nice meal, hadn't I? I'd got to thump the Goblin, and wrestle around in the rotting garbage with him? What more could a man ask for on a first date?

What made the whole misadventure at least bearable was that as I'd left her house, Barbara had made it clear that she wanted to see me again.

'Even if it's just as friends,' she said on her doorstep.

'Is that what you want?' I asked.

'Of course it isn't what I want.' She grabbed a handful of my shirt and pulled me to her. She kissed me again, hard and deep. 'What I *want* is to screw your brains out — but I can wait, if I have to.'

Her fingers feathered over the front of my trousers, where my little friend was still urgent, frantic even, for attention.

'You'll call me?' she asked.

'First thing tomorrow.'

'Better still, why not come over for breakfast?'

So we'd left it like that, Barbara waving goodnight, standing on her doorstep like a Siren on a rock, and me hobbling over to the car with a bulge in my trousers that looked like I was trying to shoplift a crowbar from the local B&Q.

Magic moments are made of this.

Henry and Maude were asleep in the guest room when I got home. I could tell that Henry had turned up to keep Maude company because I could feel his buzzsaw-like snore reverberating through the floorboards, and the downstairs loo smelled like an explosion in a septic tank. Also, there was a large fat Golden Retriever heavily asleep on my sofa with the remains of a cushion sticking out of the corner of its mouth.

Vic was snug in her cot, nested like a little squirrel. Albert was nowhere to be seen. He was probably out on the tiles again with Mrs. Webber's pretty little tabby, getting his furry, conscienceless little end away.

Lucky git.

I double-checked that everything was locked up tight and then trudged back upstairs and shut myself in the bathroom, where, over the next ten minutes or so, I rediscovered yet another old truth: cold showers do not work exactly the way they're supposed to.

In fact, scratch that — the bastard things don't work at all.

I CAME FUZZILY awake at four o'clock in the morning, wondering what had woken me. Outside my window, I could hear cats yowling like banshees. Albert's date was definitely going better than mine had. If I could have spoken Cat, I would probably have heard Alice telling Albert, 'Harder! Faster! Come on! Give it to me, big boy!'

Then the phone beside my bed rang for a second time, making me groan. With my eyelids still glued together by sleep, I simply pulled the whole phone into bed with me and scrambled the receiver to my ear.

'Good morning, Joel,' a familiar voice said brightly.

It was Lisa.

Ten

'Hello! Hello! Hello!' Lisa yodelled when I didn't immediately answer. 'Joel, hello, good morning!'

'Good morning?' I finally said — when I could speak, that was. 'What do you mean *good morning*, it's the middle of the bloody night.'

She laughed at me, which, unfortunately, was an experience I remembered all too well.

'Well, it's morning where I am, you old sleepyhead, so it must be morning where you are. Ahh, but I'd forgotten what you sound like when you get woken up so early. You're just a great big grumbly bear, aren't you, all growly and moody and spiky. Very, very sexy.'

I grunted. 'Maybe if you'd kept that in mind we wouldn't be separated now.'

'Oh Joel,' she sighed, 'we're not going rake over those old coals again, are we? Not at this late date? It's too boring. What's done is done, and what's past is past. It can't be changed, it can't be mended. You *do* know that, don't you?'

Yes, I knew it all too well, and said so.

'Well then — say good morning to little Lisa.'

'Good morning, Lisa. Where are you?'

She laughed again, but this time her laughter sounded hollow and her humour brittle.

'Yes, that's what everybody wants to know, isn't it, hubby darling? The million-dollar question on everybody's lips. Where is Lisa? How can we find Lisa? What is Lisa up to now, we wonder? Where on earth can Lisa be?'

When I didn't respond, she grew more serious.

'Joel, I have something very important to ask you now... are you with anyone?'

I started guiltily, thinking of Barbara.

'I don't see how that's any of your business, Lisa,' I told her stiffly, uncertainly aiming for the moral high ground. 'It stopped being your business when you walked out on me, don't you think?'

'No, you fool,' she said impatiently. 'I mean are you with anyone *now* — right now? Oh, for God's sake, Joel, you're such an innocent! Is anyone else there in bed with you?'

Oh, I thought.

'Well, only the usual selection of beautiful women with which I routinely stock my harem,' I said. 'A few blondes, a few brunettes, a couple of red—'

'So you *are* alone?'

'Of course I am,' I sighed. 'I'm always alone.'

'Okay, then listen to me,' she said. 'I want us to meet.'

Now this was a surprise. I had been desperate to find Lisa, but it never occurred to me that she might want to be found.

'Why?' I asked. 'And why *now*?'

'There are some things we need to discuss, Joel. Things we should have discussed a long time ago.'

Talk about an understatement.

Over the past week or so, I'd been thinking about all the many things I'd want to say to Lisa the next time we spoke, but now that I had the opportunity and could feel the words fizzing on the tip of my tongue, yearning to be set free, I realised that I'd have to keep them bottled up for at least a little while longer. Many of the things I had to say to her would probably be offensive to her delicate shell-likes, and right now I couldn't afford to scare her away.

'When do you want to meet?' I asked.

'Today.'

'Where?'

She paused for a moment before answering.

'Joel, as to the precise location, I'm going to give you some clues. So listen very carefully.'

'Clues?' I asked. 'What are you talking about, *clues?* Lisa, this is ridiculous. This isn't a game. I'm not Andrew Lipton, and I'm not prepared to—'

'Joel, just listen!' she snapped. 'The clues should let you know where to meet me. They're clues that only you and I would ever understand, and I'm sure you'll work them out immediately. But this is very important, Joel — in fact, I can't stress *how* important it is — I don't want you to say the answer out loud. You *mustn't* say the answer out loud. Keep it in your head.'

'Why can't I say it out loud? What's the point? I told you, I'm alone, nobody can hear us.'

'Do I have to spell it out for you, Joel? You of all people?'

Yes, at this time of the morning, she did.

'Sometimes private conversations turn out to be not quite as private as you'd like them to be. You never know who may be listening, or why.'

'Huh?'

Either I was being exceptionally slow, or the world was moving too fast. I felt like I was talking to someone for whom English was a second language.

But then, suddenly, I understood.

'You're trying to tell me you think your phone might be bugged?'

Lisa gave vent to a shrill, exasperated screech that very nearly burst my eardrum. 'No, you great idiot, not mine — *yours*.'

'*Mine*?' My voice had risen so high I sounded like I was auditioning for the role of pantomime dame. 'Who on earth would bug *my* phone?'

'Not now, Joel, please. Look, I'm running out of time here. We can talk about this when we meet. Are you ready for the clues?'

'All right,' I said, but I was very far from being all right. The idea that my phone might be bugged was severely creeping me out. In my time on the force I'd monitored my fair share of phone taps, but I never expected to be on the wrong end of one myself.

'Okay,' Lisa said, 'There are two clues in total. Clue number one is *Tina Turner*. Clue number two is *credit card meltdown.*'

Despite the aggravation, despite the worry, I almost found myself smiling. She was absolutely right, I immediately knew where she meant, and I remembered that day very well.

Lisa was talking about the first and practically the last time I ever willingly accompanied her on one of her mammoth shopping trips. This was in the early days of our relationship, when I was still a gainfully employed and generally respected officer of the law, my credit-score was healthy, and I still believed that everything was going to turn out all right.

The QUEEN of HEARTS

What a dink I must have been.

We had driven out to Brent Cross shopping centre just off the North Circular Road, and I had spent the whole of the morning and most of the afternoon following Lisa around an eternity of clothes boutiques and shoe emporiums while she rode all our cards up to their respective limits.

That was the *credit card meltdown* reference.

By the end of the day we had been on the verge of our very first serious argument, a battle royal which was only averted at the last moment, when Lisa whispered into my lughole that she was actually wearing some of the slinky, sexy lingerie she had just bought under her coat — the lingerie and nothing else — and she wanted to model it for me in the back seat of our car.

That was the *Tina Turner* reference: the song *Steamy Windows*.

Within moments we were in the car park, hurrying toward my car. I remembered opening one of the rear doors for her. I remembered her lying back on the upholstery and opening her coat for me, all smooth creamy skin and form-fitting black lace. I remembered smacking my head on the roof climbing in after her, and not feeling the pain until much, much later. The windows steamed over, just like in the song, leaving us in a sticky cocoon of blissful privacy, both of us steaming ourselves, and eventually boiling over like—

'Well, do you get it?' Lisa asked, impatiently breaking into the memory.

Daydreamus interruptus.

'Joel, do you *get* it?'

Oh my God, yes — I got it, all right.

The QUEEN of HEARTS

'I know the place you're talking about, Lisa,' I said, trying to sound all business, and probably failing. 'What time do you want to meet?'

'Around lunchtime.'

'Lunchtime. Okay. And whereabouts, *exactly*? It's a big place.'

'Don't worry about that. Just wander around and follow your nose. You won't see me, but I'll find you.'

'Are you sure you won't—'

'And one more thing, Joel. You better make damn sure you're not followed.'

She hung up without warning, without saying goodbye, but that was Lisa all over. Good on *helloes*, rubbish at *goodbyes*. With not much expectation of success, I hit the call-back button, and, of course Lisa had withheld her number. How come everybody but me could do that?

I put the phone back on the nightstand and lay back on my pillow, wondering about Lisa's concern that my phone might be bugged.

It was a troubling thought, if it was true, but I wasn't convinced that it was. There had been no suspicious clickings or hummings on the line that I had heard, and as far as I was aware there hadn't been any mysterious men climbing up the telephone poles or fiddling around inside holes in the ground. And if I had missed them, I was sure that Mrs. Webber, who was still on red alert, wouldn't have.

In the end, I decided that Lisa's paranoia about bugged phones was probably only a measure of how scared she was. It showed just how afraid she was of being caught by the bad man. The Big Man.

At least, that's what I hoped it was.

I WOKE UP again a few hours later. Albert the Cat was sitting at the bottom of the mattress staring, in that self-hypnotised way cats have, at my feet as they poked out the bottom of the duvet. I wriggled one of my big toes experimentally and his eyes widened in rapt attention.

I've heard that there's a type of fiction where cats turn detective to solve crimes, and I can almost believe that some of them are smart enough to do this (Albert especially). But in my experience, I'd say they were far more likely to commit crimes than solve them. For every Persian Blue Sherlock Holmes there'd be a dozen moggy Moriartys. For every tortoiseshell Clarice Starling, a score of Siamese Hannibal Lecters.

Cats are no respecters of law and order.

I wriggled my toe again, and Albert, unknowingly proving my point, immediately raised a paw to bat it.

'Don't do it, Albert,' I advised him. 'I'm not in the mood today.'

Albert gave me a cool 'Am I bothered?' sort of look, jumped down from the bed and strutted away with his tail angled up and away from his body, like the cat equivalent of a raised middle finger.

I sat up, rubbing the sleep out of my eyes. I could hear lots of noise from downstairs, which let me know that Maude, Henry and Vic were already up and doing, and I could smell breakfast cooking. And breakfast reminded me that there was a call I had to make.

I leaned out of bed and pulled the trousers I had worn last night from the chair and retrieved my wallet from the back pocket. From my wallet I removed a folded slip of paper. It was the receipt from the restaurant in Knebworth, and on the back of it I had scrawled Barbara Rawlings' home phone number. With my ears open for the sound of footsteps, either tiny or ancient, ascending the stairs, I dialled the number. I hoped that it wasn't too early for her.

Apparently it wasn't, because the phone was answered on the second ring.

'Barbara?'

'Joel!'

She sounded happy to hear from me, which made me feel good. And there was a deep, husky, treacly quality to her voice, even in that one word, that made me think she was speaking from deep in the nest of her own bedclothes. Her voice reminded me of what Lisa had said about mine in the early hours.

Sexy. Very, very sexy.

'How are you this morning?' she asked me. 'I thought about you after you'd gone. I thought about you a *lot*.'

I told her that I'd thought about her, too, although I didn't go so far as to tell her about the cold shower, and how it hadn't worked very well (or at all).

'In fact, I was thinking about you just before you rang, as well,' she said, her voice now almost a purr. 'Why don't you come over for breakfast, right now? We could even have it in bed.'

Breakfast in bed sounded like a great idea to me, and the tiny beast beneath the duvet thought that it sounded like a *fabulous* idea (especially if there was no actual food involved in the meal). But sadly, I had bad news to break, both to the beauty and to the beast.

'Actually, that's why I'm calling. I can't make it this morning, after all. I have to meet someone.'

'Someone more important than me?' I could hear the attractively playful pout in her voice.

'My wife.'

The phone went quiet.

'But it's not what you're thinking,' I told her. 'It isn't a romantic liaison, not even close. There are a lot of things going on in my life right now — mostly bad things — and Lisa seems to be at the root of them all. I need to see her to sort everything out. And amazingly, for once she actually seems to agree with me.'

'When is this happening?'

'Later today, around lunchtime.'

'So why can't you come over here now? There's plenty of time.'

'No, it won't work. In the first place, I have to get all the way over to Brent Cross to meet her. Plus, I have her parents at my house right now, and I need to get rid of them before I set off. I don't want them to know I'm seeing Lisa.'

'Why not?'

I sighed. 'It's complicated.'

'It certainly sounds that way.' She paused for a moment, and then asked, 'Am I making a mistake here, Joel?'

'What do you mean?'

'Am I making a mistake getting involved with you? Is your wife always going to come between us?'

'No, she isn't. And you're not making a mistake. I'll make it up to you, I promise.'

'Tonight?'

'I'd like to, but I can't say for certain. I'll have to call you.'

'You promise you'll try to make it?'

'Yes, I promise.'

'Are you sure you want to?'

'Of course I'm sure.'

'But do you *really* want to?'

I smiled. 'Yes, I really, *really* want to...'

The conversation went on like this for a little longer, but trust me, you wouldn't want to know exactly how it went. Suffice to say that five minutes after it ended, I was back under a cold shower. Which, once again, didn't work

As I believe it also says somewhere in the Bible, keeping your hands to yourself doesn't always keep you out of trouble.

TODAY BEING *SPLENDID Sunday*, when Vic and I would usually be spending the day with Henry and Maude anyway, I didn't anticipate any problems when it came to leaving my daughter in their care for a few hours, and there wasn't. Maude agreed immediately.

I was wearing only my dressing gown. Vic was wearing one of my old rugby shirts, a plastic Roman Centurion's helmet and a pair of yellow rubber gloves. She and Henry were putting on their shoes (roller-skates for Vic), prior to taking a walk to the newsagent to collect the Sunday papers. Maude was turning sausages under the grill, with Daisy the Dog sitting only inches away from the heat, slavering onto the vinyl flooring and trembling in anticipation of getting her laughing-gear around one of her favourite Lincolnshire bangers.

'I shouldn't be gone for too long,' I said. 'It's just some business I promised to take care of and forgot about until just now. Some guy I know needs something taking somewhere...' Could I be any vaguer, or sound any more stupid? 'Just one of those things, you know how it is.'

'That's fine, Joel,' Maude said lightly. 'We'll take Victoria home with us, and you just come along whenever you're ready.'

'Great, thanks.'

'Actually, Joel, I was hoping that you were going to help me in the garden today,' Henry said as he tied his shoelaces. He had lately decided he was going to try his hand at growing organic veg', and wanted my assistance digging his whole back garden over. 'Got to make a start soon.'

'I help you, Granddad,' Vic chipped in.

'Ah, well...' I began.

'The garden can wait until next week, Henry, or the week after, for that matter,' Maude said serenely. 'Didn't you hear, Joel's busy. And for Heaven's sake, take a look out of the window, dear — gardening's not exactly his forte, is it?'

This was perfectly true.

When we first moved in the front garden was neat and very well-cared for, with a little strip of bowling green-quality lawn beside the short drive, colourful flowerbeds, and a path to the front door edged with miniature, meticulously-trimmed conifers. Now, under my stewardship, it was nothing less than an unkempt wilderness, and the conifers looked like the kind of trees you might expect to find at the back of a wardrobe leading to another world. The back garden was even worse. I kept meaning to get around to it, but somehow I had the feeling I never would.

'I'll tell Mother Nature to hang on then, shall I?' Henry grumped.

'*I* tell Her, Granddad!'

'You go ahead and do that, Henry, my love,' Maude said. 'In the meantime, go get your precious newspapers. Breakfast's nearly ready, and if you're not back in five minutes, I'm giving yours to old Sausages here.'

Henry and Vic left via the back door, and Daisy the Dog, having heard the use of her alternative name, was now at DEFCON 3 on the anticipation-of-food scale, and looked like she wanted to lock and bolt it after them.

'I apologise for Henry,' Maude said. 'He obviously forgot where he was and got out of the wrong side of the bed this morning. Speaking of which, how did it go last night? The big date?'

Fortunately, Maude wasn't looking directly at me, otherwise she would have seen that I was blushing from the tips of my toes to the roots of my hair. I took a deep breath, commended my soul to whatever agency is responsible for souls these days, and gave her a fairly brief account of my evening.

It had to be brief, mind you, because once I'd taken out the sex and violence there wasn't a lot left to describe.

'I knew it must have gone well,' Maude said, smiling to herself as she began to dish up the food on to the warmed plates.

'Because I got home so late?'

'Because she had to call and speak to you only a few hours after you left her side,' she said, her sly feline eyes sliding in my direction. 'That *was* the phone I heard about four o'clock this morning, wasn't it? And would Barbara be the 'business' you have to take care of today?'

'Maude, it isn't what you're thinking.'

'You don't have to say another word,' she said primly. 'I shan't pry. I know that it's none of my business...'

I rolled my eyes. Never before in the entire history of the universe had anyone adopted a more inappropriate catchphrase. Maude not prying would be like Mrs. Webber not snooping, or like a dog not cocking its leg against a lamp-post.

The rest of the morning crawled by like a slug on sleeping pills, with Daisy Sausages sitting under the table begging for scraps, then a grumpy Henry dragging his heels about getting his overnight stuff together, and Vic dragging hers over collecting everything she felt she would need for the day, which seemed to include most of the contents of her bedroom. She even made me look through an out-of-date copy of the *KrazyKidz Toy Warehouse* catalogue, searching for some kind of electronic learning toy she'd been playing with over at *Tiny Minds*.

And all the while, Maude was giving me these secret little smiles, as if she was saying, 'I know what you're thinking about...' which, of course, she didn't.

It's a wonder that I didn't go out of my bloody mind.

Finally, they left. With a great sense of relief, I watched their car clear the end of the cul-de-sac, and as the last of the fumes from their exhaust dissipated into the air, I grabbed my jacket, my wallet and my keys, and ran for the door.

Which was when the phone rang.

I hesitated. Henry, Maude and Vic had already made me late, and Brent Cross seemed like a long way away when I had to be there for lunchtime. And who knew what time lunchtime was, anyway? Twelve o'clock, one o'clock? I almost closed the door. But then I thought that it would be just like Lisa to cancel or change the venue at the last minute. So I went back in and answered the phone.

But it wasn't Lisa. It was somebody called Charlie.

'Who?' I asked.

'Charlie Noble. Friend of Henry Forrester? He asked me to call you, said you wanted to know something about a boxer.'

The penny dropped. 'Yes, that's right, Mr. Noble.'

'Well, I hope I can help you. I've been following the boxing game closely for around sixty years, so I've got as much chance as anyone else. Sorry it's taken me so long to get back to you. Been a little bit busy on the domestic front, you know how it is.'

Sure did, I thought.

'Got married again, didn't you?' I asked, casting my mind back to what Henry had told me about Noble. 'For, what was it, the third time?'

'Fourth,' he corrected. Then he sighed deeply. 'And the least said about *that* situation right now the better. Temporary insanity, I suppose — just following orders from the Little Bald Colonel, as per bloody usual.'

The Little Bald Colonel? Jesus Christ, I thought. As penis euphemisms go, that's just bloody *awful*.

'Now, what's your question?' he asked.

'I'm trying to identify someone. I don't know for sure that he *is* a boxer, I just *think* that he is. Or he once was.'

I gave him a description of the little misfit who had threatened me and my daughter, including the fact that his first name might be Greg, and concluding with the name he had given his right fist.

To my surprise, Noble immediately began to chuckle, his laugh like a long, tobacco-roughened avalanche. 'The Lightning Bolt. That takes me right back, that does.'

'You mean to say you really know him?'

'Oh yes,' he said, still chuckling. 'Fella by the name of Gregory Feelen. He was a bantam contender years ago. When he got older and heavier, he tried to move up to welterweight and failed. In his glory days — not that there were very many of those, if I recall correctly — he was usually billed as Gregory *Pocket Thunder* Feelen. Either that or just *Lightning Bolt* Feelen.'

I told him that I called Feelen 'the Goblin', which made him laugh again.

'That'd be about right. Mind you, the little bugger's probably had more names over the years than I've had hot dinners.'

Or wives, I thought.

'Feelen claimed to have Irish roots somewhere down the line, so for a while he took to waving the Tricolour over his head before fights — usually that'd be just about three rounds before his corner threw in the towel. Then, when it became abundantly clear that he didn't have the luck of the Irish, he got himself a Union Jack and started calling himself a British Bulldog. Everyone else in the game had their own name for him. *Stumpy* Feelen was a popular one. I think I first knew him as *Reelin' Feelen* — as in Reelin' Feelen stares at the ceiling — because he spent most of his time in the ring on his back.'

'Was he ever any good?' I asked, although I had seen his face and so already knew the answer to that question.

'No, bloody terrible,' Nobel confirmed, laughing again. 'He always *looked* the part, mind you, tough like. And he could *talk* a good fight, but in the ring he was a complete shocker. He had a glass chin, no technique, no reach, a poor defence, and worst of all, he had absolutely no killer instinct. Hardly landed a punch of his own and got cut to ribbons every fight I saw.'

He cleared his throat again.

'Poor fella's probably got about three brain-cells left to his name. *Everybody* wanted to fight him, of course. It didn't matter how useless they were, he made them all look like Muhammad Ali.'

'Do you know what happened to him in the end?'

'Not for sure. I remember he used to fight for some management company that went down a long time ago. Some kind of scandal, as was usual with those type of firms. Last I heard, he was working security at some fancy nightclub up the West End. To tell you the truth, it wouldn't altogether surprise me if he'd drifted off the straight and narrow now and then.'

'Me either,' I said dryly. I glanced at my watch. 'Look, Mr. Noble, you've been very helpful and I'm really grateful, but I'm going to have to get off, I'm late for an appointment. Is there anything else you can tell me?'

'I don't think so. But I must say, I'm rather curious why you want to know about Feelen.'

'It's what you might call a private investigation. Sort of.'

'I thought Henry said you were a taxi-driver now. Isn't that what he said?'

'It is and I am,' I told him. 'But in my spare time, I fight crime.'

'You do, do you?' he asked thoughtfully. 'Like Batman?'

'Like Batman, exactly.'

'Only without the tights?'

'Depends on the day.'

Eleven

I took the A1 southbound to Apex Corner and then passed through Mill Hill and Hendon on my way to Brent Cross. Even though it was a Sunday, the traffic was still moderate-to-life-endangering, and negotiating it safely demanded the bulk of my attention. Nevertheless, along the way I managed to tick off in my mind all the many wonderful things I now knew about Greg the Goblin.

First, I knew that he really *had* been a boxer (and a particularly inept one, at that). I knew that at some point in the past he had been a bouncer on the London nightclub scene, and I knew that he was currently a thug-for-hire in the employ of the criminal my wife was hiding from.

And — most importantly — I now knew his real name.

This last was the key. Once I began to dig deeper, and maybe not too much deeper, it was likely I'd discover much, much more. Soon I would be in a position to start connecting the dots of this little puzzle, which hopefully would lead me to...

Stop it! a voice abruptly said, a voice so loud that I actually jerked in my seat and momentarily allowed the Scenic to wander over into the next lane, where a white-haired old lady driving a Nissan Micra flinched away, hanging onto her steering wheel like grim death.

Stop it! the commanding voice in my head ordered once more. *Stop it, right now!*

It took the intervention of this strident interior voice to make me understand exactly what I was doing — I was thinking like a cop again. I was thinking like a detective conducting an investigation, and the voice was right, it had to stop.

This situation with Lisa wasn't like breaking up a half-arsed fistfight in the street on a Friday night after the pubs had closed. (Something I had done more than once while wearing my once-a-cop-always-a-cop head.) This situation had the potential to be truly dangerous, and not just for yours truly. My subconscious knew this all too well, which was why it had chosen this moment to open its trap.

It was with a sudden sense of disbelief that I recalled myself speaking to Charlie Noble on the phone before I left the house — 'in my spare time I fight crime,' I'd glibly told him. I shook my head. What had I been thinking of? Even though it had been meant purely as a joke, what the hell was I thinking of?

'Okay,' I said aloud, 'it's time for a reality check.'

I caught my own eye in the rear-view mirror and gave myself a censorious frown.

'Face the facts, September,' I advised myself. 'You don't fight crime, and you're no superhero — not by a long shot. It's time to stop deluding yourself. You're not a cop any more, you're not even a dodgy private investigator. You are a taxi-driver, full-stop, end-of-story. *Operation Find Lisa* is all about getting the Goblin and his boss off your back. It's about protecting your daughter. It's about making it all stop, making it all go away. It is *not* about solving mysteries or putting criminals away behind bars. That isn't your job anymore, is it? So once and for all, give it up.'

I sighed heavily. This was getting slightly weird.

If talking to yourself is supposed to be the first sign of madness, what on earth is *lecturing* yourself meant to be? The second sign, the third? Or could it be the very last stop before the men in white coats drag you off to the padded cell in their butterfly nets?

TEN MINUTES LATER I was at Brent Cross, circling around the levels on my way to the top floor of the car park. It took me a further five minutes to find an unoccupied slot wide enough to comfortably accommodate the Scenic, and another five to walk around the rest of the level, peering into every car to make sure that Lisa wasn't waiting for me out here, away from prying eyes.

She wasn't, of course. Just because she clearly remembered the last time we were here together, and the intimate circumstances of that occasion, didn't mean that it was a matter of sentiment for her. Sentiment wasn't Lisa's thing, as I think we've pretty much established by now.

I passed through the car park doors and entered the shopping centre on its top-most level, which was purely a food court. Whether my estimation of what constituted 'lunchtime' was correct or not, a whole bunch of people seemed to concur with me. The place was heaving, most of the seats I could see were occupied, and some people were even queuing for their food and drinks.

I did the rounds of all the cafes, snack bars and restaurants, looking for Lisa, imagining that I'd see her sitting at one of the tables (and of course she would have been given a table to herself, in a prime location). There she'd be, calmly sipping a latte and flicking through the pages of a glossy magazine. I'd call her name and she'd look up, fixing me with those movie-star, *femme fatale* eyes, not green like her mother's and her daughter's, but a rich shade of chestnut so deep it was almost ebony.

When I'd met her for the first time, I had thought that looking into those eyes was like venturing naked into the unknown, like swimming out into a dark, fathomless pool. It was only much later I realised I was not swimming but drowning, and by then it had been far too late to save myself.

You know, when people tell you that life isn't a beauty contest, don't believe them, because Lisa's living proof it's exactly that. Her face was the face of an angel, and she had the kind of body that made men drive up on the pavements. But it was all a façade. All front. All show and no tell. Beneath the surface of that pretty face, the former apple of my eye was rotten to the core. The sexy, ball-bearing hipsway of her walk was hypnotically attractive, but it was purgatory in motion. She should have come with a warning sign flashing on and off above her head: CAUTION! MURKY DEPTHS! BEWARE!

The last time I'd seen Lisa was the night before Christmas, eight months before today, when she had swung by to bring Vic a present in the shape of a teddy bear and mayhem back into my life after only a month's separation.

On that occasion she'd looked even paler than usual, and she'd had her naturally curly dark hair straightened and cut in some kind of angular fashion that made her fringe look like a silken curtain. She had been decked out in more bling than a West Coast rapper and wore a luxurious grey mink coat that hung all the way to her ankles. She'd looked like a million dollars, which made me feel worth about three-and-a-half quid in small change.

'How many gerbils had to die to make that coat?' I'd asked her.

'As many as necessary,' she had responded, without even the hint of a smile.

It had been funny seeing her again in the house we had shared together only a month before (not funny ha-ha, I can assure you.) She was atypically subdued and thoughtful, and it was hard to shake the impression that she was looking around our small, chronically untidy home, sizing the place up and finding it wanting, wondering how or why she had ever lived here for so long.

It was an uncomfortable feeling, particularly as she seemed to be looking at me the same way.

Vic was all over her, naturally — this was her long-lost Mummy, for Christ's sake — but Lisa almost absently kept her at bay, as one might fend off an over-excited puppy. The teddy bear she had brought was cute enough, but to me it also seemed completely charmless. It reminded me of the kind of flower bouquets they sell at petrol stations, last minute purchases for the thoughtless and the uncaring. Vic loved the bear immediately, of course, and still did to this day.

At the first opportunity, I had pulled Lisa into the kitchen so that we were alone.

'Why did you come back?' I asked.

She looked at me blankly for a moment, her eyes those of a mystified stranger, and then she said, 'I don't know.'

'Can I help you?'

I glanced across at the waitress who had spoken and realised that I was standing in the middle of a café, staring off into space like a fool. I shook my head and quickly made my way out.

AN HOUR LATER I had been everywhere, in every clothes shop, shoe shop and jewellers in the entire centre, and I hadn't found Lisa. I had seen a couple of women who had a look of her from a distance, but close up they were nothing like.

I looked at my watch. It was after two now, and I wasn't sure that Lisa had any intention of showing. She may have got cold feet and changed her mind. I refolded the guide I had been following, ticking the stores off as I went, and stuck it in my jacket pocket. When I looked around, I found that I was standing just across from a shop selling educational toys, and on the spur of the moment I decided to go in.

Inside, I spoke to a young salesperson about the electronic learning toy Vic was so enchanted with at her playgroup. Although the shop didn't stock the particular model that had grabbed Vic's imagination, the girl knew exactly what I was talking about and she told me where I could buy one — it was *KrazyKidz*, after all — and I was just thanking her when I noticed her eyes drift away from me and widen.

Instinctively, I turned to see what she was looking at, and my eyes widened, too.

In the shop's doorway stood a living, breathing California-styled Barbie doll. A size-zero, perma-tanned, surgically-enhanced, trout-pouting, silicon-pumped Halloween mannequin, complete with glow-in-the-dark teeth and cascading bottle-blonde hair that fell all the way to her shoulders and beyond. Dressed in skinny white jeans tucked into white, be-sequinned cowboy boots, and a tight white blouse stretched to the seams by bazooka boobs, she was carrying about a hundred shopping bags from the sort of shops I had spent the last hour trawling through.

Without preamble, Barbie began calling out for someone called Myron in a loud, nasal New York-accented voice that immediately made you feel sorry for poor old Myron, whoever and wherever he might be.

'Myron?' she foghorned through the narrow vents left by her radical rhinoplasty. 'Myron? Where are ya, honey?

'Here I am,' I said.

It was a pretty good disguise — hell's teeth, it was more than that, it was a *wonderful* disguise — but Lisa hadn't done anything to her eyes. Her eyes were still the same.

'Gee, honey, I been lookin' for ya everywhere!'

'Same here.'

I smiled at the goggling salesperson (who, bless her kind heart, clearly hadn't had me pegged for a Myron), and then followed my estranged wife out into the lower mall, where she immediately made a beeline for the escalators up to the second level.

I caught up to her about halfway up and she turned to me and smiled her Hollywood smile.

'What do you think?' she asked in her own voice.

I looked her up and down. 'Not exactly camouflage, is it?'

'But that's *exactly* what it is, Joel,' she replied. 'Everybody *looks* at me, but nobody ever really *sees* me. They only see the tits, the teeth, and the hair. Then they hear the *voice*, and it's so bloody awful they immediately blank that out too. I'm the invisible woman.'

'*I* recognised you.'

'Only because I allowed you to.' She slipped on a pair of outsize sunglasses and my wife instantly disappeared. It was like a magic trick.

'How did you find me so easily?' I asked.

'Oh, I didn't even have to look for *you*,' she said. 'No, I just staked out that kids' shop. I knew you'd turn up there sooner or later.'

ONCE WE REACHED the second level, Lisa chose a spot at the railing looking down into the lower mall and dropped her shopping bags on the marble floor.

'Are you sure you weren't followed here?' she asked.

I assured her that I'd done my best to reach her tail-free, and then asked if she wouldn't prefer to have this discussion over a cup of coffee in the food court.

'The food court's at the top of the centre, isn't it?'
I nodded.

'Then we're staying here,' she said. 'If you get trapped at the top, there's only one way down. Didn't you ever see *King Kong*?'

She turned away from me to take a long slow look around the mall, and it suddenly became obvious to me just how carefully she had chosen this location.

From this spot, Lisa could see a long way in every direction, she could overlook all the escalators, and she had multiple avenues of escape should she have need of them. Her over-riding display of caution gave me another moment to study her, to look beyond the push-up bra, the fake tan, the blonde wig, and the bravado of the rest of her character.

She had always been slim (slim, but gorgeously curvy in all the right places), but now I saw that she was positively scrawny. She had lost a lot of weight. With the large sunglasses covering her eyes, she looked more than ever like an incognito movie-star, one who was currently lost in the limbo between rehab' and approaching anorexia.

Finally, she turned back to face me. Again, she smiled, but without the back-up of her eyes it looked more like a grimace. Who knows, maybe with the eyes it would have been worse.

'Joel, I'm not going to lie to you, I need your help.'

I shook my head in disgust, but I couldn't help laughing at the same time. 'You've got a nerve, Lisa, you really have.'

'I know, it's one of my most attractive qualities. Are you going to help me or not?'

'What choice do I have? What choice have you left me with?' I leaned towards her. 'Do you know that I've been threatened by that little creep of an ex-boyfriend of yours?'

'Boyfriend?'

'That's right, good old Greg the Goblin. Gregory *Pocket Thunder* Feelen. Remember him?'

I could tell by her sudden and complete stillness that she hadn't expected me to know the ex-boxer by name, and certainly not the fact that they'd had any kind of relationship.

Lisa recovered quickly and smiled unconvincingly again. 'Don't worry about Greg. Under all the bluster, he's a little sweetie, really. He wouldn't hurt a fly.'

'Oh really? Is that what you believe, Lisa? Didn't you see what happened to your apartment, or was that just some hallucination I had? Did you see what he did in your bedroom?'

'That wasn't—'

'Who was it beat the shit out of Andrew Lipton and trashed his flat if it wasn't little sweetie Greg? Who was it tried to abduct our daughter from her playgroup so that he could force me to tell him where you were?'

She went silent.

'This is serious stuff, Lisa,' I told her. 'This is bad news, bad with a capital B-A-D.'

'Then it's worse than I thought,' she admitted. 'You're going to have to negotiate for me, Joel. You'll have to be the middle man.'

'Why me?' I asked. 'Why did I have to be involved at all? Why didn't you just get Lipton to hand over those incriminating files. Then it'd all have been over in a flash.'

Lisa did her rabbit-caught-in-the-headlights act again. 'You know about the files?'

'Yes, I do.'

'Do you know who they belong to?'

'No, but I will once you've told me.'

She seemed relieved by my ignorance on this matter.

'It'll be much better if you don't know, believe me,' she said. 'You don't want to get in too deep. Just deal with Greg. It has to be you, Joel. There's no one else I can depend on. Andrew's loyal, but he's not strong enough.'

I had a different idea. 'Why don't I just hand the files over to the police instead, and let them take care of it all?'

'No, they'll put me in jail.'

'Maybe so. But you'd probably get away with a reduced or even a suspended sentence for cooperating with an investigation.'

'You don't understand. If I'm put in prison, even on remand, it'll be the end of me.'

We looked at each other. Her fear was obvious, and was obviously real.

'Okay,' I said. 'So stop fannying about trying to make deals and just give this Big Man what he wants.'

'I can't do that, either.'

'Why not?'

'Because a part of what he wants — a very large part of it — *is* my death.'

I stared at her again, trying to spot the tell that would let me know she was exaggerating the danger she was in to gain my cooperation. But I saw nothing. She was telling me the literal truth.

'That's why I need you to negotiate for me, Joel. That's the deal I want. I give him all the evidence I have, and in return, he lets me live.'

'Who is he, Lisa? Who is this man? And don't tell me I'm better off not knowing — not if I have to deal with him.'

Lisa glanced away again and muttered something.

'He's what?'

'He's a... a Russian businessman,' she said.

A 'Russian businessman' indeed. It was an expression that had become as transparent a euphemism as 'exotic dancer' or 'merchant banker'.

'Are we talking Russian *mafia* here?' I asked in amazement. 'How in God's name did you get mixed up in that?'

She shook her head. 'It doesn't matter, does it? It happened. Forget him, anyway. Just deal with Greg, okay? Please?'

I looked away for a moment, over her shoulder, at the figure emerging from the ant-swarm of shoppers flowing by.

'Okay,' I said.

'You'll do it?'

'Yes, I will. In fact, I'll do it right now, shall I?'

I could read the puzzlement in her eyes even through her sunglasses, and then she spun on her heel to follow my eyeline.

Standing only a dozen paces away was the man himself — Greg the Goblin, in person. I guess he was a better follower than he was a boxer. He was showing his gold teeth to me again and his little eyes were lit up like lights on a Christmas tree.

'Don't you just love it when a plan comes together?' he said, taking a step forward. 'Hello, Lisa!'

Twelve

Lisa gave a tiny little strangled squeal, like a cartoon mouse in peril, and immediately nipped around behind me for protection.

Her hands were like hot coals on my shoulders, and for an instant her whole body rested against mine. In that moment, we were man and wife again. That which God has joined together let no man set asunder, in sickness and in health, till death do us part, and all the rest of that garbage — the whole works. Instinct had taken over, and entirely against my will, I felt ready to die for her.

No doubt this was the whole idea of her touching me in the first place. Lisa had always known how to play me.

'Nice sexy outfit, Lisa,' the Goblin said, strolling slowly towards us.

He never once took his eyes off Lisa, as though he couldn't even see me now. But clearly he *could* see me, as his next, less-than-flattering words conclusively proved.

'Don't think for one second,' he said, 'that this tosspot can stop me taking you.'

I felt Lisa's hands leave my shoulders as she began to back away.

'Stay where you are,' I told her. 'There's no need to be afraid. I can handle this little fella.'

'The only little fella *you* can handle is your dick,' the Goblin said, displaying more ready wit than I had previously credited him with.

But then he went and spoiled it by sniggering. Maybe he thought it sounded sinister or menacing or something, but really he just sounded like Vic doing her patented evil-witch cackle, which she'd learned from watching *Hocus Pocus*.

'One day soon, my friend,' he added, 'I'm going to put you down.'

'In that case, you'd better bring along someone big and strong to help you. Shouldn't be too difficult to find anyone *bigger*....'

My plan to take his attention away from Lisa seemed to be working. The Goblin's smile had lost most of its sunny happiness — I couldn't imagine why. He advanced on me quickly, raising his fists in an aggressive display which (now that I'd spoken to Charlie Noble) had ceased to hold any major fears for me.

'Well, well, well,' I grinned. 'It's the return of Reelin' Feelen, the scourge of the flyweight division. How're you doing, Greg? Lost any good bouts recently? Or are you still opening doors for a living?'

This information-salvo stopped him dead in his tracks like a good strong jab. Clearly, Feelen was one of those unfortunate men born without the multi-tasking gene, and was therefore unable to move and think at the same time — which might have gone some way to explaining his conspicuous lack of pugilistic success and his shop-soiled face.

'How'd you know my name?' he asked suspiciously, obviously disturbed by the depth of my knowledge.

'Read it on a toilet wall,' I told him. 'Just below the searching question, which short-arsed little prick couldn't punch his way out of a paper bag?'

Behind me, I heard Lisa's cowboy boots slowly beginning to edge further away from us.

'Lisa, come back,' I called over my shoulder. 'Everything's going to be okay. Greg's going to be a good boy now — aren't you, Stumpy?'

'It's not *him* I'm worried about,' Lisa hissed back. 'It's whoever he's with'

'What do you mean?'

'You don't think he came alone, do you?'

Oh balls, I thought. Of course he wouldn't be alone. I had forgotten all about Feelen's accomplice, the so-far unseen driver of the black Rover.

I had a quick look around the centre, picturing in my mind's eye a sort of twin brother for Feelen, another miniature ring-relic with severe facial glove-poisoning and a losing personality — but I saw no likely candidates for this unrewarding position.

What I did see, however, was Feelen trying to exploit my moment of inattention by edging around me towards Lisa. I quickly adjusted my position and waved him back.

'I can't see anybody,' I said to Lisa over my shoulder. 'What about you?'

Lisa's reply came not in words but in the Morse code signal of her boot-heels clocking on the marble floor, a signal that grew faster as she rapidly shifted into top gear — she was hightailing it.

I turned around in time to see her weaving her way through the crowds away from me. I took a single step forward, meaning to go after her, but then I saw her abruptly stop in her tracks. She stood stock still for one second, and then turned and bolted in an entirely different direction.

'What the hell...?'

Then I heard a male voice calling out sharply, and I peered through the crowds to see a heavy-set grey-haired man wearing a black leather jacket over a shirt and tie coming down the last few steps of the escalator from the food court. He was pointing in the direction Lisa had run. A moment later, a brown-haired man about twenty-years younger and ten-stones lighter dodged past him and ran after her, and was soon as lost to sight as she was.

Oh no, I thought. Feelen had not one but *two* associates.

At that very moment, the shopping centre's high roof seemed to fall in on me — well, something heavy whacked me on the top of the head, anyway. Then something struck my chin, rocking my head back violently.

My legs lost all their strength, I crashed down to the marble floor, and for a fraction of a second all the lights in the world went out with a pop.

WHEN MY EYES eventually came back into focus, the first thing they saw was Feelen's ruined face hovering above mine like an evil apparition. His gold crowns flashed and twinkled as he opened his mouth to form an expression that in many ways resembled a human smile.

'You asked for it, smart-arse, and you got it, didn't you!' he hooted. 'How'd you like it, you fucker, how'd you like your first taste of the Pocket Storm's Lightning Bolt?'

I managed to struggle to my knees, but then the world became a carousel and for a moment or two I couldn't get any further. My head was spinning like crazy. None of the muscles below my waist seemed to be working right. I could taste blood in my mouth, and I felt an almost overwhelming urge to puke.

'Lightning Bolt?' I said, hearing myself slurring the words thickly. 'Is that what you call it? Greg, I've got to tell you, mate — I've been hit by worse carpet static.'

The joyful, fugly face went back to being just plain fugly. He raised his fist to thump me again, but then paused mid-strike and looked up sharply. Something had disturbed him.

'What the…?' he said, frowning. Then, much more loudly, 'Oh man, oh *shit!*'

Wobbling slightly, I turned my head and saw that the portly, grey-haired gent who had previously shown so much interest in Mrs. Lisa September, *nee* Forrester, now seemed to be showing an equal amount of interest in Mr. Gregory Feelen, *nee* Pocket Thunder. This was an unexpected development. I had immediately jumped to the conclusion that these other two guys were Feelen's accomplices, but his alarmed reaction to the grey-haired man's reappearance suggested that this was not the case at all.

Obviously, Feelen had been so intent on choosing the optimum moment for landing the first decent punch of his life on the point of my chin that he hadn't noticed what was happening elsewhere. Now that he *had* noticed, Feelen immediately proved beyond a shadow of a doubt that the grey-haired man's interest was not reciprocated in the least, by whirling around and running off as fast as his stumpy little legs would carry him.

Using the banister rails, I managed to haul myself to my feet, and then had to close my eyes against another rush of nausea. It had been a long time since I'd taken a punch and I had forgotten the esoteric joys of such an experience. A few shoppers were inquiring after my well-being, following what they saw as an unprovoked attack, but I rudely pushed by them and dodged away.

Still uncertain on my rubbery legs, I reeled my way through the crowds of shoppers in the direction I had last seen Lisa heading, which led to a staircase down to the lower mall. I took the stairs as fast as I dared, and at the bottom followed the signs to the exit, which took me out of the centre's front doors and into the open air.

I didn't see Lisa. I didn't see Feelen. I didn't see either of the two mystery men.

I wandered farther out into the bright sunlight, startling and all but blinding after the artificial daylight inside the mall. I staggered across a small pick-up area outside the main doors and across to the narrow access road that ran parallel to the shopping centre, looking first one way, then the other. At first, I saw nothing. Then I heard the snarl of a powerful engine and the screech of tyres.

I raised a hand to shade my eyes and saw, in the distance, light reflecting from the windows of a small red sports car as it twisted and turned its way out onto the North Circular Road, a chorus of angry horn-blowing an indication of the unexpected and dangerous nature of its desperate manoeuvres.

Seconds later, another car, this one large and dark (probably Feelen's Rover) tried to follow the sports car's erratic route, but soon found itself blocked by other traffic. If the drivers of the other vehicles had ever possessed any reserves of patience or courtesy in their urban souls, then Lisa — almost certainly the driver of the red sports car — had already used it up.

After a while, the Rover appeared to give up, and then took off in another direction with another pissed-off-sounding screech of tyres.

I was just about to head back into the centre when one of the cars driving along the access road slowed down as it passed me. The man in the passenger seat had a good look at me, and I had a good look at him. It was the grey-haired man from the mall. We looked each other in the eyes for a few seconds. It was like being eye to eye with a dead fish. Then the car accelerated away and disappeared.

I was nearly back inside the centre before I realised two things. The first was that I had the impression that somewhere, at some time in the past, I had met the grey-haired man before. And the bad taste that this impression left in my mouth led me to believe that the circumstances of that encounter had not been pleasant.

The second thing I had noticed was that the car in which the grey-haired man had been a passenger was a metallic-blue Saab — exactly like the one Mrs. Webber had reported seeing parking in our street several days ago.

Who the hell were they? I didn't know, but Lisa had run away from them as though her backside was on fire. Ditto Feelen.

The QUEEN of HEARTS

It didn't look good, did it?

AFTER TAKING A moment or two to compose myself, I went back into the centre and headed back up to the Upper Mall, intending to collect all the shopping bags that Lisa had dropped on the floor. Surely there would be some kind of clue in there that would lead me to her? A purse, maybe. And in the purse, a card with an address?

That was what I was hoping for, in any case.

When I reached the top of the escalator, I saw that most of the people who had been gathered around me had moved on — the scene had already lost its novelty for the jaded folk of north London. But the one or two who still remained had seen me coming, and as I approached they were busy pointing me out to the latest character to join the comic-melodrama of my life.

This character took the shape of a tall, skinny, nineteen-year-old rentacop, who was lethargically examining Lisa's shopping bags. As I came closer, the security guard straightened up and gave me what I considered to be a very funny look indeed.

As you can imagine, at this stage I didn't want to attract any more attention than I already had, so I started off by giving him a nice wide smile — a gesture to which he reacted as if I'd expressed an interest in using his severed head as an ornament on my mantelpiece. From this reaction, I deduced that he'd listened to the witness's accounts of my tussle with

Feelen, and consequently thought I was some kind of nutter.

I hastened to set his mind at rest.

'Hi,' I said. 'I just wanted to apologise for all the fuss.' I included the remaining witnesses in the warmth of my new (and hopefully slightly less manic) smile. 'I'm afraid my wife and I had a bit of a domestic and it got out of hand. It's all sorted now, thank goodness.'

I could see that the witnesses were succumbing to my charms and the humble candour of my admissions, but the security guard was still watching me warily. I gestured to the shopping bags at his feet.

'My wife was too embarrassed to come back for her bags, so she sent me up for them.' I shrugged at him, one man to another, and tried a rueful grin. 'You know how it is; you do as you're told, keep your mouth shut, and hopefully you don't get into too much trouble...'

Nope, he was still a statue.

'So, can I take her bags?'

'You want these bags?' the guard asked, sounding almost disbelieving. When I nodded, he quickly stepped back and said, 'You want 'em, mate, you take 'em, they're all yours. Have a ball.'

I had been expecting a little bit more resistance than this — after all, I had no proof of ownership — but I hurried forward before he changed his mind. As I left, with many a backward call of thank you, I noticed he was giving me another of those odd 'what a nutter' sort of looks.

It was a look I only fully understood a few minutes later, when I got back to the privacy of my car and was at liberty to examine the contents of Lisa's shopping bags. Each and every one was filled with nothing but old yellowing newspapers that smelled of mould.

The shopping was fake, just another part of Lisa's disguise.

I LEFT THE earthly delights of Brent Cross wondering to what extent I had to be worried about this new development.

When Mrs. Webber had first reported the appearance of the two men in the metallic-blue Saab, I had been dismissive. But now it turned out she had been right to be suspicious. It just goes to show, you should never discount the semi-senile ramblings of a fussy old busybody, especially when they were as adept at pinpointing discrepancies in neighbourhood routine as pigs were at sniffing out the location of truffles in French woodland.

Even more worrying was the notion that I might have previous knowledge of the grey-haired man.

I remembered Henry telling me that if he was walking down the street and a face leapt out at him as being familiar, he always assumed that he had last seen it in a police mug-shot. And I must admit that in this instance, I was thinking pretty much the same way. I'd mixed with a lot of criminal types in my time — even more than my wife had slept with, hopefully, although this was no longer the safe bet I would have previously assumed it to be.

But if Greg Feelen represented Lisa's 'Russian businessman', the so-called Big Man, exactly who did the grey-haired man and his younger accomplice represent? A rival faction, presumably. And if even

Feelen was deathly afraid of them, how dangerous did they have to be?

Weighed down by these and other questions, I made my way over to Henry and Maude's and spent the rest of the afternoon and early evening there, for the most part deep in speculative thought. Henry thought I was being a miserable bugger, and made no secret of the fact. Maude had a go at digging for information on what she still assumed had been a romantic tryst with Barbara ('not that it's any of my business, anyway'), but soon my obvious lack of elation made its mark on her, and she stopped.

Vic, meanwhile, had interpreted my general quietness for sadness, which meant that she tried, instinctively, to offer me comfort, first by playing games with me rather than her grandfather, and then by sitting on my lap, giving me lots of hugs and kisses. As comforting goes, this was pretty good, and I had absolutely no complaints.

After dinner, we went home and ran through the whole bathtime/reading-book/Disney-movie routine, after which I carried a semi-conscious Vic to bed and tucked her in. Downstairs again, I called Mrs. Webber and humbly asked her to put the metallic-blue Saab back on her watch-list.

'By the way,' I added, "you don't happen to speak Russian, do you?'

'What a very odd question.' She was silent for a few seconds, and then asked, 'What on earth's going on?'

I had to admit that I didn't know.

'Is it about your daughter?' she asked. 'Is it a custody battle thing?'

When I didn't answer, Mrs. W said, 'You can't go on like this. You've got to fix it. All this aggro is giving me the willies.'

What a liar. She was having the time of her life, and we both knew it.

'I know,' I sighed. 'I know, I know. I'm trying.'

'Try harder.'

But it wasn't that easy.

I SPENT THE remainder of the night in silence, sitting by the phone, waiting for it to ring. The status of *Operation Find Lisa* was no different today than it had been yesterday. No real progress had been made. I was still entirely dependent on her contacting me, and until she did, I had no option but to wait. There was nothing else I could do.

The phone rang about midnight when I was lying on my bed, half-asleep. I grabbed the phone, instantly awake, but it wasn't Lisa. It was Barbara.

'How did the meeting with your wife go?' she asked.

'Not as well as it could have done,' I admitted.

'Is she going to give it to you?'

I paused for a moment, wondering if I'd actually told Barbara anything about the Lisa situation and the incriminating information she was holding. I didn't think I had — I'm not usually so forthcoming on short acquaintance, even with women who've seen me with my pants down and my blood (quite literally) up.

'Er, what do you mean? Is she going to give me what?'

'A divorce.'

Ah, a divorce — so that's what she'd meant. Then I thought, *divorce?*

I suddenly realised that I had never even considered such a final step. But put as plainly as this, I could see that Barbara had made an entirely natural assumption. What's more, she was right. This was something I really had to think about now. More than just *think* about, actually — it was something I needed to do, to set in motion. It was time to stop pretending this marriage was a bad dream I was going to wake up from.

'Joel?'

'We didn't get that far in our conversation,' I said. 'Maybe next time.'

'You're meeting her again?'

'I hope so, but I don't know when. I have to wait for her to call me, I don't have her current number.'

'It sounds to me like she's still pulling all the strings in this relationship.'

'You're right, that's just what she's doing. I don't like it, but at the moment that's the way it has to be. Hopefully it'll all be resolved before too long.'

'I hope so,' Barbara said with feeling. 'You realise that we haven't seen each other again?'

'I know,' I replied, with equal feeling. 'Believe me, I know.'

'What's happening tomorrow?'

I sighed. 'I don't think we can do it tomorrow, either.'

I'd promised Vic that in the morning I'd take her over to the *KrazyKidz Toy Warehouse* at Stevenage, to buy her the electronic learning toy before dropping her off at *Tiny Minds*. Afterwards, I was meant to be working while Henry and Maude picked Vic up again and looked after her for the rest of the afternoon. But instead of working, I was probably going to wait at home, hoping that Lisa would get in touch again.

She had my mobile number, of course, but knowing how unpredictable she was, I didn't put it past her to turn up at the house anyway, despite the probability of lurking danger. That was the thing with Lisa — you just never knew what she'd do.

Barbara listened to all this with great patience, I thought, and she accepted my decision not to meet with her with obvious regret, but also with exceptionally good grace.

Then, out of the blue, she asked what I was wearing.

'Er, I'm in bed, so I'm just wearing boxer shorts. Why?'

'I *like* boxer shorts. What colour are they?'

'They're black.'

Yeah, maybe they'd been black *once*. Now, four or five years and hundreds of wash-cycles down the line, they were a murky, unappealing grey, and the seams were beginning to fray.

'Hmmm, I *like* black underwear. Anything else?'

Bemused, I looked down at myself. In addition to the boxers, I was still wearing my socks, in this case a novelty Christmas pair older than Vic, which took the shape of wash-faded, red-nosed reindeers, complete with wilted antlers… and (adding just that extra touch of class) on the right foot, my big toe poking out of Rudolph's arse.

'No, I'm not wearing anything else,' I said.

'Have you ever tried phone sex before?'

'You must be joking,' I replied. 'I don't even know how to withhold my number…'

'*Have* you?'

'No.'
'Do you want to try?'
'Um... okay. How do we start?'
'We already have.'
'What do we do now?'
'Now you ask me what *I'm* wearing?'

I was guessing that even in bed this lady would be wearing killer heels. But I asked her anyway, and Barbara's answer turned out to be very interesting indeed, the first of very many interesting discoveries to be made that night.

Barbara thought it was amazing that I'd never had phone sex before. I thought it was amazing that it could be done at all. Imagine it — all that pleasure, and not a cold shower in sight.

Thirteen

ALTHOUGH I HAD been half-expecting a repeat performance of yesterday's early morning call (Lisa calling to say 'wakey-wakey, rise 'n' shine,' in her isn't-life-grand voice, just as though everything was normal), dawn came and went without the slightest tinkle from the bedside phone.

Actually, I might not have heard it ring anyway, deep as I was in the refreshing sleep of the righteous and the self-satisfied.

Before last night, I would never have believed that just talking about having sex (combined with a little hands-on back-up) could be so erotic, but to my surprise the whole experience had been absolutely incredible. At one point, I got so carried away that I'd almost fallen out of bed.

When I explained what had nearly happened to interrupt us, Barbara had laughed out loud — 'oh, you silly boy,' she'd chuckled — and on we had gone. And on, and on, and on… A night to remember.

Afterwards, I was left with three distinct thoughts.

The first was that to date — my marriage and my former career not withstanding — I must have led a very sheltered life. The second was that contrary to my pessimistic thoughts on the subject, there was definitely a (sex) life after marriage, and it was well worth having.

The third thought was more speculative; if Barbara could make me feel so good over the phone, how much better would it get if we were actually to become intimate together in the same room?

Gulp!

Before I could think too hard or in too much detail about what might happen under those circumstances, I forced myself to get out of bed. Today was likely to be a busy day, and I had to meet it head on.

Be still my beating heart! Be still my throbbing loins! Down, Shep!

Any hopes that I might have been able to fob Vic off for another day with regard to her trip to *KrazyKidz* were dashed by her appearance at the breakfast table about half-an-hour later, with a crayon drawing of her desired toy fastened to her pyjama-top with copious amounts of sticky tape.

'Today!' she loudly announced.

'Today,' I conceded, with slightly less vim.

Albert paused in his morning ritual of food crunching to look back over his shoulder and give me an amused glance.

'Hey, don't blame me,' he seemed to be saying. 'She's your kid, not mine.'

I swear if that damned cat had eyebrows, he'd have been waggling them at me like Groucho Marx. In retaliation for this sass, I made a snipping motion at him with my fingers, and the next moment, in a whirl of fur and claws, Albert scrambled out through the kitchen door, leaving the cat-flap rattling.

'Allie go quick,' Vic said, her mouth full of cornflakes and banana.

'Yeah,' I growled, 'and if he knows what's good for him, he'll *keep* going quick.'

The QUEEN of HEARTS

Vic ran her spoon over the surface of the kitchen table like a racing car.

'*Meeeeooooowww!*'

'Exactly like that,' I nodded.

After breakfast I sent Vic upstairs to get changed (with a request to keep it simple, please, my darling daughter) and I turned with a heavy heart (and an incomprehensible instruction booklet written in Sanskrit or some other such dead language) to the landline phone in the living room.

Look, I'm not going to say I'm a complete technophobe... but I sort of am. I must be the only person left on the planet who doesn't own any kind of computer whatsoever (unless you count a broken laptop), and my mobile phone is a beaten-up Nokia so old and battered it doesn't even have a functioning camera. I don't do emails, I don't do Facebook, Twitter, Snapchat, Instagram, or any other kind of social media, and to be honest, from all I hear about it, I don't think I'm missing that much.

On the whole, I think I would have been far happier living in the Age of Steam, wearing a frock coat and a nice-looking stovepipe hat.

A half-hour after beginning (and after a great number of muttered curses), I finally managed to replace the existing outgoing message. This message was so old it was actually Lisa's voice on there, telling our friends that although we were out at the moment, we would instantly return their call the very moment we got back. My estranged wife's voice, which sent a severely icy shiver running down my spine, sounded completely insincere.

The new message I created was simple and straight to the point. It was aimed directly at Lisa, but being mindful of any possible illegal eavesdroppers on the line, I never mentioned her name. I only said that I would be out for about an hour-and-a-half, but after that I would be back. If my caller couldn't wait, I could be reached on my mobile, after which I recited my Nokia's number twice.

I suppose a more clued-up member of the communications revolution would have simply redirected all calls from their landline to their mobile phone, but I had about as much chance of figuring out how to do something like that as I did of learning to fly by jumping off a cliff and flapping my arms. In other words, zilch — and not even an instruction booklet in recognisable English would have changed that.

Not long after I'd recorded my terse message, Vic finally reappeared, washed, dressed and ready for the off. I'd hoped that she would choose something practical for our shopping trip. A pair of jeans or leggings, a t-shirt and trainers would have done it, I should have thought.

But Vic had her own ideas, quite obviously.

She had chosen a pair of pink plastic high-heels and a fairy costume, complete with a jewelled tiara (with integral flashing deely-boppers), a glittering wand, and a pink taffeta tutu.

Oh yeah, and fairy wings.

STEVENAGE IS ONLY about six miles or so north of Welwyn Garden City along the A1, and because we were driving against the morning traffic rather than with it, the trip was short and sweet. Very soon we were pulling into a parking space not far from *KrazyKidz*, which was located in the very centre of a large retail park.

We left the Scenic and headed to the store on the double, with Vic pulling me along by the hand, like a tiny tugboat guiding an ocean liner into a crowded harbour.

Normally when we visited this place of childish worship, Vic tended to saunter slowly along each and every aisle from first to last. She was the same in the supermarket too, exclaiming over practically everything on the shelves ('Look Daddee, a tin of *beings!*') as though we were in a Moroccan bazaar, not the local Aldi. But today, her excitement was too great to be contained, and a mere five minutes after we went in, we were on our way back out again.

There were already two customers ahead of us at the single operational till, one of them a man in the process of buying a large remote-controlled car. The other, waiting directly before me, was a young mother dressed in a grubby brown velour tracksuit which looked like it had been flayed from the rotting carcass of a three-piece suite.

The young mother took no notice of me, being far too busy grunting into her mobile and picking at the collection of yellow-heads that sprouted either side of her mouth. Her unfortunate child, a fourteen-month-old snot-monster wearing a nappy I could see was bursting at the seams, was squirming to release himself from the irksome captivity of the shopping trolley.

The stench the boy was giving off was enormous, and Vic, who normally likes younger kids, even if they do smell a bit like a cesspit, quickly bypassed this one and wriggled through to the back of the tills to wait for me. As she went through, she accidentally jogged the arm of the man with the remote-control car just as he was collecting his change, but he just smiled and ruffled her hair, entirely unconcerned. Vic smiled at him as he left.

'What a nice man,' her smile said, and as Vic was usually a pretty good judge of character, I guessed he must have been.

The young mother, still gabbing into her phone, moved forward and began slinging her purchases at the checkout girl in a way that got up my nose like a cloud of pepper spray. The girl handled it easily though, professionally processing the goods without once giving back any of the attitude. I thought she deserved a medal.

'Daddee!' Vic suddenly called. 'Hurry! Wanna *play!*'

'Won't be long now, sweetheart. Just wait for me there, okay?'

'OK.'

When I had first spoken, the young mother had turned her head to examine me like I was something stuck to her shoe. Then she turned back to pay for her goods in cash, including about a fiver's worth of loose change that she excavated from the bottom of her handbag and carelessly slapped down on the counter. She snatched her receipt from the checkout girl's hand as soon as it was offered and marched off without a word of thanks.

I stepped forward into her place, and the checkout girl and I shared a look of complete understanding. She smiled sweetly when I asked how she put up with that kind of behaviour from customers.

'I just fantasise that in the future, after I've been elected the first President of the World, I'll be able to have people like that sterilised.'

This sounded like a good plan to me, and I wished her well with it.

Finally, with the receipt in my wallet and my goods under my arm, I turned away from the till and reached out for Vic's hand — and then I realised that Vic's hand wasn't there. Just like the rest of her, it was missing.

'Excuse me?' I said to the checkout girl, who was already serving another customer. 'Did you see where my daughter went?'

She glanced around, just as I had, and then shook her head. 'No, sorry. She must have gone outside.'

I concurred. As I knew all too well, Vic had a naturally curious nature, and a bad habit of wandering off exploring, occasionally into potentially dangerous situations — a pattern of behaviour I was afraid she had inherited from me on a genetic level.

Outside the store, my daughter was nowhere to be seen, but the runner-up in this season's *Hertfordshire Young Mother of the Year Contest* (a close second to my own wife) was all too visible. She was still gabbing on her mobile, still ignoring her squalling, smelly child, and was now sucking on a cigarette for good measure. The poor kid was downwind, getting a good dose of secondary smoke.

She gave me the who-do-you-think-you-are? look again, when I asked her if she'd seen Vic come out of *KrazyKidz*, but this time I wasn't having it. Unlike the girl on the checkout, I wasn't being paid to put up with her attitude. I plucked the cigarette from her lips and tossed it away, and then jerked the phone from her bitten-down-to-the-quick fingernails with their chipped nail-polish and turned it off.

'Hey!' she protested.

'Did you see my daughter come out of that store?' I asked again.

'No, I don't know nuffink about your daughter. Give us it back!'

I tossed the phone back at her and turned away.

'I'm not your babysitter, you know,' the girl sneered at me. 'What d'you fink I am?'

'I don't know,' I sneered back, 'but your kid needs changing, and you need a personality transplant.'

I left her gaping after me and hurried off in the direction of the car park, just in case Vic had gone back to the Scenic. The car park had filled up while we were shopping, making it a much more dangerous place for unaccompanied little people, and the idea of her toddling around there on her lonesome — all two-foot-nine of her — was not a comfortable one. Along the way, I asked the people I passed if they had seen my daughter, but nobody seemed to have seen a fairy answering Vic's description.

When I reached the Scenic a few moments later, there was no sign of Vic. No sign of her around the car, no sign of her anywhere in the car park.

My annoyance at her for running off had long since departed. Now I was just worried. I chucked the computer toy in the back of the Scenic, and looked around again. A few rows away, I saw the man who'd been ahead of me in the queue at *KrazyKidz* glance over at me briefly, and then quickly duck out of sight as he bundled himself into his car.

I had already opened my mouth to call out my question — 'Have you seen my daughter?' — but now I closed it again with a snap. My heart lurched in my chest. My memory rewound and replayed itself. I saw the man ruffling Vic's hair, extracting a smile from her as he left. I saw my daughter's expression, the one that said, 'what a nice man.'

But was he? Was he really?

Or could he actually be Greg the Goblin's so-far unseen accomplice, the mystery man who usually drove the black Rover and hid his face behind its tinted windows? And was this man now on the verge of completing the task which his partner had so narrowly failed to accomplish the other day — kidnapping my daughter!

Before I knew I was doing it, I was racing and weaving through the cars, and then I threw myself in front of his Toyota before he could pull away.

I could practically hear myself shouting, 'Give me back my daughter, you pervert!', but the words never actually left my lips. Because in the car along with the man was the man's wife, a boy of around six or seven, who was clutching his new remote-control car on his lap, and a brand new baby in a car seat.

Wrong again.

The man wound down his window and asked what the hell I thought I was doing. (He didn't say *hell*, actually, but another word which drew a sharply critical response from his wife.) I quickly explained, too scared now to be embarrassed at the fool I'd just made of myself, and asked him if he'd seen Vic come out of the store after him. He was shaking his head, but his wife was tentatively nodding hers.

'Is your little girl wearing fairy wings?' she asked, and my heart went into overdrive.

'Yes, she is.'

'Then I *did* see her.'

It seemed that the wife had been checking out curtains in a different store while her husband collected their son's present (to make up for the disappointment of getting a baby sister instead of a baby brother), and on the way back to their car, she'd seen a little girl in a fairy outfit walking in the other direction.

'Where did she go?'

She shrugged. 'I'm so sorry, I'm not sure. Just further into the park.'

'Was she alone?' I asked, thinking about the Goblin's squat figure.

She hesitated, unsure, and I darted away from them without waiting for the rest.

Anybody who might have been watching me that morning would have thought I was a bit loopy — if not outright insane. Dashing from store to store in my peculiar, limping gait, dashing around inside the stores themselves, sweating like a pig and attracting the attention of salesmen, nervous customers, and security guards left, right and centre.

Finally, I found myself standing beside the collection points in the Argos store, panting and scanning the passing crowds who seemed to have materialised from nowhere. Irrationally, their sheer numbers made me even angrier than I already was — this was a weekday, why weren't all these people at work? Then I turned and saw something that chilled me to the bone.

I saw Vic walking through the crowds, away from me and towards the exit, her little pink wings jiggling with every bouncing step. And she was holding the hand of a six-foot-plus man wearing a baseball hat, jeans and a denim jacket.

Actually, I'll clarify that. Vic wasn't holding *his* hand, he was holding *hers*. And she wasn't taking bouncing steps. He was dragging her along and she was resisting him.

The old red surf instantly rose in my mind and crashed over me like a Martian tsunami. Large, ugly sounds tore themselves free of my throat and exploded in the air. People stopped and turned to look as I pushed my way though the other shoppers to catch up, the pain in my knee temporarily forgotten.

I wanted to grab the man by the throat and throttle him, but evidently he heard me coming, or figured out something was wrong from the reactions of the people around him. Either way, he turned around to face me when I was still several paces away.

'Give me my daughter back,' I snarled at him.

He gave me a confused, panicky look.

'Let her go, now!' I shouted.

'I'm scared, Daddy,' a tiny alarmed voice said.

'Don't be scared, sweetheart,' I said, my eyes still locked to those of her would-be-abductor. 'I'm here now, you're safe.'

The man frowned at me. 'Who the bloody hell are you calling *sweetheart?*'

'Daddy, who's that man?' the little voice chirruped.

I tore my eyes away from his face and I looked down at Vic. But it wasn't Vic at all. It wasn't my daughter. It was just another little girl in a fairy costume, only lacking the deely-boppers. She was about a year older than Vic, and her hair was shorter and darker. Her eyes were huge, shiny with gathering tears. I had frightened her badly.

I began to back away.

'You're a nutcase, mate,' the man said. 'If you don't leave us alone right now, I'm calling the police.'

A couple of people in the audience we had attracted expressed the opinion that he should call the police anyway. I looked at the man in desperation.

'Look, I've lost my daughter,' I said. 'She's wearing the same outfit. I've got to find her.'

'He's a right nutter, that one,' a voice croaked behind me, 'he had me phone off me earlier!' It was the runner-up *Mother of the Year*, sticking her oar in.

I ran back outside, turning around and around. Vic was still nowhere to be seen. I started to shout her name.

'Vic! Vic! Vic! Vic!'

Now even more people were staring at me, but I couldn't have cared less.

'Vic! Vic! Vic!'

I was making so much noise that I almost missed the sound of my mobile ringing.

I began moving back in the direction of *KrazyKidz*, now thinking that instead of going out, maybe Vic had actually snuck through one of the closed tills and gone back to wander around some more. And even if she hadn't, the store would have security cameras. The recordings might show in which direction Vic had been headed when she left, and with whom.

I pulled out my phone, hoping to hell it wasn't Maude calling, because I couldn't bear the thought of telling her what was happening. I doubted I'd be able to lie convincingly. She'd be able to hear the worry in my voice. And if it was Lisa? For the first time in our relationship, I would probably tell her to sod off.

One crisis at a time, thank you very much.

'Hello?' I said.

'Hello again, smart-arse,' Gregory Feelen, AKA the Goblin, replied. 'You know what, your daughter's got a really nice smile. I'm looking at it right now — so sweet! But I wonder what she'll look like when she starts to *scream*...'

IT WAS EVERY parent's nightmare come horribly true. My muscles froze solid, my mind locked up, and I couldn't speak. Only my ears seemed to be working properly, and with them I heard Feelen breathing wetly at the other end of the phone. He sounded like a dog panting in the heat of a summer's day. Not a good sound to hear over the phone at the best of times, and this was not the best of times, not by a long chalk.

'Okay, September, we're getting down to the nitty-gritty now,' he said.

As though I hadn't already got that message loud and clear.

I finally found my voice, and it was a choked, rasping noise that sounded like it had to find its way around a large obstruction in my throat. This obstruction was either my heart or my breakfast, and at this moment in time I was betting on my heart.

'What on earth do you think you're playing at?' I asked Feelen.

'You wouldn't listen to reason, so the Big Man decided you needed a little incentive. Now it's going to be a straight swap. You give us little Lisa, and we give you your daughter back.'

'Feelen, this is crazy, even *you* must see that?' I said, my voice beginning to shift up through the gears into shouting mode.

I noticed that other shoppers were still watching me curiously and I turned away, making an attempt to keep my voice low and to filter out some of the panic that must have sounded like a fire alarm.

'Listen,' I said desperately, 'Feelen, I don't care how many times you got punched in the head, you can't be that stupid you don't see it. This isn't just threats and intimidation anymore, where a court would only give you a suspended sentence or a bloody fine. This is the abduction of a small child. This is a major, indictable offence. This is real jail time, and a lifelong reputation as a nonce. Don't you realise how serious this is?'

'I know how serious it is,' he replied quietly. '*You* were the one didn't understand. Now you do. Find Lisa.'

'I told you before, I don't know where she is!'

'You found her once, you can do it again.'

'But I—'

'Put it this way, September, you better find her. 'Cos if you don't…'

Once again my voice became compressed into something that was almost a snarl.

'Feelen, I'll kill you. I'm not kidding, this is not an empty threat. If you hurt my daughter, if you harm her in any way whatsoever, I will *kill* you. I will hunt you down like the animal you are, and I will kill you with my bare hands. Do you understand?'

The Goblin gave a sick little giggle that made me want to kick holes in the nearest wall.

'Sorry, got to go now, September. I'll call later to see what progress you've made.'

'Do you understand what I said?'

'Yeah, yeah, yeah,' he said, 'my knees are knocking. By the way, I'm sure I don't need to tell you — if you try to contact the police, you'll never see your daughter again. And we'll know if you do,' he added. 'We got eyes and ears everywhere… and believe me, I do mean *everywhere*…'

And then he hung up.

Fourteen

When I was in my late teens, an old school friend and I went back-packing around Europe for a couple of months, just drifting until our meagre reserves of money ran out. At one point, we spent a whole week in Paris, staying on the fourth floor of a fleabag hotel a stone's throw from the Gare du Nord.

In the mornings (when the pair of us were almost always nursing mammoth hangovers), we used to sit in the windows, just marvelling at the Parisian traffic jams below us, where it seemed that every single inch of road was occupied by completely static vehicles. Engines would be revving as though they were poised on a Formula 1 starting grid, horns would be blasting constantly, as if noise alone could clear the way, and drivers would be screaming at each other and making ugly Gallic hand gestures.

I mention all this only to illustrate exactly how my mind felt an hour later, when I sat alone at my kitchen table. Like those Parisian roads of yesteryear, my mind was completely jammed, blocked, choked, and confused. I couldn't go forward or backward. I couldn't move in any direction. I couldn't even *see* any way to proceed.

I had already phoned Henry and Maude to tell them not to bother picking Vic up from her playgroup because she wouldn't be going, and that I'd be looking after her myself today. When Maude asked me why, I said I didn't think that we'd been spending enough quality father/daughter time together, and thankfully she bought it.

I must say, I felt like a bit of an arsehole lying to her after all the help and support she and Henry had given me, but I simply couldn't tell them what was really happening — that would be as good as telling the police. Selling them the lie would at least buy me a little time to figure out what I could do. Unfortunately, this was the total extent of my good ideas.

For the moment my anger had left me, the red tide had receded to a distant line on the horizon, and now I was just terribly, terribly afraid for my daughter's safety. Not only right at this moment, when she must have been so frightened, but also in the immediate future. Because, try as I might, I could think of no earthly way I could contact Lisa to let her know what had happened, much less deliver her to the Goblin and his master, the Big Man.

It was also something of a moral dilemma. If by some miracle I did find Lisa, was I really cold-hearted enough to do what her enemies wanted? Could I actually hand my wife over in exchange for our daughter, all trussed up like a Christmas turkey? When I knew full well what happened to turkeys at Christmas time?

Actually, faced with the alternatives, I was slowly coming around to the realisation that maybe I *could*. Maybe I really could. Vic was worth ten Lisas, easily. Twenty Lisas, thirty Lisas…

But all this was pure speculation.

In reality, I was in the same boat as I had been until Lisa called me yesterday morning. I didn't know where she was and had no ideas of how to reach her. For that matter, I didn't know for certain that the two mystery men who'd chased her out of Brent Cross hadn't caught up to her somewhere else in the meantime. Clearly they didn't work for the Big Man, because Greg 'the Goblin' Feelen had also legged it sharpish when they'd appeared on the scene. So who were they, I wondered? Some rival criminal faction Lisa had also managed to piss off?

More Russian mafia?

International spies?

Criminal injury lawyers?

And even that didn't really matter. There was something of even greater concern.

Even if Lisa *was* still at liberty, and even if I *could* find her, and even if I *could* subdue my conscience long enough to hand her over to her enemies, I still wasn't convinced that I would get Vic back safe and sound. I wasn't sure they would let either one of us live a day longer than they had to. Because now I knew Feelen's real name — as I had so foolishly insisted on revealing at the shopping centre, and then hammering home on the mobile earlier.

The Big Man, whoever he was, would know that my knowledge of the Goblin's true identity put *him* in danger, too, and he was probably ruthless enough not to want to leave loose ends like me and my daughter hanging around, threatening to trip him up at every turn.

I looked up from my gloomy thoughts. The phone was ringing.

The QUEEN of HEARTS

It looked and sounded about a thousand light years away from me, although I was able pick it up without leaving my seat. I reached out for the receiver, my arm appearing to stretch out for miles. I was very slow in answering it. Not because I wasn't worried, or because I was trying to play some kind of game with the Goblin. It was simple fear. I was afraid because I had nothing to report.

And if this was all I had to say, then Feelen might decide that I needed a little more encouragement. And then he might do something to Vic, something to hurt her. And he would make me listen. And if that happened, I knew that it would drive me stark, staring insane.

I picked up the phone, brought it to my ear.

'Hello? Hello?'

It was a female voice. Not Lisa. Not Barbara. Not Maude. Not Elaine Leigh...

It took a few moments for me to recognise that it was Mrs. Webber's voice, because in addition to the fact that I had been expecting someone else, she was also talking funny, sort of whispering out of the corner of her mouth. Mind you, I can talk — I had greeted her in a voice that, even to me, sounded like one of those speaking computers that tell you the time or ask you to close the car door.

But Mrs. W was clearly too excited to notice the lack of expression in my voice.

'They're back!' she said.

'Who're back?'

'Those men. The ones in the metallic-blue car!'

I put the receiver down on the table, stood up and walked over to the kitchen window. She was right, they were back. The Saab was parked at the curb just like it belonged there, as though its owners were local residents. The overweight, grey-haired man was framed in the passenger side window, looking at the house, and at me watching him from my own window. He wasn't even pretending not to look now.

'Joel? Joel, are you there?'

I could hear Mrs. Webber's tiny flea voice squeaking out of the phone even as I left the kitchen. She may as well have been speaking from a different world. In fact, she *was* speaking from a different world, because I was no longer on Earth. In a matter of seconds, I had been transported back to the Red Planet.

I stepped out of my front door and began to amble down my garden path, and I felt as though I was not walking at all. I felt as though I were floating, being borne along on a cloud of red mist like a passenger on a flying carpet, or maybe one of those travelators at the airport. Meanwhile, around me the sky, the houses, the trees, the very air itself, were steadily turning crimson. I felt very calm, very peaceful, and completely in control of myself.

For a Martian, that is.

All the while, I had the feeling that as soon as I reached the metallic-blue Saab, it would quickly reverse, spin into a handbrake turn and then speed away. But that didn't happen.

I stopped by the passenger window, where the grey-haired man was coolly staring back at me. I reached out and lightly tapped on the window with my knuckles. He looked away for a moment, presumably to consult the driver, and then turned back. He depressed a button and the window slid smoothly down.

'Good morning,' he said neutrally. 'Can I help you?'

'Yes, you certainly can,' I replied. 'Come here!'

Then I grabbed the son of a bitch by the lapels of his black leather jacket and dragged him out through the window.

He was a big, burly bastard, but he came out of that window like toothpaste from a tube. When all but his ankles were out, I deliberately dropped him. He hit the pavement hard, expelling a painful grunt. Even though he was badly winded by the fall, he tried to get up immediately, and I, nicely brought-up fellow that I was, decided to help him out. To this end, I grabbed a handful of his grey hair and pulled it as hard as I could, and he came up so fast he might have been filled with helium.

Once he was upright, I slammed my good knee into his crotch and watched his face crumple into a very satisfying mess. Then I threw my right arm all the way back, hand clenched into a tight fist, poised to deliver a right hook of biblical proportions. I couldn't quite remember what it said in the Bible about smiting, but I was up for it, anyway.

I also had an idea that if I caught him just right with this punch, I could make his bloody head spin all the way around, like the girl's in *The Exorcist*, and the Martian in me was very interested to see how that might look.

As I say, I *tried* to punch him, but suddenly found myself unable to — because something had attached itself to my arm.

I looked back over my shoulder and saw that the other, younger man — the man who Mrs. Webber had described as having a face like a smacked arse — had jumped out of the car and joined the dance. With the hand he wasn't using to restrain my right hook, he reached out and grabbed a chunk of my shoulder and neck and dug his fingers deep into the knot of nerves buried there. At the same time, he twisted my right arm up behind my back, then spun me around and slammed me face first against the side of the Saab.

A detached part of my mind (the non-Martian part) registered the professional ease with which I'd been subdued. It also registered that Mrs. W had been entirely correct — this guy really *did* have a face like a smacked arse. He was the sort of man you took an immediate, instinctive dislike to, even if he wasn't in the process of assaulting you.

At the periphery of my vision, I saw old grey-hair stumping heavily towards me, breathing hard and gingerly rubbing his swollen, throbbing balls. He did not look to be in a particularly good mood. When he reached us, he plucked me from his partner's clutches like I was a naughty rag doll and he was its angry mummy. Then he spun me around, planted a meaty fist in the pit of my stomach, and then followed it with an uppercut which, if it had connected, would have taken my head off at the roots.

The reason it didn't connect properly was that at the crucial moment a certain something had struck the side of *his* head, and it had struck with truly devastating force. That certain something turned out to be the heavy wooden head of a garden broom, and it sent old grey-hair spinning to the ground again.

'You dirty, dirty bastards!' Mrs. Webber growled from behind her broom. 'Two against one, is it?'

The younger man with the objectionable face stepped forward aggressively. 'Hey, old lady, if you know what's good for you, you'll—'

Without warning, Mrs. Webber hopped forward and thrust the head of her garden broom directly into his face, the sharp bristles poking into his eyes, and the younger man dropped to the ground, screaming like a little girl. Mrs. W gave him no quarter, immediately rushing forward and beginning to beat him around the head and shoulders, swinging the broom like a giant croquet mallet.

'If I know what's good for me?' she shouted. 'I *know* what's good for me, young man, don't you worry about that…'

The grey-haired man, now bleeding freely from a small gash Mrs. Webber had opened on his earlobe, staggered to his feet again. We stared at each other as he took a couple of deep breaths and readied himself to charge, and I almost smiled. It seemed that I had found a fellow Martian to play with.

'I think that will be quite enough of that, thank you very much!' a loud voice suddenly called out.

I turned around to see that a third man, who had so far remained unnoticed in the rear of the Saab, had now emerged. He was standing beside the car, leaning on the roof with both forearms, looking both ruefully amused and frankly disgusted. He was tall, with short sandy-coloured hair and a pleasant, honest face.

'Why don't you stand down now, Jimmy,' he said mildly to the grey-haired man. 'I've seen enough slapstick action for one day.'

I turned back to see that old grey-hair had been creeping forward while my back was turned (a dirty Martian trick I simply had to admire), and was almost upon me, with his hands raised and curled into claws aimed in the direction of my throat. But at this low-key command, he immediately backed away, straightening his clothes.

'Joel?' the third man said to me. 'See if you can't call off your guard dog before she kills young Dale.'

The younger man was screeching in panic and pain now, frantically trying to evade the swinging broom by crawling around the car on his hands and knees, but Mrs. W, in an absolute frenzy of bloodlust, was following him like a predator stalking wounded prey, walloping him left, right and centre with her heavy broom. Occasionally, whenever the opportunity presented itself, she reversed the broom to shove the handle right up his jacksie.

I have to be honest, it made you feel proud to be British.

'Mrs. Webber?' I had to shout to get through to her. 'Mrs. Webber! Stop!'

She paused, blue-rinsed hair and horn-rimmed spectacles awry, beads of perspiration on her brow, and anger in her eyes — anger that she had been interrupted, more than anything else, I thought. No doubt about it, this was a really big day for the Martian race.

'What?' she shouted back.

'Stop hitting him.'

'Why should I? Big bloody bully!'

She took another almighty swipe that drew an anguished scream from the unfortunate Dale.

'Mrs. Webber, you *have* to stop,' I said firmly.

'Why?' she demanded.

I sighed. 'Because he's a policeman.'

She was so surprised she dropped her broom. 'A policeman?'

I nodded. 'Yes. They all are.'

'Oh my God!' Mrs. W said, clutching her bony hand to her bony bosom. 'Am I under arrest?'

The younger copper lurched uncertainly to his feet, and then staggered forward to loom over her menacingly, clutching the broom before him like a two-handed axe.

'Yes! Yes! Yes!' he all but screamed into Mrs. Webber pale face. 'Yes, you fucking well are, you crazy old bitch!'

I POURED BOILING water into two mugs and stirred the instant coffee. Behind me, my old friend Scott Vaughan sat at the kitchen table trying to attract Albert's attention by wriggling his fingers above the cat's head. Albert, sitting on one of the other chairs like a third member of a morning coffee circle, was playing it cool, but I knew his habits all too well. If Vaughan continued taunting like this, he could expect to lose blood.

Out through the kitchen window, I could see that the street was now deserted. Mrs. Webber had instantly fled back inside her house to bathe her temples with *eau de cologne* — or snort a few lines of crystal-meth, or whatever it was she usually did to reduce her stress levels. The fat, grey-haired cop Vaughan had referred to as Jimmy had taken the younger, smacked arse-faced one, Chris Dale, over to the A&E at the local hospital, where they were to have their injuries checked out by a professional.

The scratches and scrapes Mrs. W had given them hadn't looked that serious to me, and I had a feeling that the hospital trip Vaughan had ordered was really a way of getting Dale out of the way and calming him down a bit. At any rate, I had seen some kind of silent understanding pass between Scott and the grey-haired Jimmy, who seemed to be much more in control of himself.

I turned back and took the coffees over to the kitchen table. We had already completed some of the necessary small talk — he now knew that my parents were still breathing, and I knew that his mother had survived a small stroke around Easter time and that he was currently spending most of his off-duty time helping out at her house. Not, he said, that there was much off-duty time at the moment.

He said he was very busy these days. Busy, busy, busy.

Vaughan was still tempting fate by taunting Albert, whose tail was now beginning to twitch alarmingly. His luminous green eyes had reached that peculiar level of Zen serenity that indicated the imminence of a lightning attack.

'I wouldn't do that anymore, if I were you,' I said. 'Sooner or later, you'll lose a finger.'

Vaughan laughed easily, but withdrew his hand from the danger area quickly enough (I could almost hear Albert sigh in disappointment). 'What are you like, Joel?' he asked. 'Runaway wives, killer cats, psycho neighbours...'

I sat down opposite him.

'Thanks for not pressing charges against Mrs. Webber, Scott. I have the feeling that if it wasn't for you, Dale would have had the cuffs on her in about two seconds flat.'

He laughed again.

'You'd be right, too. He's a firebrand is Chris Dale, well known for it. Ambitious as hell, and keen to get to the top of the greasy pole as fast as possible. He'd nick his own Mum if he needed to make up his quota. But he's still young. Give him time, he'll mellow. Jimmy'll help take some of the starch out of him, too. He's been around the block a few times, knows what's what.'

'Yeah, he looks like he does. Seems familiar to me for some reason?'

'Like I said, he's been around a long time. Even longer than you and me.' Vaughan looked me up and down. 'Look at you, though — looking *good*, Joel. I mean, you always were a good-looking bastard, but retirement really seems to have suited you.'

'Not exactly retirement, is it?'

'No, but you know what I mean. Lots of blokes, they lose all sense of discipline when they leave the Job, and they pork up pretty bad. You haven't. You work out at a gym?'

I shook my head. The closest I had come to working out in the last couple of years was lifting old ladies' shopping bags in and out of the boot of my car. And don't forget crawling around on all fours with a whooping Vic on my back — now that was a really painful memory flash, and one I could have done without.

'Neither do I,' he admitted with a sigh, 'but that's exactly what I should be doing. Got to fight the march of time, you see, got to hold off all those young bastards who're after my job. People like Chris Dale.'

I took a closer look at Vaughan, and found him not much changed from the last time I'd seen him. He was exaggerating for effect. His sandy hair had receded ever so slightly from his temples, and his waist was a teeny bit thicker, but that was all.

'I'm sure you don't have to worry about that little pipsqueak,' I said.

'Ah, I have to worry about everyone and everything, that's the way of the world, my old son. Besides, I already *know* your secret.'

A cold finger ran down the length of my spine and flirted with the idea of giving me a proctological examination.

'What secret is that?' I asked.

'The secret of your youthful physique, of course,' Vaughan grinned. 'It's that daughter of yours, isn't it, keeping you on your toes twenty-four-seven?'

He pointed at the selection of paintings and photos stuck to the fridge with decorative magnets, and I breathed an entirely internal sigh of relief.

'Yes, that's the secret, all right.'

'Pretty little girl,' he said. 'Where is she now?'

I paused.

For just one second, I was tempted to tell him the truth of the matter. This was my friend, after all. My good friend. But then the impulse passed. It was just too dangerous.

'She's at her playgroup right now,' I told Scott. 'Her grandparents will pick her up from there and look after her until I've finished my shift tonight.'

'Must be nice, having a kid.'

I nodded. 'What about you? Did you ever get married?'

'Nah, you know me — married to the Job. The Service is the only girl in my life.'

'Well, that's not altogether true, is it?' I asked.

Vaughan was well-known as a passionate car lover. The last 'mistress' I could remember him being obsessed with was a ten-year-old Toyota Corolla, extensively restored and pampered to a level that even Lisa would have found acceptable.

'Did you ever get that Jag you were lusting after?'

'You know me too well,' Vaughan laughed. 'No, I never did. I've got a Lexus now, though. Cabriolet. Platinum. Brand new, top of the range. Stunningly beautiful. My pride and joy.'

Vaughan and I eyed each other carefully over the table. He sipped his coffee, I sipped mine. Albert looked from one of us to the other, like he was watching a couple of gunslingers getting ready to slap leather at high noon.

'So, tell me,' I finally said, 'how long have you been searching for my wife?'

Vaughan smiled.

'Oh, for a while now,' he said. 'A good long while.'

'YOU WERE ALREADY looking for her before I called you asking for help, weren't you?'

Scott nodded.

'And you didn't think to mention this to me? What happened, did it slip your mind?'

'Be fair, Joel,' Vaughan said. 'You're the husband of a woman who's at the very centre of an on-going criminal investigation. I could hardly tell you the truth, could I?'

I shrugged, remembering his initial caginess on the phone. 'It's the business at the bank, I suppose. Morgan-Matheson?'

Scott raised his eyebrows, surprised. 'You know about that?'

'Not that much. But I know that Lisa was sacked for… irregularities.'

Vaughan smiled a little. 'Irregularities — I like that. Just vague enough to be polite, isn't it?'

'But I was told that the police weren't going to be involved, that the bank was sorting it out in-house.'

'Who told you that, Handley?'

'Yes.'

'Well, he was telling the truth, as far as he was aware. He didn't call us in, and he probably still doesn't realise that we know what was happening. It was just one of the things that came up during the course of a much larger investigation.'

A much larger investigation, I thought. *Jesus.*

'Do you know where Lisa is now?' I asked.

'I'm afraid not.'

'Did you try to track her through her credit card transactions?'

'Standard Operating Procedure.'

'But no joy?'

'No. It looks like she hasn't used any of her credit cards for well over four months. Now, from what I remember of Lisa, I was thinking that she might be dead…'

He paused and smiled to let me know that he had intended this to be a joke — which it almost was.

'But, of course she *isn't* dead, is she? She's just gone to ground, like a sexy little fox avoiding a pack of hounds. She came to meet you at Brent Cross, didn't she? How did you manage that little miracle? Don't try to tell me it was a coincidence.'

I weighed up the option of claiming exactly that, but quickly realised that it wouldn't fly.

'She called out of the blue early yesterday morning, said she wanted to meet me there.'

'Did she say why?'

'She wanted a second opinion on a new dress.'

Vaughan cocked his head and softly tut-tutted me.

'Okay, she wanted my help.'

'To do what?'

I hesitated. Unconsciously or not, Vaughan was using all his interviewing skills, plus our history of friendship, to draw out all the information I had. But there were things I couldn't tell him, places I didn't want to go, because ultimately they could end up endangering my daughter.

'We didn't get that far in our conversation before we were interrupted.'

'By who?'

'Well, by *your* men, for starters.'

He winced slightly. 'Yeah, that would have been Dale's influence. They got a bit too enthusiastic for their own good. Moved in too soon and spooked her. But there was someone else there, wasn't there?'

I nodded. 'The Goblin.'

'*Who?*' Vaughan was puzzled, but for only a moment, and then he laughed. 'That's right, that's exactly what he is — a goblin!'

He laughed some more before settling down again. He seemed to laugh a lot more these days than he used to. I thought it was probably a technique he'd developed over the years, to put the people he was questioning at ease.

'Do you know who he is?' he asked.

'No,' I lied. 'Although, I have noticed him hanging about town just lately — it's kind of hard to miss a face like that. But until he turned up at Brent Cross, I just thought he was someone new in the area, someone who I just kept seeing coincidentally.'

'But you don't know his name?'

Once again, I knew that ignorance was best, and I shook my head.

'Well, *I* do,' Vaughan said. 'He's an ex-boxer, name of Gregory Feelen. Used to fight for a management company called Top Dog years ago. Boxed at a couple of weights, was useless at both of them. Face tells its own story, doesn't it? When he left the sport, he started taking security gigs, mostly nightclub work. Also drifted into petty crime, enforcing, muscle for hire. In other words, he's a thug.'

'Why would a man like that be after Lisa?'

'He's just doing what comes naturally to a man like him — following orders.'

'Whose orders?'

Instead of answering my question, he asked another of his own.

'That management company Feelen boxed for, Top Dog Promotions, you ever hear of it?'

'Maybe,' I said, casting my mind back to my conversation with Charlie Noble. 'Didn't it go down in some kind of scandal?'

'You could say that. Ever hear of a man called Bernard Jacks? On paper he was the sole proprietor and owner of Top Dog during its long, colourful life, and he was everything you might expect from such a character. Twisted, crooked, and bent — all at the once.'

'And he's the man you're really looking for?'

'No, we know where Mr. Jacks is. Well, we know where his *body* is, at any rate, and I've got a pretty good hunch where his soul ended up, too.'

'So he's dead?'

'Committed suicide a couple of years ago. Suicide was how it was *meant* to look, anyway. Probably it was more of what you might call an assisted suicide, like one of those mercy killings you hear about all the time. Except with none of the mercy.'

'How did it happen?'

'You don't want to know that.'

He was right, suddenly I didn't.

'It was an accumulation of Jacks' business mistakes that led to Top Dog's collapse, and he was probably skimming off the top, too — men like him always do, they just can't help themselves — and that won't have helped his cause. In the end, he was made to pay the price for his failure, and believe me, he really paid in spades. The pathologists tell me it's theoretically possible for him to have killed himself in the way that it appears he did. But in practical terms, no one would ever choose to go out like that. No *man*, certainly, if you catch my drift.'

'Do you know who did it?'

I was picturing the Goblin with his filthy hands on my daughter. Suddenly, Lisa's assertion that Feelen wouldn't hurt a fly sounded extremely unconvincing.

'We don't know who did the wet work, no. But we could make an educated guess on who gave the order.'

'Who was it?'

Vaughan took another slurp of his coffee before answering.

'That would be the man who was the *real* owner of Top Dog Promotions. Who just happens to be the *same* man who owns the nightclubs Feelen used to be a bouncer at, and who is *still* employing him to this very day.'

'Who is he?'

'The same man who paid the rent on your wife's luxury flat in Bayswater. The same man whose dirty money she ran through the laundry at Morgan-Matheson — none of which we can actually one-hundred-percent prove, of course. At this stage there at least half a dozen firewalls between him and us, dummy companies, false names, and the like. It's like the six degrees of separation, the bent version.'

I'd had enough of his teasing by now.

'Scott, just tell me who he is.'

He smiled kindly. 'His name is Temple. Nicolas Richard Temple. That name ring a bell for you?'

Oh yes.

That name did more than just ring a bell. It was like a mass gathering of campanologists all tugging away for England. In a day absolutely jam-packed with thoroughly bad shocks, this had to be the worst of them all. I felt simultaneously hot and cold, as though in the grip of a tropical fever. Hell's bells were clanging in my mind.

Temple was the corrupt undercover cop on whose rocks I had come so badly aground all those years ago. The man who had ruined my police career, my physical health, and just about my whole damn life. And yet, even knowing all that, Lisa had *still* gone into business with him.

The QUEEN of HEARTS

I closed my eyes as I realised that they must have been lovers, too. As I realised that, in fact, Lisa must have left me and Vic *for* him.

This was the man behind my daughter's kidnap. The worse kind of criminal imaginable, a cop gone bad.

A murderer.

"Nick Temple…'

Fifteen

A BITTER CHILL enveloped me, sinking in bone deep, and the reality around me faded away. My kitchen simply didn't exist for me anymore.

My eyes were still tightly closed, and in the darkness behind my eyelids, I might just as well have been back there, all those years ago, in that dank tomb of a south London cellar, bleeding, crippled with pain, preparing myself for the worst. Preparing to die. A series of phantom pains swept through me, as if my body had memories and the memories had teeth.

I tend to downplay my injuries these days, both in terms of their severity and in the manner by which I came by them. But the truth is that I was taken apart with brutal precision, savagely smashed into little policeman bits.

I hadn't thought about that terrible night for such a long time — perhaps deliberately, because it was so painful. But the memories had obviously lodged fast in my subconscious, because now I hardly had to reach for them at all. I turned away from the present completely, away from Vaughan, who I imagined was watching my face like a hawk, and the memories just tumbled from the shelves of my mind, like I'd kept them close at hand for just this moment.

Maybe I had. Maybe I had never tried to hide them too well. Maybe a part of me had always known that one day I'd need them.

It was nearly five years ago now, late October, and I had been practically alone in the CID suite sometime after eight o'clock at night. For what felt like the millionth time, I was looking through the file of notes that I had assembled in my one-man pursuit of Nicolas Temple and his gang of corrupt undercover cops. Several weeks earlier, I had informed my superiors of my suspicions, but they had displayed an astonishing lack of curiosity on the subject. They were like ostriches, I thought, with their heads buried firmly in the sand.

The only thing they *had* done (which was precisely what I *hadn't* wanted them to do) was to let Temple himself know what I suspected, therefore putting him on his guard. I had expected some kind of angry rebuttal from him, but he was smart enough to just laugh it off. His official line was that undercover officers got these kinds of suspicions and baseless accusations hurled at them all the time. They came with the territory, he said. Badges of office.

My superiors told me to drop it. But naturally, I didn't, I kept digging and sifting, digging and sifting. Because in my heart, I *knew* he was bent.

That night, as on so many nights in the past, I should have gone home hours before to my lovely young wife. But I kept thinking that if I looked at my notes for long enough, just one more time, a previously hidden pattern would miraculously appear, an overlooked detail would spring out like something out of a kids' pop-up book, and then I'd know how to nail the rotten bastard.

But everything seemed to be working in reverse that night. The stars were misaligned. A bad moon was rising.

Instead of coming clearer, everything seemed murkier. Studied this intensely, even the small snippets of hard fact I'd jotted down among all the conjecture simply degraded into mush. Worse, it had begun to look like fiction, like the fabricated vendetta certain people had already begun to accuse me of.

Enough, I remember thinking. *Enough.*

I'd closed the file and then locked it away in the bottom drawer of my desk, feeling demoralised and depressed. And I was angry in a low-key but steady, relentless way. At that time in my life, anger was my constant state. I was a permanent resident of the Planet Mars.

I'd turned off my desk lamp, pulled my jacket off the back of my chair and slipped it on. I was finally on my way home. Lisa would be waiting up for me. We'd have a late supper together, and then go to bed and make love. For a little while, at least, there would be a kind of peace in my life. But the phone on my desk rang before I had taken two steps away from it.

I almost didn't go back. A thousand times or more since that moment, I've wished that I hadn't. But I did.

I said my name into the phone, and a female voice said, 'I have some information for you.'

'Who is this?' I asked.

'No names.'

'Information about what?'

The phone was silent for so long, I thought she had gone.

'Nick Temple,' she said eventually. 'Nick the Dick.'

Her voice was low, secretive, as though it would be dangerous for her to be overheard.

I sat down again, heavily. I could hear the receiver creaking in my hand and struggled to loosen my grip. As a part of his elaborate undercover identity, Temple was rumoured to run a stable of prostitutes. Another rumour was that he was his own best customer, hence the rhyming nickname. The fact that the woman on the phone had used it so easily meant that she was probably genuine, and that her information could turn out to be extremely valuable.

'Are you still there?' she asked. 'Am I boring you?'

As casually as possible, I glanced around the CID suite. There were only two other detectives around now. One was on the phone, apparently chatting to a girlfriend, and the other looked like he had fallen asleep at his computer terminal. They weren't paying any attention to me, or to anything I said. Or so I hoped.

'Who are you?' I asked in the same low voice she had used. 'One of his girls?'

'No, I'm a little higher up the food chain than that. Let's just say that I'm a concerned fellow officer. I can't bear seeing what Temple's doing, what he's getting away with. What they're *allowing* him to get away with.'

'What do you mean? *Who's* allowing him to get away with *what*?'

There was another pause. 'Not over the phone. I have to speak to you in person.'

'Why?'

'Because I have evidence to hand over to you.'

'What kind of evidence?'

'I have surveillance photographs. I have copies of fraudulent documents, and papers that he's signed in his own name. I have a shotgun with bloody fingerprints on it — the fingerprints are Temple's, but the blood isn't.'

By this point my head was pounding. 'Where did you get—'

'I will only give this evidence to *you*,' she continued, 'I will only put it directly into *your* hands. I need to know I'll be safe, and you're the only one I'm sure I can trust. I don't trust anyone else, and neither should you. Too many of them are on his side. You must come alone.'

Alarm bells should have been ringing at this point, I know. They *were* ringing, as a matter of fact — I just chose to selectively ignore them. Martians can do that sort of thing quite easily.

In clipped, precise language, the woman gave me my instructions.

There was a certain address somewhere between Elephant & Castle and Kennington Oval in south London. I had to meet her there in half-an-hour. She would wait for me no longer than ten minutes. If I didn't make this window, if I didn't seize this opportunity, she'd be gone forever. And so would my chance of getting Temple bang to rights.

She said she wasn't prepared to take this kind of risk ever again. She would step back into the undergrowth and bury whatever remained of her ideals and principles, as so many had before her. She wasn't prepared, she said, to sacrifice herself for the integrity of the Thin Blue Line.

Unfortunately, I was all too prepared to do what she was not. I should have had a neon bloody sign hung around my neck — looking for a sacrificial victim? Then look no further, for I am your man!

The address turned out to be a boarded-up house in a long residential road festooned with other such abandoned properties. It would be a number of years yet before the property developers moved in to reclaim the area, and at that time it had looked like an urban war-zone. It was full night by then, the sky clear, with sharply defined stars and a silver coin for a moon, and it was as cold as a witch's tit.

Around the back of the house, I found that the steel plate covering the back door had been partially peeled away at the bottom, like the lid of a sardine can. I leaned in and saw nothing but darkness, smelled nothing but damp plaster and garbage and cat shit.

'Hello?' I said into the darkness.

'In here,' the woman whispered.

I ducked under the curl of steel and stood up again. Invisible in the darkness, stray cobweb threads attached themselves to my hair.

'Come forward slowly,' she said, and I did. 'Okay, stop. Now take two steps to your left. Good. Now come straight on, towards my voice.'

I moved slowly and cautiously, hoping that my eyes would soon adjust to the darkness, as the woman's clearly had.

'That's it,' she encouraged me, 'You're almost here. Just five or six more steps now.'

With my hands held out before me, I silently counted each step.

One, two, three, f—

That was when the floorboards ran out and the cellar steps began.

The house was a large Edwardian terraced, and the cellar steps were long and steep and made of sandstone. I went down them like a runaway train, and a third of the way down something happened to my knee that made me scream. Then I was tumbling over and over in the darkness. The stone steps almost beat me to death. The stone floor at the bottom smashed all the breath from my body. The brick wall I slammed into nearly broke me in two.

I was a mass of pains. I had broken ribs. A dislocated shoulder. Broken fingers and a broken wrist. A fractured skull. But the pain in my knee out-sung them all. It felt like it was on fire. It was so bad I couldn't even get my breath to scream, and could only hyperventilate.

Leisurely footsteps began to descend the cellar steps behind me, echoing hollowly. There seemed to be a lot of them, as though an army was coming for me, but it turned out to be only three. Three was quite enough, as it happened.

'Whoops!' the woman said, laughter ringing in her voice. 'I forgot to stay stop.'

'Never mind,' a male voice replied. 'We all make mistakes.'

This was a voice that I knew all too well. Nicky Temple, Nick the Dick, in the flesh.

'That's right, isn't it, Joel — we all make mistakes?'

'Like the one you've just made,' I managed to gasp. 'You've gone too far this time. You're finished now.'

'No, I'm not,' he said calmly. I could hear the smile in his voice.

'I have men surrounding this house.'

'No, you haven't.'

And of course he was right, I didn't. I'd been too anxious not to spook my female informant by bringing back-up.

Also, there was a part of me that hadn't *wanted* help. That part of me wanted to do everything on my own, bring in my man hog-tied over my saddle like a bounty hunter in an old western movie. Maybe I'd been watching too many TV shows about maverick cops. Or maybe it was simply because I was a Martian, and didn't know any better.

'Let's just get on with it and kill him,' another male voice said matter-of-factly.

I sensed Temple moving toward me, and tried to curl into a protective ball. But he just squatted beside me, gently patting me on my dislocated shoulder. Groaning, I felt my body unfurl again. It simply hurt too much to stay in that position.

'I can't begin to tell you how much trouble you've caused me, September,' he said mildly. 'You've been a right royal pain in the backside. You're supposed to be a smart guy, I thought you might have got the message to clear off before it came to this. But you wouldn't have it, would you? You had to push me all the way. And just look at you now... what a mess.'

'Can we just fucking *do* him and go?' the other man asked irritably. 'I'm missing a fucking top meal for this chimps' tea party.'

Temple chuckled complacently. 'Don't worry, my friend, you'll get your meal.'

I heard him stand up, and their shoes crunching on the gritty stone floor as they all crowded in around me.

'Any final words, Joel?' Temple asked, mockingly. 'An epitaph for your headstone, perhaps?'

'Can you see me?'

'Of course. We're wearing night-vision goggles. We use them to surveil criminals.'

Temple and his cohorts laughed.

'All right,' I said, 'then surveil this!' And in the dark, I gave them just about all the resistance I was currently capable of — I gave them the finger.

'Oh, you silly boy,' the woman said wonderingly. She sounded quite charmed.

The first blow took me on the forehead, giving my skull its second fracture of the night.

Subsequently, the doctors told me that my injuries were consistent with a baseball bat beating, which seemed about right, because that first blow had felt like a home run. Too dazed to protect myself, I could only lay there while the three of them tried to beat me to death.

I don't know how long it went on. At some point one of the bats connected with my already damaged knee and mercifully, I passed out.

I came to a couple of hours later.

At first, I wasn't sure I was really alive, but eventually I reasoned that I had to be. I was fairly confident that upon death I would get to go to my first-choice destination, which was Heaven (if for no other reason that my only real sin was gross stupidity), and that this miserable, painful hole could hardly be Heaven — not unless I, and a lot of other gullible people, had been badly misinformed over the years.

Gradually, I began to realise what must have happened — they had left me for dead, left me to lay here until my body was discovered by accident, by a tramp looking for shelter for the night or a junkie looking for a place to shoot up. Not a very happy scenario, obviously, but believe it or not, my first emotion was exhilaration, actual *joy*. Not just that I was alive, but that Temple had finally slipped up. And now I had him.

It was only when I tried to move that I realised how badly they had beaten me. It took an age to locate my mobile phone, which they had overlooked to remove.

No, not overlooked. They hadn't removed it because they thought I was either dead or about to die, and dead men can't make phone calls.

After I finally managed to get the phone out of my pocket, which was under my body and wet with blood, I struggled through the pain to make three calls.

One to summon an ambulance for myself. One to my superior officer to explain what had happened to me and who was responsible. And one to my darling Lisa, telling her that I wouldn't be home for a late supper, after all.

I OPENED MY eyes and found Scott Vaughan still studying me.

I wasn't precisely sure how long I'd been away, revisiting the past, but his attention hadn't faltered. I felt a great need to explain myself to him, but of course that would have been unnecessary. He knew the story all too well.

Back then he had been elsewhere in the capital, following his own career, but after I had spilled my stories to my superiors and made my accusations from a hospital bed, *he* was the one they had sent to break the bad news.

Not that it was just bad news he had delivered that day. Bad news I could have coped with. Bad news would have been a walk in the park. It was *terrible* news Vaughan had brought me. Appalling news. End of the world news.

He had appeared at my hospital bedside about a week after the attack, thinner in the middle and thicker on top than he was now. I'd had three minor operations by that time, and was due to have at least one more, the biggie, on my right knee. They could fix it well enough for me to walk, they said, maybe even jog a little, but I'd always have the trace of a limp.

I suppose that if I'd been a professional football player they would have sent me to America to have the knee rebuilt by world-renowned experts. But I wasn't anything as exalted as a football player, I was just an unimportant, bog-standard copper, and what I got seemed to be a couple of anonymous amateurs armed with scalpels and a bucketful of scrap metal.

I could see from Vaughan's face that he was not the barer of good news, so his first words surprised me.

'There's going to be an inquiry.'

'That's fantastic!' I said. 'Temple won't be able to wriggle out of—'

I stopped because Vaughan was shaking his head.

'What?' I asked.

'The inquiry isn't concerned with Nick Temple's activities. It's about you.'

'Me?'

'About your vendetta against Temple. The slanderous allegations you've been making about him. Your attempts to sabotage his undercover team's work. Your attempt to frame him for attempted murder.'

'My *what?*'

Vaughan went on to explain that the current thinking among the great minds of the Met' hierarchy was that it was I — and not Temple — who was the one in league with major players in the criminal fraternity. According to these brainboxes, I was supposed to be trying to undermine Temple's work and besmirch his reputation among his colleagues, because of the danger he posed to my underworld friends.

The so-called 'attack' on me was a last desperate attempt to frame Temple and put him behind bars himself. Supposedly, I had agreed to be beaten half to death in exchange for a small fortune. Accordingly, my bank accounts and financial records were now being carefully sifted for evidence. My home was being ransacked by nosy coppers who I didn't know.

'I can't understand this — it's just unbelievable!'

Vaughan nodded, but did not speak.

'Temple almost *killed* me! He was there, in that cellar, and if he'd hit me one more time, I would have died! They've got to believe me! *You* believe me, don't you, Scott?'

Vaughan looked away, and I knew there was something he had yet to tell me — something even worse — and I was right.

'Temple has an alibi,' Vaughan said. 'Cast iron.'

'He *can't* have.'

'But he does. Unbreakable, unshakable. Rock solid.'

'That's impossible.'

But apparently it was not.

'At the time you claim he was attempting to kill you, he was at a party on the other side of the river. He has witnesses. Lots of them.'

'No way that's true. He's got his pals lying for him. All you have to do is dig a little and the truth will come out.'

Vaughan was shaking his head again. I'd never seen him look so sad.

'No, Joel, you don't understand. The party he was at wasn't so much a party as an *event* — a charity function.

Black tie, celebrities, the whole bit. There were over two hundred guests, a fair number of whom were Met' senior officers and their wives. One of the people personally confirming Temple's alibi is a member of the Top Brass. Another is a well-respected backbench MP, who claims he spent most of the evening with Temple and a few others in a private room, playing poker for high stakes. Apparently, Temple won.'

'It looks that way,' I muttered.

I knew what had happened. Temple was sharp as a knife, and he'd set this up so neatly there was no way out for me. They hadn't left me for dead, after all. They had *known* I was alive, and they were probably aware that I had a mobile phone on me, too. Maybe they'd even checked that it was still working before they left me. Then Temple went back to his party and his so-called witnesses, and waited for me to land myself in it. Which I obligingly did as soon as I regained consciousness.

Now I was completely discredited, and I would never be able to convince anyone that I was right. No one on the force would ever trust me again.

'He set me up, Scott,' I said. 'That cunning bastard set me up.'

Vaughan was my good friend, my best friend, but even he couldn't look at me. That was the moment I first realised that my career was over.

'YOU WERE RIGHT about him,' Vaughan said to me now. 'All those years ago, you were right. But

Temple was more than just a bent copper, more than just a crook. He was a bloody gangster. He was undercover, alright — undercover as a *cop*. Turned out he was a damned sight cleverer than anyone knew.'

'I knew,' I couldn't help saying, although, in my defence, I managed to avoid adding, 'I told you so.'

'Yeah, *you* knew. But you got the old red mist and went at it like a maniac.'

'I tried it the right way first, by the book, but the Brass didn't want to know. I had no alternative except to go it alone.'

Vaughan looked like he wanted to argue, but then decided to concede the point. 'I can see how it must have felt that way,' he said with a shrug. 'You were put in an impossible position.'

'Where's Temple now?' I asked. 'Don't tell me he's still in the Job.'

'No, he resigned about ten months ago. Left before he was pushed, you could say. The Powers That Be allowed him to go and pursue his many business interests. But a lot of questions were being asked, I can assure you. About Bernard Jacks, for one. Not to mention missing seed money from drug operations, alleged profits from prostitution... you can take your pick.'

'But if there was this level of suspicion, why was there no official investigation, no charges brought...?'

Vaughan shrugged. 'You wouldn't believe how much support Temple has going for him. Even now, a lot of the young studs secretly hero-worship him. And there are other people, older and more experienced officers who should know a lot better, who admire him unreservedly, who believe that he was a champion of law and order. These people think he's a martyr.'

'A martyr?' I said. 'That'd suit me, actually. Just let me know if he wants to be boiled in oil, crucified, or stoned to death.'

'Also, we believe he had a lot of very compromising, maybe even incriminating evidence on a number of influential figures. Chiefly meaning a certain senior officer and a certain prominent politician he'd managed to drag into his slimy world — the men, specifically, who alibied him at the time of your attack. They've been his insurance policy for years.'

Blackmail, I thought.

Which made a lot of sense. It was exactly the same sort of dirty trick Lisa had played on David Handley to stop him talking to the police. (Not that it had worked in that instance — Vaughan and his team had found out, anyway.) But no wonder she had been drawn to Temple in the first place. The two of them were cast from the same cracked mould, cut from the same bale of rotten cloth.

I looked up at Vaughan. 'How did they meet, Lisa and Temple? Do you know?'

'As far as we can figure, Temple actively sought her out, chose her above all the other women he could have had.'

'Do you know why?'

'Obviously, she was rather ideally placed within the financial world to provide the kind of specialist services he required. And I think it's equally obvious he must have seen something in her to suggest that she would be susceptible to the kind of rewards he was able to offer in return. But there are probably hundreds more like her out there, all waiting for the wrong man to come along at the wrong time. Personally, I believe he targeted Lisa simply because she was your wife.'

'Why? Hadn't he done enough to me already?'

'Nicolas Temple's not the sort of man to be content with simply slipping a horse's head under your duvet, Joel — no, he'd want to ram the hooves up your arse, for good measure. My theory is that he wanted to destroy your life entirely.'

'But why? I took my shot at him years ago, and I missed. What threat would I be to him now?'

'You still don't get it, do you? For him, it's all about revenge. Payback. What you did back then may have failed at the time, but the echoes started something. It was the first real crack in his armour, and after that it was just a matter of time. It was the beginning of his downfall.'

He left me to contemplate this for a few moments before adding something else.

'And of course he probably wanted to shag Lisa, too. I mean, he wasn't called Nick the Dick for nothing.'

Vaughan just shrugged at the angry look I sent him in response to this comment. That's the way it is, his shrug said, this is the real world. He was right.

'How could she have been so stupid?' I asked.

'Well, the promise of a lot of money does tend to strip most people of their common sense,' Vaughan said. 'But maybe she wasn't quite so stupid, after all. In fact, maybe she was smart.'

I asked what he meant.

'We believe that once Lisa had been forced out of Morgan-Matheson, she quickly realised she'd ceased to be an asset to Temple, and become instead a dangerous loose end. And Temple has a very specific way of dealing with loose ends — you could ask Bernie Jacks if he wasn't already in his grave, minus a few tender body parts. We believe that Lisa was smart enough to grab some insurance before the sky began to fall.'

He was talking about the files, of course, but I continued to play dumb.

'We believe she must have squirreled away all the hard-copy paperwork associated with her best client's accounts. Correspondence, ledgers, spreadsheets, receipts, foreign and off-shore bank details, as well as flash-drives, external hard-drives, etc. If we were to get our hands on that cache of evidence, we'd have Temple at our mercy, plain and simple. We could take him down immediately.'

He leaned back in his chair and grinned at me.

'In a way, it'd be a bit like putting Al Capone away for tax-evasion. But what the hell, any port in a storm, eh?'

'How come you can do this now?' I asked. 'Go after him this aggressively? What about all his powerful friends, what about the people he's been blackmailing for years — suddenly they don't count anymore?'

'Don't you ever read the papers, Joel? Watch the news? Surf the Net?'

Vaughan smiled, but not pleasantly.

'A certain beloved member of the Met' hierarchy died late last year of a mammoth heart attack. Surprised the hell out of everyone — no one ever knew he *had* a heart. My team and I have been on standby since then. And then just recently, Temple's favourite backbencher went down in flames, the biggest political scandal since Profumo, they're calling it.'

I recalled hearing the other taxi-drivers talking about the disgraced politician only days ago, and hadn't made the connection. And I'd never heard about the cop's heart attack at all. If I had, I would probably have danced for joy. The man in question had presided over the *in-camera* inquiry and sunk me like a gold-braided torpedo. He was the man who'd accused me of having "an excess of zeal", and solemnly concluded the inquiry by telling me that everyone was "very, very disappointed" in me.

As I'd left the inquiry rooms on my crutches, Temple had caught up to me to mockingly repeat those exact same words in my ear. Of course at the time I'd believed Temple had simply picked up on that one line because he knew it would drive me crazy. Now I realised that he had probably fed the line to his stooge deliberately.

I looked up and caught Vaughan smiling at me again, and it was a predator's smile. It was like looking at the business end of a Great White Shark.

'All bets are off now,' he said. 'Temple's lost all his protection, and you can be sure he knows it. That's why he's so desperate to get his hands on Lisa and those files.'

Of course it is, I thought. And it also explained why he was prepared to go to the extremes of kidnapping and threatening the life of a small child.

He was fighting for his own life.

Sixteen

'So, are you going to help us or not?'

This was the question Vaughan had asked me just before I left the kitchen table — in fact, it was the question that had prompted me to leave the table in the first place. I knew what Scott expected my answer to be, and in practically any other situation, I'm sure he would have been right. But he didn't know about Vic, and I couldn't tell him.

The warning Feelen had made over the phone earlier was always at the forefront of my mind. The warning about not talking to the police, because *They* would know, that *They* had eyes and ears everywhere.

'I'm waiting for an answer, Joel,' Vaughan said, his mask of patience slipping a little. 'Yes or no.'

I dashed the rest of my coffee down the sink and rinsed the mug out under the cold water tap, playing for time. Out through the kitchen window, I saw that the metallic-blue Saab had now returned from the hospital and was parked in the same spot as before. I could see the new sterile dressing stuck to Chris Dale's forehead, luminously white in the car's interior gloom. The grey-haired cop sitting beside him had a smaller dressing on his ear, too. They were chatting, chuckling.

The grey-haired cop is called *Jimmy*, I thought.

And suddenly, I knew him. Talking about Temple had brought it back, I suppose, and recalling Feelen's warning had reinforced it. I turned back to face Vaughan.

'Where did you get Jimmy from?' I asked.

'Jimmy? Why do—'

'Did you choose him or was he given to you?'

'A bit of both, if I recall. Why?'

'I told you he looked familiar, didn't I? I recognise him now. He was a hell of a lot lighter the last time I saw him, and there wasn't a single grey hair on his head. It's James Gill, isn't it?'

Vaughan smiled. 'Nothing wrong with your memory, is there?'

But I wasn't smiling, not at all. 'You know that he was a member of Temple's undercover squad, don't you? On the streets he was known as Jimmy Fish. Or sometimes just the Eel, because he was so thin back then.'

'Yes, of course I know. That's the whole reason why he was offered to me in the first place, and that's why I said yes-please-and-thank-you and practically bit their fucking hands off. As far as this investigation goes, Jimmy's my ace in the hole.'

'Yeah? Are you sure he isn't really the joker in the pack?'

Vaughan asked me to sit down and calm down, but I wouldn't.

'How do you know he isn't still working for Temple?' I demanded to know.

'Look, Joel, don't you think I'd have checked him out thoroughly before taking him on? Do you think I've gone soft in my old age?'

'No, but—'

'Jimmy's squeaky clean, and he always was. He was only ever on the fringes of Temple's team — what they called the Posse, back in the day — he was never one of the trusted inner circle. He never liked or trusted Temple, and you can bet your bottom dollar that he was never liked or trusted in return. He requested a reassignment not long after you had to resign. He *believed* your stories, and he had his own suspicions besides. But he was tough, and he decided he wasn't going to let it ruin his career the way it had ruined yours.'

I grunted. Good job Scott wasn't a doctor — his bedside manner would have left a lot to be desired.

'However,' he continued, 'he was a part of the team long enough to learn how Temple's mind works, and Temple's been his pet project ever since. Jimmy knows more about the slick bastard than anyone else alive. Temple's his Mastermind specialist subject, which is why he's part of the team that's finally going to bring the Big Man down.'

Vaughan stood up and squared his shoulders. He looked like he wanted me to come to attention and salute him.

'What about you, Joel. Are you a part of the team?'

'You seem to forget, I'm not a cop anymore. I'm a taxi-driver now.'

'That's right. Because of *Temple*. But in your heart, you're a copper. You'll always be a copper. Now, are you going to help us or not?'

'I'll think about it.'

It was plain to see that Vaughan didn't like this answer much, and I suppose that in his place, I wouldn't have cared too much for it either.

'This isn't the time to sit on the fence, Joel.'

'It's too dangerous.'

'Since when did *you* mind a little danger? What happened to the Man from Mars?'

'He got married and he had a daughter. That's when he started worrying about danger — when he became a father.'

'You know as well as I do that the best way to keep everyone safe and sound is to put the bad boys behind bars.'

'If only everything was so simple and straightforward.'

'But don't you see, it is that simple! Joel, if you can deliver Lisa to us, we'll take care of everything else. We can work out a deal to keep her out of jail. If need be, we can arrange a new identity for her, a new life. Maybe it would be a life that she could share with you and Victoria.'

Once again, all I could say was, 'I'll think about it.'

Vaughan angrily spun away. He grabbed his jacket from the back of the chair and pulled it on as though he hated it.

'I don't get it,' he said finally. 'Don't you want to see the man who ruined your life go down? Don't you want to see that arrogant prick behind bars? This is the man who smashed your leg and screwed your career. This is the man who fucked your wife behind your back and turned her into a criminal.'

I glared at him. Maybe he saw that he'd gone too far. But he wouldn't apologise. He wouldn't take it back.

'I'll think about it,' I said quietly.

'Don't think about it too long. Time is running out. You have my number.'

I saw that he'd left a card on the kitchen table.

'I'll be expecting your call. Make it soon, Joel.'

I PEERED OUT through the kitchen window as Vaughan stomped his way down the overgrown garden path, slammed the gate behind him, and then stalked back to the Saab. While he was still a dozen paces away, Chris Dale all but leapt out of the vehicle like a jack-in-the-box, and ran around to open the rear door for Vaughan to slip in. On top of everything else, it looked like Dale was a major arselicker — my prediction was that he'd go far.

Jimmy Gill's head turned to confer with his boss, and all I could see of him was that veil of grey hair and the heavy jowls that had masked his true identity. When he turned back, the engine roared to life. Gill guided the Saab through a swift, professional three-point turn, and then sped off.

On the kitchen table, Scott's card waited for me, displaying a host of numbers. Office 1, Office 2, home, mobile, e-mail. It was the card of a man determined not to be left out of the loop. I considered tossing it into the trash, but then decided against it. I popped it into my overstuffed wallet, just in case. Because you never knew.

Never ever.

Vaughan was certainly a lot more ambitious than he used to be. It used to be that *I* was the ambitious one, and he used to be the easy-come, easy-go type. Now everything had changed, and Vaughan was as conscious of that as I was. Confident of his own power, he'd given it his best shot at coming on like a friend, and he'd done pretty well, all told. But in the end, he'd slipped, revealing himself to be what he really was, which was a cop using every resource he possessed in order to get a result.

But that was okay. I understood it, and I understood him. If you can't play hard, you need to get out of the game, and I sensed that these days, my old friend could play pretty hard. Vaughan had barely flexed his muscles at me, and yet on more than one occasion I'd been tempted to spill the beans to him, tell everything and hope that they could save my daughter.

I might have done it, too, under different circumstances. God knows, I *wanted* to.

But I didn't like it that James Gill was a member of Scott's team. I didn't like it at all. It had always been my impression that Gill had been more than just a fringe member of Temple's undercover operation. Contrary to Vaughan's claim, I had assumed that Gill was a full member of the Posse, and at one point I'd even had him down as the second man in the baseball bat ambush.

But that isn't saying much, really. Back then my soaring paranoia levels meant that just about everyone I knew had been in the frame at some point. Even Scott Vaughan himself, for a brief while.

There was something else, too.

It didn't matter that Scott Vaughan was an old mucker of mine, and one of the few people I had ever completely trusted. The fact was that he was in the employ of the Metropolitan Police Service, and I didn't much trust that institution any more.

Don't forget, they'd already sold me down the river once, and at the time I'd actually been one of them, one of their golden boys. Now that I wasn't one of them anymore, I was nothing. It'd be a case of you scratch our backs, we'll stick a knife in yours. They'd promise me the earth, no doubt, but I'd probably come out of it with my head on backwards.

And maybe a dead daughter for company.

Wearily, I left the kitchen, went through into the living room, and slumped down on the settee. Albert, seemingly at a loose end, joined me and curled up in my lap. Cooperating with Vaughan was a moot point in any case, as I was completely dependent now on the whims of my estranged wife. It was gnawing away at my guts, but there was nothing else I could do.

Nothing.

I leant my head back and closed my eyes. On my lap, Albert was making little cat-snores. I made myself completely still, gradually slowing my breathing and forcing everything out of my mind, every worry, every fear, every conscious thought. It was an old trick from my days on the Job. It was a deliberate attempt to form a mental vacuum.

Because Nature hates a vacuum.

Something needs to fill that space. And if you can keep everything you *think* you know at bay, sometimes you learn that there are other things floating around in your brainpan. Things you didn't know you knew. It was like the memories of the cellar and the baseball bats. The pain. The expectation of death. The footsteps in the darkness. The last-minute gesture of hopeless defiance, giving them the finger, and then the home run with the baseball bat. It was all there, just waiting to be discovered.

My mind was a black void, just like the cellar.

Then I heard a *giggle*. And a mocking female voice *spoke*.

'Oh, you silly boy,' it said. 'Oh, you silly, silly boy...'

My eyes flew open of their own accord, absolutely astounded at what I had found. I shot to my feet, and Albert hurtled away with a long yowl of complaint. I ran out into the hall, threw open a cupboard, and rummaged around until I found what I wanted.

The Yellow Pages.

I ALL BUT tiptoed up the last few steps of the gravel drive, anxious not to spoil the surprise of my visit. My caution was probably unnecessary — from inside the house, only slightly muffled by the double-glazing, I could hear a hi-fi system banging out a steady pulse of dance music anthems at a volume loud enough to send Ibiza crumbling back under the sea.

Once on the doorstep, I quickly went through a little checklist. My hair was tidy — check. My shirt was buttoned correctly — check. My fly was properly zipped up, my breath was minty fresh, and I had nothing gnarly and embarrassing depending from either of my nostrils — check, check, and check.

I hadn't had a lot of time to get ready, because this surprise visit was a bit of a surprise to me, too, but I figured I'd done the best I could under the circumstances. If I wasn't exactly attractive, I was at least presentable. I'd left the Scenic parked outside on the road, out of sight of any of the house's windows. The small bunch of handpicked wild flowers had been a last-minute inspiration.

I knocked on the glossy black front door. I waited a few seconds and then knocked harder to compete with the music. Almost immediately the door swung open.

'All right, all right, keep your bleedin' hair on! Where the—'

Barbara finally saw that it was me and froze mid-sentence.

She was dressed as casually as I'd ever seen her, in a pair of faded jeans and a lightweight black sweater with the sleeves rolled up above her elbows. Her hair was scraped back into a functional ponytail and she wore no make-up. She was wearing boots today, not shoes (but they were boots with four-inch heels), and bright pink rubber gloves on her hands. Her forehead was beaded with perspiration. She had been working hard.

Behind her, the thumping music track juddered to a halt and another one, totally indistinguishable from the first, immediately began.

'Joel!' She didn't look anything like as overjoyed to see me as she made herself sound.

'In the flesh,' I replied with a wide, beaming smile. I held out my small bouquet of dandelions, daisies, buttercups, and a sprinkling of unspecified weeds (I think there might even have been a nettle in amongst them). 'These are for you.'

She looked at the flowers for a moment as though I was trying to hand her a poisonous spider, but then decided to accept them.

'Funny,' I said, cocking an ear to the music, 'I would have bet money that you were a classical music kind of gal.'

'Well, I like a little bit of everything.'

'As the actress said to the bishop...'

I could see that Barbara was just as puzzled by my strange manner as she was by my visit itself, but she tried her best to smile, and her smile was almost good enough. *Almost.*

I took a step toward her. 'Mind if I come in for a minute?'

'Well...'

As though she had already invited me, I stepped past her into the hallway.

A bucket of soapy water stood on the bottom step of the staircase, and I could see that the water she had used to wash the banister rail was still drying. There was a thick, artificial lemony odour to the house that was almost as loud as the music. At the other side of the hall, two medium-sized unmatched suitcases stood side by side with a coat draped over them.

I turned back to Barbara. 'Are you going somewhere?'

'Yes. I have an important business meeting.'

'You packed two suitcases for a business meeting?'

'Well, actually it's a series of meetings, over a few days. Abroad.'

'Like a conference?'

She smiled in what looked like relief. 'Yes, that's exactly what it is. It's a business conference, in... in Italy.'

'Italy? Wow, that sounds fantastic! Although, it's all a bit sudden, isn't it? You never mentioned it when we spoke last night.'

'I wasn't thinking about *business* when we spoke last night, Joel,' she said with a touch of the old smoulder. 'Were you?'

The QUEEN of HEARTS

I shook my head. No, I definitely had not had my mind on business last night. But I now believed that *she* had.

'Besides,' she added, 'I didn't learn until this morning that I had to go. One of my colleagues was scheduled to be there, but they had to pull out at the last minute. Some kind of family crisis.'

Family crisis. I nodded sympathetically. Yes, I knew all about family crises.

'So why are you spring-cleaning when you should be heading to the airport?'

She blinked. 'It's just a habit of mine. I like to give the place a good clean before I go away for any length of time. Then I know I'm coming back to a spotless house. It makes me feel better.'

If that was the case, she was a far better housekeeper than Lisa had ever been. Lisa regarded all housework, even as minor a task as washing-up after dinner, as she did serious diseases — all right for other people, but not really her cup of tea.

'Who did you think I was?' I asked abruptly.

'What?'

'When you answered the door, you were obviously expecting someone else.'

She double-blinked. 'I thought you were my lift to the station... the airport, I mean.'

I frowned and contrived to look a little upset. 'Why didn't you call me? I am a taxi-driver, after all. I would have been more than happy to take you to the airport. I could have held your hand until departure time.'

'Sorry, it was all arranged at the last minute. A colleague is going to take me.'

'Another colleague? Tell you what, why don't you call them now and tell them not to bother coming. I'd be delighted to take you. What time's your flight?'

'No, I can't do that. They have to give me a briefing before we leave.'

'Is it a he or a she? I don't have to be jealous, do I?'

Barbara was looking increasingly worried the longer this conversation went on. I laughed to relieve the tension, just like Scott Vaughan had done to me earlier.

'Don't worry, Babs, I'm just pulling your shapely leg.'

She hoisted another uncertain smile in my direction, this one only about half as good as the first.

'Still, it's a good job I called over,' I said. 'At least I get to see you once more before you leave. When will you be back?'

'I'm not sure. Why don't I call you from my hotel when I get there?'

'That would be nice. But what about the time difference — what country did you say it was, Italy? Which city?'

'Rome,' she replied in a flat delivery that made it sound like the first place that had come into her head. Probably it was.

'Lovely city. And the time difference is only about an hour, isn't it? But is it forwards or backwards?'

She triple-blinked. 'I — I don't know.'

'Oh well, it doesn't matter, does it?' I smiled warmly again. 'Do you like the flowers?'

'Yes, they're…'

She stared down at the moribund bouquet in her hand as she struggled for an appropriate compliment. I think it was probably the nettle that confused her most. Yes, I was saying it with flowers — but exactly *what* was I saying?

'... they're beautiful,' she eventually managed.

'Aren't they?' I reached out and caught the hand not holding the flowers. 'Come on, I've got another surprise for you.'

Barbara tried to protest but my bubbly enthusiasm won her over — or, at least, she couldn't come up with a good enough excuse to yank her arm away, which is what she looked like she really wanted to do.

I pulled her across the hallway and guided her through a doorway on its right-hand side, which led to the sitting room in which we had almost made love before I had an attack of the guilts. Once we were inside, I let her go.

This room was where the music originated, issuing from a battered old CD player, incongruous in the understated middle-class ambience of the rest of the house. A few china figurines had been carelessly pushed back so that it could rest on a dark sideboard beside Barbara's very serious briefcase.

'Do you think we could have the music off for a moment or two?' I asked.

Barbara crossed the room and turned down the volume, but not by much. 'Favourite track,' she shrugged

I shrugged back. At least I could hear myself think now.

'Come over here,' I said, holding out my hand.

She hesitated for moment, but then came.

I held her shoulders in my hands as though I meant to kiss her. But instead I turned her around so that she was standing at an angle to the window, which looked out over the grounds in all their summer splendour.

'Look over there, past that big Silver Birch. Just to the left there? That's where I picked your flowers.'

I felt the muscles in her shoulders stiffen.

Abruptly, and none to gently, I shifted her across to the other side of the window, and swung her to the opposite angle, so that she could now see the other half of the garden.

'When I was collecting the flowers, I found *that* as well.'

Planted in the centre of the lawn was the sign I had discovered thrown in the undergrowth about ten minutes ago and hurriedly stuck in the ground for just this moment. It was a sign from a local estate and letting agency, which advertised a *Luxury House to Let*.

'It was stuffed against the wall, back in the nettles,' I told her. 'Care to explain?'

She shrugged in an attempt at nonchalance, but the tension in her shoulders gave her away.

'Well, I *did* rent out the house for a while,' she said, carefully easing herself out of my grip and turning away. 'After it had been reconstructed... after the fire... I didn't know whether I could live here again. What with all the memories of my parents and the way they died, you know? Eventually, I decided that I could, that the good memories outweighed the bad.'

I turned her around to face me again, and saw the unshed tears pooling in her lovely blue eyes, and on the spur of the moment, I decided that it was time to stop acting. She was much better at it than I was. I was better at the truth.

'Come on,' I said. 'Let it go. I know everything.'

'What do you mean?'

'This house isn't yours at all. The real owners have retired and now live abroad. In Italy, coincidentally, where your business conference is. Or isn't, as the case may be.'

She shook her head in puzzlement. 'Joel, I don't know what you're—'

'Oh, of course you know what I'm talking about, Barbara — if Barbara's your real name, that is. Frankly, I'm assuming it's not. The real owners originally wanted to sell the property, but at the time there was a slump in the housing market, and they decided to rent it out instead, through the agency I spoke to less than an hour ago.'

Again she tried to interject, and again I forestalled her.

'Two weeks ago, you rented this house for one calendar month, paying in cash. But you went back to collect your deposit this very morning.'

'There must have been some mistake, some mix up at the agency. Maybe it's another house they were—'

'No, it's *this* house. No mistake. I spoke to the agent who handles it, on the pretext of renting the place myself. It's a relatively new build — on the site of a much older house, that's true — but there never was a fire here.'

She tried to pull away, but I held on to her. Her teary eyes now looked a good deal more convincing.

'Please, let me go,' she said. 'I need a tissue.'

I let her go, and watched her walk over to the sideboard, where she carefully laid down the flowers and begin to root around in her briefcase. I slowly moved until I was between her and the door to the hallway, blocking her exit.

'There's no need to pretend anymore,' I told her. 'I know that everything you've ever told me was a pack of lies. There is no conference, there's no flight to Italy, and no hotel in Rome. I know you didn't grow up around here — the day I first met you, you didn't even know the name of the Howard Centre. How dumb was I not to pick up on that?'

Not deigning to answer, Barbara delicately turned her back on me to blow her nose.

'Mind you,' I said, 'I've been a lot dumber than that, just recently. What about that wonderful romantic date of ours? I was so busy looking at the rest of you, I failed to notice that the grazes on your knees had completely vanished in a couple of hours. That was a great piece of selective perception by the Little Bald Colonel, wasn't it?'

'By *who*?' Barbara sniffed, sounding distinctly puzzled. 'The Little Bald—?'

'Never mind!' I snapped. I really hadn't meant to let that dreadful penis euphemism slip out — damn you, Charlie Noble.

I began to move towards her.

'The point is, I'm on to you, sweetheart. I know that when your 'colleague' — the person you were expecting to see when you opened the door — comes to pick you up, he will be driving a black Rover with tinted windows, and he'll have a face like a dog's bum with a hat on. And I know that you set me up, not just once, not even twice, but *three* times.'

I could feel myself growing angrier. I realised that I wanted to grab her and shake her to pieces, and I put my hands behind my back so that I wouldn't be tempted.

'I went to meet Lisa in secret, and as if by magic the Goblin turned up. Then I went shopping with Vic, and the Goblin just happened to be on hand again to snatch her. *You* were the only person who knew where I was going to be at those times.'

She sniffled something, shook her head. I took a step closer.

'The other time that you set me up — the very *first* time — was when you lured me to a derelict house in south London. It was a good few years ago now, granted, but you should still remember the occasion. You told me I was a silly boy, and then you tried to smash my head in with a baseball bat. You called me the same thing on the phone just the other night. Remember now?'

I moved even closer, well within throttling range.

'I know the scumbag you work for, lady. Now, you tell me where my daughter is, or there's going to be trouble.'

Still with her back to me, she mumbled something that I couldn't hear for the music. I reached past her and snapped it off.

'Tell me where she is, right now, or I won't be responsible for my actions.'

And then, in the middle of the silence that followed my threat, I heard other sounds coming from upstairs, sounds that the music had masked — sounds that I now realised the music had been *meant* to mask. Little fists banging against a locked door, and a little frightened voice calling out. *Crying* out.

'Daddeee!'

It was Vic! Vic was here!

Rage took me instantly, like being plunged into a red ocean. I spun Barbara around. I don't know what I would have done — it was in my Martian mind to strangle her — but I was saved from having to make a decision.

Barbara had something in her hands besides a tissue.

It was a black oblong object, slightly larger than a mobile phone, with a couple of silver prongs at one end. Barbara's eyes were completely dry, despite all the snivelling, and her face looked maliciously triumphant. She reached out and pressed the silver prongs against my throat before I could stop her, and I only realised what this device was in the second that she pressed the button.

The electric charge hit me hard, and for a moment I felt that someone had thrust an arm all the way down my throat and then pulled me inside out.

In what felt like super slow-motion, I collapsed to the floor, and in the second before consciousness left me, I had time for one brief thought:

The cowbag had tazered me!

Seventeen

'*SHE TAZERED ME...*'

Just before my eyes fluttered open again, I actually heard myself speak my final thought, like an echo from the great beyond. When the world came back into focus, the room around me, the walls, ceiling, the furniture, all seemed gigantic, tilted to extreme angles like something out of one of those old German silent horror movies that make you feel seasick.

As a matter of fact, I *did* feel nauseous, and there was an immense throbbing pain engulfing my right eye, as though I might have hit my head as I collapsed. There again, a small part of my nausea may have had something to do with the rather rank smell of the wildflower bouquet Barbara must have scattered over me while I was out cold. I couldn't see what had happened to the nettle — maybe she had kept it to remember me by.

All in all, I felt pretty bad, but I rolled over anyway, trying to get up as quickly as possible. From the little I knew about tazers — which, admittedly, wasn't that much — depending on the strength of the charge Barbara had hit me with, I might have only been out of it for as little as a few seconds. If I was quick, I might even have a chance to catch her before she could get Vic out of the house.

I had a horrible moment at first when my legs simply refused to act on the commands my brain was sending them, as though all the lines of communication were still down. But finally, I was able to stand, leaning back heavily against the sideboard and knocking over a few of the china ornaments. Barbara's CD player and briefcase were both gone.

'Vic!' I shouted. My voice rolled back at me as if from a deep cave. There was no reply.

I shook my head to clear it still further. By now the world was losing its expressionistic slant, and I was able to take more in. I could now see that the light in the room was subtly different, which made me suspect that I'd been unconscious for a lot more than the few seconds I'd hoped for.

I glanced at my watch and received instant confirmation. It was a few minutes before four now. As I'd walked up the drive with my hastily gathered bouquet, it had been a few minutes after three-thirty. I totted up how long our conversation had taken and calculated that it had been more than ten minutes since Barbara had turned the juice on me.

That was too much time. Barbara had to be long gone, and Vic with her.

Nevertheless, I hobbled across the room and out into the hallway. Barbara's suitcases and coat had gone, too. I called Vic's name a few more times, but there was really no need. The house was empty, devoid of life, I could feel that clearly. No one was home. I searched the entire ground floor of the house only to have my first impression confirmed.

When I returned to the hallway once more, I caught sight of my face in a mirror on the wall by the front door. I had a world-class black eye forming, which was now beginning to swell and colour up nicely. The epicentre of it was a half-inch wide black spot just below my eye. I could think of nothing in the sitting room I might have fallen against that could have given me such an injury.

Then I remembered checking out Barbara's casual clothes and noticing those armour-plated, high-heeled boots, and I knew exactly what had happened. After she'd zapped me, my 'girlfriend' had viciously stamped on my face and almost blinded me.

Turning away from the mirror, I looked up the stairs.

I really didn't want to go up there, but I knew that I'd have to. Just to make sure. I had to be sure that the phrase 'devoid of life' was relevant only to the house, and not to my little daughter's body.

It was an appalling thought, and yet I had to think it. I knew exactly what sort of people I was up against now, and I knew just how high the stakes were. The sickly, heavy scent of the lemon detergent was all around me, and in my mind's eye, I saw Barbara working her way steadily around this large house, carefully washing all the surfaces she had touched or thought she might have touched clean of all her own fingerprints. Then she could disappear, and might never be traced.

I went upstairs.

No, I kept telling myself over and over, they wouldn't have done it. If for no other reason that Vic was their lever on me, and they needed my cooperation to get to Lisa.

But still, every door I opened was like opening a door on to a nightmare. Every empty, lemon-scented room I searched and dismissed seemed like a blessing. I went through every room, every bedroom, bathroom, closet and wardrobe on each of the two upper floors, and found no indication that my daughter had ever been there.

Finally, there was only one room left.

It was a small attic room right at the top of the house, and my heart was beating wildly with every step I took closer to its small door. It took just a few moments for me to realise why my heart was beating this way. It was because I could *smell* Vic, I could smell her own particular, individual scent. This was the room where they had kept her.

I closed my eyes.

Now, I'm not a praying man, I never have been. As it says in the Bible, you better help your bloody self, because no other bugger will. But as I reached out to the door handle, I found myself saying a prayer. I didn't feel like a hypocrite, either. I felt like an honest sinner. I said a prayer to the God Who's supposed to care if even a bloody sparrow falls, let alone a little innocent child.

And I hoped that for once the deaf old Sod was listening.

I swung the door open and the sense of Vic's presence doubled, trebled, quadrupled. My imagination ran riot, and for one brief moment, I really saw her there, a tiny featureless bump under the duvet, unmoving, lifeless... but thankfully imagination was all it was. Vic wasn't there.

But something was.

I walked over to the bed on legs made wooden by fear. Vic's fairy wings were propped up against the pillow. One of them had a tiny rip in it, shaped like a teardrop. I picked them up, my hands trembling and making them flutter, and held them against my face for a moment, inhaling, thinking crazy thoughts. Somebody had pulled my daughter's wings off. How would she ever fly again?

Underneath the wings was a brown Jiffy bag, with the words READ ME printed on it in block capitals. Inside the Jiffy bag was an ugly, anonymous-looking black mobile phone and a short note, written in the same difficult-to-analyse block capitals. It told me to go home and keep the ugly phone with me at all times. They would be in touch.

They. I was really beginning to hate *They*.

I FOLLOWED THE note's instructions, and soon found myself sitting at my kitchen table once more. This time, instead of sitting across from Scott Vaughan, I found myself opposite Albert the Cat. It used to be I was afraid that one day he might answer me back when I was telling him about my troubles, but now I sort of wished that this day was that day. He might be able to tell me what to do.

Just before sitting down, I had been to the loo, and belatedly discovered what had happened to the nettle from the wildflower bouquet — Barbara had tucked it inside my fly zipper, and I had no idea how the Little Bald Colonel had avoided getting stung.

The note Barbara had left me said nothing about taking a shot of whisky to steady my rapidly fraying nerves, but that was exactly what I did. The bottle was about half-full (or half-empty, I suppose, considering my current frame of mind), and I doubted that I'd be really drunk even if I emptied the lot. My level of shock and despair was so deep, I thought nothing could touch me.

I was wrong.

On the table between me and Albert were three phones. One was my mobile phone, one was the house phone, and the third was the ugly black phone Barbara had left for me in the Jiffy bag. One of the three now began to ring, and for the life of me I couldn't tell which one. But then I looked at Albert, who was staring fixedly at the phone in the centre. My mobile. I picked it up.

'Hello, Joel?'

It was Maude. As always when she called me on the mobile, she shouted her conversation, as though we were speaking over some antiquated hand-cranked ship-to-shore lash-up during a north Atlantic gale. She wanted to know how our day was going, so I made up a day for her.

After visiting *KrazyKidz*, Vic and I had decided that it was such a lovely day, we'd go to the park at Stanborough. Vic had frolicked in the play area, then we had paddled in the river, and eaten ice creams while our feet dried off in the sun.

Maude liked our day almost as much as I did. Could she speak to Vic?

'You won't get a word out of her at the moment,' I told her. 'She's just turned on this new learning toy computer thingamajig, and now she's completely engrossed.'

In fact, the damn thing was still in its box in the carrier bag on the work surface by the fridge. I could see it from where I sat. The pessimistic side of me wondered if my daughter would ever get the chance to play with it.

Maude had another bright idea. They'd just come back from the supermarket with lots of two-for-one deals — if Vic and I wanted to come on over, she'd get Henry to fire up the barbecue.

'Great idea, but another day if you don't mind.'

I could feel Maude's disappointment, but I told her I'd promised to take Vic out for a meal. I didn't know exactly where yet, but that didn't matter. This was our special day together.

Eventually, Maude got the message. She told me to get some rest later, because I sounded tired. What was happening tomorrow? Again, I told her I wasn't sure. Once again, she sensed something off-kilter. She was sure it was none of her business, but was I positive that everything was all right?

'Right as rain,' I assured her.

Then, just as she was about to ring off, however reluctantly, she recalled something else. She had bumped into Elaine Leigh at the supermarket, who had asked after Vic's health because I hadn't bothered to inform her that my daughter would be absent from the playgroup today.

'She also mentioned something about your *brother*, Joel — you don't have a brother, do you?'

I hastily explained that on Vic's first day there had been some kind of mix-up with another child's relatives, and then got off the phone as quickly as possible. At her worst, Maude was something like a human lie detector, and I could feel her cruising around my fibs like a rogue shark circling a group of stranded skin-divers.

The QUEEN of HEARTS

AN HOUR LATER another of the phones rang. Albert had stalked off ages ago, bored with my company (and I didn't blame him), but this time I didn't need his sharp ears to help me out. There was no mistaking which of the phones was ringing.

The black mobile Barbara had left me made a sound I'd never heard before, a harsh metallic chirruping sound, as though it were a robotic insect. It even *felt* like an insect when I picked it up, unpleasant to the touch and dangerous, as though I were holding an enormous scorpion. I pressed the receive button and put the phone to my ear.

'Hello, Nick,' I said.

'Hello, Joel,' Temple affably replied.

His voice took me all the way back. Back to that dark, damp cellar, when he'd asked me what I wanted carved on my headstone. Back to the afternoon when I walked out of the *in-camera* inquiry, which had condemned me and exonerated him. I remembered the way he'd sidled up to me, smirking, whispering with faux sorrow and barely subdued glee: 'We're very disappointed in you, Joel. We're all very, very disappointed...'

Temple laughed at my silence.

'Take a few deep breaths,' he advised. 'It can be difficult talking to old friends after such a long time, can't it?'

I cleared my throat, and said, 'We were never friends.'

'No, I suppose not. What would you call us, then? Colleagues? Contemporaries? Acquaintances?'

'Nothing. We were nothing.'

'If you say so,' he laughed again, more briefly. 'All right, Joel, let's cut to the chase, shall we? And don't worry, we can speak quite freely now.'

'What do you mean?'

'Come along, my friend, I know the boys have been sniffing around you — young Vaughan and his swarm of eager bluebottles, pursuing their doomed investigation.'

'How do you know that?'

'Oh, I keep my ear to the ground, and I know lots about everything. For example, I know they finally got the warrant to tap your home phone a couple of days ago. I also know at some point they'll try to recruit your unlimited cooperation in their righteous quest to bring me to justice, and in return they'll offer you some kind of deal they'll never be able to live up to. Actually, what time is it now — yes, they've probably already made that offer, haven't they?'

I quickly weighed up my options, and found them not so much slim as anorexic. What was the point of lying?

'Vaughan was here earlier,' I said to Temple, 'and I told him I'll think about it. But that isn't what I meant. I meant, how do you know the investigation is doomed?'

'The same way I know everything else. I still have lots of friends in the Service, Joel. Lots of good, loyal friends.'

I thought of grey-haired James Gill, the former Jimmy Fish, the Eel, who Scott Vaughan believed was his secret weapon — but was it the other way around?

'I guess you must.'

'Now, with regards to our privacy, in the light of your tapped landline... In amongst all my other business interests, I also happen to own the controlling share in a major security firm with its own research and development department. The phone you're using at this moment is completely scrambled using the very latest technology, totally state-of-the-art. It can't be surveilled remotely in any way, neither recorded from nor listened into. So while we're having our little tête-à-têtes today, you — and more importantly, *I* — can be sure they're completely private. We are free to speak plainly.'

'Okay,' I said, 'then let's see if this is plain enough for you: if anything happens to my daughter, you are a dead man.'

I basically told him what I'd told Feelen earlier in the day, when I'd been about a thousand years younger. That I'd track him to the ends of the earth, hunt him down, and slaughter him.

'Yes, I believe you would,' Temple said, although he didn't sound too worried about the prospect. 'Well, at least I believe you'd *try*. That's why it's in both our interests to make sure this deal goes through without any hitches.'

'And what is this deal you have in mind?'

Temple paused, presumably to ponder, but I believed that he was really trying to tease me. When he spoke again, his voice had gained a bogus reflective quality, and I knew I was right.

'You know, I remember the first time I ever saw Lisa. This was many years ago now, quite a while before our little professional disagreement. I was with some business associates in a fashionable nightspot late one evening, probably when you were slaving away on the nightshift, and there she was, out on the dancefloor with a couple of friends, boogying her hypnotic little arse off. Needless to say, she looked absolutely ravishing. The dress she was wearing, a skin-tight little black cocktail thing, looked like it had oozed out of her pores.'

I remembered that dress, and against my will I found the idea of Temple ogling Lisa wearing it absolutely infuriating.

'I had absolutely no idea who she was at the time, of course, but I was all set to go over, introduce myself, and buy her a drink — *lots* of drinks, if she'd let me. I was definitely smitten. But then one of the people I was with recognised her and told me who she was married to. And that shocked me, knocked me back on my heels. Do you know why?'

I said nothing. I didn't trust myself to speak.

'It was because I knew what she *was*. Even at a single glance, I knew *exactly* what she was, because I can read people. It was the same with you, Joel. You had a bit of a reputation as an ice-man, but I knew better. I knew you were one of those men — light the blue touch-paper and stand well back, because you'd be all too ready to blow yourself up. And I was proved right, wasn't I?'

I didn't reply, although I wanted to tell him that the touch-paper wasn't blue, it was red.

'I read Lisa just as easily. I could see she was about as bent as a three-quid note. And I knew that she wasn't married to anyone or anything, not really. Oh, on paper, maybe — but in her *mind*, no way. She was up for anything.'

He waited for me to respond, but when I didn't, he went on, raising his game at the same time.

'You know, Joel, before I took your wife to bed for the first time, I already knew she was going to be hot stuff. Although, now that I think of it, it wasn't a *bed*, it was more of an office desk... but that's by the by. The point is, I had no idea just how hot she really was. There was literally *nothing* that woman wouldn't do in the sack, and I simply wasn't prepared for all that passion, all that wildness, that total lustful abandon—'

'Have you had enough fun yet?' I snapped.

He laughed again, louder and harder. 'I suppose so.'

'What's the deal you're offering?'

'Well, of course you understand that in the best of all possible worlds, I'd want Lisa dead? I don't suppose I could offer you a financial incentive to help me out that way? Or at least to physically hand her over to me? No, I didn't think so. But, as you are well aware, there are certain items belonging to me that she is currently holding in storage.'

'The evidence, you mean.'

'The property,' Temple emphasised. '*My* property. Which, naturally, I would like returned. And that's the deal. Quite simply, I want it back. All of it. Every flash-drive and photocopy, every single document, bond certificate, order, receipt, fax, notebook, and ledger. All of it, without omission. In return, I will allow Lisa to live.'

'And I get Vic back.'

'And you get your charming daughter back, all safe and sound.'

Which was precisely what I wanted. And which sounded just about what Lisa had indicated she was after during our brief meeting at Brent Cross. But that still left one major problem.

'Listen, that's all fine,' I said. 'I'm sure Lisa would accept those conditions—'

'She'd *better.*'

'But when I told your boy Feelen that I didn't know how to reach Lisa, I wasn't bluffing, it was the truth. Much as I might want to, I can't contact her unless she calls me.'

'I believe you, Joel. But I think she *will* call, and soon. Believe me, Lisa is far from stupid. She'll know it's in her best interests not to make me too mad for too long.'

'But even if she *does* call, if Vaughan is listening in, won't that—'

'Joel, put your brain in gear, for Christ's sake. Just get her to call on *this* phone, and it won't matter. Do you have a pen?'

I leaned back on my chair and snatched one from the jar by the breadbin. He reeled off the number of the phone he'd given me, which I furiously jotted down on a piece of cardboard torn from a cornflakes box.

'It doesn't matter if young Vaughan overhears you telling Lisa this number, it won't help him listen in to further calls, or triangulate your location from the signal. Even if he calls the number himself, he won't be able to do anything but talk to you.'

I thought of how angry Scott would be if he thought I was screwing him around, working with the enemy behind his back, ruining his investigation. That wouldn't be a good conversation.

'How would I explain it to him?' I asked.

'I really don't care, as long as it isn't the truth. That's your problem, not mine. And if you were to make any mistakes… well, there'd be a very unhappy little girl who wouldn't be seeing her daddy ever again.'

I felt my fingers tighten on the phone. 'Is that it?'

'So eager to be rid of me, Joel?'

'Believe it or not, you're not exactly my favourite person in the world.'

Temple chuckled. 'I imagine not. But before I let you go, there are a couple of other non-negotiable conditions attached to this trade.'

Here it comes, I thought.

'The first is that after our business is concluded, Lisa must leave the country immediately, and never return. *Never*. If she does ever come back and I get to learn of it — and believe me I will — then all bets are off. I'll take out a contract on her, there and then.'

'I don't know if—'

'Out of sight is out of mind, Joel. Tell her that. She'll know it's for the best.'

'All right. What else?'

'Well, the *money*, of course,' Temple said, sounding surprised. 'I want the money back.'

Money, I thought. What money?

I suppose my long silence told Temple everything he needed to know.

'Oh *dear*,' he said. 'Lisa didn't tell Joel about the money, did she?'

'No.'

'I should have guessed. This is the last batch of cash I had entrusted her with to invest for me, and which she still had in her possession when the bank booted her out.'

'How much are we talking about?'

'A million, and change.'

'Oh *shit*.'

'Precisely speaking, it was one million, two hundred and thirty-seven thousand pounds sterling.'

So now I knew how Lisa had managed to survive so long without recourse to her credit cards — she had a petty cash fund Bill Gates would have been proud of.

Temple cleared his throat.

'Do yourself a big favour, Joel. Be smart for once in your pathetic, mediocre little life. Meet Lisa to collect the files, but don't even think of mentioning the word *money* — not until you're close enough to grab her by the throat.'

'I want to speak to my daughter now.'

'Okay,' Temple replied. 'Stand by.'

Then he hung up.

Eighteen

STAND BY, TEMPLE had said. *Stand by.*

As if I would ever need any more proof that the man was a sadist, this was it. *Stand by*, which anyone normal would take to mean, 'Hang on, fella, be with you in a minute or two.'

But the evil bastard kept me waiting for more than half-an-hour.

During this time, which felt more like a bloody lifetime than a piddling half-hour, all I could do was sit at the kitchen table and stare at Temple's ugly black phone, willing it to call out to me in its abrasive, insectile buzz. At one point, Albert sauntered back into the kitchen, polished off the food in his bowl, looked at me reproachfully for not immediately offering him a refill, and then sauntered out again, muttering under his fishy breath. Shortly after, I heard him sharpening his claws on the living room sofa in revenge for my inattention.

When the phone eventually rang, I snatched it up from the table so quickly I almost dropped it.

'Vic?'

'She'll be here any second,' Feelen said.

'Where is she? Is she okay?'

'Don't worry, she's safe in the other room.'

'Let me speak to her.'

'Soon.'

'No, not soon!' I shouted. 'Now! Right now!'

'Not like this,' Feelen said. 'Listen, September, you need to calm down before you speak to her. It's taken me ages to get her settled down. If you start her off again, it'll take even longer. She doesn't need any more upset today.'

'I'm not the one who upset her in the first place, am I?' I growled.

'Look, you either promise to behave or I won't let you speak to her at all.'

Tough choice.

'What have you told her?' I asked. 'How have you explained why she's staying with you?'

'I said that you had some work to do away from home, and you asked me to look after her till you got back.'

'And she accepted that?'

'Eventually.'

'Okay, put her on.' I listened to the unchanging silence on the other end of the line, and I sighed. 'All right, I promise not to upset her.'

I heard Feelen's footsteps as he began to walk the phone through from one room to another, first as sharp tappings that sounded like someone rapping on a hard-wooden door, and then as softer, almost muffled thuds. Moving from a hard surface, tiles or laminate, to a carpeted one — kitchen to living room? Had they just transferred her from one rented property to another? Might they have used the same letting agency? No, they wouldn't be that foolish.

The next sounds I heard were explosions, and hurtling runaway trains, and smashing crockery, and howls of pain. The familiar soundscape of the animated world coming from a living room TV. Under this cacophony, I heard Feelen mutter something, his brutish voice sounding surprisingly gentle, and then...

'Daddee? Daddeeee!'

'Vic, sweetheart!'

The relief swept through me like a drug, made me feel light-headed and knock-kneed.

'Hello Daddee, I'm watching TV.'

'Are you?'

'Yes. Their TV's gooder than our TV. It's big with lots of toons. I'm watching Tom Jerry and Roadrun and Bug Buns and—'

'That's great, darling. How are you doing, are you well?'

'I'm OK.'

'Yeah?'

'I was scared first,' she said, and then added in what I had come to think of as her telling-off voice, 'why didn't you tell me you gone way?'

'I'm sorry, darling, I forgot.'

'That's what Greggy said. He said you're a silly Daddee.'

'Greggy?'

'He don't like the Goblin name,' she whispered. Then she giggled. 'Greggy's so funny.'

'Is he?'

'Yes. He's my friend.'

I closed my eyes at this, this betrayal of childish trust. It was all but unbearable. I saw the red rolling tide of the Martian ocean rising, rising, and in the far distance the setting sun bleeding into it...

'Oh, OK,' I heard Vic say to someone else. Then, 'Bye Daddee!'

I opened my eyes. 'Vic? Vic, wait!'

'That's enough for now,' Feelen said.

I heard him reverse his short journey, his footsteps becoming audible once more as the sound of the TV diminished and then faded altogether, taking a sense of Vic's presence with it. It was like seeing her face through the rear window of a stranger's car as it sped away into the darkness. Her beautiful face becoming indistinct, then vanishing, then gone forever. It was like having my heart torn out.

'See?' Feelen asked. 'She's okay.'

Yes, she'd *sounded* okay, and she *said* she was okay, but that didn't mean she really was. I'd hoped that talking to my daughter would reassure me of her safety, but in fact it had only made me more fearful. Probably that was the point Temple had wanted to make by allowing the conversation to happen at all.

'Why does it have to be you?' I asked Feelen suddenly. 'She's a little girl, for God's sake. It's totally inappropriate. If it had to happen at all, why couldn't Barbara have looked after her?'

'Barbara? Oh, you mean Angie…' He managed to stop his mouth churning, but too late. Now he'd given me a name. 'Oh shit, you didn't hear that from me, okay?'

Angie? I filed this information for later use.

'Whatever her real name is, I want her looking after my daughter, not you.'

'No, you really don't,' Feelen said, and then dropped his voice. 'She's horrible, a total bitch.'

'Now there's a word you seem to like,' I snapped before I could stop myself. 'You carved it into Lisa's dining table and sprayed it all over her bedroom walls, just before you took a shit on her bed!'

'Hey!' Feelen yelped in protest.

I had lots more to say, but I forced myself to stop. This animal had Vic as his captive and I couldn't afford to make him angry at me, not when it was Vic who would pay for it.

"Hey!" Feelen said again, sounding not so much angry as offended. Very highly offended. 'What're you talking about? That weren't me did that filthy thing!'

'Then who did it — the Shit Fairy?'

'It was Angie.'

Which sort of knocked the wind out of my sails.

'What?'

I tried to reconcile the two things in my mind, the soiled and scarred wreckage of a once-smart apartment and the classy, sophisticated woman I'd taken out to dinner the other night. The two simply didn't seem to match up. I tried to see Barbara — or Angie as it appeared she was really called — climbing up on to Lisa's bed in her elegant high-heels, dropping her knickers and squatting to do her business. I just couldn't do it.

'I don't understand,' I said feebly. 'Why would she do that?'

'Jealousy,' Feelen immediately replied.

'Jealousy? Jealous of what — because Lisa had stolen you from her, or because she'd stolen Temple?'

'Jealous of just about anyone who got too close to Lisa — because Lisa had dumped her.'

'Dumped her? Are you saying that Lisa and *Barbara*...?'

I was quite numb now. This was one sexual entanglement I certainly hadn't seen coming. I remembered asking Andrew Lipton if there was anybody in this game my wife *hadn't* slept with, but it wasn't meant to be a literal question.

'Listen to me, September,' Feelen said in a much lower voice. 'That nice woman you met called Barbara Rawlings? That wasn't a real person. And Angie? She's not a real person either. If you knew what she really was, you wouldn't want her anywhere near your little girl. She's pure evil.'

While I was still pondering this provocative, troubling statement, Feelen said that he had to go.

'When are you going to call again?'

'When I'm told to.'

I swallowed a lump in my throat. 'Feelen, you'll look after her for me, won't you?'

'I'll try,' he whispered. 'But you better get hold of Lisa, pretty damn quick. Otherwise, I don't know what they'll do to her…'

AFTER FEELEN ENDED the call, I went to the kitchen sink and put my head under the cold tap, desperately trying to cool down before I fainted through fear or anger. I could sense that Feelen's heart wasn't in it anymore, which was good, but that last sentence of his had absolutely terrified me. If what he'd told me was the truth, the Goblin, for all his menace, wasn't the one I had to worry about.

The optimistic side of my mind kept insisting that everything was sure to work out fine in the end — that it simply *had* to work out fine — because my daughter and I were the good guys in this cosy little mystery, we were the heroes of the piece. But at the same time, the dark side of my mind was busy reminding me this was

The QUEEN of HEARTS

no story, and that in the real world things seldom turned out that way.

As it says somewhere in the Bible, bad things *do* happen to good people. As a matter of fact, they happen so often it's a wonder anyone ever bothers to be good.

This negative side of my mind kept showing me things I didn't want to see. It showed me this Angie creature deciding that I needed a little more of an incentive to find Lisa, and calling me on the scrambled phone to make me listen to her applying her tazer to my daughter's arm.

I turned off the tap and used the tea towel to roughly dry my neck, face and hair. I looked at myself in the small mirror on the windowsill above the sink and saw the face of a terrified man.

'How did it come to this?' I asked my reflection, but my reflection didn't know.

My skin was ghastly pale and the bruise below my right eye had contracted and darkened almost to a black dot. I realised it reminded me of something. Or rather, of *someone*. But who?

Then I got it. Andrew Lipton.

I now understood exactly how he had come by those strange, spot-like bruises on his face. They weren't the result of being stabbed with an umbrella, as I had speculated. They had been caused by Angie's stiletto heels, just like mine.

With the benefit of hindsight, and Feelen's confidences, I could see it happening. All those framed pictures on Lipton's walls, all of them smashed directly over the image of Lisa's face, the lover who had jilted her. I could even imagine Angie standing over a helpless Lipton, repeatedly stamping on his face, trying to torture Lisa's whereabouts out of him.

But Lipton hadn't cracked. Was that because his love for Lisa had kept him strong, or because he really hadn't known? And what about now? Did he know *now*?

I went back to the table and then hesitated. If I tried to call him on either the landline or my mobile there was every likelihood that our conversation would be listened into by the police. That was no good. Then I looked at Temple's scrambled phone, which could not be surveilled in any way. Was it able to make calls as well as receive them?

I picked it up, pressed a button, and immediately got a dialling tone.

Yes!

I pulled out my wallet, shuffled through the latest layer of strata (call it the Horrific Period), retrieved the scrap of paper with Lipton's home number on it, and then dialled it. The phone at his basement flat rang and rang without answer and eventually I hung up. A few seconds later, I dialled again. This time his answering machine cut in after just three rings. I hung up without leaving a message, and then grabbed my jacket and my car keys.

Activating the answering machine had been a mistake. It meant that someone had to be there to switch it on.

The QUEEN of HEARTS

IT WAS BEGINNING to get dark by the time I arrived at Lipton's address, but down in the shadowy recesses of the basement flat, night had already arrived. As I slowly descended the steps to the front door, I saw that the thin curtains were closed, but behind them all the lights were on.

I approached the door but did not knock. I waited and watched Lipton's shadow occasionally flit across the curtains, and listened to the sounds he was making. The thud of his crutches, other bangs, rattles, rustling. Even a low murmuring that might have been him talking or singing to himself under his breath.

When I eventually knocked on the door, everything stopped immediately. There were no more sounds, and a couple of seconds later all the lights went off, as though he had pulled a master fuse. Despite everything that was happening, I almost laughed.

I gently knocked again and then bent down to speak through the letterbox.

'Come on, Andrew, I know you're there. It's Joel September. I hate to be the one to tell you, but you're really rubbish at hiding. You can't switch on the answering machine after your phone's already rung once — it's a bit of a giveaway. Also, you can't switch off the lights after someone's already knocked at your door.'

I heard him approaching, the clatter of his crutches. A second later a key turned, a chain was withdrawn, and the door opened. 'Come in if you're coming in,' he said without even glancing at me.

I stepped past him as he relocked the door. It was curiously similar to our first meeting a couple of weeks ago in Lisa's apartment. He lurched past me and ducked into a hall cupboard. I was right, he had pulled the fuse.

One quick snap and all the lights came back on, and I was able to see what he had been so busily doing before I arrived. He was packing.

Two tea-chests stood against the wall, a pile of old newspapers beside them. He was using the yellowing newspapers to wrap up his vast collection of framed photographs. Still refusing to look at me, he went back to this task, plucking another picture from the wall, the sticky pad on the reverse of the small frame ripping away the surface of the painted lining paper beneath.

'I don't know what you want,' he said, 'but I hope it won't take long. I'm busy, in case you haven't noticed.'

The wrapping was difficult for him, but he was becoming increasingly adroit with the crutches.

'You're moving out?'

'Yes. I can't stay here anymore. Not after the what happened. I keep having panic-attacks. I can't relax or sleep. I'm going to sell up and move on.'

I could understand that.

'Where will you go?'

'Back to my parents' home for the time being, most likely,' he said.

'What about those?' I asked, indicating the boxed photographs. 'What will your parents think of them?'

'My parents will never see them. They'll go into storage along with the furniture, until I decide what I'm going to do, where I'm going to live.'

'You should burn them all,' I told him.

'Yes, I know.'

'You're not going to, are you?'

'No.'

'Andrew, look at me.'

'What?'

'Look at me.'

He wedged the latest wrapped photograph in the tea-chest with an exasperated sigh, and then reluctantly turned to face me.

'What?'

Then he finally saw my face, saw the bruise below my right eye, so similar to those on his own face.

'Why didn't you tell me the truth?' I asked.

He looked down at the floor, then back at my face, and then away again.

'I was embarrassed,' he admitted. 'Being beaten up by an ex-boxer doesn't sound so bad. Being beaten up by a woman sounds completely pants.' He was already close to tears. 'And against all the odds, I found myself liking you. I didn't want to appear weak.'

'You know, you could have saved me a lot of heartache and aggravation if you'd told me about Angie up front. She came after me too, you know, but she came dangling the carrot instead of wielding the stick.'

He glanced at me again, as if wondering where she'd stuck the carrot.

I nodded. 'She only did this to me after I'd found out the truth — electrocuted me and then stamped on me when I was unconscious and helpless. Andrew, I need your help.'

'I can't help,' he said quickly. He stumped through the doorway into the living room before I could speak again. I followed him through.

There were more boxes in here, all of them full. The living room's walls had already been stripped of photographs, and were now covered by an all-over rash of tiny rips where the sticky pads had snagged the wallpaper. It looked like the bedroom of a teenage girl who had abruptly outgrown all her boy-band posters.

Or maybe he hadn't outgrown them, I suddenly thought. Maybe he'd *upgraded*.

After all, who needed photographs of their heart's desire if they had instant access to the real thing? All the newspapers he was using as packing material were old and yellowing, just like the ones Lisa had filling her prop shopping bags at Brent Cross.

'Andrew, I need you to talk to Lisa and get her to call me as soon as possible. It's a matter of life or death.'

He looked at me.

'Not my life or death, or Lisa's,' I said. 'Our *daughter's* life or death.'

'What do you mean?'

'They've kidnapped my daughter, Andrew. They've kidnapped Vic, and if I don't get them what they want…'

I was unable to finish, but Lipton got the point. He stared at me in absolute horror. But he was still shaking his head. 'I'm sorry, I don't know where she is. Really.'

I plucked my wallet out of my pocket, and gave him the strip of cornflake pack with the number for Temple's scrambled scorpion phone written on it.

'What's this?'

'If Lisa should contact you, give her this number. It's the number of a mobile phone that is totally unbuggable. It's a completely secure line, and it'll be safe for us to speak openly. Tell her I've made the deal. Tell her it's exactly what she wanted.'

Lipton caught himself nodding and made himself stop.

'What happens if she doesn't call,' he asked in a hollow voice.

'I don't want to think about that. The woman who did that to your face and put you on crutches, set loose on a defenceless little girl? I *can't* think about that. I think I'd go mad.'

I stared at him, willing him to say that he was mistaken, that he *did* know where Lisa was, after all, but it didn't work.

I turned around and walked away. I unlocked the door and let myself out. I was halfway up the steps when I heard Lipton's voice.

'I'll try,' he said. 'I'll try.'

Just that, and no more. But it was enough.

Nineteen

Driving home, I suddenly realised that I was famished. The last time I had eaten was breakfast, and then it had been no more than a slice of buttered toast. On top of that, I'd had a tot of whisky, and although it'd had little effect on my sobriety, both it and the day had taken a lot of my energy, leaching it out of me like lifeblood.

I was beginning to feel weak, and I couldn't afford to be. I needed to take on-board a little fuel. As soon as I came off the A1, I stopped at a Chinese takeaway and took a couple of dishes home with me.

Back home, I took the cartons straight into the kitchen and began to dish it up. Albert came in through the catflap like a little furry bullet with his nostrils flaring. The aroma was making my mouth water, too. It was only after I located a bottle of Soy sauce in the cupboard and snatched a couple of forks from the cutlery drawer that I realised what I'd done.

Not only had I bought the two dishes that Vic liked best whenever we had this occasional treat, I had also served them up on two plates, one of them Vic's *Toy Story* plate. But Vic wasn't here to enjoy it with me, was she?

Once I'd realised this, my appetite vanished completely, and after separating out a bowlful of prawns for Albert, I scraped the rest of the unwanted food into the recycling bin.

A MINUTE OR so later, I went through into the living room and discovered that there were two messages waiting for me on the answering machine. The first was from Maude, who it seemed had not been entirely fooled by the story I'd spun for her earlier. She wanted to know if there was anything wrong.

I knew the best thing to do would be to call her, put on an Oscar-worthy performance and set her mind at rest. But that wasn't going to happen. My first performance obviously hadn't been too convincing, and now it was that much later, and I was that much more frightened. She'd know from the mere sound of my voice that something was terribly wrong, and I just couldn't risk it.

The second call was a hang up. Someone had waited through the whole of the recorded message, and then hung up without speaking. Maude wouldn't have called back without identifying herself, even if the redial was an accident, so it wasn't her. There was only one person I could think of who might have made a call like this, and that was Lisa. If so, then she would have got the answerphone message containing my mobile phone number. And depending on what time she'd rung...

On cue, I heard my mobile phone, still in my jacket pocket in the kitchen, begin to ring. I ran through and grabbed it.

'Yes?'

'Hi, Joel?'

I let out my breath. For a moment I had managed to convince myself that it was Lisa, but it wasn't. It was Elaine Leigh.

'Hi, Elaine,' I said, less than enthusiastically

'Hello there,' she said, 'I'm so sorry to bother you at home — again. Just thought I'd call to see how Victoria was doing. She didn't make it to the playgroup today, is she okay?'

'Yes, she's fine.'

'I thought she might be ill at first, because there's a bug making the rounds, as usual. But then, after speaking to Maude earlier, I wondered if it had something to do with what happened last week… I was concerned.'

'So Maude told me,' I said. 'But there's no problem. Everything's fine.'

I wanted to get Elaine off the phone quickly, and not just because it was becoming harder and harder to keep up this façade of normality. I also wanted her off the phone so that the line would be clear for a much more important call. But because Elaine seemed reluctant to let me go that easily, I gave her a potted version of the same tissue of lies I'd laid out for Maude. Shopping trip, quality father-and-daughter time, etc.

'Now she's tucked up in bed, fast asleep,' I finished.

'From the sound of it, that's where you ought to be yourself,' Elaine said. 'You sound terrible. Are you coming down with this bug?'

'Maybe,' I lied. 'A cold or something.'

'Have a shot of whisky and get off to bed yourself.'

'I had one earlier, but it didn't seem to do me much good. Now I don't know whether I've had too much or not enough.'

'If that's the way you're feeling, I'd say you've had enough. Just try to get some sleep.'

'I will.'

The conversation paused there. It was the perfect point to say goodbye and hang up, and it would have seemed perfectly natural to do so. It was exactly the cue I'd been waiting for. But I *didn't* hang up, somehow finding, against all expectations, the sound of Elaine's voice soothing. Elaine didn't hang up either, and eventually it was she who broke the silence.

'Actually, there *was* another reason I rang,' she said. 'I wanted to apologise for last week. For calling you egotistical, when you thought I wanted you to ask me out on a date. Remember? It was only today that I realised I was being fairly egotistical myself — by saying no even though you hadn't actually asked me.'

I smiled despite myself. 'That's just too complicated for me right now. Why don't we just agree to blame Maude for dropping us both in the soup?'

'Yes, good idea — she really did a number on us, didn't she?'

We laughed together. I sounded very tired, even to myself.

'Maude hasn't changed a bit since I was a girl with braces on my teeth,' Elaine said. 'I even remember my Mum complaining about her from time to time, for trying to run our lives for us. But they were always the very best of friends. I suppose that was why everyone expected me and Lisa would also be best friends.'

'But you weren't?'

'I thought we were, for a long while. But she changed in the last year before we had to move away. I was glad to leave her behind, if I'm completely honest. I didn't like the people she was beginning to spend her time with. They seemed like bad influences.'

You should take a look at her new playmates, I thought. They'd blow your mind.

'Oh, by the way,' Elaine said, with the air of someone very deliberately changing the subject, 'I understand congratulations are in order?'

'What for?'

'Maude told me that you went out on your first date on Saturday.'

'That's right,' I confirmed, wondering if I was ever going to have anything like a private life with Maude taking such a huge interest in it.

'That's great, it's a really positive step,' Elaine said. 'How did it go?'

I thought back. Instead of genuine memories of the candlelit date itself, I saw an image of Barbara morphing into Angie, like something out of a horror movie.

'Not so well,' I admitted.

'Oh, I'm sorry to hear that. Will the two of you be going out again?'

'I don't think that's very likely.'

Elaine made some more sympathetic noises. 'In terms of finding a new relationship, it's probably going to take a lot more time than you think,' she said. 'It can be very difficult to let yourself trust someone new. And even when you finally do, you always feel like you're betraying your ex'.'

I told her it sounded like she was speaking from personal experience.

'Yeah, well, like I said before, whatever doesn't kill you...' She seemed to take a large breath. 'You know what, Joel, maybe we *could* go out sometime. Just for a drink, just as friends. Nothing too...*involved*... just casual?'

'I thought the playgroup rules prohibited any fraternisation with the parents of children?'

'Well, *I* wrote the rules,' Elaine said. 'It'd be easy enough to amend them. What do you think — should I do that?'

I hesitated. 'I ...think I'd like that. But I need to sort things out with my wife first. Got a lot of unfinished business to take care of.'

'That's something I understand, believe me. My ex-husband... oh, that's a story for another time, maybe when I've got a few drinks under my belt. Okay, I better let you get some rest...'

A few seconds later we finally said our goodbyes and hung up. I didn't know if I was relieved to get rid of her or not. I glanced across at the bottle of whisky, still standing on the kitchen table, the glass waiting beside it.

Too much, or not enough?

I went over, passed the bottle by, and put on the kettle instead.

AN HOUR LATER I was sitting at the kitchen table, absently leafing through one of our old photo-albums. Pictures of Lisa in a hospital bed just after delivering, looking utterly baffled by the little screaming bundle in her arms. Vic, so tiny in her first car seat as we brought her home for the first time. Lisa attempting to breastfeed (for the first and last time). Vic crawling, still in nappies. One of the three of us on Vic's first birthday, taken by Maude, all snuggled together in a family hug. It was like looking at someone else's life.

The scorpion phone rang. I picked it up, brought it to my ear.

'It's me,' Feelen said.

I sat up sharply. 'What's wrong with Vic?'

'Nothing's wrong,' he replied, but I could tell that something was. There was a strain in his voice that hadn't been there earlier. He sounded desperate, and under pressure. I wondered aloud what could be responsible — and soon had an answer. 'Jesus,' he said, 'how do you do this every fuckin' day? I'm fuckin' shagged out!'

I almost smiled in relief. 'Childcare's not as easy as it looks, is it?'

'Tell me about it! She never stops! I haven't had five minutes peace all day!'

'I can help you,' I said.

'Yeah?'

'Sure. Just bring her home and I'll take the responsibility off your hands.'

'Very funny, September,' he said. Then he whispered, 'She keeps wanting me to take her to the *toilet!*'

Somehow, the sheer amount of embarrassment I heard in his voice made me feel a little better about him being in a position to do so. So I bent a little.

'It's a bit of a friendship thing, I think. She must like you.'

'Yeah?' He sounded pleased. 'Well, I like her too. I just wish things could have been different…'

Didn't we all.

'Feelen,' I said, 'bring her back to me. I'll pay you anything you want, I'll give you everything I've got, just bring her back.'

After a brief silence, he said, 'I'd like to, September, I really would. And I wouldn't ask for a penny. This isn't my kind of thing, you know, kidnapping little girls, this isn't what I'm about.'

'Then bring her home.'

'I *can't*. Temple and Angie, they're not normal people. They'd kill me. They kill anyone who gets in their way.'

'Then what did you call for? Just to moan?'

'No. Vicky needs some stuff to see her through the night.'

'I can have her overnight bag ready in five minutes.'

'Okay. In about twenty minutes take the bag to the end of your street. Leave it on top of the postbox, then go straight home again. You know not to try to stop the car, or try to follow the car, right?'

'Right.'

'Okay, do it.'

AND SO IT was that twenty minutes later I was carrying Vic's pink backpack down the dark street. Out of the corner of my eye, I saw a chink of light appear at one of the windows of my neighbours' houses, and when I turned to look, I saw that Mrs. Webber was watching me through a narrow gap in her curtains. I nodded a greeting at her and she nodded back. I saw her looking at the backpack and I shrugged.

Don't ask.

Mrs Webber was still at her window a couple of minutes later as I walked back. I knew she'd noticed that I no longer had the backpack, but again I just shrugged.

Really don't ask.

A couple of minutes later the scorpion phone rang again. It was Feelen ringing to complain that I had forgotten Vic's favourite bear. He was right, I had. He left me with instructions to repeat what I had done with the backpack, and I went upstairs and got the bear. This was the same bear that Lisa had brought on her single visit at Christmas, which Vic loved and I, of course, detested.

I repeated my journey to and from the post box at the end of the street. I don't know if Mrs. W saw me this time around. I made sure that I never glanced at her window.

Another half-hour passed and the scorpion rang yet again. This time Feelen wanted to know what kind of story he could tell Vic. I told him to tell her the usual kinds of stories grown-ups tell children. Princes and princesses, witches and goblins, and good overcoming evil.

'Fairy stories?'

'Yeah, that's right. Fairy stories.'

After this, I went through into the living room and sat down on the sofa, putting all three phones on the seat beside me. At any second I expected Feelen to call back for another piece of childcare advice, but time passed and that didn't happen.

At last, irritated and intimidated (and, frankly, scared witless) by the ominous silence in the house, I turned on the TV and began flicking through all the channels at random. It was a pointless exercise, because I didn't understand anything I saw. All the people looked either fake or dead. Eventually, I found myself on one of the smaller home-shopping channels, watching some has-been ex-children's' TV presenter trying to explain the benefits to be gained by buying something called a dreamcatcher.

Dreamcatchers, apparently, were an invention of the Native Americans. They were a sort of web-like charm or ornament that you hung over your bed and which were meant to snag your nightmares before they could get to you, and the has-been made it sound like they were pretty good things to have.

They were of no earthly good to me, of course. All my nightmares seemed to happen while I was wide awake.

YOU OCCASIONALLY HEAR people talk about something called the 'long night of the soul'. You read about it sometimes in magazine articles, or maybe hear it mentioned on news reports about people who have lived through catastrophes; wars, floods, famines, earthquakes, terrorist attacks, tsunamis — all the big hits. People who have suffered the very worst that life could throw at them. People who have faced the kind of despair that holds you prisoner just like chains.

It's supposed to mean a time spent in hopeless solitude, I think, a time where you are forced to confront your deepest fears, your darkest imaginings. A time when the world with all its weight, all its fearful gravity, descends upon you, crushes all the breath from your body, all the hope from your soul. You are at one with everything you never wanted to live to see, drowning in a darkness so vast that you believe there can never again be any kind of light. A darkness so terrible that you understand no one will ever find you and save you.

Fool that I am, I thought I'd already had *my* long night of the soul. In fact, I thought I'd had it *twice*. Once lying on a stone-cold cellar floor in south London, waiting to die, and once when Lisa left me, shattering my heart into a hundred-thousand pieces. I really believed that I'd paid my dues, but apparently I was wrong, because here I was once again. It was all too familiar, and yet the darkness was no less engulfing, the fear no less unmanning.

There are many layers to hell, it seems. But only one real question: why me?

Some of us are just lucky, I guess. Or as it probably doesn't (but certainly should) say in the Bible — shit happens.

I DIDN'T SLEEP. I didn't doze. I scarcely closed my eyes. Dawn found me wide-awake, freshly-shaved, showered and dressed. I sat at the kitchen table drinking black coffee, watching through the kitchen window as the sun rose above the roof tops.

The scorpion phone rang at six o'clock exactly. I placed my mug carefully on the table and picked up the phone.

'Hello.'

'Up early this morning, Joel?'

I closed my eyes in relief, and sent out a silent prayer of thanks to poor-little-rich-boy Andrew Lipton... the lying little rat bastard.

'Hello, Lisa. I spoke to Temple yesterday.'

She was silent for a few seconds, and then I could almost hear her shrug. 'Well, so now you know.'

'Yes, I know.'

'Don't blame me,' she said defensively. 'I didn't want you to find out. I tried to keep it from you.'

'Was that for my benefit or yours?'

'Yours, actually. It would have been safer if you didn't know.'

'But now I do.'

'Yeah... so let's move on, shall we. What have you got for me?'

There was no fake bonhomie this morning, no aimless flirting. It was straight down to business. For the first time in a long while, it seemed that my wife and I were on the same wavelength again.

'I got the deal you wanted,' I said. 'It's exactly what you asked for. In return for handing over all the evidence you possess, Temple is willing to let you go. He'll call off the dogs, and you can walk away without retribution.'

'*Hmmm.* What else?' she asked, in the voice of someone who knew all too well to wait until the second shoe had dropped.

'You've got to get out of the country and stay out. If you ever come back, the deal's off. Temple will put out a contract on you immediately, and no amount of bargaining will take it off.'

She considered this for a moment, and then asked, 'And that's it, that's everything?'

The QUEEN of HEARTS

I thought about the money, a million-plus, and about Temple's advice not mention it until I had her within reach.

'Yes, that's it all,' I said.

Lisa was silent for a long time. Then she sighed, and said, 'Good. That fits in with my plans perfectly.'

I felt a small spike of anger, a needle-thin icicle sliding into my brain. 'Oh, there was one more thing.'

'What? What else does he want?'

I knew that she was thinking about the money. Me, I was thinking about something much more precious.

'It's nothing Temple wants. It's something else that *we* get, in return. Our daughter, Vic. Remember her, that little lump you carried around for nine months a few years back? We get her back safe and sound. Doesn't that sound good to you?'

'Joel,' she began, 'I know you don't think I—'

'*Stop*. I'm not interested in listening to you trying to justify yourself. Just tell me where to come get the stuff.'

'Look, Joel, I'll be honest, I'm nervous about us meeting up. Maybe a drop would be safer. Or I could even post it.'

'Absolutely not. Posting it would mean that they'd keep Vic for another night at least, and that is unacceptable. A drop isn't certain enough, anything could go wrong. We have to meet face to face. I will guarantee your safety. You know that I wouldn't let anything happen to you.'

'Yes,' she said, 'I know that. Okay, Joel, it's riddle time again.'

'What?'

'I'm going to give you some clues that only you and I will underst—'

'No, not again! What's the point, Lisa? I told you, this is a completely secure line, no bugs, it's untappable.'

'Oh yeah? And who told you that?'

'Temple.'

'And you believed him?'

'Yes. He gave it to me so the police couldn't listen in on our conversations. Believe me, Lisa, he's said a lot of very incriminating things on this phone. If there was the slightest chance he could be overheard, he'd never have said them in a million years. The police can't hear us.'

'Oh, I'm sure they can't. But I'm pretty sure that *Temple* and his goons can. Don't you see, it'd be too good an opportunity to miss? Hello, Nicky, if you're listening in! Good try, better luck next time!'

She laughed a little, and I could see her in my mind's eye, her head thrown back, dark hair tumbling over her shoulder, the pearlescent skin of her white throat, the perfect image of a beautiful woman laughing.

'Okay,' she said. 'Ready for this?'

'In a second, there's one other thing I want to say first. I want you to remember that you brought this on us. And if you arrange to meet me and you don't turn up, and if anything happens to Vic because of that, I'm going to hold you responsible.'

'Joel, I—'

'Shut up, I haven't finished. I'm going to hold *you* responsible. I'm going to blame *you*. Do you understand? And if you think Temple is bad, just wait, because I won't make a deal.' I eased back in my chair, loosened my grip on the phone. 'Go ahead, give me the clues.'

The QUEEN of HEARTS

Lisa was silent for a long time. Then, as before, she spoke two apparently meaningless and unconnected sentences.

'The Weather Girls,' she said cryptically.

'Cardinal, I drink to you,' she added, even more cryptically.

As she had said, only we would be able to connect these clues and make sense of them, and I did immediately.

'You're joking?' I asked.

But she wasn't.

WHEN WE HUNG up, I looked at the cooker clock. It wasn't even six-thirty yet and the place she wanted to meet didn't open until ten. The journey to meet Lisa might take me anywhere between forty minutes to an hour-and-a-half, depending on the traffic. Hard to predict, especially as rush hour seemed to last twenty-four hours these days. I had time to spare, but I thought it would probably be better if I set off immediately, before anybody else was tempted to interfere in my life.

I stood up and took my mug over to the sink to rinse it out. And that's when I saw that the metallic-blue Saab was back.

Jimmy Gill and Chris Dale were clearly visible through the car's windscreen, and were busy munching what looked suspiciously like bacon rolls. Steaming takeout coffee cups rested on the dashboard. They had made a very early start today. Did that mean they knew something — like that we were now coming down to the wire?

I went back to the kitchen table, and from the phones on the table selected the scorpion once more. It didn't matter if Temple could eavesdrop on this conversation, just as long as the cops couldn't. I dialled a number that had only become familiar over the last few weeks or so. After half-a-dozen rings, it was answered.

'Good morning, Mrs. Webber,' I said. 'How would you feel about doing me a big, big favour?'

Twenty

I GRABBED MY keys and pulled on my jacket while I stood at the kitchen window, waiting for the signal to make my move. Over in the Saab, it looked like Gill and Dale had finished the bacon roll section of their breakfast and had moved on to what was probably not only their favourite part of their meal, but also of their job — emulating the dietary excesses of their cinematic counterparts, by chowing down on a box full of donuts.

There were a lot of guys like that in the Service, seduced by the movies and obsessed by the trappings. Only if they had been carrying Magnum .44s in shoulder holsters and conducting their stakeout from a Crown Vic could their lives have been more complete.

When Mrs. Webber stepped out of her front door, Gill glanced across at her and said something to his partner. Dale then glanced across at her, too, scowling, as she locked her front door.

I watched her approach the old Volvo parked on her short drive, climb in, and then immediately fasten her seatbelt. A gust of dirty blue smoke came out of the exhaust as she started the engine. She 'accidentally' flicked on her hazard warning lights, and then flicked them off again. This was the signal that she was ready for action whenever I was. I waited for yet another moment, and saw her fumble around to get something out of her handbag before readjusting the angle of her rear-view mirror. I watched the policemen notice her begin to powder her nose and apply lipstick. I saw them chuckle together, and I could almost hear their conversation.

She doesn't need Max Factor, she needs surgery...

Why doesn't she just get a plasterer in to give her a skim...

Ha-ha, I thought. In a minute or so the laugh was going to be on them.

I turned from the window and headed out the door. I didn't look at the Saab directly, but I sensed increased activity inside the car as I unlocked the Scenic. The box of donuts disappeared onto the back seat. The coffee cups vanished from the dashboard. I started the Scenic, eased out of the drive and drew level with the Saab.

I powered down my window, Gill powered down his.

'Morning,' I said, peering past them into the back seat. For the first time, I was sure that Scott Vaughan wasn't with them.

Gill nodded a greeting at me.

'I'm going shopping, is that okay with you?'

Gill shrugged. 'Go wherever you like. But wherever it is, we're going with you. Orders.'

I returned his shrug. 'Fine, I guess I'll see you in the frozen peas aisle.'

I slowly pulled away and trundled up to the end of the street. There was no cross traffic, but I waited anyway. In the rear-view mirror, I saw Gill start the Saab, then roll forward and turn into my neighbour's drive before reversing out again, turning the car neatly around. As he started forward again, he saw me waiting at the junction for him and flashed his full beams for me to go on. And that was the moment when Mrs.

The QUEEN of HEARTS

Webber reversed out of her own drive at Warp Speed Seven.

After I had quickly explained about Vic's kidnapping, Mrs. W, bless her, had been ready to do anything that might help get her back. And if it entailed getting up the nose of DC Chris Dale, to whom she had taken an instant and venomous dislike, then all the better. She had agreed to pull out and block Gill and Dale's exit from our narrow cul-de-sac, and then, while keeping her doors firmly locked, to play for time.

Maybe she'd pretend that her Volvo had stalled and wouldn't restart. Or accidentally-on-purpose drop her keys under the seat and struggle to find them. Or pretend to faint. Or pretend an injury, like whiplash, or a heart attack, even. At least, these were some of the ideas I had furnished her with. Any one of them would give me the precious moments I needed to get clean away.

I suppose that an adrenaline rush must have got the better of her... Either that, or, as an expatriate Martian, she was living with an awful lot of repressed rage. But whatever the reason, she reversed out of her drive like a killer whale launching itself from the surf to grab a juicy seal.

The rear of her ancient Volvo rammed into the Saab's left wing, crumpling it like tissue and shunting the whole front of the vehicle about forty-five degrees to the right. The right tyre burst as the wheel jumped the kerb and the headlight above it imploded as the wing struck a lamp-post. High above, the lamp's glass fitting swung loose on a hinge, dangled for a microsecond, and then plunged downward, smashing into the Saab's sunroof and showering the two cops inside with broken safety glass.

The QUEEN of HEARTS

Having seen my plan succeed — to an extent beyond my wildest expectations — I tore out of my street, leaving twin ribbons of tyre rubber across the road surface. I know it sounds strange, the situation being what it was, but it was five minutes before I could stop laughing.

What finally stopped me was the sound of my mobile phone ringing, which only reminded me that I'd left Temple's scorpion phone behind in the kitchen. Which meant that if and when I met Lisa and got what I needed to secure my daughter's release, I was still going to have to go home to collect the phone, so that I could contact Temple to arrange the exchange. Which would mean bypassing Gill and Dale once more, which I assumed wouldn't be so easy next time.

I slapped the dashboard in frustration. As it so very wisely says in the Bible (Obscenities 3:11) — bollocks!

I extracted my own mobile from my jacket pocket and brought it to my ear — and then snatched it away again when my hearing was assaulted by what sounded like the hunting cry of a rabid mongoose. In actual fact, it was the sound of my very good old friend, Scott Vaughan, venting his spleen.

Now, I'm no expert, but he seemed to have a dangerously large spleen.

'What the ugly bloody fuck do think you're up to?' he all but screamed. 'Are you out of your tiny, fevered fucking mind?'

'Scott, I'm—'

'You fucking *shithead!* Have you any fucking idea of the trouble you're in now? You are neck deep in a steaming fucking quagmire of septic, maggot-infested shit, and right now it would be my absolute fucking delight to stamp on your flat fucking head and fucking drown you in it!'

'Scott, I can sense you're a little *upset*, so—'

Another strange, inarticulate sound came squawking over the line, not the cry of a furry hunting animal this time, more the sound of some other creature, a large bird perhaps, which had accidentally impaled itself on a TV antenna. I switched to the handsfree setting.

'Upset?' Vaughan yelled. 'Up-*fucking*-set! Let me—'

'Scott, listen—'

'No, you listen to me! What just happened outside your house was sheer insanity! If Gill hadn't had to call an ambulance for the old woman, Chris Dale would have fucking strangled her — *honest-to-God, fucking strangled her* — and what the fuck is going on with this scrambled phone business? Where in fuck's name did you acquire a fucking scrambled phone?'

It was good to hear that Mrs. W was carrying on with my plan as arranged, pretending injury to escape the policemen's immediate wrath. Mind you, after that scene from *Mad Max*, I only hoped that she *was* faking.

'How is Mrs. Webber? I hope she's—'

'And I hope she's fucking dead! Well?' Vaughan demanded. 'What the fuck is going on? Talk to me!'

'It was more a case of I *had* to have the scrambled phone, Scott, because you forced me into it. You had all my phones tapped, and you were listening in to my calls.'

Scott at least had the grace to fall silent for a moment. When he came back on, much of the raw anger had gone from his voice.

'Yes, okay, we *were* listening. But at least we were professional about it. We didn't eavesdrop on anything that didn't have to do with the case. We didn't listen to your heart-warming conversations with your mother-in-law, for example, or to the sweet, fledgling romance with the playgroup leader totty. And we *certainly* didn't listen to you having rampant phone-sex with Angie Edwards.'

Oh Jesus. Talk about being caught with your pants down. Talk about being led into trouble by what old Charlie Noble was pleased to call the Little Bald Colonel. Even in the privacy of the car, my face had gone beet red.

'You may still know Angie as Barbara Rawlings,' Scott said, 'but she was the one who gave you the phone, wasn't she — on behalf of Temple?'

There seemed to be no point in lying at this stage, so I told him he was right.

'I don't know if you realise this yet, Joel, but Angie Edwards is not your friend.'

'Thanks, I'd worked that out for myself.'

'Angie and Temple have a very long and convoluted history together, and believe me, none of it makes for pleasant reading. Back in the good old days, when Temple was untouchable, Angie was the first prossy in his stable.'

I recalled thinking how professional she had been at all the sexy stuff, and now I knew why.

'She recruited most of the other girls, lots of them straight off the buses from the provinces, and she ran them for Temple. Ran them with a rod of iron. Not one of those girls stepped out of line more than once, because Angie's punishments were bloodcurdling. She was also one of his best spies, sleeping with the right people and collecting evidence on them so they could be blackmailed later. She may be beautiful, but she's also vicious, amoral, and completely ruthless. Back in the old days, I always thought she was a suitable companion for Temple, and she hasn't changed one iota.'

'Why are you telling me this?'

'So you'll understand that you can't trust her any more than you can trust Temple. You can't trust them to stick to any deal they may have offered you.'

'Funny, they say exactly the same thing about you.'

'Joel, if you do it their way, you're going to get hurt. And so will Victoria.'

'Why didn't you warn me about Angie sooner? If you knew that she was going to be...'

Then what Vaughan had actually said struck me like a gutshot. My whole body reacted, and it was a miracle I kept the car on the road.

'When you came around to ask me to join your team, you already *knew* Vic had been kidnapped, didn't you?' I asked.

Vaughan grunted. 'I actually saw it happen. We'd followed you on your shopping trip, hoping you'd lead us to Lisa. Unbeknownst to us, Feelen and Edwards must have done the same thing. From where we were parked, we saw Victoria come out of that toy store alone. We kept looking for you following on, but you didn't come.'

I only took my eye off her for a minute, I thought bitterly. But sometimes that's all it takes. I wasn't the first parent to make that mistake, and sadly, I wouldn't be the last.

'Angie must have been as surprised as we were,' Scott continued, 'but she thought on her feet. She raced over, told Victoria off as though she were her own daughter who'd run away, then snatched her up and rushed her over into their car. You wouldn't think anyone could move so fast in heels that high, but the whole thing took about five seconds flat. Your daughter was so surprised she didn't make a peep, and nobody else paid the slightest attention. Feelen pulled away before the door was properly closed. It was smartly done.'

I was absolutely stunned.

'You *saw* it happen,' I echoed. 'You saw it happen, and you did *nothing* to stop it.'

'We got video footage of the snatch,' Vaughan said defensively. 'Totally incriminating, if it ever goes to court. The original plan was to follow them to their hideout, and then call in reinforcements. Get Victoria back safely, and then convince Feelen and Edwards to give evidence against Temple, in return for leniency on kidnapping charges. Don't you get it? Then we probably wouldn't even *need* Lisa.'

'But it didn't work out that way, did it?'

'No,' he admitted uncomfortably. 'I'm afraid we lost them.'

'Scott, you gambled with my daughter's life.'

'I made an error. I had a lapse of good judgement. But if you cooperate with me, we can get over that.'

'No, we'll never get over that.'

'Joel, listen to me—'

'No, Scott, I'm done listening, and the next time I see you, you better have a raygun handy. Because the Man from Mars is going to rip your head off.'

I disconnected the call on his squawking voice. The phone immediately began to ring again and I switched it off completely, angrily tossing it on to the passenger seat.

The QUEEN of HEARTS

I PASSED THROUGH London Colney and then joined the M25, heading in the direction of Heathrow International Airport. If Lisa intended to leave the country, then Heathrow seemed like a reasonable place for her to be hiding out. But I wasn't meeting her at Heathrow. I was meeting her in just about the last place anyone would think of looking for someone on the run.

The clues she had given me were these:

The Weather Girls.

Cardinal, I drink to you.

Together they added up to one more mutual experience that I would never forget — even though this was one I wouldn't mind being lost in the ether.

It was a date we'd had long before our marriage, and one that perhaps should have alerted me to the major, irreconcilable differences in our characters. I liked sober reflection. I liked my feet on the ground and the world (or my part of it, at any rate) under my control. Lisa liked a chaotic world turned upside down, with the only certainty being the satisfaction of her immediate needs. So our date had fulfilled every aspect of her criteria, but none of mine.

It was a pattern for our future life together.

I don't know if you remember, but The Weather Girls were one of those one-hit-wonder bands that come around now and again, and their hit was called *It's Raining Men (Hallelujah!)*. And *Cardinal, I drink to you* is a reference to a variation of a charming drinking game most commonly played at stag parties (including mine, unfortunately), where the combatants are requested to down all manner of drinks (mostly unpleasantly mixed concoctions) in one liver-crippling draft, and are eliminated from the game when they vomit.

So the two clues added together made up the song Lisa had so hysterically sung to me at the conclusion of our date, which was: *It's Raining Puke. (Hallelujah!)*

The date had been at an amusement park, and the song related to the moment she had forced me on to one particular ride against all my better judgement, a twisting loop-the-loop sort of ride that on my own I would never have gone on in a million years. At the top of the biggest loop, my guts had finally given up the ghost, and my lunch had gone airborne. At the bottom of the loop, just about to go up on the next, myself and thirty other people (but of course excluding Lisa) had reconnected with the falling puke, and had become instant sick bags.

By the time the ride ended twenty-seconds later, a dozen other people had also vomited as a result, and the ride had to be closed for an hour to be hosed down with disinfectant.

I remembered Lisa laughing at me afterwards, singing her little song. And I'd *still* wanted to marry her. Gives you some idea of her power, doesn't it?

Sheer volume of traffic and the latest in a never-ending sequence of road works meant that it was almost an hour-and-a-half later when I finally saw the sign I had been looking for, and I indicated to pull into the slip lane.

I had nearly reached Lisa's secret lair.

Thorpe Park.

The QUEEN of HEARTS

EVEN THIS EARLY, the queues at the amusement park's ticket booths were enormous, and I had to wait half-an-hour before I reached the window. The woman directly ahead kept looking back over her shoulder at me, casting suspicious glances, and it took me a while to figure out why. I was alone, you see. A single man entering a theme park full of kiddie-packed families.

I could see her point of view.

I began to glance back into the car park, and then went up on my tiptoes to see ahead in the queues, making sure that she noticed my charade. Eventually, I tapped her on the shoulder and asked if she might have seen my family. I described Vic wearing her fairy outfit, and Lisa as I had last seen her at Brent Cross, the All-American Barbie. Of course, the woman hadn't seen my family, but my inquiry did its job of diminishing her suspicions. I had to be careful though, to make doubly sure the woman was out of earshot before I purchased my single Billy-No-Mates ticket.

As I passed though the theme park's main gates and walked over the footbridge across the river, I started to hear the screams from the first riders of the day, and my stomach instantly felt uneasy. My body remembered the sound of those screams and the internal eruptions that had followed, and it was very afraid that I was going to force it to undergo the same trials and tribulations as the last time I'd been here.

The QUEEN of HEARTS

No fear. The only thing that had got me up there in the first place had been love. And I wasn't in love anymore. Was I?

To get into the Park proper, you had to pass through a large entrance hall in the shape of a dome. At the centre of this dome, a large screen showed video clips of the park's so-called attractions, while people sat at tables eating and drinking from the variety of coffee and snack stalls encircling the hall. A set of stairs led down to the customer toilets, lockers and public phones.

I took a couple of minutes to scan the crowds at the various kiosks and tables, as well as those just passing through, but I didn't see Lisa. It would be like Brent Cross all over again, no doubt. I wouldn't find her, she would find me. I resolved to let her.

I followed the crowds out into the daylight. Everyone seemed happy and excited at the prospect of being strapped helpless to pieces of heavy machinery that would be hurled hundreds of feet into the air at alarming speeds and then allowed to hurtle back to the earth.

As it says in the Bible, people are just weird.

JUST OVER FORTY minutes later, I had made a more or less complete circuit of the theme park. There were a hell of a lot of people here and more arriving every moment, making it difficult to move or see in a straight line. I'd kept my eye out for Lisa's California babe outfit, but all I saw were the usual Essex girls. The queues for the rides were already gigantic.

The smell of fast food mixed with the sounds of thundering machinery and screaming people had already combined to make me feel queasy. I was also jumpy, waiting for that nasal, foghorn voice to start calling, 'Myron! Myron!' I found a free bench and sat on it.

The ride in front of me was basically a log flume on steroids, where a large carriage hurtled down a sharp incline of fast-moving water and crashed into a pool far below. As it careered through the pool, the carriage sent up a vast sheet of icy water as though there had been an explosion, which then rained down on the silly buggers inside. The spray of water also showered over a covered bridge which led away from the ride, and then showered down beyond it on to the pavement directly in front of me.

A large group of boys aged between nine and twelve, already completely soaked, hung around this spot with their shirts off, waiting for another *al fresco* shower. Off to the side, an adolescent blonde-haired girl in matching pink shorts and halter top, who must have been one of the boys' older siblings, watched from just out of range of the falling water, shaking her head in mild disgust at their antics. After the next shower had descended on them, the laughing boys decided that it was time to move on and as one ran away, leaving the girl behind without a backward glance.

The girl turned around, shrugged in what I took to be resigned exasperation, and then began walking in my direction. Her short blonde hair was kinked with a natural wave, her eyes covered with pink-framed, heart-shaped sunglasses. Her limbs were long and gangly, she was wearing far too much make-up, and her pre-adolescent chest was still as flat as a board. And yet I thought that when she grew up she was going to be beautiful.

And what's more, she was going to *know* it.

The girl came and stood directly in front of me. She opened her little pink clasp handbag on its faux gold chain. She brought out a cherry-flavoured lollipop and stuck it in her mouth.

It was Lisa.

Twenty-One

'What's this supposed to be,' I asked, 'the Lolita look?'

'Something like that.'

She had led me away from the bench and we were now walking completely aimlessly, changing direction as dictated by the whim of the crowds.

'I must admit, it's hard work acting natural with my tits strapped down like this, but the whole effect works, doesn't it? I mean, you saw me just a few days ago, and even you didn't recognise me.'

'Maybe without the sunglasses…'

She smiled to herself, knowing that I was lying. She could have walked away at the same time as the boys she'd been watching and I would have been none the wiser. It was only because she came to stand in front of me, and stayed there, that I'd eventually recognised her. Her continuing weight-loss had taken her figure into the androgynous territory. Even her voice had changed.

'Still, at least you made it,' she said.

'Why here, of all places?'

She shrugged. 'It's unexpected, for one reason. Unexpected means *unsuspected*, and that's good. For another reason, it's one of the few places I was sure you'd get the clues for. Also, at the moment, it happens to be a convenient location for me.'

'Because of the airport,' I said.

'That's right.' She gave me a little sidelong glance. 'To tell you the truth, I was thinking about leaving the country pretty soon, anyway,' she said. 'But having it as one of Nicky's conditions of the deal made the final decision easier.'

I noticed her familiar use of the diminutive of Temple's first name. It annoyed me that it annoyed me as much as it did. When was I ever going to learn? What was it going to take?

'How did it happen?' I asked before I could stop myself.

'Me and Nicky, you mean?'

Lisa sucked on her lollipop thoughtfully for a moment. If the question caused her the slightest embarrassment, it didn't show. I figured that by now she was beyond embarrassment. If she'd had even a single shred of it left in her body, she probably wouldn't have been sucking that lollipop the way she was in public.

'He called me up at the bank one day, completely out of the blue,' she said. 'He introduced himself as a businessman and investor, and told me I'd been recommended to him by several acquaintances. All the people he name-checked were completely kosher, so I accepted him at face value. We met a few times, and talked. Money at first, and then other things, too. He flirted with me, I flirted with him. Nothing out of the ordinary. But soon we were having long business lunches in very expensive restaurants. Soon after that, it was room service in very expensive hotels.'

She looked at me directly for the first time since she'd started talking. The sunglasses hid anything that might have been in her eyes, but her voice had become both deeper and lower, throwing off, just for a moment, the little girl act.

'I couldn't resist it, Joel. The glitz, the glitter, the pampering. I just couldn't resist. Not when the alternative was a life back in the sticks that I'd already escaped from once. Not with a glorified Uber driver for a husband and a wailing baby that I never wanted in the first place.'

She turned away again.

'Then, when I was well and truly hooked, Nicky told me what the real business was. He told me exactly what I'd have to do, what I'd have to risk, and what I'd have to give up — and everything I'd stand to gain in return. He kept dangling all the rewards in front of me, there for the taking. The luxury lifestyle, the swanky apartment, the money... and eventually I gave in. Which, to be fair, was only what I'd wanted to do from the very beginning.'

She hooked her arm through mine.

'You see, Joel, you always thought that I was a good girl, trying to be bad. But it was always the other way around. Always.'

She stopped walking and looked up. I did too, and I realised that we were now underneath the very ride that had made me blow my chunks mid-revolution all that time ago. Above us, screams rose and fell, like the soundtrack to a disaster movie. I looked back down at Lisa, who was watching the looping progress of one of the carriages.

She may have been dressed in baby pink right now, but Lisa was one of those people who lived their lives in black-and-white. She was still that *femme fatale* movie star that had enthralled me from the first moment we met, and every gesture of her hand, every artful turn of her head, seemed to have a weight of meaning behind it. Lisa had been born at the wrong time and in the wrong place. She should have been one of those darkly sparkling actresses with brilliant careers and tragic lives, dramatically and unnaturally cut short. Fifty years after her premature death, successive generations of teenagers would still be pinning posters of her on their walls, unaware that their beautiful icon had the all the morality of a cockroach.

She suddenly looked down from the ride and caught me staring at her. She took off her sunglasses and pinned me with her attention. I could see an almost obscene lustre in her dark eyes, an excitement raised by the screams, by the thrill of being so close to the ride that we could feel the airstream as the carriage passed overhead.

She stepped closer to me, her charm on full wattage, like low grade radiation I could feel invading my body, saturating my cells.

'Let's go on this ride again,' she said. 'Come on it with me now. Just for fun.'

And just for a moment, I wanted to do exactly that. I really did. More than anything else in the world.

'No,' I said.

She studied my eyes for another second and then took a step back. 'No, you won't, will you.'

Before she slipped her glasses on again, I literally saw the life die in her eyes, the vitality fade. It hurt that I was the cause of it. It hurt that I had *always* been the cause of it. But I hardened my heart, and told myself that she was just an actress playing a role. I didn't really believe that I had hurt her feelings any more than I believed that she was really a pre-adolescent girl.

'Tell me something, Lisa,' I said harshly. 'Aren't you worried about Vic's safety? Weren't you sick with fear when you heard she'd been kidnapped?'

'Yes, of course I was.'

'And yet you haven't once asked after her — asked if I knew how she was holding up, or how they were treating her. You haven't demonstrated even one iota of concern. The only person you care about, the only person you have *ever* cared about, is yourself.'

She said nothing.

'For God's sake, Lisa, this is your daughter we're talking about. Whether you wanted her or not, she's your own flesh and blood. Doesn't that mean anything to you?'

Abruptly, Lisa walked away, and I quickly followed her, before she could disappear into the crowds.

I must have called her name a dozen times, but she either couldn't hear me or was pretending not to. In the end, I broke into a limping trot and snagged her arm, yanking her to a stop. I was a little rougher with her than I had intended to be and several people turned to look at us, at the picture we made, the young jail-bait girl and the man who appeared easily old enough to be her father.

One woman in particular gave me what had to be the mother of all glares, and I realised with a sinking heart that it was the woman I had spoken to in the ticket line earlier. Lisa didn't look like either of the family members I had described to her. Now I was just a single man again, alone in the park, harassing a young, underage girl. She stomped away, and I could only hope that it wasn't to alert security

I turned back to Lisa angrily. She was sucking her lollipop again, in a manner that went well beyond the obscene. I saw one passing man stare so hard he walked into a fence.

'Okay, this has gone on long enough. Where's the evidence?'

'It's right here,' Lisa replied mildly.

She looked to her left and so did I. I saw a bank of about twenty free-standing lockers, placed there by the side of the footpath for the convenience of those who couldn't be arsed to walk all the way back to those in the entrance dome. Lisa reached inside her pink clasp bag again and scrambled out a key.

I looked around and saw a low wall where we could have a little privacy. 'Go sit over there and wait for me.'

I took the key over to the locker and opened it. Inside was a large black sports bag. When I lifted it out, it was so heavy it almost hit the ground before I could adjust my grip. I carried it over to the wall and set it down beside Lisa. I pulled open the zipper and looked inside. Papers, files, notebooks, ledgers, and a long clear plastic box packed with flash drives. It looked like a police investigator's wet dream.

'Is this everything?' I asked Lisa. 'That's part of the deal. No omissions, no copies. Temple wants everything.'

'That's everything.'

'You're not holding out on me? If anything's missing, Vic could get hurt.'

'It's everything.'

Now it was time.

'And what about the money?' I asked.

'What money?'

There was no tell-tale hesitation before Lisa's response, but fortunately, I knew she was lying. I snatched her clasp bag out of her lap. She tried to pull it back, but the gold-effect plastic chain snapped. I opened the bag, rifled around for a second, rummaged through tissues and make-up (plus a number of ribbed and flavoured condoms, damn it), and then came up with a second locker key — to fit the locker right beside the first.

Lisa threw her lollipop aside. There was a litterbin only a step away from where she sat, all she would need to have done was lean across and drop the lolly in, but instead she'd just thrown it on the floor at her side. Just something else she was finished with.

'I could scream, you know?' she said under her breath, but with more genuine emotion than I had seen from her in years. Now I knew what really made her heart beat faster. 'People are already looking at you like you're dirt. If I scream, they'll grab you and tear you apart.'

I tossed her handbag back. 'Go ahead and scream. I still have my old warrant card in my wallet, which identifies me as CID.'

I went to the second locker and opened it. Inside was an identical sports bag that was even heavier than the first. I took it back to the wall, jerked the zip partway open, and then shut it again immediately. The bag was full of cash. Lots and lots and lots of cash.

Lisa was still seething. 'You know, if anyone looked at that warrant card closely, they'd see that it's expired.'

'Only if they knew what they were looking for, and only if they bothered to look very closely. And even if they did, they'd only call security, and security would only call the police. And how would that help either one of us?'

'I want that money, Joel. I *need* it.'

'I need it more. To buy our daughter's safety. To save her life.'

She thought for a long time. Then she took a deep breath, and let it out very slowly.

'Okay,' she said. 'I suppose I'll survive somehow.'

There was something about the way she said it that raised my hackles. I hefted the bag again. A lot of cash. A million and change? How would I know without sitting down and counting it?

'You've already split some off for yourself, haven't you?' I asked.

'Of course.'

'How much is missing?'

'Not much. A couple of hundred thou'. Tell Nicky it's severance pay. I've lost everything else, and if he wants me to disappear forever, I'm going to need it to start over.'

I looked at her. She looked right back at me. Even through her sunglasses I could feel the directness of her gaze. She meant it. She was sticking to her guns on this one.

'I'll tell him,' I said.

She stood up and lightly stepped into my arms. Into my traitorous arms, which first opened to welcome her and then closed to hold her. To hold her tight. She pressed her lips to mine. Her body leaned into mine, and I could feel the heat of her, the firmness of her strapped-down breasts, through her little pink top.

'Thank you,' she murmured into my mouth, and I pushed her firmly away.

I could feel people looking at us again — judging me by what they thought they were seeing — but that isn't what made me push her away. She disgusted me. I disgusted *myself* for still wanting her.

'Don't thank me,' I told her. 'I'm not doing it for you.'

She smiled. 'Yes, you are. Just a little bit, you are.'

She glanced back at the ride as another clutch of suicidal thrill-seekers screamed their way around another loop. The corners of her mouth twitched into a smile.

'Are you sure you don't want to come on that rollercoaster with me, after all?' she asked. 'You know, we really could have a lot of fun together this time around... now that you know what to expect of me.'

For once she seemed serious. And despite the smile, almost sad. I wondered if she was really asking what I *thought* she was asking, or was it just another role she was playing.

But in any case, I shook my head — no.

'Too bad,' she said. 'It could have been wild. But that's okay, I'll go on alone.'

She began to turn away, heading toward the ride entrance, but turned back when I called her name.

'Changed your mind?'

'No,' I said. 'But when you get wherever you're going, and you're settled, make sure there's somewhere I can reach you. Even if it's just a post-office box in Rio.'

She smiled again. 'Are you going to write me a love letter, Joel?'

'No. But I imagine my solicitor will.'

She understood what I meant at once, that I meant to divorce her. I thought I saw a shadow cross over her face, some small sign of regret. But like most everything else about our relationship, I probably had that wrong too.

She smiled once more, this time a little crookedly.

'Finally washing your hands of me, eh, Joel?'

'No, sweetheart, not so much washing my hands of you,' I said. 'More like scraping you off my heel.'

I bent down to pick up the matching sports bags. When I stood up again, Lisa was gone.

HALF-AN-HOUR later, I was back in the Scenic with the bags safely resting on the back seat. I followed the exit signs and at the roundabout beyond the park's main gates, I paused. A turn either left or right would eventually take me back to the motorway. But if I were to go straight ahead, directly opposite the theme park was a large sign that said, 'Welcome to Penton Hook Marina' — which was, apparently, the largest inland marina in Britain, giving almost instant access to the Thames.

I thought of Andrew Lipton, and how he had been able to reach Lisa to give her the number of the scorpion phone. And my mind went back to the first time I'd visited his basement flat, on the day I'd taken him home from the hospital. All those smashed photographs on the floor. All those photographs still on his walls. All of them featuring Lisa. Some of them featuring both Lisa and Lipton. And some of *those* taken on a sail-boat, a yacht, moored in a marina.

Because David Handley had been in a couple of those pictures (and because at that stage I had been unaware of Lipton's family wealth), I had assumed that the boat belonged to the bank chief. Lipton had even confirmed my assumption when I asked, but it seemed now that he'd lied. Even back then this plan must have been well in motion.

The fact was that Lisa was still being ultra-cautious, pretending to be leaving the country by plane from Heathrow, but instead intending to quietly slip away on a slow boat to China. (Well, on a slow boat to the south of France, probably.) Lisa was playing to her strengths again.

Behind me a horn sounded, another car urging me to choose a direction, and I pulled away, turning left, retracing my route back to the motorway. A part of me would have liked to have gone into the marina and found Lipton's boat. A part of me would really have enjoyed standing on the deck, waiting for the moment when Lisa returned. I'd have loved to have seen her face. But a larger part of me (the better part, I hoped) wanted to get on with the important business of the day.

An image of Andrew Lipton standing on the bridge of his boat wearing an Admiral's hat came to me and almost made me laugh. Well, good luck to him. Judging from that fine selection of condoms in Lisa's little bag, it looked like he might finally have achieved his heart's desire. But if he knew what was good for him, he'd do well to keep his ears and eyes open on the voyage across the channel.

Otherwise, he might suddenly wake up in the middle of the night to discover that Lisa had decided he was fish food. And with all that plaster on his leg, he'd probably sink like a stone.

I WAS STILL about twenty-or-so-minutes from home when a police patrol car settled in close behind me on the inside lane, dominating my rear-view mirror. It was with a certain amount of resignation that I saw the cop in the passenger seat speaking into his radio — I had been expecting something like this ever since turning my mobile phone back on again. Five minutes later the patrol car peeled off, overtook me and disappeared. When I checked my rear-view mirror again, I saw that it had been replaced by a metallic-blue Saab — a metallic-blue Saab that looked rather like it had recently taken part in a stock car race.

The Saab pulled out and accelerated until it was running directly alongside me. Two angry-looking cop faces glared at me, their hair billowing in the wind streaming in through the broken sunroof. Chris Dale, nearest me in the passenger seat, pointed vehemently at the hard shoulder, ordering me to pull over. I nodded and started to indicate.

As I braked to a grinding halt, Jimmy Gill pulled the Saab in front of me, then reversed up until we were almost bumper to bumper. A split second later, a third car, a gorgeous silver Lexus, pulled up behind me, only inches from my rear bumper, effectively boxing me in. In my wing mirror, I saw the Lexus' driver's door thrown open and Scott Vaughan hurl himself out, heedless of the traffic hurtling past only a couple feet away.

Scott looked fairly angry. Angry like the Incredible Hulk on the day his pants shrank in the wash. As you can imagine, after the day I'd already put in, this was just what I wanted to see.

The QUEEN of HEARTS

I got out of the Scenic, more than ready for this encounter, and slammed the door behind me as I turned to face him. Behind me I heard the Saab's doors opening as Dale and Gill came to support their boss, but Vaughan angrily waved them back. He wanted me all to himself, it seemed, which suited me just fine.

'We've been trawling for you for hours,' Vaughan snarled at me. 'Where the fuck have you been, Joel?'

'Where I needed to go.'

'You've seen her, haven't you? You met with Lisa. Have you got my evidence?'

My reply was silence, which in this case was as good as a real answer. He glanced over my shoulder and tried to see inside the Scenic's windows. To distract him from the bags I had left on the back seat, I prodded him in the chest hard, stopping him in his tracks.

'I thought you were my friend, Scott,' I said, reaching out again. This time I didn't prod, I *shoved* him.

'What do you think you're doing? Why don't you stick to what you're good at, Joel, and keep your hands to yourself?'

This time I used both hands to thrust him away, and he went skipping back on his heels until he collided with his own car, and nearly ended up sitting on its bonnet. Once again, he had to wave his hands at his men to keep them back.

'Better let them come,' I said. 'You're going to need them to stop me tearing you apart.'

'What the hell's got into you?' he asked, seeming genuinely astonished by my anger. What an actor.

'You need to see a doctor, Scott,' I told him. 'Get him to check you for early-onset Alzheimer's or something. Your short-term memory seems to be on the fritz. Only a couple of hours ago, you admitted to letting my daughter be abducted by murderers. What the hell do you *think* has got into me?'

'But I explained that. It was a mistake. It was for the good of the case.'

'She's not even three-years-old, Scott.'

'Joel, all I'm saying is listen to reason…'

But it was too late for that now. Reason was a dead duck. It was *War of the Worlds* time. The Man from Mars was back. I pretended to turn away, but that was only to take my arm back, twist my shoulders, and generate a little torque. I saw Dale and Gill hovering half-in and half-out of the Saab, waiting for the order to move in.

Vaughan said, 'No, Joel, wait!'

Not a chance. I spun back around, swinging my fist in a long, looping right cross. Vaughan should have been expecting it. It was such an unsubtle blow, he should have seen it coming a mile off. He should have had time to duck under it and tie his bloody shoelaces if he wanted to. But he didn't.

Instead, he emitted the kind of grunt made by American football players as they crashed into each other like mad bulls. Then he flew backwards, sailing gracefully over the bonnet of his Lexus, and crashed to the ground out of sight.

Only seconds later, two large coppers body-slammed into me and ungracefully crashed me down directly on to the Lexus's bonnet, which crumpled beneath our combined weight. My arms were forced up behind my back and I heard the unmistakable sound of handcuffs being pulled out and readied for action.

'What the fuck have you done!' Vaughan screamed.

Everyone looked up, including me.

Vaughan had sharply risen to his feet, clutching a big clump of handkerchief to his nose and mouth. The handkerchief was saturated with bright red blood, and still more was dripping from it down his shirt. His voice, even when screaming, sounded as though he had a peg on his nose. But at the moment the injury to his hooter seemed to be the last thing on his mind. He was staring over the bloody handkerchief in absolute horror at his car's severely damaged bonnet.

'Guv!' Dale said. 'We were just—'

'Get the bastard off my fucking car, you morons!'

They yanked me off the car and back on to my feet, in the process pushing my arms so far up my back I should have been able to scratch my head. A low moan of despair fluttered Vaughan's bloody handkerchief as he saw the full extent of the damage. He wasn't acting now — this reaction was real.

Gill cleared his throat. 'I'm going to cuff him now, yes, Guv?'

'Yes,' Vaughan seal-barked. Then, 'No.' Then, 'I don't know! How the fuck am I supposed to think straight when I'm in this much pain?'

He seemed to gather himself, finally dragging his eyes away from his beloved car. He looked at the three of us.

'Let him go.'

My arms were released and I felt the blood rush back into them in a wave of pins and needles.

'Dale, you need to take me to the hospital. I think my nose is broken.'

Dale nodded and immediately trotted around to the driver's side of the Lexus.

'No, you fucking idiot!' Vaughan snapped. 'Do you want my upholstery covered in blood, on top of everything else? We'll take the Saab.'

Dale, in top arselicking mode, abruptly about-faced, and went to take Vaughan's arm.

Vaughan shook him off. 'I'm not a fucking invalid! Gill, you take my car and escort Mr. September to his home. Stay there until further notice and do not let him leave under *any* circumstances. Understand?'

'Yes, Guv.'

'By then I should have decided what we're going to do with him.'

'Yes, Guv.'

Vaughan limped over to the Saab, and took one last agonised glance at the injured Lexus before getting in. Dale revved the engine a few times and then pulled out into the knot of vehicles that had slowed down to a crawl to get a better look at the show we had just given them.

Gill and I faced each other for a few seconds, and neither one of us would drop our eyes. We both knew that the die was cast. We both knew what was going to happen next.

I got in the Scenic and headed for home. Gill got in the violated Lexus and followed me.

Twenty-Two

An hour later, I was once again at my kitchen window, looking out on another perfect summer afternoon. I had pulled a stool up to the sink and now sat with my elbows on the draining board, my head in my hands, my life in pieces, and my family's fate hanging in the balance.

Mrs Webber's house had looked empty when I got back home, so I presumed that she was still at the hospital, being checked out. I wondered if she and Scott Vaughan would meet up there at the A&E and bond, swapping their favourite war stories from the September front line. That would make for an interesting conversation.

Gill was still parked outside, just as he had been since I'd pulled up in my drive and very obviously carried both of Lisa's sports bags from the Scenic and into the house. He wasn't able to park in exactly the same place as he usually did, though. Someone in the cul-de-sac had a visitor who'd parked an ancient red Fiat with a lot of rust on it under the lamp-post the Saab had been shunted into earlier. Although Mrs. Webber's Volvo had already been hauled away, granular lumps of safety glass still glittered in the gutter.

Once inside the house, I'd dumped everything, the bags, my jacket and my mobile phone, in the living room and then returned to the kitchen, where the hated scorpion phone was still on the table where I'd left it. In a crazy five-minute spell, I'd raided the fridge and eaten almost everything I had found in there, including a piece of Camembert so far gone that I practically had to drink it.

Now, apart from a slight sensation of nausea, I was calm, and resigned to what had to happen. Maybe I was *too* calm. It'd already been a very long day, having seamlessly merged with the night before, and I had no idea when it might end. My eyelids were getting heavy. I might even have nodded off, except that another car suddenly pulled into the cul-de-sac.

I sat up quickly, wondering what this was, and so, I noticed, was Jimmy Gill. The car, a dark blue Peugeot saloon, slowly cruised forward and stopped alongside Vaughan's Lexus — by which time I had recognised it as a taxi, and a familiar one, at that. The driver's name was Tel, a mate of mine.

Tel was originally of Afghan extraction, and although he looked somewhat like a militant Muslim cleric, he was actually born and raised in Walton, Liverpool, so whenever he opened his mouth, he sounded exactly like one of The Beatles. He was a really nice guy, but you didn't ever want to get him on to the subject of his religion — Tel was a devout fundamentalist, and at the drop of a hat was always ready, willing and able to indoctrinate you into the Church of Liverpool Football Club.

What's he doing here now? I wondered. If this was a social call, he couldn't have chosen a more inappropriate time.

I watched as Tel got out, walked around his car without even a glance in the direction of my house, and opened his rear passenger door. I breathed a small sigh of relief as I saw him assist a shaky-looking Mrs. Webber from the back seat and then escort up her garden path to her front door. Mrs. W was wearing a cervical neck collar, and I experienced a twinge of guilt. I could only hope that she was still faking it.

Tel strolled back to his cab a few moments later, incuriously glanced at my house without noticing me at the window, and then reversed down the cul-de-sac and out on to the main road, leaving Gill and I to resume our study of the empty street. Thank God for that. I didn't think I could bear any more complications right now.

A quarter of an hour later, I was broken out of my half-doze yet again, this time because Gill had moved. When I looked more closely, I saw that he had a mobile phone held to his ear. He spoke for a few seconds, then listened again, and then hung up. He started the Lexus's engine, and before he spun it around (bumping up over the kerbs in a way that wouldn't have done the suspension much good and would have caused Scott Vaughan to throw a major hissy fit), he paused to give me a wide, knowing smile. Then he tore away.

On the counter beside me, the scorpion phone immediately rang.

'So did you get everything?' Temple asked when I picked up.

'You know I did.'

Temple chuckled. 'Yes, but I enjoyed asking you anyway. You can bring it to me now, it's time for the exchange.'

'Bring it where?'

'Well, we'll get to that later, because we have to be very, very careful now, don't we, for all our sakes? For yours, mine, and especially for Victoria's. Otherwise, this could still all end unhappily ever after.'

'What do you want me to do first?'

'In a moment, you're going to pick up those two lovely sports bags Lisa gave you and leave the house. But first, you're going to leave your own mobile behind on the kitchen counter and turn the phone I gave you on to speaker-mode. Understand? I want to hear every move you make.'

'All right.' I did so.

'Good. Once you're outside, I want you to go across to that red piece of shit parked under the lamp-post. See it? The door is unlocked. Under the driver's seat, you'll find the key. With me so far?'

'Yes.'

'Lovely, then make a move.'

I did as Temple had bid me. I popped the scorpion phone into my shirt pocket, collected my jacket and the two sports bags from the living room, and then left the house. I bypassed my Scenic and walked out into the road. The piece of shit Fiat was unlocked, as Temple had promised. I threw the bags into the front passenger footwell and then climbed in after them. I retrieved the keys from under the driver's seat.

Then I saw Mrs. Webber at her window, looking out at me. She waved. I waved.

'So far, so good,' Temple said from my shirt pocket. 'Anything to report?'

'One of my neighbours just waved at me.'

'Which neighbour — not the old woman in the car?'

'Yes.'

Temple burst out laughing. 'Fabulous, I *loved* that. What a getaway! And that fight with the garden broom the other day! Bang! Bang! Bang! Fantastic stuff!'

'Glad you're enjoying yourself,' I said. 'Can we get down to business now? I want my daughter back.'

'Of course you do. And so you shall. Very well, Joel, if you will start your engine…'

I did. The engine farted loudly, belching blue smoke from the exhaust, but it ran.

'Now, if you will drive to the end of your street and hang a left, that would be lovely. After that, keep straight on until you hit the second set of traffic lights, where you will be turning right.'

Temple sounded like a driving instructor. He also sounded like he was having fun.

'Then, if you carry on for precisely…' He broke off abruptly. 'What was that noise? What are you doing?'

'Relax, I just rolled down the window.'

'Why?'

'Because it's about ninety degrees in this sodding car and it smells like something died in here not too long ago.'

'Oh, I see.' I heard the tension leave his voice, and in its absence, the jarringly false sense of good cheer returned. 'Smells like something died in there, does it? Well, oddly enough, now that you mention it…'

THREE-QUARTERS-OF-an-hour later, I was lost. *Really* lost. I had kept a handle on my sense of direction and my knowledge of the roads and landmarks for just over the half-hour mark, with Temple forever waffling in my ear like some little tin-pot demon: Take a left at the water tower. Hang a right at the Red Lion...

But towards the end of that half-hour, the specific directions began to break down. Soon it was vague instructions that sounded entirely random: In a mile or so turn right. The next time you see a postbox, turn left, then immediately right... Actual road signs were now non-existent.

In between all these increasingly vague and seemingly unnecessary directions, Temple amused himself by regaling me with what seemed to be his two chief fascinations in life. The first was his relationship with my wife, although applying the word 'relationship' to whatever they'd had was kind of pushing it. Basically, in his head he had a list of the times and ways they had indulged in sexual congress. It was a depressingly long list.

Temple's second hobby seemed to be killing, beating, and torturing the people who got in his way. The stories about Lisa made my blood boil, and the stories about those poor unfortunates who got on his bad side chilled it almost to freezing point.

He was trying to rattle me, obviously, but after a while it seemed to have exactly the opposite effect, as the sheer repetitive quality of the stories wore me down, numbing my capacity to be shocked. Once I was past this, I was able to think more clearly, and see what he was doing with all these pointless directions.

'You've got the car bugged, haven't you?' I said, breaking into his latest gruesome monologue.

'What was that you said?'

'You don't care *which* way I go, do you, because you're tracking this car. You've got some kind of GPS tracker in it. That's why you wanted me to take this shit-heap and not my own car.'

'Ah, the penny drops!' Temple laughed. 'Busted!'

'In that case you can stop leading me around in circles now. I'm already lost and you know nobody has followed me.'

'Fair enough, Joel,' Temple said. 'Wait just a moment...' His voice seemed to fade a little as he examined something, then came back. 'Okay, carry along on this road for another two and a half miles, and then, at the unmarked crossroads, turn right. Carry on for approximately three miles and then keep an eye out for an old oak tree on your left-hand side, which we have marked for your convenience...'

'Presumably by tying a yellow ribbon around it,' I muttered.

'No,' he said. 'By nailing up the dress your daughter was wearing yesterday.'

Which shut me up.

'Any more sarky comments, Joel? No? Good. Now, beside this tree is an overgrown mud track. Turn in, nice and slow, and drive down this until it intersects with a narrow gravel access road, where you'll turn left. You'll see where to go from there. Got it?'

'Got it.'

'I'm *so* pleased we're going to have this time together.'

I followed Temple's directions to the letter and soon found myself on the narrow gravel road. But even as I drove down it, the disturbing image of my daughter's fairy outfit crucified on the oak tree stayed with me. The whole thing had been grubby, and part of the taffeta tutu was torn and hung loose.

'You see the gates ahead of you now?'

I did — a couple of eight-foot high rusting metal gates set in an unbroken stretch of ancient chain-link fence. And I saw what lay beyond. A vast flat open plain, covered in abandoned, half-wrecked buildings, including one that looked like it was once a hanger for aircraft. The most complete building, actually attached to the hanger, was a long, low concrete building, some kind of factory or assembly line, I presumed. Beyond this, largely hidden by the tall summer grass, I thought I could see the crumbling remnants of a wartime landing strip.

'Joel?'

'Yeah.'

'Get out to open the gates, drive through, then get out and close them again.'

'And then?'

'And then drive towards the buildings you can see ahead of you.'

As soon as I had done this, a black Range Rover came bounding at me out of the tree-line like a predatory cat. It surged up behind me and forced me faster down the pot-holed access road and around the back of the factory. I stopped when I had to, my forward progress halted by the presence of a weathered but still solid brick wall. I had stopped between two other cars, one a black Mercedes sports car, and the other Feelen's black Rover.

Just the sight of the Rover made my heart beat quicker. If Feelen was here, so was Vic.

The Range Rover crunched to a halt directly behind me, blocking the Fiat in. In the rear-view mirror, I saw a man climb out. A big man. He was well over six feet tall, wore a black leather box jacket and had a shaven head. Like Feelen, he had his fair share of old boxing injuries, but by no means as many.

I opened the car door to face him and immediately found a large hand wrapped around my throat. The thug pulled me out of the car and then pushed me back and held me against it one-handed, using the other to pat me down. He did a thorough job and missed nothing. It was instantly clear that he was nothing at all like Feelen, in that he was a heavyweight, had probably once been a half-decent fighter, and was more than likely a fairly serious villain.

Once he had finished cleaning out my pockets and checking which way I dressed of a morning, he let go of my throat and stepped back. He stuffed my wallet into his jacket pocket, then turned off the scorpion phone and tucked that away too. Then he rolled his big shiny head toward an open black doorway in the side of the vast building and grunted at me to move.

I leant back into the car and pulled out the two sports bags. The heavyweight tried to take them from me, but I held on tight, and something about the way I did it seemed to make an impression on him. I had been prepared to concede the man-handling and the intimate frisking, but the bags were a different story.

'They're for Temple,' I said. 'I'll only hand them over to him.'

He shrugged, then headed for the dark doorway. Just before he disappeared into the interior gloom, he looked back over his shoulder to check that I was obediently following him. I was.

The doorless doorway led into a rabbit's warren of corridors leading to offices and smaller workshops, some linked by doorways and others separated by frosted glass panels, now mostly cracked or entirely broken. Almost every surface was blackened with soot, as though there had been a fire here at some point. Damp had penetrated the building and clumps of plaster from the walls and ceiling had fallen to the ground. I could even feel the chill damp of the concrete floor through the soles of my shoes. The whole place smelled of smoke and rot.

The huge thug moved steadily ahead of me, a darker shadow in the general gloom, turning first one way and then the other, and I was reminded of the dreams I'd had at the start of this little adventure, of somebody being chased through a dark maze by some beast, some minotaur. But in those nightmares, Lisa had been the one in the maze. Where was she now?

On a boat, quite probably, I thought, perhaps even now on its way downriver. She'd be sunning herself on the deck, telling Andrew Lipton that she loved him back... and secretly eyeing up one of the crewmen at the same time. Meanwhile, I had taken her place in the nightmare.

I realised that I had been wrong the other night when I'd been watching the shopping channel — if anyone ever needed a dreamcatcher, *I* was that person.

The thug turned yet another corner and when I turned after him his bulk was suddenly outlined in a brilliant white light that made me squint. I followed him out of the narrow corridor and into the main body of the building, the part that was like a hanger. It was a vast open concrete area, littered with gravel and cinders and dotted here and there with rectangular holes, like inspection pits in a garage, and large rust stains tracing the outline of the heavy machinery that had once stood there.

The QUEEN of HEARTS

The arched roof high overhead was made of large corrugated sheets, most likely asbestos, and held together by rusted bolts the size of clenched fists. It was dotted with half-a-dozen paned skylights, some of them broken, others green with algae and moss. Pigeons flapped around the steel rafters, casting shadows in the dusty sunlight.

At the centre of all this open space, Nicolas Richard Temple stood waiting for me, his hands loosely clasped behind his back, like visiting royalty. Angie Edwards stood about fifteen-feet to his right, smirking at me. She was wearing a light summer dress, white with little red flowers embroidered on it, and white shoes with harpoon-like heels that would have worried a blue whale. Between them was a rusty fifty-gallon oil drum with several lengths of freshly split timber poking out of the top. I smelled petrol.

'Joel!' Temple cried happily. 'So nice to see you again!'

'Wish I could say the same. To me you still look like something that crawled out of a sewer.'

Temple just laughed.

I could bitch all I liked, but in truth the years appeared to have been more than kind to him. His cap of dark hair was still smooth and thick, untouched by grey, and his face seemed equally smooth and boyish, and totally line-free. Obviously, frowning wasn't a large part of a conscienceless being's facial routine. (*Want to avoid those troublesome wrinkles? Forget Botox — be a sociopath!*) It looked as though life had been just as generous to him as the years. His bespoke suit, not that I was any expert, looked like it may have cost several thousand pounds, and his highly-polished handmade shoes were like works of art in a posh gallery.

I followed the large thug across the expanse of concrete, cinders crunching under my cheap supermarket-bought shoes. I stopped about fifteen paces away and watched him hand the contents of my pockets to his employer. Closer up, I could see the one clear mark the advancing years had left on Temple — a growing paunch that had been hidden only by the superb cut of his suit.

Temple saw me looking at his waistline.

'Yes, one of the unfortunate drawbacks of a successful life, I'm afraid — not that you'd know anything about that, of course. I don't suppose you'd have any quick tips on how to lose about ten or eleven pounds of unsightly flab?'

'Why don't you try cutting your head off?'

'Sticks and stone, Joel, sticks and stones.'

He looked at the scorpion phone briefly and smiled.

'Just to let you know,' he said, 'the GPS tracker isn't in the car. It's in the phone. A miracle of modern technology. Everywhere you took this phone, you took me along for the ride. Imagine how pissed off I was when you left it at home when you went to meet Lisa. If only your memory was a little better, I'd have everything.'

'Happy to have disappointed you.'

He tossed the phone over to Angie, who caught it deftly and immediately dropped it into the oil drum.

'This is everything he had on him?' Temple asked the thug, holding up my bulging wallet.

'Yeah. He's clean now.'

'Good.' Temple opened my wallet, and said, 'Christ Almighty,' when he saw how much crap was in it, and then began to thumb through the contents. 'Big shot,' he said to Angie, holding out the only bank note my wallet currently contained.

Her permanent smirk widened. 'Wow, a whole twenty quid!'

'No wonder Lisa left you,' Temple said. 'Probably just wanted someone with a bit of class — a bit of the old *crème de la crème*.'

I cocked my head. 'You're not talking about yourself, are you? You could get done under the Trade Descriptions Act.'

'You know what they say, Joel,' Temple said. 'Cream rises.'

'Yeah, I've heard that. Mind you, they also say that shit floats...'

Temple tut-tutted me.

He had worked his way through to the photographs at the back of the wallet. Mostly they were photos of Vic, but there was one of Lisa in there too, which was the one Temple looked at most closely. He snorted in amusement as he stuffed them all back in, and then tossed my entire wallet over to Angie.

'No!' I said. 'Not the photos.'

'I'm sure you have more at home,' Temple said. 'I mean, even *I* have a few photos of Lisa — videos, too,' he leered. 'Maybe I'll post them online when all this is over.'

Angie made a teasing motion to drop my wallet into the oil drum and I swore at her.

'Language, language, Joel. I don't want you sullying the ears of my ladyfriend.'

'You mean the whore?'

Angie bristled immediately, but Temple only laughed again.

'No need to get all offended, my dear. You *are* a whore — and let's face it, a damn good one.'

Angie conceded the point. 'Got *your* pecker up, didn't I?' she asked me. 'Although I must admit that our last encounter was a bit of a shocker. *Buzzzzzz....*'

Temple laughed loudly as Angie mimed tazering me, and even louder when she carelessly tossed the wallet on the floor between us and I went scrabbling desperately to recover it.

When I stood up again, he had his eyes on the sports bags. 'Bring them over here,' he told me.

'I want to see Vic first.'

'I hardly think you're in a position to bargain right now, Joel. Do as you're told, like a good boy.'

'My daughter first.'

Temple sighed and then shrugged expansively. 'Okay, whatever you say.' He reached inside his expensive suit jacket and produced his own mobile phone, hatched from the same bug-cocoon as the one he'd given me. He speed-dialled a number that was immediately answered. 'Bring her through now.'

He closed his phone and put it away. Then he looked at me expectantly. I hefted the bag containing the money in my right hand and tossed it over to land at his feet. He opened the zip a few inches, just to verify the contents, and then slid it over to Angie.

'Count it.'

I was about to begin explaining why they were going to find it short, but suddenly found all my rational thinking processes disrupted. I could hear my daughter's voice.

I turned about, almost tripping over my own feet. I couldn't see her yet, but her voice was growing louder and louder. She was speaking to someone else, probably

Feelen. Then I saw her. She stepped out of the same dark corridor that had brought me here, hand in hand with the Goblin. I sighed in relief. She looked to be in good spirits, and unafraid, and clearly had not been harmed in any way.

Vic saw me the very second that her eyes adjusted to the brighter light, and her face exploded with joy. She dropped Feelen's hand like a hot coal and came racing over the concrete floor towards me.

'Daddeeee!' she happily squealed. 'Daddeeee!'

I thought my heart would burst.

Twenty-Three

I WENT DOWN on my knees to meet her and she slammed into me like a kind of infant-shaped missile. She wrapped her little arms around my neck and almost choked the life out of me, and covered my whole face with little wet kisses that pierced my flesh like knives. I held her tightly to me, so very tightly, wondering how I had ever imagined that the feeling I had for Lisa was love.

No, that emotion had been some pale echo, *this* was love. Love without question. Love without limitation. Love without parallel.

I buried my face in the place where Vic's neck, shoulder and chest met, and I inhaled as deeply as I could. It was the sweetest smell I'd ever known. And I remembered when I had smelled the faintest traces of this beautiful scent back at Angie's rented house, how absolutely terrified I had been that the memories of it were all I would ever have.

I opened my eyes, blinking back tears, and saw Feelen standing behind Vic. He was awkwardly holding Vic's stuff, her overnight bag and her teddy, and he looked uncomfortable and ashamed, as well he might. On the other hand, clearly he had looked after her as well as he was able to, which, judging from her appearance, seemed well enough.

I gave him a small nod to acknowledge that he had done as he had promised. But it didn't seem to raise his spirits.

'Ahh, what a lovely little reunion this is, so very touching!'

Temple's voice came from close behind me, and then I heard the second bag being pulled away from my side, sliding over the gritty floor.

I stood up, lifting Vic with me, and turned. Temple had dragged the sports bag back to his original position. Now he opened it and briefly considered the contents. Then he smiled.

'Mr. Staines, if you would like to do the honours?'

The thug grunted and walked toward the oil drum. From the pocket of his jacket he produced a box of matches.

'How's it looking over there, Angie?'

Angie was methodically counting the cash in the sports bag and then transferring each wad into another bag she must have brought with her, a long green canvas bag that looked something like an army kitbag.

'Okay so far,' she said. 'I'm not sure, though — it looks like it might be a little light. How're things over there?'

'Good. I think everything's here.'

The thug, Staines, struck a match, held it for a second, and then dropped it into the oil drum. There was an immediate thumping explosion as the accelerant they had poured on the timber inside the oil drum ignited, and Staines leapt back. Orange fire erupted like a plume of dragon's breath and flared two or three metres into the air before settling down.

Temple was looking at me speculatively, his eyebrows raised. 'Do you know anything about the money, Joel? Any of it missing?'

'Lisa kept some of it back,' I admitted. 'About two hundred grand. She said you should think of it as severance pay from her bank job. She also said you'd understand that if you want her to disappear for good, she'll need it.'

Temple took a double handful of files out of the sports bag and stepped forward to drop them into the flames. He watched the fire eat the paper, and considered.

'I suppose she's right,' he said after a while. 'Difficult to disappear without a decent wedge in your back pocket. Although she does have Mr. Lipton's generosity to fall back on now, doesn't she?'

He smiled when I didn't take the dangling bait. He picked the box of flash drives out of the bag, opened it, and then tossed the sticks one after the other into the oil drum. The smoke issuing from the drum grew darker and foul smelling, and the flames licked higher.

Angie finished putting the last of the money into the long green bag and stood up. 'Two hundred and ten grand short,' she said.

Temple nodded in acknowledgement, then stepped away from the bag of evidence, indicating that she should carry on with the cremation.

'I'm not worried about the missing money so much,' he said to me. 'That's fair enough. But the real question is, Joel, do you think Lisa will stick to the deal you made for her? Will she stay out of the UK, and keep her mouth shut?'

'Yes,' I said. 'She's too scared to do anything else.'

'Good, good...' He nodded again, then grinned. 'Because if even Lisa is prepared to stick to the deal, then she'll believe that *I'll* stick to it, too. Which is going to make her a lot easier to catch up with.'

My blood seemed to stop dead in my veins.

'What are you talking about?'

'If she isn't looking over her shoulder all the time, then eventually she'll make a mistake, and then I'll have her.'

'But the deal...'

'Come on, Joel, you know Lisa — or you *should* know her — almost as well as I do. She won't have told either of us the whole truth. I'll bet she's copied a lot of these files and stashed them somewhere, just as a safeguard in case I go back on the deal. Or, more likely, until she's bled Lipton dry and moved on again. What do you think, Joel — if that happened, would she get a job in a bar to pay the rent on some grotty Tenerife apartment? Yes? No? Or would she wake up one morning at dawn, as is her wont, dial a few numbers, and then demand more money from me in return for her continuing silence?'

Yes, now that I thought of it, Option Two was definitely more my wife's style.

'I know what you're thinking,' Temple grinned. 'Lisa, keep her mouth shut? Ha! She's more likely to keep her legs shut — and believe me, that's very unlikely.'

'But even if you did capture her,' I said, ignoring this last jibe, 'you'll still be in the same bargaining position. She's clever enough to make sure that her copies would find their way to the right people if anything should happen to her.'

'Yes, she is. But once I have her in my hands, she'll tell me anything I want to know, including how to retrieve the copies safely. There'll be no secrets between us then.'

'She wouldn't tell you. Not if keeping the secret was going to save her life.'

'There are worse things than dying, Joel, I can assure you of that. I'll turn Lisa over to Angie, who's been crazy to get her hands on her for a long time — eh, Ang?'

Still feeding the flames with incriminating documents, Angie's smirk looked monstrous.

'You see,' he went on, 'whoring is just one of Angie's many specialities. She enjoys the sex, but she really has a passion for torture. You've probably never heard of a man called Bernard Jacks…'

But I had. This was the former boss of the Top Dog management company which had promoted Feelen's boxing career. The man who, according to Scott Vaughan, had 'committed suicide' in way so unbearable that no man could have conceived of it. I had news for Scott Vaughan. No man *had* conceived of that death. It had been woman's work.

'…but you did meet him once,' Temple continued. 'You may not recall, but Mr. Jacks was with us in that Kennington cellar all those years ago — the man who wanted his dinner, remember?'

I did. *Let's get it done, I'm missing a fucking good dinner for this chimp's tea party…*

'Well, soon after that, he went a little bit soft on us, started getting flaky.' He was shaking his head slowly at some memory I wasn't sure I wanted any part of. 'Oh well, he was coming apart at the seams anyway. Angie just sort of helped him along…'

He looked at me and grinned.

'You know, I hear that Andrew Lipton's parents own an absolutely magnificent villa on the Cote d'Azur. I believe we could look for Lisa there first, even make a little holiday of it...'

'I don't care,' I said suddenly. 'I don't care who's got what, or what anybody's done in the past or is going to do in the future. I'm walking out of here, right now. Me and my daughter, we're leaving.'

Angie tossed another load of papers into the flames and a cloud of ashes and sparks flew from the top of the oil drum.

And Temple quietly said, 'No, Joel, you're not going anywhere.'

Angie stooped and reached into the strange long green bag which I now recognised as an old-style cricket bag, the sort of things stumps, pads, and bats were carried in to the field of play. But what she brought out from under the bundles of cash wasn't a cricket bat. It was a baseball bat, of course. She carried it across to Temple like it was a holy relic.

The wood was stained with old blood. *My* blood. Temple had kept it safe all these years. To finish the job.

'I was only playing with you last time,' he said, 'but now I'm going to do it for real.'

I took a step back, aware of Staines somewhere over to my right, and Feelen directly behind me. Angie stood by the oil drum, happily burning, but she was watching me too. I was boxed in. Surrounded.

'What's the point of this?' I asked Temple. 'What would you gain?'

'The same thing I'd gain from killing Lisa, even though, ultimately, it might mean my ruin. The score would be settled. Because nobody — absolutely no-

fucking-body — takes Nick Temple for a ride. Nobody screws me and gets away with it. Because I'm like an elephant, I never forget. And if you can never forget, you can never forgive.'

'You were always going to do this, weren't you?'

He nodded slowly. 'It's long past due. I only let you live the last time so you'd set yourself up, to draw your teeth. It worked in the short term, but in the long run, it turned out to be a mistake. One of the worst of my life. Dead, your suspicions would have counted for nothing, fizzled away, and I would still be on the force now. Up on high. Brass. Royalty. With you still alive, those suspicions grew, festered, until the only smart move was to get out.'

Temple raised the bat and rested it on his shoulder.

'Now, I suggest that if you don't want to see your daughter's brains on the floor before you die, you'd better put her down.'

Until this moment, Vic had kept her face scrunched into my shoulder, but now she looked up and pointed at Temple angrily.

'You a bad man!'

'Yes, but I'm not *all* bad,' Temple replied, looking only at me, looking me dead in the eyes.

It was like being in a staring contest with the devil. One blink and my soul would be lost.

'Don't worry, Joel, I'll make sure Victoria's taken care of. There are lots of markets throughout the world for young girls these days — the younger the better, in some places. I'm sure that Angie, with all her experience, will be able to groom her and negotiate a good asking price.'

'No!' To my surprise, Feelen had stepped forward to stand beside me. 'That's not right, Mr. Temple. That's just sick, you can't—'

'Shut your fucking mouth!' Temple bellowed. 'Never presume to tell me what I can or can't do!'

'But...'

Temple nodded once, and I heard a loud thud. Out of the corner of my eye, I saw Feelen fall to his hands and knees, stunned. Staines had slipped up behind him and clubbed him with a length of wood that matched those which had been set alight in the oil drum. Vic looked down at him with her hands held to her mouth.

'Oh, poor Greggy!'

I put her down on the ground and pushed her lightly towards him. Blood was running down the side of his shaved head from his cauliflower ear, which had been split almost in half by the blow. Vic put her arm around him, sternly wagged her finger at Staines, and told him that *he* was a very bad man too.

Unlike Temple, Staines didn't bother trying to justify himself — not even when Vic told him he'd have to go sit on the naughty step now.

Feelen raised his head a little, and I saw that he was dazed but not altogether out of it. Our eyes met, and I also saw that he understood I'd have to try something now. *Anything.* I willed him to keep Vic out of it, and by some miracle he understood this too.

He put his arm around my daughter's slim waist, as if he just needed a little cuddle, and not so that he could hold her back out of danger while her father was being battered to death.

'But here's what I'll do for you, Joel,' Temple said, as though offering me a great kindness. 'Purely out of the sheer goodness of my heart, I'll save Victoria from a terrible fate in a far-off country. I'll forgo the small fortune I'd make by selling her. I'll save her from the perverts and the sadists… and keep her for *myself*. I'll bring her up at my own expense, and I'll break her in when she's old enough. Later on, when I'm bored with her, I'll see that she's gainfully employed. I'll put a roof over her head, and Angie will put a mattress under her back.'

He smiled.

'But I'll only do all of these things if you *beg* me.'

But I didn't beg him. I wasn't anywhere near begging him. I had an ace up my sleeve, and I was about to play it.

'You know, Nick, when I found out you were the one looking for Lisa, I was a bit puzzled. I found myself wondering why a serious player like you would employ a henchman as inept and stupid as Gregory Feelen to do your dirty work.'

I ignored Feelen's muted protest from behind me.

'And it was all so *visible*, too. I wondered why would you let that happen, especially when you had Angie working undercover so subtly? It was really out of character. But now I realise why you chose him. Even back then, you knew that you were eventually going to need a fall guy, and you couldn't have chosen better, could you?'

'Huh?' Feelen asked.

'What have you got planned?' I asked Temple. 'Some kind of murder/suicide thing? Me as the victim, Feelen as the suicide?'

'Something like that,' Temple smiled.

'Hey!' Feelen said.

'It's worked before, it'll work again.'

'Not this time.' I shook my head. 'Scott Vaughan will never believe it in a million years. But you don't much care about that, do you? You don't care what he thinks, as long as he can't *prove* anything. And if the cops need another little nudge in the wrong direction, you can always have your inside man plant some false evidence to move things along.'

'How true.'

'At first I thought it was James Gill — formerly Jimmy Fish, Jimmy the Eel — but it isn't Gill. And then I got really paranoid and started to think you'd nobbled Scott Vaughan himself. But it isn't Vaughan, either. It's *Dale*, isn't it? Chris Dale? Young, dumb, ambitious, and greedy. How did you get your hooks into him?'

'Oh, that was simplicity itself,' Temple admitted smugly. 'Angie made the first approach, I made the second. It was the old classic one-two. Honey and money.'

'Do you know where Dale is now?'

'Probably still at the hospital, holding Vaughan's hand while he has his nose reset,' Temple laughed.

'No, you're wrong. He's right here.'

Temple glanced around the empty space theatrically.

'Not in *here*, obviously, but outside. In the back of a squad car, with his hands cuffed behind his back.'

Temple glanced at Angie and Staines, who both shrugged.

'You're bluffing, Joel,' he said.

'No, I'm not bluffing. I finally figured out your inside man was Dale just after I'd collected the bags from Lisa. Something Vaughan said to me earlier came back to me — something about how a lot of the younger cops still hero-worshipped you. Suddenly, I just *knew* he was the one. And I also knew how to get you. Before I set off home from meeting Lisa, I stopped and called Vaughan from a pay phone.'

'No, you didn't,' Temple shook his head. 'Dale would have found out. That's what he's there for.'

In fact, to bypass Dale in the chain of communication, I had actually phoned Vaughan's *mother* and asked her to call her son over to her house urgently. Mrs Vaughan's number had been scrawled down on the back of half a London Pride beer mat more than ten years ago, and it had been sitting there in my wallet ever since then, just waiting for the right moment to serve its purpose.

'Didn't Dale call to tell you that Vaughan had dashed off to see his poor, frail old mum? Of course he did. But it didn't trouble you, did it, because that kind of thing has become a regular occurrence ever since her stroke?'

Temple said nothing, but his face went very still.

'As soon as Vaughan got to her house, his mother gave him the payphone number I was waiting at, and he called me straight back. I told him about Dale, and about you, and together we came up with a plan.'

'I think you're absolutely full of shit,' Temple scowled. He smacked the baseball bat meaningfully against the palm of his hand. 'It's going to be very interesting to see what actually comes out of your head when I crack it open.'

'I'm not lying,' I told him. 'The fight between me and Vaughan was a complete set-up. He had a joke-shop blood capsule in his mouth and a stained handkerchief ready in his pocket. I threw a punch at him, and he jumped over his car out of sight. When he came back up, spitting blood with his hankie over his face, how would Dale know any better?'

Angie shifted on her stiletto-shod feet. 'Nick, maybe we'd better...'

'Be quiet!' Temple snapped at her. 'Let him speak.'

'Thanks, Nick,' I said. 'So then Vaughan told Gill to escort me home and make sure I didn't leave, and he got Dale to drive him to the A&E. From that moment on, Dale was under constant surveillance. Obviously I wasn't there, but I would guess that this was pretty much what happened: Vaughan got himself taken off by a nurse for treatment, leaving Dale to his own devices in the waiting area. Probably he called you straight away to let you know I had the bags, yes?'

Temple didn't answer, didn't make any movement at all.

'Knowing Vaughan like I do, for the next half-hour or so, he probably flirted with the nurses and got them to bring him tea and biscuits. Then he went out with a dressing taped over his nose and told Dale he wanted Gill to take his damaged Lexus around to the body shop, ASAP. As Dale well knows, Vaughan loves his car, and this was to be a priority. But, Dale asks, what about making sure that the troublesome Joel September stays put at home? Ah, Vaughan replies, just send a couple of uniforms in a patrol car...

'Then Vaughan disappears back into the treatment area, and Dale makes the necessary calls. One to Gill, telling him to take Vaughan's car to be repaired, and one to *you* to say that the coast would soon be clear. And then, belatedly, he calls the local station, telling them to despatch a patrol car to my house to take over the surveillance. Is it an emergency? they ask. No, Dale replies, it is not...'

Temple's flat glare was murderous.

'And as soon as Dale walked back into the hospital after making those calls,' I finished, 'he was arrested.'

I smiled at Temple, letting him feel it. Letting him *taste* it.

'Any of this sounding remotely plausible, Nicky?'

Once again, no response. Not from Temple or any one of his cronies. They were attentive but carved in stone, like gargoyles on a church roof.

'Now,' I continued, 'I bet you're just dying to ask why there was such a long delay before Dale was told to send Gill to the body shop — almost an hour in total. Was it just Vaughan maintaining the fiction of medical treatment? Well, actually, no, it wasn't. It was to create a window for us to work in. You see, after Gill had followed me home, I took the bags into the house and left them in the living room while I had a cup of coffee in the kitchen — and in my living room was a team of police tech' guys, waiting to make copies of the evidence.'

Temple had now paled beneath his tan.

'They'd come in the back way and taken over the whole room, pushed all the furniture back and everything, frightening the life out of my cat in the process. They had two huge photocopiers, about five or six laptops, video cameras, scanners, the whole works... Limited time, you see, had to get as much as they could as quickly as possible. I thought they might have had a little trouble with the memory sticks, but apparently they broke all Lisa's passwords easily enough. In fact, they got absolutely everything they wanted. By the time Dale had called Gill and Gill had driven off, the tech' boys already had the bags packed up for me again. Then *you* called, Nick, and the game really began.'

I felt like finishing the story with a triumphant *ta-daaah!* but decided against it. Temple studied me intently for the longest time.

'I believe you,' he said finally. 'You've beaten me, Joel. You've won. I'll have to leave the country immediately, and I'll never be able to come back.'

To my surprise, he managed to smile again.

'But fortunately, I've been prepared for this eventuality for years. I have any number of false identities set up and ready to go. The majority of my money is already banked abroad, in countries which don't believe in income tax — or indeed extradition, if it should ever come to that. And although it looks a bit overgrown now, the landing strip outside is still perfectly functional — I can have a Cessna here within the hour.'

Temple shifted his stance and took a firmer grip on the baseball bat, waggling it experimentally in my direction.

'So what have you really won, Joel? *Nothing.* All you've really done is to forced me to make my move a little earlier than I planned to. Hardly an inconvenience at all. But that doesn't help you, does it? Not in this position. I'm still going to kill you. But now…'

He adjusted his grip on the bat and dropped his eyes to a point behind me.

'…now I think I'm going to make you watch your daughter die first…'

Twenty-Four

At this threat, Vic broke free from Feelen's encircling arm and ran to my side, wrapping her arms tightly around my legs. She was crying hard now, and trembling badly. I picked her up, held her to me, and told her not to worry, not to be scared, because everything was going to be all right, Daddy would make everything right.

'Even *I* know you shouldn't lie to little children,' Temple said softly. 'Don't promise what you can't deliver.'

'I'm still not lying. You've forgotten something, Nicky — earlier I told you that Chris Dale was outside this building in the back of a squad car, under arrest. Remember that? A whole lot of cops would have brought him here, which means that right now you are surrounded.'

'I didn't forget. That's the one bit of your story I didn't believe. It's exactly the same tired old "you're surrounded" ploy you tried all those years ago, down in the cellar. You really should have learned some new tricks by now, Joel.'

On cue, his sidekick Angie snickered in mirthless amusement. Temple slowly began to circle in my direction, finessing his grip on the bat. I slowly began to circle away.

'Nobody could have followed you here along the crazy route I put you through, not without us knowing about it,' Temple said. 'Staines was behind you for a part of the journey too, just to make doubly sure. And Chris Dale, under duress or not, didn't know the location for this little jamboree. Therefore, no one knows where you are, and no one can save you.'

'You're right,' I admitted, 'I haven't learnt any new tricks. But I'm older now, and a little bit wiser, and I know a man who *has* — so do you, his name's Scott Vaughan. You know that little GPS chip you put in your phone to track me? Well, guess what, Scott's tech' team had some of them too. They sewed one into the lining of the evidence bag, and one into the lining of the money bag.'

Temple looked around at the empty sports bags. No one and nothing else moved.

'Also, I have a bug sewn into my jacket. Every word you say is being recorded for posterity.'

'If that's true, where are the cops?' Temple asked, turning back to me. 'Where's Vaughan? Why haven't they rushed in to save you?'

Which, now that I thought of it, was a bloody good point, actually. Where on earth *was* the cavalry? I hoped to hell nothing had gone wrong.

'They're not here, are they?' Temple grinned. 'They'll *never* be here. Christ, you almost had me going there. But it was a bluff, after all. Joel, if I knew you could lie that well, I might have asked you to work for me years ago.'

'I told you before. I don't bluff and I don't lie. Do I, Scott?'

The silence seemed absolute, eternal. You could have heard a pin drop. A mouse squeak. A sparrow fart.

The QUEEN of HEARTS

'*Do* I?'

Temple picked up on the new note of desperation in my voice, and it made him laugh.

And then Vaughan finally broke cover, stepping into the body of the building from a patch of darkness behind Temple's back.

'Nope,' he said happily. 'You told the truth, Joel. The truth, the whole truth, and nothing but the truth. You are to be commended for your honesty.'

Jimmy Gill swaggered out after Vaughan, unable to keep the joyous grin off his face.

'Hello, Nicky,' he called out, and actually waggled his sausage-like fingers in a mocking little wave. I don't think I'd ever seen a fat, grey man as happy as Gill was at that moment. He looked like an elephant after a few glasses of champagne at a Christmas party.

Then, like a dance troop from a Gilbert and Sullivan revival, dozens of uniformed officers began to filter in behind them, fanning out across the vast concrete stage. Both Angie Edwards and Staines panicked and tried to leg it, heading back towards the corridor from which we'd entered the hanger.

They were almost there when another legion of cops swarmed out of that darkness, too. Angie Edwards and the stoic Mr. Staines were seized and forced to the ground, their wrists immediately forced behind their backs and looped with plastic ties. Staines took it like a man, strong and silent. Angie Edwards took it like a mythological harpy, spitting, scratching, biting, kicking, screaming, and swearing.

I exhaled shakily. It was finally over.

'You took your bloody time,' I called to Vaughan.

Vaughan very slowly — ecstatically, orgasmically slowly — began to close the twenty-five-metre gap between us. 'We could have come in a lot sooner, but Jimmy and I were quite curious to see just how much further you could get Mr. Temple to incriminate himself. It was a stunning performance, Joel. Absolutely *stunning*.'

Gill, just a step or two behind him, began to applaud me. Vaughan joined in a moment later. They weren't applauding me really, they were applauding themselves, the pair of them almost drunk on their success.

Vaughan locked eyes with Temple, who had simply been staring at him as he approached, absolutely shell-shocked by the turn of events. 'What about you, Nick?' he asked. 'Was it good for you?'

'Yes, it was a great performance,' Temple replied, his voice hollow. Then he began to speak with a new urgency. 'But if you want to see something really *stunning*, just you watch this — this is how to end things with a real bang!'

Temple's back was to me and I couldn't see his face. But I could see Vaughan's, and as Temple's voice rose to a full-bodied roar, I saw the alarm appear on Vaughan's face like a bloodstain racing through cotton.

As Temple began to raise the baseball bat and spin back toward us, I saw Vaughan lurch forward, skip to break into a sprint, and heard him began to shout for help. Gill, heavier and slower, pointed at Temple and shouted for assistance, his face wild.

At the moment Temple completed his turn, his upswing reached its apogee, and immediately the bat began to sweep down again with lethal force.

I tried to turn away, to lower my head and raise my shoulders, to provide some cover for Vic's precious head. But I already knew that it was too late.

Too late.

The QUEEN of HEARTS

Then something flew past us, whirling, a dervish, a blur, and in the next instant there was a loud grunt, the sound of flesh and bone striking flesh and bone, and then Temple's baseball bat was twanging about harmlessly on the gritty concrete floor.

I turned back.

Temple himself was laid out cold, his mouth all bloody, and his jaw hanging awry in a way that suggested serious dislocation. Standing triumphantly above his inert body was his conqueror and our saviour.

It was Greg Feelen. The Goblin.

I felt like cheering. Vic actually *did*.

Feelen stared down at his previously all-powerful boss with an expression that said he couldn't believe the enormity of what he'd done. Then he raised the fist that had done the damage — the fabled (though much-maligned) Lightning Bolt — and stared at it incredulously.

Then his expression of amazement dissolved into one of absolute agony, and I realised that Temple's jaw wasn't the only casualty here.

'My fingers!' Feelen suddenly screamed. 'I broke my fucking fingers!'

A SHORT TIME later, Jimmy Gill walked Vic and I through the rabbit warren of dark and gloomy corridors and back out into the daylight. The afternoon was now giving way to evening, and the golden sunlight was warm and sweet on our faces.

The QUEEN of HEARTS

Vic, emotionally and physically exhausted by the day's events, was all but conked out in my arms, her head on my shoulder, her little sparrow-legs dangling loose. The strength-sapping weight of her reminded me that she was growing day by day, and that I was likewise getting older day by day. I could feel the strain of carrying her for so long in my shoulders and in my back, not to mention my knee, which was making ominous creaking sounds.

But I would not have relinquished my hold on her. Not for the world, not for anything. Let my shoulders and my arms ache like rotten teeth, let my back complain to its heart's content, let my knee creak like a rusty hinge. Screw them all, I had my daughter back, and that was all I cared about.

Gill left us and went over to join Vaughan, who was standing at the centre of a phalanx of cop cars and other emergency vehicles, including two ambulances. In the back of one of the two squad cars, I saw Chris Dale staring blankly out at nothing. I guessed that a part of his mind was already banged up in prison, wondering how his new roomie would take the news that he was sharing his cell with an ex-cop, and becoming increasingly afraid of the developments that lights-out might bring.

Vaughan was speaking on his mobile phone, looking a lot like a man whose fondest dreams had all come true at the same time. Without breaking off his conversation — with a superior, I assumed — he and Gill gave each other a high-five, then a low-five, and then finally a sequence of hand clasps that completed their transformation into teenagers.

Inside one of the ambulances, its back doors open for ventilation, Greg Feelen sat waiting for his lift to the hospital. That trip was currently being delayed because of the nuisance Nick Temple was making of himself back in the abandoned hanger, which was bad enough to require the paramedics from the second ambulance as well as the first.

After Staines and Angie Edwards had been dragged away and placed in the back of separate patrol cars, the paramedics had arrived with a collapsible gurney to collect Temple. Moments after they had carefully lifted him onto it, I saw that Temple was beginning to regain consciousness.

When his eyes had first flickered open, he had seemed confused and disoriented by the two paramedics leaning over him. Then he was stricken by nausea, and turned his head to emit a thin stream of vomit on to the shoulder of his expensive suit jacket. And once he had moved his damaged jaw, he'd started to grunt and screech like some kind of wild animal on the wrong end of a pitchfork, and his eyes had crossed with pain.

The fact was that not only had his jaw been dislocated by Feelen's Lightning Bolt, it had also been fractured in two places — once just to the left of his chin (the primary injury) and again just under his right ear (which the paramedics referred to as a *contre coup*). To put it in plain terms that even a dumb layman like me could understand (understand and thoroughly *appreciate*), Temple was in absolute screaming agony.

As soon as the paramedics tried fitting him with a cervical collar, Temple reacted by punching the first paramedic in the eye and kicking the second paramedic in the stomach. Then, unbelievably, he vaulted off the gurney and tried to make a run for it, one hand holding his slack jaw in place.

The QUEEN of HEARTS

He managed to get ten or so paces away from the gurney before three large uniformed coppers landed on him in a none too gentle way and hauled him back to the gurney, where, under the direction of two now extremely pissed-off paramedics, they strapped him down again. By this time Temple was out and out wailing. He was also frothing at the mouth, and his eyes looked like they had sprung out of the sockets on springs.

It was a terrible thing to hear and a terrible thing to see, and I have to admit that I loved absolutely every single moment of it. Had it not been for the distress it had begun to cause Vic, it was a show I could have watched all day long.

As it says somewhere in the Bible, very, very occasionally, very, very bad things happen to very, very bad people — and it's so very, very *satisfying!*

'Wanna see Greggy,' Vic suddenly said, startling me. I had assumed she was fast asleep by now, but apparently not.

She raised her head from my shoulders, pushed a lot of sweaty hair out of her eyes and glanced around, finally spotting Feelen sitting morosely in the back of the ambulance.

'Wanna say bye-bye.'

'Okay.'

I supposed that I should say bye-bye, too. And thank you. If not for his intervention, this day would have finished very differently.

I carried Vic over and she squirmed to be let down. I set her down on the ambulance's top step and she hurried inside the vehicle, and gave Feelen the sort of hug I thought she reserved only for me. Maybe I should have been jealous, but I wasn't. He deserved it.

While they were hugging, I heard a small commotion behind me and I turned. They were now just in the process of bringing Temple out of the building and transporting him into the other ambulance. The four paramedics were carrying the gurney between them over the uneven ground, and a squad of policemen escorted them fore and aft. It was like a funeral cortège for a premature burial.

Temple, even his head strapped down at this stage, was raving like a madman, despite the considerable pain it must have been causing him. And then it occurred to me that this could be the optimum moment to cause him a little *more* pain.

Just a little, you understand. What we might call the icing on the cake.

I glanced back into the first ambulance. Feelen and Vic had now broken their embrace, and Feelen was holding out his injured hand for Vic to inspect, like a puppy with a poorly paw. She was okay.

I turned away and started across to the other ambulance just as they began to load Temple inside. Both Vaughan and Gill saw me move at the same time, and they both shouted a warning and then started running. They reached the ambulance doors before me and placed their own bodies between mine and Temple's. Vaughan, who knew all too well the extent of the Red Planet's hold on me, tried hard to get my attention.

'Stop, Joel. It's not worth it. We've got him now, and he's not going to get away, I promise. He's going to pay for everything he's...'

And more and more in this vein.

'I just want to speak to him,' I said calmly. 'I just want to say *one* thing. One *little* thing. Just *one* sentence.'

I looked at Vaughan, who looked deep into my eyes and saw that I was telling the truth. Maybe he even knew what it was I wanted to say.

'Wait,' he said, stopping one of the paramedics from closing the ambulance doors.

He and Gill allowed me to advance into the narrow opening that was left. Temple saw me immediately and his screams stopped. I waited until he was completely focussed on me before speaking.

'Nicky,' I said. 'I just wanted to say something before you go.' I smiled a sunny smile. 'We're all very disappointed in you...'

The pain in his bloodshot eyes instantly gave way to crazed homicidal anger and the ranting began again, more frenzied and more painfully than before.

'Yes, we're all so very, *very* disappointed...'

Satisfying though the moment was (and believe me, it was), it was with some relief that I finally closed the ambulance doors on Temple's contorted face, just as his bulging eyes began to swivel in opposite directions. I closed the doors and it seemed to make the ending final and real, like closing the cover on the last chapter of a very long book.

The bad guys had lost.

The good guys had won.

Everybody I cared about had come through unscathed.

Well, what do you know — a happy ending.

Twenty-Five

I PULLED INTO my driveway and killed the engine with a satisfied flick of my wrist. I felt in an almost hallucinatory state of well-being. It had been a couple of weeks since I'd had the pleasure of seeing my nemesis Temple hauled away under arrest, and at the moment — fingers firmly crossed — things seemed to be going well.

Extremely well.

My chief concern through everything had been Vic's reaction to her abduction and the violence she had been made to witness, but she seemed to have weathered the whole experience incredibly well, as though the adventure had been nothing more than an interesting sleepover. And indeed, she did still seem to regard Gregory 'Greggy' Feelen with great affection, which was why I'd spoken to Scott Vaughan on his behalf. Now I understood that he was cooperating with the police investigation in return for a little leniency in his own sentencing.

As, it seemed, was Angie Edwards.

Pretty funny for the boys in blue. Angie was busy tattling on Temple, and at the same time Temple was busy ratting on her. It seemed that they both knew where a lot of bodies were buried (in this case, the phrase wasn't merely a metaphor) and who put them there. No honour among thieves. Scott Vaughan was having the time of his life, I think, playing them off one against the other.

The whole truth about what had been going on for the past few weeks never made it into the papers or onto the TV news. Vaughan had more than enough on Temple without bringing me and Vic into it, and he very kindly didn't try to put me on the spot concerning Lisa's whereabouts. In the light of the wealth of evidence she had inadvertently provided, her prosecution would have been an irrelevance anyway.

The other good news is... wait for it... I'm dating again.

After a little soul-searching, I finally phoned Elaine Leigh and we met for lunch one afternoon. The lunch went well, and it was clear that the initial sparks of attraction we'd both felt weren't caused by crossed wires. The next evening we went out for dinner together, which went even better.

I can't honestly say that it reached the giddy heights of my last dinner date, with Angie Edwards, but then I never expected it to. It was *better*, though. Elaine, after all, was a real person, a real woman, and she wasn't trying to play me. We had a great time. And when I dropped her off at home, we smooched in the car like a couple of teenagers, and I got to drive home with a satisfyingly uncomfortable bulge in my pants.

Which brings me back to today.

A little earlier, I had dropped Vic at Henry and Maude's house, where she would, on this fine Saturday evening, be over-nighting. I had just been to the supermarket to gather the ingredients necessary for one of my more edible homemade meals (pasta bolognaise

The QUEEN of HEARTS

bake), which I was making in honour of my dinner guest this evening — Elaine, obviously.

It wasn't written in tablets of stone (actually, it hadn't even been openly discussed), but there was a gentle undercurrent of understanding that Elaine might — just might — be over-nighting herself. Here. With me.

Hot stuff, eh?

I climbed out of the Scenic in a hurry, dragging my shopping bags after me. I had my plan and I was determined to stick to it. First, food preparation. Second, change the bedclothes. Third, take a long (coldish) shower. Fourth, open the red wine to breathe. Fifth... say a fervent prayer to the fickle gods of love, lust, and whoopee — for Heaven's sake, give us a bloody break!

As I began to walk down the garden path, I saw Mrs. Webber waving at me enthusiastically from her window, and I thought, *oh no*... To be fair, I couldn't be anything other than grateful to Mrs. W after the things she'd done for me and Vic, but I sensed that she was one of those people who, if you once allowed them into your life, felt they had the right to be there for evermore.

And let's face it, I already had one bossy old woman with a full nelson on my life, and Maude had absolutely no need of a tag partner.

So I nodded back at her briefly and hurried along to my door. I had just slipped my key into the lock when I felt a presence behind me. I heard the overgrown shrubbery bordering my garden path suddenly rustle and saw a tall shadow rise up the wall at my side.

Too late, I realised that Mrs. Webber hadn't been waving. She had been gesticulating, frantically trying to warn me that someone was lying in wait for me. I had no idea who it might be, but I had a pretty good idea who had sent them.

It had to be Temple. This was his way of reaching out from his jail cell — by setting another of his attack dogs on me.

Even as I dropped my bags and began to turn, I knew that I had already been too slow to react. But I turned anyway, raising my arms to shield my head, leaning back against the door, ready to kick out.

But I didn't have to.

The man who had been lying in ambush for me had paused a few steps away, and was holding up his empty hands to show that he meant no harm.

Not that I believe he could have *done* a lot of harm. At first glance, he looked to be about ninety-years-old. Although he was still tallish, around the six-foot mark, there was nothing to him at all. He was rail-thin, and his clothes flapped about on his frame as though his weight loss had been both sudden and recent.

'Sorry if I alarmed you, Joel,' he said. 'It wasn't intentional.'

The voice sounded familiar, but I couldn't place him at all.

'How is it that you know me and I don't know you?' I asked, straightening up myself. 'Who are you?'

'Oh, but you do know me,' he replied, giving me a lop-sided smile that revealed a lot of discoloured denture. 'I'm Charlie — Charlie Noble.'

Aha, I thought. So this was the four-times married boxing expert who'd given me Feelen's name in the first place, setting me on the road to understanding. Henry's golfing buddy, one of The Boys.

I reached out to shake the hand he was offering, and I invited him into the house for a moment — not seeing a polite way of immediately telling him to go sling his hook. As he passed me, I waved across to Mrs. W, to let her know everything was okay.

In response, she shot me a crisp thumbs-up signal I was afraid she had picked up from old cops shows on the *Alibi* channel.

TO MY CHAGRIN, Charlie gratefully accepted my fake offer of coffee. I did, however, make a point of plonking my shopping bags on the table directly in front of him, sending what I hoped would be a none-too subtle message that I was a busy man with little time for idle chit-chat.

'It's nice to meet you face to face, finally,' he said when I had sat down across from him.

'Same here. I wanted to thank you again for the information you gave me. It helped. I meant to call you back and let you know how it all came out, but somehow everything got out of hand.'

'That happens,' he shrugged. 'Anyway, I got the whole story from Henry last week in the club house.'

I sighed. 'Yeah, well Henry and Maude aren't too happy with me at the moment. They thought I should have told them what was going on at the time, and not when it was all over. But...' I spread my hands. '...I didn't think it would help them or me or Vic, so I didn't.'

'For what it's worth, I think you did exactly the right thing, and the proof is in the pudding, isn't it?

Everything came out right. Henry and Maude are taking your daughter on holiday next week, is that correct?'

'First thing Monday morning. They're taking her to Disneyland Paris for a five-day break, as a special treat. She's going to love it.'

'And you're staying behind?'

'Someone's got to pay the mortgage.'

'How true. What about the future — do you have a plan?'

Of course I had a plan. Didn't everyone? Personally, I had a very well thought out ten-step plan. However, the last nine steps didn't amount to much without the first, which involved matching all six numbers on a Saturday night rollover. It's only forty-five-million to one, and someone's got to win, right?

'You know, from what Henry was telling me, I gather that you're a very handy and resourceful young man, and you've still got a lot of copper in you.'

'Well…' I smiled away the compliments and half rose from my chair, hoping to hurry him along. But Charlie hadn't finished.

'Which brings me to the *real* reason I'm here today. It's by the way of being a business proposal.'

I looked at him. He looked at me. If he was jolly before, he wasn't jolly now. I sat down again.

'When you left the Job, did you ever consider working as a private investigator?'

'Only very briefly. I already knew a few ex-coppers who'd gone the PI route, but from what they told me about the job, it didn't sound like it was for me.'

Charlie's face fell yet more, like a deflating balloon.

'That's a shame. I was hoping I could convince you to do a bit of detective work on my behalf. I would be prepared to compensate you very generously for your time…'

Then he named a sum of money so large that it was all I could do to stare at him in astonishment.

Before I could speak, before I could react in any way at all, old Charlie produced a photograph out of nowhere, like a conjuror forcing a card on an unsuspecting punter.

Foolishly, I took it.

The photograph turned out to be an enlarged colour photocopy of what, originally, had been nothing more than a snap taken with a cheap, pre-digital camera. It had been taken in a pub or club somewhere around Christmas time, with the long saloon bar decorated with balloons and tinsel.

The central figure was a very pretty young woman, really not much more than a girl, an appearance not helped by her dark, shoulder-length hair having been tied into bunches at each side of her head, or the extremely skimpy St Trinian-style schoolgirl outfit she was almost wearing. She held a bottle of beer in each hand, and looked like she'd already had many more than she could handle.

I noticed that the photocopy had been folded around the edges, obviously to fit a missing frame, and when I unfolded it to its full size, I saw that the drunken girl was flanked by a couple of equally drunken men, both considerably older than her. One of them was looking down her cleavage, and the other had his hand on her thigh, above her stocking-top and below her skirt. I think it was safe to say that the girl's moral well-being did not appear to be their main concern.

I sighed sadly. I'd seen it all before, of course — the offspring of good coppers going off the rails. It seemed to be something of a pattern. Just look at Henry and Lisa.

I looked up from the girl's pretty but over-made-up face — about eighteen, I was guessing, or maybe even a year younger — and looked at Charlie Noble's seamed old walnut of a face, now worried and haggard enough to pass for a hundred or so.

'So which is she,' I asked gently, 'your daughter or your grand-daughter?'

Insofar as a man with a face like his *was* able to blush, he did so now.

'Neither,' he said softly. 'That's the wife.'

I looked down again at the girl in the picture — so heartbreakingly young — then back up at Charlie Noble — so backbreakingly old.

'I know what you're thinking,' he said.

Which was more than I did. I couldn't decide whether he was a cradle-snatcher or she was a grave-robber.

'Believe me, I know how it looks. I've heard all the jokes, but I don't care, she's the light of my life.' Huge tears suddenly appeared in his eyes, like rainfall in the desert. 'And now she's gone, disappeared without a word, without a trace...'

Suddenly, Charlie leant across the table and clasped my hands. He was openly weeping now, all but sobbing.

'Find her for me, Joel!'

'Look, I...'

'*Please*, Joel! *Please!*'

'But...'

'I *beg* you!' Alarmingly he slipped off his chair and fell to his knees at my side. 'I *beg* you, I *beg* you!'

I stared at him in amazement and despair, and I thought, Oh *shit*...

The End
of
THE QUEEN OF HEARTS

Hopeless Optimist
Blithering Idiot
Soft Touch
At last, a hero you can believe in

Joel September will return
in
THE GIRL IN THE PICTURE

If you enjoyed this novel, please leave a review on Amazon and spread the word

Other Works

Crime
The Queen of Hearts
The Girl in the Picture
Perfect Day
Perfect Peace
The Hunted Man 1: Old Dog New Trick
The Hunted Man 2: Identity Crisis
The Crime Short Story Collection

Horror
(writing as Jim Mullaney)
Comeback – a novel
The 1st Horror Short Story Collection
The 2nd Horror Short Story Collection

Please visit me at:
pjshann.com
or my **Amazon Authors Page**
or contact me at:
pjshann121@gmail.com

Thanks for Reading

Printed in Great Britain
by Amazon